THE HIDDEN PATH

ROSALIE E F ROSS

FOR CHLOE AND HARVEY

FOR WHEN YOU ARE READY

PROLOGUE

1970

SCOTLAND

Alexander felt light of heart - if not of body. So preoccupied had he been with the heady combination of prayer and feasting upon the sights, sounds and smells of the land he had grown to love, that he had walked further than he had intended. He took his jacket off, laid it across the soft roadside cushion of heather and carefully lowered himself down. The afternoon sun had warmed the ground, and he would have been comfortable, if not for the gnawing pain which threatened to spoil this most pleasant of afternoons. Massaging his left thigh, he tried to control the concern he was starting to feel about the walk back. It took several minutes before the acute stage passed; now it was just the usual constant ache.

Able to think clearly again, he leaned back on his elbows, his face turned towards the sun, and breathed in the sweet, country air. There was something about this wild, untamed place that was intoxicating, and, like a drunk, he could have curled up there and then and slept. But time was getting on; there was one more issue he wanted to add to the list he had already submitted for consideration to his Invisible Companion. He asked his question and was rewarded with an immediate answer, delighted, he sat up, made a fist of one hand, banged it into the other, and said out loud, *'Yes! Of course; that's it! It's obvious. Thanks Boss.'*

The girl was just twenty or so yards away when he first noticed her. She must have heard him, and knowing that he was not able to get to his feet without scrabbling about like a crab, resigned himself to staying put. He began to feel embarrassed and decided that, for decency's sake, he ought to say something and at least try to sound normal. When she came level, he smiled and said, 'Good afternoon, lovely day.'

She gave a tart reply and walked quickly past. He stared at her departing figure and decided that she had not been beautiful, but no Plain Jane either. In fact, what little he had seen of her had been acceptable enough, and he might well have been interested - before. He looked away, then back again, then away, only to find that some magnetic force was compelling him to turn his head once more in her direction. Curious, he asked, 'Right Boss, so what's all this about? She's no head-turner, so why can't I turn mine?'

The girl was walking faster. She snatched her beret off and he watched fascinated as the breeze caught fine strands of her hair to form a wispy, sunlit halo around her head. Now that was eye-catching. Guardedly, he asked, 'Okay, You wanted me to look at her. I'm looking. So who is she?'

The answer came. Incredulous, he remained silent for several moments before asking again, a colder edge to his voice, 'What was that? *What* did You say?'

He received the same answer. Totally dumbfounded now, he gasped, and then, unable to stop himself, began to laugh out loud. Obviously alarmed, the girl turned and looked back.

'You are joking?' he exclaimed, 'there's no way on Your green earth that I'm up for … that! Especially to a complete stranger! And who is she anyway?' Too late he realised that he had not spoken as quietly as he had intended, and now he began to feel ashamed of his outburst. Lowering his head between his knees to strike a pose of unfamiliar humility, he said in a more conciliatory tone, 'Sorry, Boss. That was insubordinate of me. But there must be some sort of mix-up, crossed wires, or maybe I misheard you? You know I can't be doing with complications like that right now, what with the Manor … ah!' He stopped short. 'The Manor, I get it. A woman. But that doesn't mean I'd have to…You're having a laugh, right?'

He didn't wait for the reply as an overwhelming urge to get going came upon him. But where to? She was heading in the direction he needed. He reviewed his options. She had been dressed casually and not for hiking and would have to turn back sooner or later, and the thought that she would pass him again and find him still sitting here was very unappealing. He could go to the Inn, but that might cause some suspicion if he turned up hours before he was due. There was just one thing for it. Keeping a good eye on her, he clumsily hoisted himself to his feet and made his way up the gentle slope. It took him exactly eight seconds to find a suitable lookout spot, from where, expertly camouflaged by a convenient boulder and the useful heather, he watched and waited.

*

The girl kept up her fast pace. She had given the man a terse reply when he had spoken and fixed her gaze determinately on the road ahead, thinking that he was remarkably coherent for a drunk. But maybe she was overreacting and he was just practicing some sort of speech whilst waiting for a lift or a bus - or something. Bother! All she had wanted to do was to go for a short walk and clear her head, but now here she was actually wondering if it was safe to go on. Beginning to feel warm, she snatched impatiently at her beret and tried hard not to look back, even though everything in her wanted to. For all she knew he could be following her, creeping up behind, ready to grab her and - do what? The Inn was too far away, and probably no one would hear her even if she did manage to scream, and there didn't appear to be another living soul around for miles.

Another noisy outburst, sounding very much like laughter, came from behind. Now she did not hesitate and spun around to find that he was still staring at her. That settled it, the time for indecision was over. She had two choices: to get back to the Inn as fast as she could, or keep going - but where to? The first choice meant passing him again, and she didn't fancy that, but the second could put her even further away from any help.

She strode on and was nonplussed to see no sign of him when she braved another look a few seconds later. Surely he couldn't have walked on so far and be out of sight already? She felt a mixture of relief, alarm and annoyance that her very first walk in such a lovely place had been ruined - thanks to some crazed man. Who was he anyway? And what on earth was he doing, sitting alone out here in the heather? And that laugh - and *now* he'd gone and vanished into thin air! Had she imagined the whole thing, or had some sort of hallucination? What was it they said about fairy folk up here? Scolding herself for being so fanciful, she made her decision, turned around - and made a dash for the Inn.

CHAPTER 1

KING'S LYNN

1959

The young girl returned to the empty, cheerless house after work one bone cold evening. Propped up against the ketchup bottle on the kitchen table was an envelope, previously used, with his name and the address crossed out and the word **Important** printed in heavy pencil to the side. She opened the flap and took out the note; it was unsigned but written in her father's usual curt style, the letters squeezed together so tightly that they would have suffocated if they had been organic. The words seemed to spit out at her:-

> *Doley,*
> *I'm going away and putting the house up for sale.*
> *I want you out by the end of the month.*
> *My mail is being re-directed, but if anything comes, take it to Allen & Partners on your way to work. You will leave everything clean and tidy -*
> *OR I WILL KNOW ABOUT IT!*
> *PS. The enclosed should get you into a bedsit. DON'T WASTE IT!!!*

'Oh God, Oh God!' she cried, forcing herself to read the note again. Slowly she lowered herself onto a chair, its legs screeching on the faded lino, the awful noise jolting her out of the shock that felt as though it had been slammed into her. He had given no warning, not even so much as a hint that he was planning to leave. And she had done her level best for him all this time. Her mother, Mary, had died six weeks earlier, but well before she had been too ill to manage, Yvonne, at just

7

sixteen years of age, had willingly taken over the bulk of household chores. The house was always clean and tidy, his clothes washed and ironed, and a hot meal ready for him every night. She put her rent money on the kitchen table each Friday and he had taken it without as much as a nod of acknowledgement. She had given him no cause to complain, no reason to do this to her. She did not deserve this.

Her anger grew as her shock abated; now the implications of the note began to hit her with full force. She was about to be thrown out of her home - cast aside like a worn-out shoe. *How dare he - how dare he!* She picked up the small bundle of well used pound notes and counted them; it did not take long. *Ten quid - was that all she was worth - just ten quid?* Noises seemed to claw their way up from somewhere deep in her chest and broke out as sobs. 'Oh Mum ... Mum, if only …'

Now she needed to move, to do something, *anything* but sit here and feel all this pain. She rushed up the stairs to her father's bedroom and gasped, even the bed had been stripped bare. She pulled out drawers and flung open wardrobe doors. Empty. He had not left behind so much as a twisted metal coat hanger.

She walked around the rest of the small terraced house in a daze, the tears drying on her face, willing herself to wake up from this nightmare, desperate to find something to convince her that none of this was really happening. But there was nothing. Owen Williams had done a thorough job of completely eradicating himself; it was as though he had rubbed himself out. The man - her so-called father - had gone. Although, he had never really been there at all, had he?

Face it Doley!

Doley! Of all things to think about at a time like this, why did it have to be the hateful name he had always called her? A tiny trace of relief crept in, at least she wouldn't have to hear him sneer that word at her again, nor it's incessant, accompanying mantra:-

You're nothing but a hole in the Durex. A Durex hole dolly! You weren't planned, just you remember

that my girl. You're nothing but a nuisance; a millstone around my neck. You'll never amount to anything. Good for nothing. Never were, never will be. Sneaking in through a hole like that. You shouldn't be here, taking up someone else's space. You're a waste of time. Ruined my life, you hear, ruined - and don't you ever forget it!

She had never discovered the cause of his venomous tirade, but she had learnt how to cope with it - by forcing it to bypass her conscious mind and letting it sink somewhere deep and hidden inside her.

She had to get out, escape the place where the very air itself seemed hostile, the same air he had breathed just hours before. Throwing the letter and money into her bag, she ran out of the house and kept running until she reached a large Victorian detached house several streets away. She stumbled awkwardly as she climbed the iron steps at the side of the building. Hearing her noisy approach, Sandra, her good friend who had been there for her throughout the past dreadful year, hurried to open the door to her small first floor flat and let her in.

It took a while for them both to calm down and rational thinking to return. At last, Yvonne's passionate outbursts at the unfairness and cruelty of the situation became less frequent, and Sandra began to insist that she stop overnight. 'I'll make up the sofa. I've got to go in in the morning, but the three o'clock perm's cancelled and I'm sure Tanya'll let me off early if I...well, you know. And the Chronicle's out tomorrow, so you go through the places to rent and try to set-up some appointments. There's bound to be something going down Cromwell Avenue.'

*

Success came in the form of a large bedsit very close to the town centre. She moved in the following Saturday and set about trying to reconstruct her life. However, her heart just wasn't in it. She missed her mother more with each passing day and felt as though a heavy, oppressive cloak of gloom had enfolded itself around her and was slowly suffocating the life out of her. Sandra tried hard to jolly her friend along, but all her efforts proved as ineffective as a plaster on a constantly bleeding wound.

Then Tom had appeared on the scene and Sandra's focus shifted. He was a kind-hearted soul and it was not long before he felt that he would like to do something for his girlfriend's best friend. Closing the door one evening after watching Yvonne descend the steps and walk away, alone again, he put the idea he had been mulling over for a few weeks to Sandra. 'I've been thinking, do you think she'd agree to go out with a mate of mine?'

'What, you mean, make a foursome? Like a blind date?' she asked, immediately taken with the idea.

'Well, it's an idea, isn't it? I told you about Tony being dumped; might help take his mind off things a bit.'

'Can't do any harm I suppose. Go on then, fix it up, and I'll try and get her to go along with it.'

Pleasant though they had been, after the third blind date Yvonne felt it only fair to ask Tom to stop his well-meaning efforts on her behalf. She really could not be bothered with the whole boyfriend-girlfriend thing; somehow it seemed so trivial, and all just too much effort.

After another three months she came to the conclusion that she was actually more depressed now than the day she had first moved into the bedsit, at least then there had been a tiny portion of hope mixed in with the unhappiness. Now there was just an unshakable, aching wretchedness. Even her office job was as mundane as it was soul-destroying, and now it looked as though her days there could be numbered. What was it her boss had said just the other day, making a point of looking in her direction?

'One more account down the swanny and we'll have to start thinking of laying someone off.'

She should probably start looking for another job; if only she could drum up some enthusiasm.

Later that week she wandered into the local labour exchange and half-heartedly read the cards. There appeared to be nothing suitable. She made herself go around again and pay more attention. As usual, there were plenty of vacancies for invoice or accounts clerks and comptometer operators, but days of constant figure work and punching endless figures into a machine did not appeal at all. Maybe she could try factory or shop work, places full of girls her own age. It was something to think about.

She reached the *Vacancies In Other Areas* board, which was something she had ignored on her first circuit, and her eye was caught by one of the cards in the *Hotel and Domestic Vacancies* section:-

Well-known Holiday Camp on the East Coast
requires seasonal staff for all departments. Ideal
for students. Must be hardworking, willing and
adaptable. If you like the idea of spending summer
by the sea, then we can offer free board & lodging,
plus small wage. End-of-season bonus. Contact ...

She read it again, then again. Well, why not? She was not afraid of hard work, and all she needed was a bed and a place to hang her clothes anyway. Why shouldn't she give it a try? What had she got to lose? She was going slowly mad here, and whatever it turned out to be, it would definitely be a change, and it would be nice to spend the summer by the sea.

It was so easy. After a brief telephone conversation with the Camp Director she was offered a chalet maid position. The man had sounded pleasant enough, although she did find it strange that he didn't seem interested in her work experience, nor had he asked for her current employer's contact details.

She worked a week's notice, packed her suitcase, said a tearful goodbye to Sandra and Tom, and turned her back on King's Lynn. Hope, which had been elusive and absent from her life for so long, had returned, making her steps quick and light as she walked to the railway station. They said that the world was a big place; it stood to reason that somewhere out there must be a new life just waiting for her. Now all she had to do was to find it.

CHAPTER 2

EN ROUTE AND ARRIVAL

1970

Yvonne watched the yellow ribbon of light coming from a long line of still open-curtained kitchen and sitting room windows stream past. Minutes later, only the occasional glow from an isolated farmhouse pierced the thick blackness outside. Sitting alone in the darkened compartment, she felt that the last ten years had flashed by just as fast.

She sighed and looked away, trying to remember where she had packed her references. She opened her duffle bag and sighed with relief. Yes, there it was, the plastic wallet containing the precious collection; the only tangible evidence she possessed to show for all that time and effort. As complimentary and detailed though they were, these hard-earned testimonials failed to express some of the other skills she had developed over the years, amongst them the ability to fit into diverse groups of floating, temporary people, at saying 'Hello' and being 'the new girl', and at packing and saying 'Goodbye.'

At first it had been an exciting and stimulating way of life. She knew that she was different from her contemporaries back in King's Lynn, many of whom seemed to be too frightened to spread their wings and try anything new. Like Sandra, most of them were still working in the same job they'd had since leaving school. She used to pity them, but not anymore. In fact, given the opportunity, she would gladly change places with any one of them. Now she found herself continually wondering what it would be like to have walls around her that did not change with the seasons. It was getting harder to protect the small, bright flame of hope that flared within her whenever she packed for yet another job in yet another area, wishing that maybe, just maybe, and by some miracle, this would turn out to be *the* one. But things would inevitably turn sour. And each time it had been her fault. Something hidden and secret inside her, something that she was not able to control, would agitate and irritate her so much that she would feel compelled to move on. And it had happened again. If this carried on much longer, she felt sure that it would soon be almost impossible for her to continue to show the expected, cheerful face to her constantly changing world.

A small group of noisy, youthful passengers banged into her carriage door as they made their unsteady way along the corridor. One of them looked in and mouthed, 'Sorry'.

She stood to pull down the blinds and switch on two of the small overhead lights. Folding her long sloppy joe cardigan into a cushion, she stretched out along one of the narrow rows of seats and carefully poured a cup of cocoa from her flask, deciding that it was pleasant having the whole compartment to herself; there were some advantages to the solitary way of life after all.

The train rumbled on through the night, occasionally disturbing its passengers with sudden jolts and violent whooshes of air as it met and passed those going south.

Morning came, and a voice from the end of the carriage called, 'Edinburgh next stop. Next stop Edinburgh.'

Soon they were approaching Waverley Station. She positioned herself by the door's open window, the blast of cold air shocking her into a much-needed alertness, but still she was not prepared for the unexpected lurch the train gave as it finally juddered to a stop. The ground seemed to sway beneath her feet when she stepped out and she was obliged to hold onto a nearby trolley until the sensation passed. Steady again, she heaved her faithful old suitcase onto the trolley base and set off in search of the station café.

A cup of strong tea and several slices of toast helped to revive her as she watched the hustle and bustle of life on the platform outside. Anyone looking her way would have seen an unremarkable young woman, dressed for warmth and comfort in a sensible dark green duffle coat. Her face had often been described as being 'pleasant', and, as usual, this morning it was framed by many unruly tendrils of dark, auburn hair, the main part of which hung in a long plait down her back.

What they would not have seen was the young woman's inner resolve that today was to be the start of a new way of life. For some time now she had been aware of a flaw, or weakness, for she was never quite sure what to call it, in her character. The annoying defect consisted mainly of the ability to effectively jettison herself out of any relationship that threatened to become serious. No amount of persistent, gentle coaxing had ever succeeded in persuading her to think again and change her mind. She would give some spurious but plausible sounding reason as to why it was essential for her to leave as soon as possible. The realisation of its existence had led to alarm, then shame, when she found herself unable to change, no matter how hard she tried, and she really did try. Eventually, tired of the battle, she was forced to accept that this was a permanent and very unpleasant part of her personality.

Now, at the age of 27, she had made what she considered to be a very sensible decision: she would live without the unwelcome complications and added burdens of anything even remotely romantic. Life was fraught enough without wasting energy hauling all that unnecessary, confusing and painful baggage around. If only she had come to her senses before; for all she knew she might have already missed several opportunities to settle down. So then, from now on, all types of close association with men were out, and hopefully a more controlled, and, therefore, peaceful existence, was in. Naturally she would have to have some dealings with them, but she would make sure that these would be strictly limited to only what was really necessary or genuinely unavoidable.

Such was her frame of mind as she sat back to enjoy her second cup of tea. She was resolved; the decision had been made; the time was now. And, with a bit of luck, the place might even be Scotland.

*

14

The world seemed to have woken up, and half of it appeared to be boarding the Inverness-bound train with her. At last, doors were slammed, a long shrill whistle pierced the air like a knife, and they were off. There were five other passengers in her compartment, and it was not long before cigarettes, newspapers and magazines were being offered around. Her contribution was a packet of Spangles and a depleted stock of sticky toffees. It was pleasant to be part of such a friendly group, even if it was just for one small part of this otherwise long and lonely journey. Declining another cigarette, she gave herself an invisible pat on the back for the way she was handling the social interaction between herself and the two male passengers. If all her contact with the opposite sex could be as satisfactory as this, then she would have no trouble. They chatted amiably as the train sped on. Only one of them, a scholarly looking, pipe-smoking gentleman, claimed to have ventured as far as her destination.

'Good luck to you, lassie,' he called over his shoulder as he stepped off the train at Aviemore, 'you'll enjoy the peace, no doubt.'

So, she was going to a peaceful place then? She nodded, and hoped her face did not betray the growing concern that had been gradually creeping back into her mind since leaving King's Lynn. She had fought hard against it since her search through the various travel books in the local library had revealed only the barest facts about the area, and nothing at all about the Tananeach Inn. Now the man's well-intentioned comment had brought it all back, and along with it, her doubts about accepting a job in what sounded to be such a remote and distant place. But it was too late now to indulge in second thoughts - or even third.

There had been another change at Invermaden, after which the train hugged the shores of a large estuary, stopping frequently at barely discernible halts and small, quiet stations. The few remaining passengers who left were rarely replaced, and she began to suspect that soon the only two people left on board would be the unseen driver and herself, and the thought made her feel uneasy.

They arrived at Braegarroch Halt at thirty-five minutes past four, the expected time. Stepping down onto the deserted, pocket-handkerchief sized platform, she felt an almost overpowering urge to get straight back on-board and be taken away from this wild and lonely place. 'Get a grip,' she told herself, as she stood watching the train creak to a slow start before disappearing from view, its comforting mechanical rumble gradually fading away. 'This is the right place, and they're probably on the way. There a bit late, that's all.'

A chilly breeze picked up. Afraid that she would get cold and not be able to do anything about it, she started pacing back and forth along the narrow path leading away from the platform, going a little further each time. Something would have to be done if the expected lift did not come soon. She listened for any traffic noise nearby, but there was none. In fact, there was no human type of sound at all, just birds singing, the whisper of gently swaying branches, and the plaintiff calling of countless newborn lambs. It was indeed a very peaceful place.

More anxious minutes passed, and she was still debating what to do, when she heard the reassuring sound of a car engine approaching. It stopped some distance away, and what sounded like a car door slam shut a few seconds later. Footsteps came swiftly towards her and soon an elderly man appeared. He was a shabbily dressed individual; his jacket was seriously faded and his badly stained trousers were held up by a wide, leather belt.

'Miss Williams, is it?' he asked, squinting at her from beneath the peak of his grimy, threadbare cap.

'Er, yes,' she replied cautiously. 'Are you from the Tananeach Inn?' hoping that she had pronounced the name correctly. It appeared that she had when he stepped forward to pick up her case and began leading the way along the path.

'Och, in a way lass. Come along now, we're running late.' They walked on in silence before reaching a clearing where a mud-spattered land rover stood. 'In you get,' he instructed, carelessly flinging her case in the back, before hopping nimbly into the driver's seat.

She paused uncertainly, struggling to take stock of the situation. To begin with, there had been no proper station, not even a platform, just a block of concrete in the middle of nowhere, then this strange, unkempt little man had turned up, and now she was expected to get into his dirty old car! She didn't even know his name, and what did he mean by saying that he was from the Inn, 'in a way'? Now what on earth had she let herself in for?

Resigned to her fate, she clambered unceremoniously up beside him, and had just enough time to take her seat before being thrown sideways as he executed a jerky three-point turn.

'And is it so that you've come a long way this day?' he asked, straightening-up the vehicle.

Holding on tightly to the door handle with one hand, and gripping the side of her seat with the other, she managed to reply, 'Yes, from King's Lynn.'

'And where would that be now?' he asked.

'In Norfolk.'

'And how many miles would that be?'

'About seven hundred I think.'

'Och, and did you come all that way by the trains?'

'Yes. It's been quite a journey, and I actually left yesterday morning.' Bright flashes of something blue-grey between the trees caught her eye, and now she had a question for him. 'Is there a la ... er ... a loch through there?'

'Aye, that would be Loch Laith, and the river end of it. It's fine and deep and good for the fishing. You'll maybe have some for your tea this night.'

She felt a pang of hunger at the mention of food and hoped that there would be something substantial to eat waiting for her at the Inn, however, experience had taught her not to expect too much. These few thoughts came and went, as did the small lochside village of Braegarroch. They were steadily climbing, the line of trees beside the roadside eventually giving way to dark, still sleeping hedgerows. Grey boulders lay scattered on the lower slopes of the surrounding hillsides. Descending again into a more gentle, tree covered area, he broke the silence by announcing that they had just entered Ardgealish. This turned out to be a tiny hamlet of about a dozen or so well-spaced detached cottages, each framed by the fresh greens, yellows, purples and whites of slowly awakening spring flowers and hedgerows that surrounded the whole delightful scene.

'What a pretty place!' she exclaimed enthusiastically, unable to let such a sight pass without making some sort of appreciative comment.

The old man was satisfied with her reaction, and, trying not to sound too smug, replied, 'Aye, it suits me well enough. You can keep your bright city lights.'

They journeyed on. After a particularly nasty jolt, she enquired hopefully, 'Are we near Tananeach yet, Mr … er?'

'Och, the name's Murray, and there's no such place. The Inn will be all there will be.'

'Really? Just the Inn?'

'Aye.'

'Oh, I see.' She spent several moments digesting this piece of information along with its implications before asking, 'What does Tananeach actually mean? I tried to find out before I left, but couldn't find the word in the Gaelic Dictionary.'

'Aye, and you wouldn'a either. It's been mucked about, and *Taigh nan an T'Eirrach* in the Gaelic. You'd be saying *House of Spring,* and built in that season, so I'm thinking.'

By now they had reached the edge of another loch, its surface disturbed by small, windblown ripples. He gestured towards it. 'Loch Nan Solas, and the Inn just by.'

They were approaching a long, unexceptional looking building, the starkness of its whitewashed walls and black painted window surrounds softened only by the presence of several mature rowan trees standing, sentry-like, either side of a glass vestibule. A public telephone box stood to the right of the entrance. To the left extended a large conservatory, situated, no doubt, to take advantage of the view of the loch and imposing slopes and snow-capped ridges of a distant mountain range.

A turning circle, surrounded by a substantial rockery of roughly hewn stones and swathes of white, red and purple heather, led them to a parking area on the other side.

Yvonne sighed with relief as she climbed out of the car. She stood for a while, staring into the distance, and began to wonder at the sheer beauty and vastness of it all. She was used to the low, flat terrain of the Fens; land that just lay there with its far-reaching expanses of hedgeless fields, interrupted only by arrow-straight dykes and canopied by seemingly endless skies.

The seconds passed, and, with some satisfaction, the old man noticed that the early evening sun was casting a soft, golden glow over the whole scene, turning the colours even deeper and more vibrant than usual. He glanced over at the *quine**; he had seen this same, hypnotic effect before and decided to let the land weave its powerful spell a while longer. A full minute was to pass before he broke into her reverie. 'Come away in now, lassie. They'll be expecting you.'

Reluctantly, she forced herself to rally and look away from the intoxicating scene as she turned to follow him. And then, trying to convey a confidence she did not feel, she entered the Tananeach Inn for the first time.

Quine: Gaelic - young unmarried woman or girl.

CHAPTER 3

'Hello, it's Yvonne isn't it? Do come in,' said a slightly older than middle-aged woman standing behind a small reception counter. She was compact and dumpy, and flawlessly dressed in a matching twin set and a row of what looked like real pearls clasped around her neck. 'I'm Georgina MacMan. Come on through,' she trilled, opening the flap.

Before Yvonne was able to offer any type of reply, the woman turned and began leading the way into a surprisingly modern kitchen. 'I expect you'll be wanting a cup of tea before you go Hamish?'

Feeling that a wee dram would have suited him better, Hamish doffed his cap, and replied in a dull, flat tone, 'Aye, that'll do,' thus making his dissatisfaction obvious.

'You too, Yvonne?'

'If it's no trouble.'

'No trouble at all, is it Niall?' she said, addressing the profile of a small, stocky figure, clad in chef's whites, whose whole attention appeared to be on the knife he was holding menacingly over a large, dead fish on a wooden block. The man made no response. Georgina tut-tutted loudly and marched over to stand beside him, her face coming perilously close to the ominous looking blade. With a very obvious edge to her voice, she repeated, 'No trouble at all, is it Niall? Look sharp now, this is Yvonne who's come to help us. The kettle's boiled, hasn't it?'

'Aye, that it has, Mrs Mac,' came the somewhat begrudging reply.

Georgina let out a forced sigh and turned to face Yvonne. 'Excellent. Well now, Yvonne, this is Niall, our chef.'

The man shot the swiftest of glances in Yvonne's direction.

'Hello Niall ...' said Yvonne, stopping short of the customary, 'it's nice to meet you,' which she felt at that moment would have been an outright lie.

He mumbled something incoherent and began to decapitate the fish.

Hamish had been standing in the doorway, and deciding that no mug of tea was worth all this mither, muttered something about 'lambs awaiting,' and made a swift exit. His reaction had not been lost on Georgina, who felt that a more positive slant on the situation was needed. Flashing a quick smile at Yvonne, she walked over to the hob and began tentatively tapping the side of a large enamel kettle on one of the hot plates.

'We're so glad you've come to join us, Yvonne, and just as well you came now, you'll have time to find your feet before we get too busy.' She darted a warning look across at Niall. 'Isn't that right, Niall?'

'Aye, if you say so, Mrs Mac,' came the unconvincing reply as he proceeded to pull out the fish's backbone.

'Indeed I do. Good, good. Well now, Yvonne, the staff corridor's through there and up the stairs.' She pointed to a door at the far end of the room. 'Your room's the third on the right. Go on up and I'll bring you a drink in a minute. Tea ... coffee?'

Yvonne placed her order, picked up her suitcase, and carefully negotiated her way past the disagreeable little man.

She had already unpacked most of her belongings when Georgina appeared a few minutes later, panting slightly and with a mug in her hand. 'Here we are then. Er, by the way, you won't mind Niall now, will you? You know what these chefs are like.' She rolled her eyes dramatically. 'So temperamental! But I'm sure you two'll get along just fine once you get used to his little ways.'

Yvonne took the mug and thanked her, hoping that the man's 'little ways' would not turn out to be big ones.

'Well now,' said Georgina, giving the room a cursory glance, 'it's nothing fancy, but I think you've got everything you need. You'll find more pillows and blankets in the cupboard by the bathroom if you need them.' She pointed to a room at the far end of the corridor. 'Down there, and the staff room's next to it. Oh, and you might need to put the gas fire on later, but do make sure you turn it off before you turn in. Flora's left you some matches somewhere. Staff breakfast's at half past seven, but we'll let you have a bit of a lay-in tomorrow; just this once mind. I'll get her to bring you up a tray.'

'That's very kind, but I don't mind coming down ...'

'No, no! She's keen to meet you; you'll be working with her most of the time. You can spend the rest of the day getting your bearings, and then make a start on Thursday.'

Pleasantly surprised at such unusual kindness, Yvonne tried to make an adequate response, but could only manage an uninspired, 'Thank you, that sounds lovely.'

Satisfied that she had conveyed all the information needed at this stage, Georgina said, 'Well then, I'll leave you to get organised,' as she turned for the stairs, then called back, 'Oh yes, I nearly forgot, you must be peckish, dinner's in half an hour, in the kitchen. Well, good night for now, and we'll be seeing you tomorrow.'

Yvonne briefly considered refusing the meal, not relishing the idea of facing that surly little man again so soon, but hunger won. 'Thank you, Mrs MacMan. Till tomorrow then.'

*

Niall hurled himself down at his place at the staff table. He was a worried man. The ruddy girl had arrived. Ever since he'd heard that she was expected he'd tried to convince himself that she would back out, but here she was, and as bold as brass. Now he was in a rare old fix. It was so unfair; so ruddy, ruddy unfair.

Six months had passed since he'd had to hightail it out of town after that bungled off-licence job. He wasn't going to stick around to get slammed-up like the rest of those stupid sods. Everyone knew that Niall Turvey was too canny for that. Yes indeed, fate had dealt him a good hand when he'd landed up here. The Chiefs hadn't asked too many questions and had been only too glad to have him, and too right too; a damn good cook like him didn't come along every day of the week!

It took him a while, but he'd even found some use for the countryside; now he could move about at any time of the day or night without having to watch his back. And then he'd come up with the idea that would secure his position here, permanently. No more seasonal jobs for him! He'd heard about a certain local spinster, and an only child at that, called Maggie MacKay. They said that her family owned a tidy croft - and an even tidier bit of land to go with it.

It didn't take him long to make his move, and it had worked like a treat; the soppy hen had almost fallen into his arms. Okay, so she wasn't much of a looker, and a bit soft in the head, but she'd suit his purposes very nicely. Very nicely indeed.

Now all he had to do was to get her away from those ruddy parents of hers, and he'd almost succeeded, but then the Chiefs went and put the kibosh on the whole thing when they announced that they'd already filled the newly created post of General Assistant. Bang went his grand plan! Why hadn't they listened to him when he'd hinted that he knew someone fit for the job? Sometimes even they were so ruddy thick. And they'd sounded so pleased with themselves, saying that this new girl was 'very experienced' - and he knew only too well what that meant. She'd turn out to be just like all the others; another vodka-swilling floater, shrieking around the place like a banshee and hopping into bed with any moron daft enough to unzip his flies. That was one good thing about Maggie, she knew her place and did what she was told alright. But this English girl was going to be a ruddy nuisance. Hadn't she just proved it? She'd only been here five minutes and already caused grief between him and the Chief. Why'd they have to go and get her in and ruin all his plans? Oh yes, he was worried alright, and it was all her fault.

*

Yvonne finished her unpacking, then washed her face and hands in water the colour of weak tea. She entered the kitchen at precisely six o'clock. Having persuaded herself to give Niall a second chance, she succeeded in sounding upbeat as she greeted him with a friendly, 'Hello again.'

He jerked his head towards a large, rectangular table in the corner, and barked, 'Over there!' Then, hands and arms laden with serving dishes, he pushed his way through a door and disappeared into what she assumed to be the dining room. She crossed the room and sat down, convinced now that this chef was definitely temperamental, and might well prove to be even bossier and ruder than some of the others she had had the misfortune to meet.

He returned a few moments later, and without a word, bent to retrieve a covered plate from the bottom of the large oven. He pushed it none to carefully across the table in her direction before turning to busy himself in the cold store, hoping that she would get the message loud and clear that he wasn't about to start pandering to the likes of *her*.

Yvonne enjoyed her meal of minced beef in a rich gravy with mashed potatoes, swede and carrots, and decided that the peas were the sweetest she had ever tasted. Every so often Niall would emerge from his cold hideout to hurry back into the dining room, returning soon after with empty serving dishes. On his third trip, and overcome with curiosity, she ventured to ask, 'Is it the waitress's night off?'

He almost spat out his reply, 'There's only three in, and the Chiefs do the waitin' on table, but they're off tonight. They're okay people, and don't need no messin' about, see, so don't you go causin' them no grief.'

Now she felt her own hackles begin to rise, nevertheless, she managed to ask calmly, 'Why on earth would I do that? I was only asking because it seems to me that you're kept pretty busy.'

'Aye, and that's the way I like it, see. We run a tidy ship here; it's a good team and we don't need the likes of you comin' to scuttle it.'

She was shocked, not only with his undisguised animosity, but at the knowledge that, apparently, here was a hotel that had no need of a waitress! If the place was *that* quiet, then maybe he had a point - what was she doing here?

She made short work of the desert, a particularly good crème brûlée, and wondered how such tasty food could have been prepared by such a sour character. Then, tired though she was, and resolving not to let herself sink to his level, she gathered up her dishes and walked towards the sink, saying, 'Thanks, that was very nice.'

'Leave them!' he ordered, 'what d'ya think the ruddy dishwasher's for?'

'Hey, keep your hair on! I was only going to rinse them.' She was just a few feet away from him now and noticed a thin, jagged white line running down his left cheek and disappear into the corner of his mouth. It looked like an old scar. Somehow, she was not surprised.

It was with some relief that she returned to her room and shut the door firmly behind her. She bathed, watched television and read before turning-in, telling herself that tomorrow was another day, and she would face whatever - and whoever - needed to be faced then.

CHAPTER 4

A light tapping sound seemed to be coming from somewhere nearby, followed by a woman's voice, 'Hello-o, hello-o-o-o. Are you awake in there, quine?'

Struggling to surface from a deep sleep, Yvonne tried to remember where she was, as she replied, 'Er, hello.'

'I've your breakfast here. Shall I be bringing it in?' called the voice.

'Oh ... yes. Come in.'

The door opened to reveal an elderly woman holding a tray laden with breakfast things. She spoke in a clear, slightly clipped Highland accent as she crossed the room to deposit the tray on the table. 'Good morning, lassie, and how are you this day? Did you sleep fine?'

Yvonne managed a sleepy, 'Yes, yes thank you.'

Twitching the curtains open a few inches, the woman turned to take a look at the bleary-eyed English girl who was attempting to sit up.

'I'm Flora, Hamish's wife; he came to fetch you off the train yesterday.' She made one last inspection of the tray's contents. 'There you are now; it's good and hot, so eat-up before it gets cold.' Satisfied, she turned for the door and began closing it behind her, calling a musical, 'Cheery-bye for now,' as she left.

'Okay, and thank you again.'

'Aye, aye,' sang the disjointed voice, whose owner was now even more curious than ever about the girl who had already managed to upset Niall. Muttering quietly to herself as she descended the stairs, she decided that Mrs MacMan was right about that accent, very English to be sure. And wouldn't she be quite the pretty thing if it wasn't for all that paleness.

Bemused and still slightly disoriented, Yvonne rubbed her eyes and tried to focus on her surroundings. Yes, everything was the same as when she had closed them the night before, although now she noticed that the mat and curtains had obviously seen better days, as had the chair and table by the window. The wardrobe and chest of drawers had proved more than adequate for her belongings, but the objects that pleased her the most were the sink and the small, mounted gas fire. All in all, it was a really nice room, and such a difference from the usually shared and shambolic accommodation she had been given throughout her scattered and varied career. And it was hers - all hers!

She stepped out of bed and shivered as she wrapped her dressing gown tightly around her and hurried to the bathroom. Returning, she lit the fire and settled herself at the table, feeling more like a guest than a member of staff as she made short work of the porridge, before tackling the mound of scrambled eggs and the strange, square shaped sausage. She told herself to count her blessings and make the most of it; all this was surely too good to be true. No doubt things would go downhill from now on. She rinsed her empty dishes and washed in the tea-tinted water. As she dressed, she wondered at how the neat looking Flora could be married to someone as scruffy as Hamish; now there was a case of opposites attracting if ever there was one! Finally, she re-read the Inn's advertisement in the February issue of *The Lady:-*

> *General Assistant needed to be part of small team*
> *in the remote but lovely Highlands of Scotland.*
> *Comfortable accommodation provided.*

All true enough; the team certainly sounded small, the area was definitely remote and lovely, and her room was comfortable. But it had been the next sentence that had really attracted her:-

> *Temporary position with the possibility of*
> *becoming permanent for the right person.*

There, that was the hook. And now only time would tell if she was indeed 'the right person'.

*

She walked into the kitchen at ten o'clock and was met by an awkward silence. She guessed that the four occupants had been talking about her, and was relieved when a man, his face well hidden behind a pair of large, tortoiseshell rimmed glasses, and a bushy, salt and pepper coloured beard, rose and walked towards her, a wide smile breaking through the hairy mass.

'Ah, hello there! It's Yvonne isn't it? Come on in. We've been expecting you. Here, let me take that.' He relieved her of the tray and put it on the draining board. Turning back, he looked down at her, with, what she felt, were pleasant and kindly brown eyes. 'I'm Donald MacMan, but you can call me Donald. And I think you've already met the rest of the crew,' he gestured towards the table, 'Mrs MacMan, Flora and Niall?'

Yvonne turned towards the group, and said to no one in particular, 'Yes, hello again. Thank you for the breakfast. It was a real treat.'

'Och, that's no trouble quine,' responded Flora, who found herself being impressed by the pale and polite girl, who, having undertaken such an arduous trip only the day before, had made the effort to present herself in a fresh and tidy sort of way.

A disgruntled, 'Humph!'was all Niall could manage, conveniently forgetting his own first day when he had been given the same breakfast in bed privilege.

Patting the empty chair beside her, Mrs MacMan invited Yvonne to sit down. 'Sleep well? It was a touch cold last night. You remembered about the fire?'

'Yes, and fine thank you, very comfortable. It's a really nice room.'

'Good, good. Well, come along, help yourself to some coffee.'

Yvonne looked with some wonder at the elegant silver-plated coffee and milk jugs and plate of chocolate biscuits. Surely they didn't do this every morning, did they? She could only think that it must be some sort of special meeting. And what did that word *quine* mean?

Donald saw the slightly awed expression on her face, and offered to pour for her. 'Here, let me do the honours. Half-and-half is the order of the day.'

Niall fidgeted in his chair and began to exude an air of restless discontent; either he was unaware of, or unable to stop one of his legs from twitching rapidly under the table.

Little flurries of conversation broke out amongst the group, giving Yvonne the opportunity to study Donald and Flora more closely. Like Georgina, Donald spoke with a refined Scottish accent. Tall and gangly, with limbs that seemed to stray in all directions, his heavily bearded face hid any clue of his age, which she guessed was probably about the same as his wife. His hair was fairly long and touched the collar of his shirt, which he wore open-necked and with the sleeves rolled-up. All this, along with a slightly baggy pair of faded corduroy trousers and worn suede shoes, gave him the air of a casual, mellow type of individual.

Flora looked to be in her mid to late sixties. Like Hamish, her face had been aired and coloured by years of wind and sun, although, unlike his, which had deep grooves and dark moles, hers was unlined and unblemished. Her short, fine grey hair was straight and neatly trimmed to cover the top of her ears. She had clear blue eyes, which looked upon those around her now with what could only be described as a faint air of alarm and disapproval. 'Tut-tutting'frequently to herself at the foolishness of their chatter, she intervened now and again to remind them 'of the great need to be wise'. It soon became apparent to Yvonne that although Flora's frequent forthright personal observations and mild-mannered censorships were accepted with good humour, they were, nevertheless, totally ignored.

Remembering the discoloured water, she searched for any evidence of peat-tinted skin tones, and was not disappointed. Flora, Mrs MacMan, and what little she could see of Donald's face, really did seem to have a light tan. Not so Niall, whose badly pitted countenance had a florid, puce hue; no healthy radiance there.

Eventually Georgina decided that it was time to get down to business. If Yvonne had not already met her, she would have quickly guessed that she was the top dog around here. There was a natural air of authority about the way she conducted herself, which, although not overbearing, was still very obvious.

'Well now, here we are. I think it would be helpful for Yvonne's sake if I explained what we all do. Mr MacMan and I are the owners-cum-managers, that is until our son takes over. Mr MacMan runs the bar and helps out in the dining room, as well as covering the kitchen on Niall's days off. In-between all that, he still finds time to do all the general handyman work around the place.'

A smile broke through Donald's beard as he gave his wife one of his benevolent, ponderous looks.

Flora, who had a strong dislike of male facial hair, saw her opportunity and spoke up, 'Aye, aye, indeed it is so. A busy soul if ever there was one, but never working-up to a great steam, which is wise indeed. You have a good, healthy glow about the ears now, Mr Mac, but as for the rest of your face, well, goodness only knows!'

Yvonne would have liked to have laughed, and it was only with some difficulty that she managed to control herself.

Georgina continued, 'Yes, well thank you Flora. Now, as you already know, Niall is our chef, and Flora is the housekeeper. I run the office and reception as well as keeping tabs on the dining room…and so forth. Between us, we manage to tick-over very nicely, although it should be a touch easier now you're here, Yvonne. Robert, that's our son by the way, is away at the moment learning the finer details of hotel management; he's due back in September. He's keen to put us more on the map, as it were, and one of the ideas he's come up with is that we start taking advantage of Art and Craft breaks, as well as the touring coaches that pass by; you know the kind of thing, coffees, light lunches … and so on.'

'Yep, probably working their way up to Kiliebeath for the ferry,' explained Donald. 'We'd make a good stopping-off point; give them a chance to stretch their legs. Going back to our roots, you might say. In days of yore we used to be a coaching inn, so I think it's kind of poetic that we'll be offering sustenance to weary travellers on the highways and byways again.'

Georgina, always the more down-to-earth half of the couple, found it necessary to add, 'Yes, dear. Only now they pass by a lot quicker and miss us. Some have started already; a bit early in my opinion. Anyway, we really don't want to take on too much to start with. He can develop things when he comes. But your main role, Yvonne, will be in the dining room and helping Flora with the housekeeping. We've fifteen rooms, and that's more than enough for us to cope with. I'll give you the tour and show you around afterwards. Oh, and yes, you mentioned that you can type, so I could do with some help in the office. You'll also be involved with the coaches when they start; serving and clearing-up afterwards ... and so on.'

Niall looked up quickly, and exclaimed in a broad, Glaswegian accent, 'Och, Mrs Mac, she'll no be needed in the kitchen!' There was no way he wanted the girl hanging around his territory any more than necessary.

Donald frowned, his eyebrows almost meeting to make one large caterpillar-like ridge across his forehead. 'What's the problem, Niall?' he asked.

'For goodness sake, Niall, be reasonable,' interjected Georgina. 'I'm sure Yvonne won't get under your feet. And it should only be two or three times a week, if that. She'll be in and out before you know it.' For some reason that she could not fathom, Niall had been more difficult than usual to manage recently, and now he was even making a fuss about this.

But Niall was not going to let the matter drop. 'Why can't Flora do it?' he asked, jabbing a finger in Yvonne's direction, and adding, 'and let *her* do the beds. Flora's always whinin' on about her back.'

Georgina stared hard at him. As far as she was concerned there was no need for any further discussion; matters had

31

already been decided. And that was that. 'Flora and I have already had a chat, and you're happy with the arrangement, aren't you Flora?'

Flora nodded. 'Indeed I am Mrs Mac; indeed I am. And I'm thinking it will work out just fine.'

'Good, good. That's settled then, and Yvonne, you can make a start with Flora tomorrow morning.' She rose, then remembered the phone call that had come in just before the meeting. 'By the way Niall, there'll be one more for dinner tonight. Well, I think that's everything. Things to do; busy, busy, busy.' Keen to leave before Niall could find anything else to cause difficulties over, she hurried out, calling behind her, 'Donald - a word.'

Draining his cup, Donald slowly raised himself to his feet and gave Yvonne a noticeable wink as he followed obediently behind. 'Bye for now folks.'

Flora stood and harrumphed. 'Well now, isn't that just the thing! She's forgotten about showing you around.' She glanced at the wall clock. 'Och, but let me see now, I'm ahead of myself, so I could be fitting it in. And I'm thinking twelve o'clock would be a fine time.'

'That would be great, thanks,' replied Yvonne.

'Just you come and meet me in reception then,' said Flora, leaving the room and calling one of her musical 'Cheery-bye's' behind her.

Yvonne stood and began making her own way towards the door to the staff stairs. The combination of the coffee and biscuits on top of the substantial breakfast seemed to be laying heavy, so she looked in Niall's general direction and said, 'I don't think I could fit any lunch in today Niall. Bye for now,' and left without waiting for any reply.

*

Even at a leisurely pace the tour could have been completed in less than fifteen minutes, instead of the best part the forty which it actually took, mainly due to Flora's encyclopaedic knowledge of the Inn and its owners, past and present. They began in the guest lounge. The sun was shining and several windows were open; a breeze catching the white lace curtains, causing them to float gracefully into the room. From there, they went into the dining room, which, apart from the impressive views, Yvonne considered was much the same as any other to be found in most medium sized establishments.

She learnt that Donald was the creator of the large silk flower displays that nestled away in some of the darker corners. Standing before a particularly large one, Flora commented, 'More dusting. Och well, I suppose some folks are that way inclined and like having such fripperies around the place,' making it clear what *she* thought of such things.

Prints of famous Scottish faces, places and historic events hung on cream, wallpapered walls. Mrs MacMan had let it be known from the start that she had no intention of wasting her energy, nor anyone else's, tending the large open coal fires in the public areas, and no time had been lost in replacing them with modern electric ones, each one boasting an artificial log or coal display.

The guest bedrooms were pleasant and had a more modern feel. Flora pointed to a group of prints depicting contemporary Highland scenes as they walked along the guest corridor. 'See now, young Robert's stamp on the place. All the way from Edinburgh, and I'm thinking none too cheap. But what that lad wants, that lad gets.'

The tour ended leaving Yvonne with the overall impression that the Inn was an unremarkable but comfortable place. She had worked and lived in far worse. Satisfied that she had done the place justice, Flora led the way to the housekeeping storeroom, saying, 'There's just the back. Then I must away.'

The air was chilly when they stepped outside. Yvonne crossed her arms tightly across her chest. Pointing to some metal steps, Flora said, 'It's a fire escape mind, but handy if you don't want to be bothering the inside. So, there you are now, I'd better away; Hamish will be fixating on the empty table. Till tomorrow then, eight o'clock, like I said.' She retrieved an ancient looking bicycle from a nearby lean-to, and called her usual 'Cheery-bye,' as she rode off. She came to an abrupt stop after a few yards and signalled Yvonne to join her. 'Now mind what I said quine, take no heed of Niall. He's a tricky mix of a soul, but a fair enough cook. Aye, you'll be needing to feel your way with that one.' She leant forward and patted Yvonne's arm. 'And I'm glad you've come, lassie, aye, truly glad,' and with that, she re-mounted the cumbersome device and pedalled slowly away, waving and calling another tuneful, 'Cheery-bye,' behind her.

Yvonne was sorry to see her go, but comforted herself with the thought that she would be seeing the kindly soul again in the morning. She climbed the steps and was relieved to find the door unlocked. Reaching her room, she decided to lie down for a while and think about what she should wear the next day, knowing that whatever she chose would need ironing. The place was so quiet, and still being travel-weary, she soon dropped off. She woke-up some time later, feeling stiff and thirsty. The water from her tap was ice cold and helped revive her as she stood looking out of the window. It was too good a day to shut herself in, so she changed into some slacks and a thicker jumper, and left the Inn a few minutes later.

Once outside, her eye was caught by the sight of countless sparkling silver ripples dancing along the surface of the loch; the sight appealed to her - it seemed the natural way to go.

CHAPTER 5

There was no one around when Yvonne reached the Inn. Disappointed that her first walk here had been ruined, she ran up to her room and went to look out of the window - no, no sign of *The Mad Man in the Heather*. Relief flooded through her. She would have to try and find out who he was and learn something of his habits; she didn't fancy having any more encounters like that! It would probably be best not to ask the MacMan's, or they might start thinking of her as a nervy type; it would have to be Flora, she was bound to know all about the local eccentrics. She felt taut and restless and wondered what she could do to unwind, then remembered the ironing. Fifty minutes later she hung her limited and rather old but carefully maintained garments back in the wardrobe, having pressed each one to within an inch of its life.

At six o'clock she braced herself and walked into the kitchen, her heart sinking when she realised that it would be just Niall and herself again.

'Over there!' he barked, jabbing a thumb at the table where a plate of sandwiches and a bowl of tinned peaches lay waiting, all uncovered. 'That'll be the lunch you did'na bother yourself turnin' up for.'

'I did tell you I didn't want any. Don't you remember?'

'Och, stop your greetin' and just get on with it!'

She would rather have taken a tray up to her room, but at least the oppressive silence was slightly dissipated by the sound of some indiscernible pop music coming from a transistor radio on the window sill. He began grating something, one arm moving furiously up and down like a pneumatic drill as he watched her out of the corner of his eye. She took a mouthful, and was pleased to find that although the bread had dried, the grated cheese and apple filling was still moist. As she ate, she reflected how much healthier the food was up here, so different from all the countless, greasy fry-ups and reheated leftovers she had endured over the years. It was just the atmosphere that was off. She finished and took the dishes over to the sink.

'Leave them!' he snapped.

'Alright, alright!' she replied, 'and I'd appreciate it if you'd stop talking to me like that. Good night!' There was no reply, but then she hadn't really expected one.

*

It had just gone half past six when she entered the telephone box and dialled Sandra's number. Soon she was answering the usual barrage of questions.

'Yes, fine. Tiring, but I got a few hours ... a few, at Inverness I think ... no, no sign of any bagpipes yet … they seem really nice ... I think she'll be okay, very efficient, businesslike, you know. Her husband's a bit of an old hippy, the laid-back type; I get the impression she wears the trousers. The food's good, can't see me going hungry here, but I seem to have got on the wrong side of the chef already. What? Hang on, I 've got to put more money in.'

With her back turned, she was unaware of the steady crunch of tyres on the gravel as the approaching car slowly curved its way into the parking area. Nor was she aware of the driver.

'What was that? Oh yes, you should see it, it's one of the best I've ever had, even got a gas fire. Can you believe it? Yes, I expect so ...'

The driver saw her and recognised her back view immediately. He had also seen the stag that had been ambling its way towards the telephone box; he had often come across the animal when out walking and knew it to be tame. But did the girl know that? The car slowed to a crawl before coming to a stop just yards away from the scene now beginning to unfold before him.

Yvonne felt a heavy thud behind her and turned quickly, half expecting to see Niall glaring in at her, and was, therefore, totally unprepared for the sight that met her. 'Oh no!' she exclaimed.

'What's up, what's the matter?' asked Sandra.

Stunned into silence, Yvonne had dropped the receiver and stood frozen to the spot, transfixed at the sight of the animal and its alarmingly pointed antlers, looming large on the other side of the glass panes.

Sandra's voice shrilled from the hanging receiver, 'Yvonne? Are you alright? Hello, hello. Yvonne? What's happening? Are you alright? *Yvonne. Hello, hello!*'

The stag had turned its head and was looking in at her with one curious and very dark eye. Obviously unconcerned, it resumed its laborious shoulder rubbing against the corner of the box, then began to emit a series of low, ominous sounding groans as it swayed back and forth.

Yvonne slowly, very slowly, pulled the cord and lifted the receiver back up to her ear. 'Sandra, shh, be quiet!'

'Why? What's happening? What's making that noise?'

Keen to stop her friend's continued high-pitched quizzing, which, for all she knew, could be aggravating the thing, she replied in as low and steady a voice as she could manage, 'There's a … a reindeer, no, I mean a deer … I think, with enormous antlers ...' Just then, the stag gave one almighty push, and lifting its impressive head, made a blood-curdling groan that vibrated menacingly throughout the box. Now she felt sure that the thing was gearing up to do...whatever these things did. 'Oh dear, I think it's going to - '

Thankfully, Sandra had the solution. 'Hang on. I'll get Tom,'and off she went, yelling loudly for the only person she could think of who just *had* to do something about this awful situation - and right now!

If Yvonne thought that she'd had enough shocks for one day, then she was soon to be proved wrong. For, there, with one hand grasping one of the ferocious beast's antlers, and the other signalling her to be quiet, was none other than *The Mad Man in the Heather!* She watched, open-mouthed, as he spoke soothingly to the animal whilst calmly stroking the side of its powerful neck. A full minute passed, although it felt far longer to her, and then, to her astonishment, he began to lead the ferocious beast away. Relief flooded through her as she noticed the man's bad limp and how heavily he leant on his stick.

Sandra's voice broke in, 'Hello Yvonne, are you there, he's in the bath. Typical! Isn't there anyone you can call? Nine-nine-nine, or someone? Oh Tom … *at last*, didn't you hear me calling? *Do something!'*

There was some muttering, then Tom's bemused voice came over the receiver. 'Hello, Yvonne. What's up? Sandra says you're being attacked by a huge reindeer in a telephone box. Tell me she's wrong!'

By now, the man and the stag were well clear, and all Yvonne wanted to do was to get out of her metal trap and put an end to the whole embarrassing situation.

'Hi Tom. It … it's alright. *The Mad* … a man came and took the thing away. Please tell Sandra I'm alright, and I'm sorry if … well, I'm going now. I just want to get out of here. Tell her I'll phone again later. Bye for now.' With that, she hastily gathered up her loose coins, pushed open the door, and ran into the Inn, giving only the swiftest of glances behind her.

The MacMan's had been laying tables in the dining room when they become aware that something out of the ordinary was happening outside. They had seen the car drive in and a man lead Rabbie away soon after. Giving each other a quizzical look, they rushed out and quickly assessed the situation. A shamefaced Georgina confessed, 'Oh no! I forgot to warn her about Rabbie. Poor girl.'

Donald began to experience several strong emotions all at once. On the one hand, he was doing his level best not to laugh out loud, but thought better of it when he saw how pale and obviously shaken Yvonne was; on the other, his heart went out to Rabbie. Poor Rabbie, the dear old boy wouldn't hurt a fly, and he had probably only called in for his usual titbits and a good old chin rub anyway.

Georgina immediately took charge. 'Do come in Yvonne, come on now. Donald, you'd better get her a brandy.'

Yvonne found herself being firmly led into the lounge and guided to a seat. A small glass of brandy was thrust at her, and not wishing to offend, she sipped it cautiously, grimaced and gave an involuntary shudder. Donald watched her negative reaction to the drink with interest. Recovering, she felt her anxiety levels begin to rise yet again when she noticed *The Mad Man in the Heather* walk past the windows and heard the vestibule door open. She stared over at him with a mixture of horror and fascination when he came to stand in the lounge doorway. This was really awful, not only had that animal just tried to push her and the telephone box over, but now she began to wonder if it might actually belong to him! Why else would they appear at the same time - and what on earth was he doing, going around the place with such a wild animal? Why couldn't he get a dog like every other civilised person? He and his dangerous pet should be locked up in a zoo. And why was he looking at her like that - was he actually *smirking?* Yes, he was! What a cheek!

Alexander was indeed trying to prevent his smile from becoming a smirk, but it was proving difficult when his overriding thought was that poetic justice had been done; now they were even. Her embarrassment must surely rate as high as his had been that afternoon when she had walked past him out there, although, magnanimously, he recognised that hers was of a more public nature.

'Mr and Mrs MacMan? I'm Alexander Grant. I called this morning.' Yvonne noted that he spoke with an English accent, but then, some Scots did.

As usual, it was Georgina who was the first to speak. 'Oh yes, goodness me! What a way to find us. Please, do come in. And thank you so much for, er, helping Yvonne. Poor girl, nasty shock, but of course, you already know. Still, no real harm done and, er ...' she gave a tiny, dismissive laugh, 'these things do happen.'

He approached and they shook hands. 'Pleased to have been of service.' Then he turned to Yvonne. 'We meet again, Miss ...?'

Yvonne knew that she had to play along and follow the rules of polite society. Making an effort to appear nonchalant, she took his hand and replied, 'Williams, Yvonne Williams.' Steel, that was the word that came to her as she looked into his eyes and felt his firm, cool hand in hers. She held his just as firmly in an attempt to convey that she was no shrinking violet, despite the evidence so far. However, this proved almost impossible, for he was observing her with such intensity that all she could do was stare back, perplexed.

He made no effort to let go of her hand as he continued his steady gaze. 'That was quite an experience you just had, Miss Williams.' He had not expected to see the girl again so soon and decided that there was no harm in looking. A bit young for his liking, and were those eyes green? Yes, definitely green. And he wasn't one for freckles, but the few she had dotted around her very pink cheeks were kind of cute. His initial assessment of her earlier on that day had been right, she was no great beauty, although very easy on the eye, even with that look of consternation and bewilderment. At last, he released her hand and took his seat.

Yvonne felt decidedly uncomfortable as she did her best to regain a modicum of dignity. Georgina had watched the scene closely and thought she could detect some kind of tension between the two apparent strangers. She turned to Donald, but was frustrated to see that his attention was elsewhere as he stood peering out of the windows, and guessed rightly that his whole concern was for that stag again. Ever the diplomat, she gave another dismissive laugh, and said, 'Er, yes, rather unfortunate timing. We must apologise Yvonne. Donald should have told you that the animal is really quite harmless,' and then addressing her still non-attentive spouse, added pointedly, 'Isn't that right, dear?'

Grateful for the opportunity to defend the honour of his old pal, Donald turned his attention back into the room. 'Aye, not a nasty bone in his body. He's a proud old man; probably just wanted a good old rub. You'll get used to him, Yvonne. He's a bit of clown, and you'll find him trying to shove that big head of his through the windows and doors. Trouble with that is he can get his antlers wedged; frightened one old lady near to death in the dining room last year. But most guests take it in good turn and reach for their cameras. He'd stay there all day if there's any titbits to be had.'

Alexander nodded knowingly. 'Actually, I've come across your illustrious tourist attraction several times when out walking. Seems a harmless enough fellow.' So, he thought, the girl was going to be here long enough to get used to the stag; obviously not a guest then.

Donald was well away now. 'They love him, and he enjoys all the fuss, especially around the - '

'Well, goodness me! Look at the time,' interrupted Georgina, knowing that her husband was on the verge of launching into one of his full-scale lectures on the wonderful world of Rabbie. 'What about an aperitif before we eat, Mr Grant, or shall we go straight in?'

Recognising that this was her cue to take her leave, Yvonne stood, and began manoeuvring her way around the table.

A smile flickered across Alex's face. 'Straight in, I think. Going so soon Miss Williams?'

'I've got one or two things to do,' she replied, addressing the table, before looking up at Georgina and Donald, and adding, 'And I'm sorry about all the fuss.' Then, unsmiling, with her back straight and her head held high, she made herself face *The Mad Man in the Heather* again. 'And thank you for … what you did, Mr Grant.'

Her coat had fallen open allowing Alex to see something of her figure. He made a quick scan and liked what he saw. 'My pleasure, Miss Williams. And I'm sure we'll … encounter each other again soon.'

Not if I see you first, she thought, attempting to walk with as much dignity as she could out of the room. At any other time or place she would have challenged him about his crazy behaviour that afternoon, but it appeared that he was the guest of the MacMan's; and goodness knows who, and what, he was! She was only the hired help around here and would have to remember that she was in a strange, wild sort of land now. There could be hundreds of those animals roaming around out there, and maybe even worse. Maybe the man was some sort of hunter, and that was why he had been lurking in the heather. That would make sense, although he couldn't be much of one with that bad limp of his. And those eyes, hard and searching, they'd suit a hunter alright, not that she knew much about such things - nor did she have any intention of finding out!

CHAPTER 6

Alex had considerable difficulty trying to get Yvonne's image out of his mind as he and the MacMan's chatted politely over their soup. 'It's good of you to agree to meet with me. I've been meaning to call before, but I've been a rather preoccupied lately.'

Georgina was immediately on the defensive. It was well known that the Tweedie's occasional soldier visitor had set his sights on the Manor, and she was keen to discover what his plans were for the place, especially if they could somehow affect the Inn. They already knew something of him from Dot and Angus: he was single, had family down south, and had taken a shine to this part of the world, often spending his leaves in their small bed and breakfast. Dot had been very guarded about the 'unfortunate accident' he had suffered, only revealing that it had been almost fatal, and had eventually resulted in a medical discharge. It had come as a nasty shock when they heard about it, and they had not expected to see much more of him from then on, so they were surprised when he had telephoned a few weeks after Hogmanay and asked if he could come and stay for a while. But this was nothing compared to their astonishment when, soon after, he told them that he had submitted a bid for the Manor. Somehow the news had leaked-out, and the rumours and speculations had started immediately, causing many a head to be scratched in puzzlement as to, 'what a single man could be wanting with such a big barn of a place'.

Georgina looked over at Donald. As usual, his attention was elsewhere, and knew it was up to her to get to the bottom of this mystery. She remarked, almost casually, 'Yes, we did hear something about you putting in a bid for the Manor. Have you heard anything yet?'

There was no disguising the delight in Alex's voice as he replied, 'Heard just this morning, our bid's been successful. We've got it!'

'We?' Asked Georgina, assuming that there must be a woman involved somehow.

'My partners and myself.'

'Oh, so you have partners?'

'Yes. They'll be joining me later.'

She looked questioningly at him, obviously expecting to be told more. Alex was happy to oblige, that was the reason he was here after all.

'Maybe I should explain. We're planning on opening a convalescent home. Actually, that's one of the reasons I've asked to meet with you. You're in the business of looking after folk, and I'd really appreciate your advice on one or two matters.' He paused, noticing a frown appear on her face.

At last Donald turned to look at their guest, then at Georgy; she appeared to be on top of things, so he turned back to the window and resumed his scanning. Alex decided to leave him be and concentrate on the little woman, who was definitely on full alert now.

'You look puzzled, Mrs MacMan?'

'Er, well, we naturally assumed that anybody who bought the place would continue to use it as a private home. But another convalescent home! Don't tell me they're closing Cairnsbrook House? Oh dear! That will upset a lot of people, and it's such a lovely place. Isn't it, Donald?'

Donald recognised the keen edge to her voice, and reluctantly shifted his focus inwards as he dutifully replied, 'Yes dear, lovely.'

Not a good start, thought Alex, and quickly responded, 'Not that I know of, and our plans have nothing to do with Cairnsbrook House. We intend to be more of a specialist convalescent home.'

Donald perked up noticeably and felt himself sufficiently stirred to ask, '"Specialist," eh? Sounds interesting?'

Georgina's mind began to work overtime. This 'specialist' thing did not sound too good to her. What was the man going to inflict on them: infectious diseases, alcoholics, or - Heaven forbid - drug addicts? This was most disconcerting. '"Specialist?"' she asked, 'In what way? Only, you'll understand, the local community has a right to be consulted about such things, and as far as I'm aware, no such consultation has taken place. One has to consider the impact of bringing, er, such people into the area. And to put it frankly, we do have our son to think about.'

Alex was fully prepared for this, as well as the many other such concerns and objections that would, no doubt, be raised before the evening was over. Even Dot and Angus had needed a fair bit of reassurance. 'Your son?' he asked.

Georgina gave Donald a look, which could only have been described as conspiratorial. He nodded, knowing that it would be almost impossible to stop her anyway. 'Don't suppose it'd do any harm. You might as well Georgy.'

Georgina's voice took on a sharper, more clipped tone as she proceeded. 'If you insist dear. It's like this, Mr Grant, Robert, our son, will be taking over here towards the end of the season, and naturally we have a duty to look after his interests.' She hesitated when she noticed that Donald looked as though he was preparing to say something, however, he was being too slow about it, so she continued. 'The thing is, he's discovered a few...er...let's say, gaps in the market, and he's extremely keen to explore them. We really bought this place for him several years ago and have just been nursing it along until he's ready to take over the reins. He got his degree in Hotel and Catering Management last year and is doing some fine-tuning in one of the more prestigious hotels in Invermaden. And, naturally, we'd be concerned about any new concern moving into the area, especially if it affected us here in any way.'

'Affected you, in what way? asked Alex.

'Well, Mr Grant, anyone who knows the area must surely realise that it can only support *one* hotel.'

'Ah, I see! Competition. And please call me Alex. Well, let me put your minds at rest on that score right away. I can't foresee any way that our two concerns should clash, or have any detrimental effect on each other. In fact, I believe the opposite could prove to be the case.' Although keen to get on, Alex was beginning to realise that he would have to find a way of allaying any unfounded fears the couple might be having. Then too, his own cause might well be served if they could be softened-up a bit, and it sounded as though this son of theirs might be the key. He went on to ask, 'But I am rather intrigued to hear about those "gaps" that your son has identified.'

Donald began to feel slightly easier at hearing Alex's reassurance, for, like Georgina, he too had been starting to feel more than a flicker of concern at hearing something of the man's plans. He pondered, then decided that it was probably safe to give him a few more details. After all, their own plans were hardly top secret, especially as they had already announced them to the staff earlier that day. 'Ever heard of the Arts and Crafts Movement?' he asked.

Alex looked at him, his surprise evident. 'You mean William Morris, Mackintosh - '

'That's the ticket. He developed a passion for such things when he went off to university, and came up with the idea of running Arts and Crafts themed holidays here. You know the kind of thing: talks, sketching, painting, throwing a few pots and so on; give folk some hands-on experience. He's also a keen amateur ornithologist and hiker, and I'm hoping he'll include something along those lines as well.' He had to pause for breath; it had been a long time since he had been able to make such a long speech without being interrupted. He turned and pointed at two prints hanging on the opposite wall. The first was of a golden eagle in full flight, its wings shining bronze against a clear blue sky; the other, a particularly becoming one of Rabbie, standing proud and erect in front of the Inn, a range of purple-blue mountains brooding dramatically in the background. 'That's some of his work. I wouldn't be surprised if he throws in some photography.'

Now that the floodgates had been opened, Georgina felt duty-bound to rush in. 'But I liked that Scottish literature idea. Did you know, Mr Grant, that Arthur Conan Doyle was Scottish? And that *Whisky Galore* was based on real events from up this way? And I'd like to think that there was a real

Monarch of The Glen; I'm sure there's still quite a few of those old patriarchal types around. Have you read it? Such an entertaining book, so amusing; I've read it several times. It always cheers me up! And I'm sure I don't have to tell you how popular Gavin Maxwell's *The Ring of Bright Water* is.' Then her animated expression quickly turned to one of almost disapproval. 'But I'm not one for poetry; personally, I don't care for it. Give me a good book any day.'

Donald looked mildly affronted. 'No Georgy, I keep telling you, it really touches some folk. And in these surroundings,' he made a long sweep of his arm to take in the view outside, 'it would be criminal to ignore our famous bards.' Turning to Alex again, he continued, 'I suggested he should combine it with some sessions on the local flora and fauna, maybe a bit of flower arranging; that would pep things up.'

'Oh Donald!' exclaimed his exasperated spouse, '*so* tame. Can you honestly see the Maxwell's going for that kind of thing?' Addressing Alex, she explained, 'They're a large family group that come for the Easter weekend every year. A lively lot, and far more interested in taking long hikes than listening to endless dirges about bonnie bluebells! And Robert knows that; he's got far more sense than to try to interfere with their routine.'

Alex sipped his fruit juice. It was obvious that they were on the verge of launching into an already much rehearsed family disagreement, and decided that the time had come for him to intervene if they were to get anywhere. He hoped that that son of theirs would have enough gumption to do whatever *he* wanted to do, and that these two would leave him alone to get on with it. Placing his empty glass on the table, he replied, 'Really? All Scottish you say? I didn't know that. And I've got to say, it sounds like your son's got his head screwed-on; and the fact that he's prepared to spread his net pretty wide should help.'

They were silent for a few moments as the main course arrived. Then he continued, 'You know, one or two of those activities you mentioned might have a therapeutic aspect to them and could well be of interest to some of our guests.'

There was no doubt now that he had gained their full attention. He quickly shot a silent arrow prayer Heavenwards: *Here goes Boss, please let them accept what I have to say with understanding and without prejudice.*

Georgina looked askance and leant forward holding her fork, precariously laden with a small mound of garden peas, over her plate. 'Oh? But I really can't imagine that any of your ... patients could have any interest in any cultural activity that we hold here. Surely convalescing people need peace and quiet?' She popped the fork's contents into her mouth with one precise movement, and then added reproachfully, 'And, to be frank with you, Mr Grant, our guests might feel rather awkward having to rub shoulders with people who've got some ... well, to put it bluntly, antisocial problems.'

Alex smiled patiently at her, recognising that, at last, the time had come for him to explain what the real purpose of Breagarroch Manor was going to be. 'Now then, Mrs MacMan, and it's Alex remember, it might help if you would allow me to tell you a bit about myself, and explain why many of our guests will have similar stories. And by the way, we shan't be referring to them as "patients"; just guests.'

Georgina frowned, and asked, '"Similar stories"?'

'Yes ma'am. You see, the Army was my life. I was a career soldier - until this happened,' he slapped his thigh, 'and I ended up being given a medical discharge. Then I had to regroup - think again. My original plan was to start my own outward bound centre when my contract was up, but obviously that wasn't going to happen. The unfortunate thing was that I just couldn't imagine doing anything else. I was out of a job, handicapped, and clean out of ideas.'

This was a sorry tale. And now Georgina found it necessary to be on her guard against the heady combination of the man's sad story and his good looks, for she had decided that he was indeed rather handsome. Glancing at Donald, she recognised that his whole demeanour was one of sympathy, and knew it would never do for them both to get carried away. 'Oh dear! How very unfortunate. But didn't the Army try and sort something out for you? And what about your family? Weren't they able to help you in some way?'

Alex nodded. 'No, there was no official help, especially of the type I needed. And my family was very supportive, although there was only so much they could do. After a while I came to the conclusion that it was down to me; it was time to take the pressure off and let everyone else get on with their lives.'

How could he tell them how bleak and utterly lost he had felt lying in that hospital bed, month after endless, painful and hopeless month? For over twenty years he had lived by the steel-hard military rule. Excellence, or at the very least, success, had been the only results he would accept, and he had needed them like he needed his daily bread and butter. Then, in one explosive, hellish moment, his whole life had been blown into kingdom come. The lower half of his once perfect body had been shattered, and what remained had been refashioned into an unsightly and scarred collection of flesh and bone. The whole, fully functional and confident person he had once been was gone forever. Cancelled out. Eliminated. And then Charles had entered his life, or to be more accurate, had been brought into his life, and it was he who had encouraged him to think about a change of scenery. Somehow the idea had taken root, and it was not long afterwards that he had picked-up the telephone and made that long-distance call to Dot and Angus.

CHAPTER 7

Alex genuinely enjoyed the meal and was generous with his compliments. He had gained a fair idea of how the land lay, and came to the conclusion that the couple had always inhabited a comfortable and secure world, albeit hardworking. His main task now was to help them to understand something of the experiences and needs of those who had lived very different lives, and, in particular, those who found themselves back in the almost alien civilian world many had left behind as just youngsters years before. He began, 'You're probably aware that I've spent some of my leaves with the Tweedie's, and that I came up for another stay soon after Hogmanay?'

Two heads nodded.

'Well, to cut a long story short, that turned out to be the best thing I could have done.' Then, appearing to change the subject, surprised them by asking, 'What lot were you in during the war Donald?'

There was such a note of authority in his voice that Donald found himself involuntarily sitting upright. A series of unbidden, unhappy memories of the years he had endured trying to put as much distance between himself and some power-crazed N.C.O.'s flashed across his mind. His reply, when it came, sounded as dismal as the expression he now wore on his face. 'Army. Cook in the Service Corps. And I don't mind telling you, a complete waste of six years of my life.'

'And what happened when you were demobbed? Did you have a plan, something to fall back on? Or did you just hope for the best, and drift into the first job that came your way?

I have my reasons for asking.'

'Oh, I knew exactly what I wanted to do alright! No offence to you, but I couldn't stand the life and just wanted to get back to my *real* one. Georgy kept the hotel going - we owned a small one in Edinburgh then.' He paused and began nodding, looking the picture of dejection. 'Not a good time for either of us.'

'I see,' said Alex, attempting to sound understanding and even sympathetic, 'but knowing what you wanted to do afterwards, and having someone waiting for you back home, that must have given you some comfort?'

'You can say that again! They were the only things that kept me going.'

'And I'm guessing that you rubbed shoulders with some who didn't? No one and nothing to go back to when it was all over?'

Donald's shoulders gradually returned to their usual relaxed position as he considered the question, his meal forgotten. 'Y-e-s. Hard to remember after all this time, but there were some like me, just marking time till being demobbed. Other blokes just sat around drinking their pay away. Poor devils! Couldn't see further than the bottom of the next bottle.'

'I'm afraid that's often the case, even today. But there's plenty of others, like you, who think ahead. Which brings us back to the type of work we'll be doing at the Manor. It'll be mainly with those who are getting on a bit by the time they're discharged, or out sooner than they'd bargained for. If there's no one and nothing to go back to, they soon begin to miss the life, especially the camaraderie. So I guess it's easy to see how they can end up propping-up the bar of their local ex-servicemen's club.' He paused and added thoughtfully, looking down at his leg, 'Easy enough thing to do, especially when you've come to the end of your own resources, which I had. And it was at that point that I found myself confronted with a choice. To cut a long story short, you've probably heard the saying, "Let go and let God"?' Two faces stared back at him, neither knowing exactly how to respond. 'Well, that's precisely what I did. I began to look seriously into the Christian Faith, and no one could have been more surprised than me when I found it starting to make some kind of sense.'

'Ah, now then!' exclaimed Donald, attempting to quickly empty his mouth so that he could enquire further.

However, Georgina was at a loss to see where all this retrospection could be leading, and feeling the need to bring the conversation back down-to-earth, asked, 'Well, of course, we know what you mean about that drinking problem. That's something we've always been very careful about, and we've always been strict about not allowing any such behaviour in any of *our* establishments. No one likes having a drunk around the place, but there's no harm at all in enjoying a few sociable drinks in pleasant company.'

'I'm delighted to hear it, Georgina, and it's a crying shame that other licensees don't follow your example,' said Alex, determined not to allow the conversation to be led off course. 'But getting back to when I came to stop with the Tweedie's - it turned out to be a blessing in disguise. There's something about this area: the peace, its separateness, so much space and sheer beauty. All I can tell you is that I feel very close to God here.' He ignored the small sigh that escaped from Georgina, but was pleased to notice that Donald appeared to be becoming more interested.

Georgina was remembering that Dot had mentioned something about how religious 'their soldier' had become, and knowing how those types did like to harp on, she decided to quickly intervene. 'Er, yes, it is lovely around here, and you must have some impressive views from the Manor? And are you ready for some dessert?'

'No thank you,' replied Alex, 'and yes, pretty special. Anyway, I got to wondering, what if it could have the same restorative type of effect on others that it had, and still has, on me? Then I heard that the Manor was up for sale, and - eureka! - the idea struck. What if I could get hold of it and try to create ...' he paused to look around him, 'I suppose, something like you've got here, a comfortable, friendly type of atmosphere, but with some kind of structured routine to the day? There could be some counselling and career advice on offer, maybe excursions and other recreational type of activities, things to help take people's minds off themselves for a bit. I reckon it could work.'

'Really?' exclaimed Donald, whose eyebrows now appeared to have become fixed in the raised position. 'My word! How interesting. You know, I've just had an idea - that is if you don't mind me making a suggestion - have you thought about keeping some animals? You know, caring for them? Might go down well, looking after the needs of others and all that. That would definitely help take peoples' minds off things.' Of course, he was thinking of Rabbie. There might be something there for him, after all, the dear old boy was aging fast, and who knows what would become of him when he wasn't around to keep an eye on him anymore.

Georgina appeared not to have heard this last exchange; she wanted to get back to the thorny issue of those heavy drinkers. 'Donald, why don't you pop in and tell Niall we're ready for coffee. I think we'll have it in the lounge. Come along now, Mr ... Alex,' she instructed, standing and leading the way.

Donald obeyed. Heading for the kitchen door, he turned to say over his shoulder, 'You'll let me know if anything like that does come off, won't you Alex?'

'Of course.'

Georgina lost no time in picking-up the drinking strand of the conversation again once they were settled. 'But why should you get involved with people with drink problems? Why can't you leave all that sort of thing to the A.A?'

'Right, well, drinking won't be the main issue for most. And, by the way, alcohol won't be allowed on the premises. Our main aim will in providing a place where people can come and think, a sort of retreat; help them to step out of their lives for a bit. Some may have physical problems, but they won't need much in the way of nursing care by the time they get to us. We'll be looking for ways to help them to come to terms with what's happened to them, and then encourage them to consider their options. Ideally, we'd like to try and give them some hope and purpose before sending them back into life, but armed with a realistic action plan.'

However, this explanation still did not satisfy Georgina.
She pursed her lips and frowned heavily. All this talk about
'retreats' and 'getting away' from life was far too airy-fairy for
her liking. And now she needed to find out what those
'physical problems' were all about. There was no mistaking
the disapproval in her voice as she asked, 'And these "physical
problems", I take it then, that these people will have been ...
what ... wounded, like you? In the line of duty?'

Alex shrugged and tried to sound matter-of-fact as he
replied, 'There might be the odd one, but our main emphasis
will be ...'

'Oh! So you will be having some then?' she interrupted.
'Don't tell me you'll be bringing shell-shocked cases here? Oh
dear! We know all about things like *that*. Personally, I can't
understand why they can't just pull themselves together, and
get over it. And to inflict that sort of thing on the local
community! It could be very disconcerting to suddenly find
such a ... a deranged person on the loose amongst us.'

Donald was beginning to feel very uncomfortable at his
wife's unsympathetic remarks, and said, placatingly, 'Oh,
come on Georgy, that's a bit rough.'

She bristled. 'Well it's okay for you men, but it's us
women who have to bear the brunt of it. Remember Fred? You
weren't there a lot of the time when I had to deal with him.
Behaved like a scalded cat every time there was the slightest
noise. I'll never forget all fuss and commotions he caused;
most embarrassing.' Addressing Alex, she explained, 'Fred
was our porter in Edinburgh, and gave us some very awkward
moments, I can tell you!'

Alex nodded knowingly. 'Don't worry, all our guests will
have been through the system and medically cleared before
they get to us. We'll be more concerned about their spiritual
well-being. Only those who've been vetted and are genuinely
keen to think about where they're going in life will be referred
to us.' Then, unexpectedly, the image of the eye-catching,
sunlit corona around a certain young woman's head came into
his mind. 'There may be a few who wander around talking to
themselves, but don't we all at times? I don't know about you,

but I certainly do when I've got a problem I'm trying to think through. In fact, I often pray out loud when I'm alone; doesn't mean to say that I'm mad, or disturbed.' He paused, hoping that this off-the-cuff explanation would neutralise any negative comments that that same young woman might have made to the couple about their encounter, just a few hours before.

Georgina, knowing herself to be an habitual self-conversationalist - although certainly not as bad as Flora - stubbornly refused to be mollified, and went on to ask, 'So, you will be taking in such ... cases?'

For some minutes Alex had been feeling that he was in an interview situation. Georgina MacMan was letting him know, in no uncertain terms, that anything and everything he was planning to do anywhere near the Inn would have to be met with her approval. Nevertheless, he went on to patiently explain, 'We prefer not to think of our guests as "cases", and there may be the odd one or two. But it's like I said, they'd have been treated and stabilised before they come to us.'

Donald had been peering up at the ceiling, and now seemed to find written there the answer to a riddle he had been puzzling over. 'Ah, I think I'm getting your drift. You'll be taking in people who've got themselves into a bit of a state ... and need a helping hand to adjust to life back in Civvy Street. That's about right, isn't it?'

Alex felt a wave of relief; at last one of the pair had finally got the message, or at least part of it. 'Exactly. Only there'll be another very important aspect to the care we'll be offering. For some, it will be more of a retreat. We want to help people who've come to the end of their own resources and realise that they need something, or more importantly - Someone - to help them. At some point in our lives we all need to take God seriously and acknowledge our need of Him.' He paused for effect, then added, 'Before we meet Him.'

The thought of meeting God somehow bounced off Georgina, who now found herself starting to become concerned about the unpleasant prospect of having some religious fanatics around the place. 'Er ... when you say '"retreat", you're not talking about starting up one of those dreadful hippy kibbutzes are you? Oh dear! Heaven help us!'

Alex knew that this was exactly how the Manor and its ministry could appear to the locals, and was about to reassure her, but before he could utter a word, Donald broke in. 'No, no, Georgy, calm down! You've got it all wrong. Try and imagine something along the lines of a…a toned-down military kind of monastery.' Pleased with himself, he gave Alex a self-satisfied, man-to-man smile.'

Alex smiled widely back, amused at Donald's description, and stored it away to share with Charles and Izzy later. 'Almost, Donald. Just try to think of it as another convalescent home, only one with Christian counsellors and career advisors on-board, then you'll get the idea.'

Georgina felt her panic subside slightly, but only slightly. Thank goodness there were to be no pot-smoking layabouts wafting around the place! But, just to be on the safe side, she went on to ask, 'And where will these counsellors come from?'

'All the mainline denominations: Church of England, and Scotland of course, Methodist, Baptist, United Reformed, Pentecostal. The usual. We've already got several civilian ministers and counsellors signed-up, as well as quite a few retired padres, many of whom would have gone through similar experiences to our guests and will be able to talk their language. It seems that the chance to spend a few weeks in the Highlands is proving very appealing.'

'Ah, so, normal vicars then, nothing highfalutin?' asked Donald, who had been imagining clusters of purple and scarlet-robed bishops, chanting and drifting eerily around the loch.

'All very normal, I can assure you,' confirmed Alex.

The whole scheme sounded fascinating to Donald and he was keen to hear more. He promised himself there and then that he would pay the Manor a visit as soon as it was up and running.

Georgina began to wonder if the place might prove to be harmless after all. But one could never be sure, so just to be on the safe side, went on to enquire, 'And does that mean that you'll have professionals involved; experienced people, good at dealing with … such matters?'

'Very professional, extremely experienced. One or two are actually quite well-known.' This was no exaggeration; Charles was already in discussion with two such popular conference speakers who had declared themselves interested in the project.

Now it was Georgina's eyebrows that were raised. 'Really?'

Alex continued, 'That's one of the main reasons I wanted to see you tonight, to ask if you'd be willing to put the odd one up from time to time, especially if we find ourselves pushed for space.'

Her eyes lit up. She was thinking quickly now, and wondered if this might actually turn out to be something of a coup. After all, it wasn't every establishment that could boast about having well-known guests under their roof. Robert would be pleased. 'Well, we might consider having the odd one or two, if we're not too stretched.'

Donald's gaze shifted to the walking stick hooked onto the back of Alex's chair. 'Do you mind telling us what you'll be doing in all this, that is, if you don't mind?'

'Not at all. My role will be mainly logistical, working in the background - more as a facilitator. It'll be my job to make sure the place runs smoothly and everyone has everything they need. There'll be a medical officer and trained nurse permanently on-site to handle the official side of things.' Smiling, he looked directly at Georgina, and added, 'Everything will be done by the book, but with a bit of imagination; a bit like it sounds your son wants to do here.'

'I see,' she said, deciding that this man certainly had all the answers when it came to all the airy-fairy stuff, but now she was curious to find out what plans he had made about the more important, down to earth matters. 'So you'll be responsible for the staff then? I hope you're prepared; it's an onerous task you know, running an establishment and catering for people's needs. You'll find it hard to find an experienced cook and other staff around here. We're lucky to have Flora and Niall, but we had to search further afield to find Yvonne; she came to us from King's Lynn of all places!'

Alex found himself more than a little interested to learn this piece of information about Yvonne Williams, which was something he would certainly have to think about later. 'The staffing's all organised, but I would value your advice on one or two other matters: reliable wholesale suppliers, milk deliveries, window cleaners, laundries, any special arrangements about refuse collection, things like that.'

Now these were things that Georgina had a wealth of experience about, and relieved that all the talk about feeble minded people wanting religion was over, she replied enthusiastically, 'Yes, of course! I'd be delighted. You've come to the right place.'

*

By the time he pulled away from the Inn, a well-worn copy of *The Monarch of The Glen* on the passenger seat beside him, Alex decided that things had gone far better than he could have hoped. But then, he had prayed. It had been a bit tricky for a while, but thankfully the couple's initial cautious reaction to the idea of the Manor appeared to have been replaced with one of enthusiastic acceptance by the one, and a tacit acceptance by the other.

He considered again how easy it could be for him to be misunderstood; Charles had been dead right when he had warned that he might be seen as some sort of eccentric religious fanatic. But protecting his own reputation was infinitely less important than that of the Manor; it could cause all sorts of problems if the place started life on any potentially harmful footing. For the venture to succeed, apart from The Boss's Hand on it, it would need the goodwill of the local community, including that of one of its nearest neighbours - the Tananeach Inn.

At the moment, he would have to conclude that the evening's mission had been a success; a small but significant sign had been when Georgina had started to use his Christian name, and their invitation to attend the next ceilidh had sounded genuine enough. No doubt Miss Yvonne Williams would be there - Miss Williams from King's Lynn. Now that was a long way to come to work in a hotel; might there be a bit of a mystery there? Maybe he should think about going to the ceilidh; he wouldn't mind taking another look at her.

CHAPTER 8

Yvonne knocked on the office door at exactly nine o'clock the following morning. 'Come in,' trilled a voice from inside. 'Ah, there you are Yvonne. Close the door; it's none too warm in here yet.'

Georgina looked tired, but managed to smile as she pointed to a chair on the other side of an enormous desk. 'That's your spot.'

'Good morning Mrs MacMan.' Yvonne glanced around as she took her seat. The room appeared to be as neat and organised as its owner.

'First things first.' Georgina reached over and handed her two copies of the Job Description she had spent a considerable amount of time on some days before. 'Read through this and sign both copies; you can keep one for yourself.'

This was a new experience for Yvonne, who had never before been offered one of these documents. She read the long list of requirements, and her doubts about being kept fully occupied in this place melted away. She signed both copies then handed one back.

'No questions?' Asked Georgina, quietly relieved not to have been challenged, as she slid the item into one of the drawers on her side of the desk.

'No, but I'll ask if anything does crop up.'

'Good, good, good. Well now, that's out of the way, let's see what your typing's like.'

The next hour flew past, leaving Georgina more than happy with the young woman who appeared to be able to quickly grasp what was required of her and perform each task to a very satisfactory standard.

*

Georgina yawned daintily into her hand as she poured her second cup of coffee. Due to Niall's absence, this morning's gathering was a far more relaxed affair than that of the previous day. Yvonne learned that it was his day off, and, as was his habit, he had skipped breakfast and hitched a lift into Braegarroch. She wondered what he would find to do all day in such a tiny place.

Georgina yawned again. 'Do excuse me. It took me ages to drop off last night. I couldn't stop thinking about all that business up at the Manor.'

A large hole appeared in Donald's beard as he yawned back. 'Me too. Mind you, I liked the man; got a feeling he'll shake the place up a bit.'

'Shake the place up? Oh dear, I hope not!' exclaimed Georgina. 'Let's hope he really does know what he's doing and can keep a tight rein on things.'

Flora, who had known all about Alex's proposed plans for several weeks, added, 'Aye, but Dot and Angus thinks he's the sort who'll do just fine.'

'Oh, so you knew all about it then, Flora?' asked Georgina indignantly. 'I wish you'd have told us what he was up to. Poor Donald had quite a nasty shock!'

Looking mildly affronted, Flora quickly responded, 'Och, away with you Mrs Mac! There's nothing for you to be fretting yourself about, and I'm sure it wasn't my place to be doing any such thing.'

'And I wasn't shocked, dear,' said Donald, 'just a tad surprised. He's taking on quite a challenge there, especially with that leg of his. But I can't see him putting up with any nonsense; doesn't seem the type.'

Trying to sound unconcerned, although quite keen to hear exactly what it was that might need keeping 'a tight rein' over, Yvonne asked, 'Are you talking about your guest last night?'

'That's right,' replied Georgina, 'and would I be right in thinking that you two have already met?'

'No ... well, yes ... that is, I passed him when I went out for a walk yesterday.' Yvonne could have taken the opportunity to comment about his peculiar behaviour, but somehow felt it would be wrong - although as to why, she had no idea, and reminded herself to ask Flora about him later on.

Feeling her feminine intuition cranking up a gear, Georgina sipped her coffee, and quietly agreed with herself that there had definitely been some sort of connection between those two, and she would do well to watch points there.

'Apparently he likes taking long walks, but I don't expect he'll have much time for that when things get going,' explained Donald, who then went on to give a short summary of the previous evening's meeting.

And so Yvonne learned that Alexander Grant, alias *The Mad Man in the Heather*, was lodging with one of Hamish's cousins, that he regularly attended the local kirk, had family down south, and was single. As a result, she came to the conclusion that her initial impression of him might need some adjustment; now it appeared that he was, in fact, a rather caring, sensitive individual, even a bit of a Good Samaritan. Maybe she should start thinking of him as *The ... Man in the Heather* from now on, and miss out the *Mad* bit. But then, why should she even bother? What did it matter to her what type of man he was, mad or otherwise?

Donald finished with his belief, that, 'There's always been a crying need for such a place,' and that, he, for one, 'was jolly glad to know that someone was finally going to do something about it!'

Georgina knew that Donald's soft nature had been touched, however, she would not allow herself to be so easily swayed. Alexander's reassurances had diminished in her mind overnight, and only time would tell what impact having such people living nearby would have upon them all. If Robert's plans succeeded, the last thing he needed would be the emotionally disturbed running amok around the area and upsetting the guests.

'Well dear, we shall just have to wait and see, won't we?' she said. 'Time will tell. And gracious me, talking of time, Yvonne, we'd better be getting back to the office.'

*

The rest of the day passed pleasantly enough. Georgina kept Yvonne busy, but there were times when she had a few moment's lull between jobs. During these times, and despite repeated attempts to shrug off the whole notion of Alexander Grant, curious thoughts about him would keep popping uninvited into her mind.

At five o'clock, she slowly climbed the stairs to her room. If Georgina's thanks had been anything to go by, then she had done her work well. She stretched and yawned. The air was different here, the water too. It would take her a few more days to acclimatise, but she had a feeling that she was really going to like it. She appreciated her room, and had every reason to believe that she would find the job enjoyable - certainly not boring. The Inn had a sort of homely feel about it, and she was looking forward to discovering more about the area. And she and Rabbie might even become good friends! If this wholesome, quiet and remote place wanted to wrap itself around her, then she wasn't about to complain. The only fly in the ointment was Niall, but if that problem could be resolved, then this might well turn out to be the place she had been looking for all this long, long time. Of course, there was that peculiar Alexander Grant lurking in the background. Now why on earth should she be thinking of him again?

CHAPTER 9

It was early morning when Alex silently eased the car away from Rosedale Croft, having already said his farewells to Dot and Angus the night before. His best suit lay across the back seat, along with the briefcase containing his speech and plans for the Manor. He had worked hard on them both, especially his speech, which he hoped would do justice to Charles and Izzy's special day. He had been looking forward to making this trip for some time and relaxed back into his seat, enjoying the freedom of the empty road and the fine scenery. Angus had assured him that the fair weather would hold, which was just as well, considering the challenging three-and-a-half hour drive ahead.

However, about forty minutes into the journey, he was rudely jolted out of this pleasant state when a loud bang came from somewhere behind, causing the car to lurch sideways. Remaining calm, he performed a classic emergency stop, opened his door and stepped out. All was quiet. A quick inspection of the vehicle revealed a series of newly formed scratches on the nearside panel, just above the wheelarch. He looked behind and spotted the likely cause, a large rock lying in the middle of the road, some thirty yards away. Obviously, it had chosen the precise moment he was passing to become dislodged and roll down the hillside.

Offering heartfelt thanks to The Boss for his deliverance, he walked back and began pushing and rolling the culprit out of harm's way. It would do no good to get stuck out here; another vehicle might not pass by for hours, and he must not miss his flight, and, therefore, the wedding. Satisfied, he climbed back into the driver's seat and drove on, keeping a good eye on the hillside and road ahead.

He felt calm and not even mildly shaken. How different from the not too distant past, when any loud and unexpected noise had the ability to turn him into an uncontrollable, quivering mess, his mind splintering into as many fragments as the landmine that had blown him so violently out of his old life. The memories may still be there, but they had no more hold on him - and no more power to control. His body may be slow to heal, but his mind had been made whole and strong again; it had been permanently, wonderfully and miraculously healed. And this latest incident only went to prove just how much.

*

That healing had started some fourteen months earlier when a smiling, sandy-haired man approached his hospital bed and introduced himself as the Reverend Charles Harmer, the hospital's Free Church Chaplain. Alex was prepared. Earlier that day he had overheard a couple of nurses talking about the Chaplain who had recently returned from one of his frequent trips away with the Territorial Army. As a rule, he would have been reluctant to enter into any sort of dialogue with any member of the clergy, but this man was ex-Army, and that made him just that bit more interesting.

The two began to talk, and to his surprise, Alex found himself warming to the diminutive figure standing at ease beside him. The man did not pontificate, or insist upon spouting weird religious stuff; instead, here was a quiet individual who exuded a peaceful sort of confidence and a winsomeness that he found very likeable.

Alex was to learn something of Charles' own background during the next few months. An Army Medical Officer in his former life, he had received the call to the civilian Church at the end of his contract, and had gone on to retrain as a Methodist minister. After ordination, he was given the responsibility of three small rural chapels, deep in the heart of the Cambridgeshire countryside. Unencumbered by wife and family, and finding that he had some spare time on his hands, it was not long before he volunteered to join the Chaplaincy team of the local hospital.

It was during one of his routine ward rounds that he had met Sister Isabelle Blair, who had just been transferred from theatre to the male orthopaedic ward. There was something very appealing about her, and he was delighted to learn that she was an outgoing and enthusiastic member of the local Assemblies of God Church. Just as interesting was the news that she was a year off retirement, had never married, and had been alone in the world since the death of her widowed mother, some years before. The couple began to meet, and it was not long before a delightful friendship began to blossom, which eventually turned into an even more delightful romance.

*

Charles was warned not to expect too much when he first walked into Alex's room; the patient had been very seriously wounded and was still in considerable pain. Suitably prepared, he was not surprised when he had been met with little enthusiasm. He called in briefly whenever back on the same ward, and by the fourth visit was to be rewarded with some promising signs when the troubled soul began to cautiously reveal something of his inner turmoil.

Alex found that he was able to let down his guard and permit his pent-up anger, confusion and frustration to surface without any feelings of shame or embarrassment. And it was he who introduced the subject of religion as he asked his questions; the fierce sectarianism he had witnessed in Northern Ireland had left its mark on him in more ways than one. Charles would reply in such undogmatic, almost matter-of-fact ways, that he found himself becoming interested in hearing what the Christian stance on several other controversial subjects. At times, he would find some amusement in challenging or disagreeing with them robustly, especially when the subject touched a still-too-raw nerve.

These mostly good humoured debates continued to entertain and stimulate Alex for several months, until, one day, he became aware that there was a small corner of his mind that was reluctant to continue being quite so argumentative. 'You keep talking about Jesus,' he asked, 'it's almost as though He's at the centre of everything, but is there any *real* historical, secular proof that the man actually existed?'

'There most certainly is!' replied Charles emphatically. 'He's mentioned in the writings of various scholars and historians. Unfortunately, we know that the Romans invaded and destroyed large areas of Israel and most of Jerusalem and its people in A.D. 70, burning whole cities to the ground. We can only imagine how much documentary evidence, especially by eye-witnesses of Jesus Himself, perished at that time. But there are other sources still remaining. Of course, there's always those, especially amongst the more liberal scholars, who try to discredit them, but if they applied the same rules of rejection to *all* historical evidence, then they'd have to claim that Alexander the Great - and even Julius Caesar - were myths as well!'

'Interesting,' replied Alex. 'I wouldn't mind taking a look at some of that evidence. Where is it? But, then again, now you're going to tell me that it's filed away in some obscure library, and written in some ancient language.'

'Afraid so, unless you can read Aramaic, Latin or Greek. And if you're that interested, I could let you take a look at some articles *The Open-Minded Reviewer* came out with a few years back.'

'*The Open-Minded Reviewer*, eh? Fair enough. As long as there's no subtle form of brainwashing's involved.'

Charles laughed. 'Oh, you'll be safe enough. As long as *you* can keep an open mind!'

'Okay. Bring them in, and I'll give them a go.'

Charles took the small pile of magazines in on his next visit. Alex studied the articles closely. The subject began to fascinate him, and Charles was duly despatched to find and purchase any further contemporary literature covering the topic, with the instruction that he should bring in an equal amount of secular as well as Christian material. He was thinking long and hard now, and beginning to realise that there was a great deal of logic and plain old common sense in what Charles had been saying. And it was about this time that he began to reach behind his bedside locker and take out the book that the hospital provided for each patient: the *Gideon's New Testament.*

*

At last he was able to get about on crutches, and soon he would be discharged into the care of his family. They were having one of their regular walks around the grounds when he confided in Charles that he'd had 'some sort of religious experience' the night before.

'The dayroom was empty and I took myself off to read, then something strange happened. I'd reached that bit about God loving the world and giving His only Son - you know the bit I mean?'

Of course Charles knew, and went on to quote the famous words of *John 3:16:*-

> *For God so loved the world that he gave his one*
> *and only Son, that whoever believes in him shall*
> *not perish but have eternal life.*

'That's the one. It was ... I found it ... kind of disturbing.'

By now they had reached the ancient yew tree, and, as was their custom, stopped to rest and sit on the bench under its wide canopy. Alex stretched out his legs and began to slowly massage his left thigh. 'That bit about *the world* got me thinking.'

Charles leant back and looked thoughtfully at the younger man's profile. Even at this angle he recognised the familiar pain etched across his brow, but there was something else, something he could only describe as a sort of lightness about his manner. 'Aha. And how do you see yourself fitting into that picture?' he asked.

'Well, as far as I can tell, it was the Romans and some of the Jewish leaders who organised and carried out the...the killing. But other references seem to claim that the sin of the whole world was actually at the root of it. Am I right?'

Charles felt that there were too many generalisations there for his liking, and went on to ask, 'Absolutely right. And how do you see that as relating to you, personally?'

'Well then, I guess that He ... He ... died for me too!'

Charles nodded. 'That's exactly what it means. But do you know why?'

By now, Alex had stopped rubbing his thigh and was leaning forward, his hands clasped tightly in front of him. As though pained by the words, he spoke them out, 'Well, I guess … for my sin too.'

'Ah yes. Sin. Not a word we bandy about much these days.'

'Er, it is kind of antiquated,' commented Alex, 'but according to what I've been reading, seems we're all guilty of it; that whole world thing again. And shepherds and sheep seem to be a significant and recurring theme. He gave a short, mirthless laugh. 'I've never thought of myself as a sinning sheep.'

'And now?'

'I'd … have to say … guess I was mistaken.'

'Hmm. What else have you read about those sheep?'

'They needed, we need … *I* need … a shepherd, to find and rescue us all. Rescue me. And that Shepherd was Jesus Christ Himself. That's what Easter's all about, isn't it? His death and resurrection? He came back because He wants to...to be with us?' He let out a great sigh, relieved to be able to put into words the amazing truth he had been confronted with the night before - and was still struggling to come to terms with.

Charles nodded, 'And to show us how much God loves us, by sending His only Son to pay the price for our sin. He paid it, once and for all, by taking the punishment we all deserve - no exceptions.'

Alex looked up. 'Man! What could I do? It was mind-blowing! And I don't mind telling you I was in a bit of a state. To suddenly realise that He, *Jesus Christ Himself,* chose to … to die … for *me!* I felt I had to do something about it, to make some kind of response.'

'And did you?'

'I think so. I just prayed and told Him that I'd got the message … I hadn't known … hadn't realised … and was sorry, *really* sorry that He'd had to go through all that for me.' Eager now to tell all, he continued, 'I tried to remember all the things I'd done wrong over the years, and apologise, but...it was impossible.' Hesitating briefly, he turned to look questioningly, almost despairingly, at Charles. 'In the end I just apologised for what I could remember.'

Charles had no doubt now that Alex had had a real touch from God. It seemed that this troubled man had made the longest journey of his life, and one that each soul is free to make: the average eighteen to twenty-two inches from head to heart. And what an incredible journey it was. For Alex, it had started with an initial curiosity about the historical fact of the man, Jesus Christ, and had finished with the understanding of why, and for whom, He had allowed Himself to be crucified. Along the way he had come to recognise his own need for forgiveness and the need to make a wholehearted repentance.

Charles smiled and nodded reassuringly. 'God understands. And don't worry, if we're truthful, we all have the same problem. Sin is a general term for everything you've ever thought, said and done that falls short of His holy standards. None of us can really ever know the full extent of our wrongdoings, but it's good to confess them as soon as they come to mind, and they will. And when they do, we should get them dealt with quickly, or they can become a sort of stumbling block. We all need to keep short accounts with God and be genuine about wanting His forgiveness. And you don't have to be a murderer or a hardened criminal; everyone's sinned, just by going their own way and ignoring Him as though He never existed.'

Alex gave a long, low whistle. 'In that case, boy, am I guilty!'

Charles saw his anxious expression and felt that some reassurance was needed. However, before he could say anything, Alex spoke again, 'So, let me get this straight. You're saying I'm right in thinking that that's what the Cross was all about? Paying the price to put us right with God, and satisfying His justice?'

'Partly, but His love is the main message of the Cross. The kiss of the Cross I like to think of it - God's kiss to us. He longs for us to accept His love. Free of charge now. And think about it, we all want justice, we want to see the guilty party pay for their crimes, so why shouldn't God? Like I said, the price has been paid; His Son came to Earth to pay the full price for us all. He took your place Alex, willingly, because He loves you, and wants to bring you back into a right and proper relationship with Him. Think of Jesus's arms stretched out on the Cross, in a way they were like a bridge, one arm touching you, and the other touching His Father. By accepting Jesus's sacrifice on your behalf, you cross that bridge and become a child of God, and He becomes your Heavenly Father.'

'That's kind of amazing. I ... well, you know ...' Alex closed his eyes as the full impact of what he had just heard began to sink in.

As he waited, Charles started to quietly sing some of the verses of a hymn that seemed particularly appropriate for this moment:-

There is a green hill far away,
Outside a city wall,
Where our dear Lord was crucified,
Who died to save us all.

There was no other good enough
To pay the price of sin;
He only could unlock the gate
Of Heaven, and let us in.

'As a child, I never could understand the *He only* bit. It always sounded as though that was *all* He was capable of. Shame the writer didn't say *Only He*, being the *only* One who could open Heaven's gate for us. *Only He* loved each one of us enough to take our place on the Cross, the place that each one of us deserves. It was *only He* who sacrificed Himself. That's why He's called "The Lamb of God", He was the final sacrifice; there's no more needed.'

A breeze caught some of the fallen autumn leaves from the nearby beech trees and blew them around their feet. Alex took hold of one of his crutches and began to prod and push them into a small heap. Somewhere, a bird began to sing.

'It all makes sense now. You know, Charles, I actually imagined myself looking up at Him, on the Cross. Somehow, it ...' He paused inhaling sharply as the emotions of the previous night threatened to flood back and overwhelm him again. 'Man, it was so ... *real!*' He had to stop; this was hard. He had never spoken like this before, never talked about such deep, soulful, intangible things.

'I know what you mean. You saw Him there, in your mind's eye. I remember standing there too - that first time.'

'That first time?' asked Alex.

'It's a place many of us need to go back to from time to time. But go on, if you can.'

'Er, well, I seem to remember asking if He was hanging there because of me ...' He paused, then said quietly, 'And He said, "Yes".'

A long silence followed, and it seemed that the very air was holding its breath. Charles closed his eyes and silently thanked the Lord for being allowed to play his part, well aware that no human agency could have reached so deeply and touched a man's dead spirit, igniting it with the gift of faith, and bringing it, at last, into divine life. This was the work of God.

Now Alex felt - wanted - needed - to know that it was okay, that others had felt these strange new emotions too. It sounded as though Charles had, but he was a minister, a man of God, and therefore special. But he, Alexander Grant, was a normal, everyday bloke. Why had it happened to him? Had everything that had taken place since the blast finally caught up with him, and was causing him to have some sort of delayed, religious nervous breakdown? What other reason could there be for this strange, inexplicable light and alive, *so* alive feeling...and even happiness? He was having trouble trying to compose himself, but managed to say at last, 'Seeing Him up there ... it's hard to describe ... but if I could, I would have got Him down. Charles, please tell me I'm not going mad!' He couldn't go on, the memory of the image was burning into his mind again, so powerful and real that he could almost have reached out and touched the blood-soaked, flesh-torn feet.

'You're probably saner now than at any time in your life. And you did.'

'I did?'

'Take it from me, by recognising that He was hanging there in your place, and being absolutely sincere about wanting His forgiveness, you freed Him. You got Him off that Cross.'

Alex stared at him, speechless now.

Charles laughed. 'And my advice to you is to keep reading your New Testament, and you'll find that everything will start falling into place. So, what happened next?'

'Er, phew! Let me see ...' The feeling of relief was almost palpable, and Alex attempted to sound coherent as he continued, 'I seem to remember promising that I'd do my best from now on, but that He'd have to help me out, I'm no saint. And that was it.' He gave a short laugh. 'I tried to get some sleep, but it was useless. I found I just wanted to keep thanking Him.'

'Sounds like you still do?'

'Yes, I do. I'm tired, but I'm feeling good, well, more than good. I've got this, and don't laugh, this kind of excited, *really* good feeling going on inside me. It's as though ...' but this was going too far. How could he explain the deep sense of relief and the extraordinary sensation of peace that he had been experiencing since his encounter? 'I feel ... disorientated.'

Charles laughed delightedly, recognising it for what it was: the amazed and mystified expressions of a newly freed soul. '*Hallelujah!*' he exclaimed. 'God's in your heart; you invited Him in when you got Him off that Cross. Now He'll stay with you forever, you're His child, a Child of God, and He's your Heavenly Father. You've been born again into a new family and have a new life. He lives in you by His Spirit, The Holy Spirit, His very Self inside you.'

'He's ... *inside me?*' Alex asked, incredulously.

'Well, you took the time to study the evidence for yourself, didn't you? And realised that it made sense? Now you've trusted God's written Word, and believed with your heart.' He paused, making a mental note to discuss baptism with him later on as he patted him on the shoulder. 'Well done lad, your name's written in *The Book of Life,* and you've got your ticket to Heaven!'

Alex still couldn't quite come to terms with it all; it couldn't be as easy as that - could it? Didn't people have to be churchgoers for years, or pray all night long before getting that close to The Almighty? Isn't that what pilgrims and saints spent their lives suffering and striving for? But all he'd done was to do some research, then spend time thinking about, and accept, what was written in the first half dozen books of the New Testament. If it was true, and God really had come to live in him, then it was incredible, amazing, wonderful. Miraculous!

'Tell you what,' said Charles, 'there is one more thing you can do.'

'One more thing?'

'It might be an idea, and something you might find beneficial, especially later on. You could formally invite Him into your heart; a sort of inking-in of what you pencilled-in last night. And it's something you can point back to in the future, especially when things get tough and the doubts start - as they will. It's something you can stand on, and say, "Yes, I did it there and then, and here's the proof."' He drew out a small leather-bound Bible from his side pocket and retrieved a card from the back. It was his habit to keep a selection of prayer cards on his person, and this was one he found particularly useful when ministering in a sickroom situation. He handed it to Alex, 'Take a look at this.'

Alex looked at the heading: *The Prayer of Christian Salvation.* There was a short prayer, and above it, the Scripture that had exercised him so much the night before: *John 3:16.* Underneath was a space for a signature and date.

Charles continued, 'Think of it as a sort of spiritual birth certificate. You could read it out, or you may prefer to take it away and pray it in private. But most folk find it encouraging having someone with them when they say it, you know, have a witness to the time they planted their flag in the ground and made their stand.'

Alex reread the prayer, and liked the idea that here was something tangible he could do; a way of making a more, formal response. 'Okay, and I'd like it if you stayed.'

'Wonderful! Just take your time and read it out slowly.'

Alex shifted his position as he cleared his throat loudly. This was a strange situation, but he'd known many stranger. He began to read:-

'Dear LORD,
Thank You that You found a way of helping me
to know and understand how much You love me.
Thank You for the gift of faith to believe that You
sent Your only Son, the Lord Jesus Christ, to
come and die in my place on the Cross.
I confess that I am a sinner in need of a Saviour,
and ask that You forgive me for all the times I have
knowingly, and unknowingly, sinned against You.
I gladly and willingly open the door of my heart
to You.
Please come and live in me now by Your Holy Spirit.
And, Lord, I acknowledge that You died and paid the
price for every part of me.
Please help me to accept Your healing of my spirit,
soul and body.
Thank You Father.
In Jesus' Name,
Amen.'

As he prayed, he became aware again of that same extraordinary sense of peace. Every sense alert, he marvelled at the sensation, knowing that he was not dreaming, but wide awake. Wide, wide awake. This was real, it was really happening to him. God had truly forgiven and accepted him. He was awed; did God really love him *that* much? Yes, he knew the answer to that now: He did, and from the inside out. He, Alexander James Grant, was loved, *really* loved by God.

Charles handed him a pen and he signed the card with a bold, if not slightly, shaky hand.

*

Now he was on the way to the wedding. Over time, Charles had become not just his hospital Chaplain, then pastor, but a close and firm friend as well. The older man's patient and unpretentious way of guiding and teaching, as well as his sociable and relaxed company, had been exactly what Alex had needed.

In time, he had come to know Izzy as well, and had grown to admire her refreshingly forthright character and bold way of sharing her faith. He smiled again as he recalled his conversation with Charles the previous night.

'How are you faring? Everything ready?'

'Can you believe it, I'm nervous? I ask you, a man of my age feeling like a raw recruit! But don't worry, I'm not suffering from any cold feet. Izzy's fine; as cool as a cucumber. She's got the whole thing organised down to the last bit of confetti. But I'll be glad when you get here; moral support and all that.'

'Makes a change for me to be there for you, and to tell you the truth, you won't be the only one who'll be glad of some support. There's a situation here that I'd value your opinion on, Izzy's too. It's only just cropped-up, and I'm still struggling to come to terms with it myself.'

'Oh? Sounds ominous? A problem with the Manor?'

'No, everything's going great guns there. Wait till you see the plans. Actually, it's of a more personal nature.'

'Personal? Okay, now I am intrigued. Personal, hmm.'

'I shan't say any more about it just now, except to say that The Boss has told me to do something ... unusual. But if there's an opportunity, I'd really value a brief session with you both. Then I fully intend to put it on the back burner, at least for the time being. There's enough to think about right now.'

'Aha. Fair enough. So, you'll give me a ring when you get to the hotel?'

'Roger and out.'

Alex replaced the receiver and felt some relief. Although he had only hinted at the problem, it had been good to mention it, albeit ever so vaguely. Ever since that day in the heather he had made sure to appear disinterested whenever Dot and Angus mentioned anything about 'the new quine at the Inn'. He guessed that they would be keen to cast an eye over her at the ceilidh on the following Saturday - which was something he was actually beginning to look forward to himself.

He drove on, once again feeling relieved and grateful that Charles and Izzy had come into his life. How much he had needed them over the past year, and now they would be the perfect couple to confide in. After all, hadn't they recently become more than a little experienced in dealing with unexpected matters of the heart?

CHAPTER 10

Yvonne was frustrated. She also needed to confide in someone, but knew that the telephone box, situated just outside the main door, was not the most appropriate place to unburden herself. Sandra was used to receiving long letters from her, but now she felt the need to hear her friend's comforting voice again. It would have to wait until her day off when she would go into Braegarroch and try to find somewhere more private.

She had awoken after a fitful night's sleep, during which she had been considering whether to postpone her decision to confront Niall for one more day. She gave herself until seven o'clock to deliberate, and then she would definitely make up her mind. The target hour arrived, and she forced herself to admit that the longer she delayed to deal with the issue, the harder it would probably be to do so when she did; she would go into action as soon as breakfast was over.

Georgina and Donald had a small kitchenette in their flat so it was just Niall and herself who ate the first meal of the day in the main kitchen. He had usually finished by the time she came down, and this morning was no different. He was busy at the sink when she sat at the staff table to begin her meal, grateful that the room's tense atmosphere was partially eased by the radio's noisy, but cheerful, contribution. A few minutes later, she crossed the room to put her empty mug and bowl in the dishwasher before turning to him.

'Niall, could you please turn that down. I've got something to say.' He ignored her, so she reached over and turned the volume down herself. 'Look, you've made it very clear that you've got a problem with me being here, and I think it's time we sorted whatever it is out.'

He turned to face her, and she was alarmed to see something like disgust on his face. Feeling her courage waver, she hurried on. 'Well, you've got to admit that you've made it pretty obvious that you can't stand me, and I'd like you to tell me why.'

'*Get lost!*' The words seemed to explode into the air as he turned the radio's volume back up to blaring level, before turning both taps full on. The cascading water splashed onto the front of his jacket. He jumped back, cursing.

She had been expecting a negative reaction, but even this was more than she had imagined. 'No, I will not "get lost". For goodness sake, Niall, just what *is* your problem?'

'You! You're my ruddy problem; I told you before, you should'na be here. We managed fine before. You're not needed. Get it? *You're not needed!*'

A nerve-shredding screech was heard from somewhere in Starold as a lucky housewife received the thrilling news that she had guessed the identity of *The Mystery Voice,* and had won a copy of the latest Beatles L.P. Startled, Niall dropped the pan he was holding, causing lumps of porridge to splatter indiscriminately over unit doors and a wide expanse of the quarry tiled floor.

'*Hell!*' he shouted, picking the pan up, and hurling it furiously into the sink before heading for the door. His desire to lash out and do some harm was dangerously near the surface now, and he knew he had to get out of there, and fast.

Yvonne was aghast. The violence of his words and actions had momentarily stunned her, and she stood motionless, surrounded by globules of the thick, slowly dripping mixture. Quickly forcing some composure to return along with her determination, she followed, and called after him as he sprinted up the stairs, 'Reception, two o'clock this afternoon. Be there. Or ... *just be there!*'

*

She spent the morning working with Flora, trying hard not to let her preoccupation over her clash with Niall to interfere with her work. She had decided not to confide in the nice old soul, feeling sure that she had her own misgivings about him. If anyone had to get involved, it would have to be the MacMan's, and only then if it became absolutely necessary. Neither had she quizzed Flora yet about Alexander Grant. However, she had learned that he was very religious and keen on taking long walks. Maybe he had just been praying out loud that day in the heather, or singing hymns; it was a possibility.

Flora was not oblivious to Yvonne's pensive manner, but put it down to the usual 'women's problem', or the after-effects of the long journey finally catching up with her. At last the morning's work was done. Flora lay down her duster and inspected the polished lounge, her hands pressing hard into her aching lower back. She exhaled a long, satisfied sigh, thinking how much easier it was now with another pair of willing and hard-working hands around. The quine had arrived in the nick of time; things were getting a wee bit too wearisome these days.

*

Yvonne braced herself as she entered the kitchen at lunchtime. Niall was sitting at the table, writing quickly, and appeared to be totally absorbed with the task. She helped herself to a bowl of soup and a bread roll.

'I'll eat this in my room. See you at two in reception, and I suggest you make sure that you do come. After all, we don't want to involve the MacMan's, do we?'

He ignored her and continued writing. That gave her an idea; maybe she should try to put her thoughts down on paper. She could try to imagine what complaints and objections he could have against her; it might help focus her mind when they met up later. She returned to her room, and began to compile a list as she ate:-

Prejudice: Was he one of those red-hot nationalists, a Scot who hated the English 'Sassenachs'? Unlikely - the MacMan's weren't fools and would have done something about him before now if that was the case.

She glanced out of the window. It looked threatening; the weather forecast had been right; rain was on the way. Threat - that gave her her second option.

Threatened: Was she some kind of threat to him? But that was plain daft! She was just a mere general assistant, and he was the chef - a far more important member of staff. No, that couldn't be it either.

Personality clash/Instant dislike: Maybe it was as simple as that. If so, the feeling was mutual. But that still didn't explain his hostility towards her before she had even spoken one word to him.

She reminded him of someone: Thinking about it, he reminded her of someone from the distant past, and someone she really didn't need to be reminded of: her so-called father.

She was forced to admit defeat after spending ten more minutes of not being able to think of another cause for his behaviour. Life was full of uncertainties, but of one thing she was sure, and despite her threat, she was determined to sort this problem out without involving the MacMan's. She didn't want to give them any reason to regret taking her on, which could very easily happen if she went running to them so soon after her arrival. Philosophically, she resigned herself to the fact that this was going to be yet another time when she would just have to find a way of dealing with the problem herself.

CHAPTER 11

Niall added another item to his list and sat back, he was still mad. The *bitch!* Why did she have to come along now, and just as he'd managed to get Maggie - the soppy hen - back in-line? She'd given him a few tricky days, before seeing sense and coming round to his way of thinking. And just as well, for how else was he going to achieve his 'Grand Plan'?

His face twisted into a self-satisfied grimace as he remembered what a soft touch she'd been right from that first ceilidh. He'd made his move, and she'd almost jumped out of her skin when he'd asked her to dance, and he'd never forget the look on her face when he sat down next to her afterwards and began giving her the old spiel.

Margaret Leila MacKay was indeed thrilled that such a man of the world had chosen to spend a little time with her. My, she thought, he was so interesting and cosmopolitan! She smiled coyly at the many nods and winks cast in her direction by inquisitive friends and neighbours. She could almost hear them now as they made their way home, 'Did you see Maggie and that wee chef from the Inn? Very cosy they looked!' No doubt, she would be the subject of local gossip for a day or two, but she didn't mind, in fact, she would make the most of the attention, however short-lived.

Her happiness was almost as great as her relief when the night was over and the dear man asked if they could meet again. It was a shame the reeling was over, for she could have danced all the way up to the top of Ben-An-t-Earrach and back again!

But the pleasure was not hers alone, for Niall had enjoyed being so openly admired, and by the time the evening came to a close, had made up his mind that she would do. Right enough, she was no Mona Lisa, but at least she had a good bit of flesh in all the right places; more than enough for a man to feel and squeeze. Yes, she was a definite prospect alright. And about ruddy time too!

Soon a tentative and rather childish association began. Although neither had any experience of how to conduct such a potentially serious relationship, both expected something significant, and, hopefully, life changing, from the other. The weeks passed, and Niall gloated privately as he schemed and pushed things along, whilst Maggie remained in a state of constant elation at being appreciated for her body as well as her mind. Now she was having to shave her legs and wash and set her hair *every* week.

It was natural that her Mam and Dad were not so thrilled, and were quick to warn her, 'Och, he'll be after that one thing ... he'll be the flighty one ... shifty. You watch yourself now dearie ... hotel folk, is it indeed! No, no, Maggie lass, not for you.' She knew that they were only looking out for her, but she also knew they would come around - once they got to know him better.

It had been a good ten years since Callum and Ailsa MacKay had reluctantly accepted the fact that their only child was a firmly established spinster. 'Pleasantly plump,' and not pretty by any stretch of the imagination, she was, nevertheless, a good, hard-working lass who never brought any trouble home. Now they were worried. What was that wee chef up to? Heaven help them if she had fallen into the hands of some fly-by-night Lothario! They couldn't help being suspicious of his motives, and found themselves at a loss as to how to cope with this new and alarming situation that had unexpectedly come upon their happy, tight-knit little family. However, they began to wonder if there might be something in it after all when the weeks turned into months, and the relationship showed no signs of cooling. It would be a fine thing if the lad turned out to be one of those rare breed of men who had the ability to see past the plain exterior and focus on the hidden beauty within. Maybe they could allow thoughts of grandchildren to filter into their hopes and plans after all!

*

Winter settled in, and Niall decided to shift his Plan up a gear. Not for them a long engagement; what would be the point? He would propose at Hogmanay. Enough time had been wasted, a whole ruddy eight weeks of it! They would marry as soon as the thing could be arranged, and that would be easy enough, for there was to be none of that fancy stuff to fork out for - unless her folks paid for it. The Chiefs were bound to offer him the double room in the staff corridor, and Maggie could carry on with her cleaning job at the school until Flora left. The old biddy was always going on about that trick back of hers, and she must be due to retire soon anyway. Two wage packets would come in very nice, very nice indeed. How many bosses would give their eye teeth for such a couple: an excellent chef, with a hard-working woman in tow? He'd be doing them a favour, and could almost hear their fawning now. As for kids - no fear! The pill would make sure of that!

So, all things considered, he was sitting pretty. He'd concocted a win-win situation for himself; a woman to meet his needs, and who came with a house and some land to go with it, enough for at least two building plots - maybe three at a push. A man his age should have some property, and how else was he going to get his hands on some? As for her old sods, for that is what he privately called her parents, well, there were plenty of old folks' homes out there. Yes sir, life was looking very rosy for him just now, very rosy indeed.

He crossed the days off his calendar as the December storms brought more than the usual amount of snow and ice with them. Then something happened on the eighth day of that month that threatened to put an end to all his scheming. Maggie's father, an arthritic sixty-four-year old, slipped and fell hard, sustaining a bad concussion, a shattered shoulder blade, and a compound fracture of the right leg. As if the unfortunate man did not have enough to contend with, five days later he came down with a near fatal dose of pneumonia.

The family coped well at first, mainly because Maggie took over all the heavy manual tasks around the croft, as well as keeping her part-time job going. Her mother was not a robust woman, and stubbornly insisted on taking the twice weekly ninety-minute bus journey to visit Callum in the hospital. It wasn't long before the stress and worry began to take their toll on her, and she developed a dry, irritating cough, which quickly turned into one of her bi-annual bouts of bronchitis. Maggie battled on; her load made heavier now by having to nurse her sick mother.

Initially, Niall had offered to lend a hand at the croft on his days off, but it quickly became obvious that he was more of a hindrance than a help. He was unused to handling live animals; his forte was in the preparation and cooking of dead ones. Whenever he did turn-up, within minutes he would find an excuse to leave, unable to bear the sound of all the violent, gurgling spasms coming from the old woman's room.

His irritation turned into frustration, and then into a slow, burning resentment towards the parents as the cold weeks turned into endless, colder months; how dare they interfere and force him to put his all-important Plan on hold!

At last, Callum was allowed to return home, the plaster still covering nearly half of his body. He was relieved to find the croft and beasts well cared for and his wife almost recovered, although Maggie looked tired and her shoulders more stooped than he remembered. But it was a fine thing to be assured that 'he mustn't fret', and that the routine of the past few months would continue 'for as long as needs be'.

Eventually, all the plaster has removed, but the pain and stiffness stubbornly remained; it seemed that no amount of anti-inflammatories or physiotherapy could ease or loosen the problematic joints. Osteoarthritis had set-in, and it became clear that his crofting days were over. But Callum was a proud, obstinate man, and railed against the idea of receiving an early pension from the state. However, Maggie could be stubborn too, and after a while and a great deal of persuasion, he eventually gave-in, and grudgingly allowed her to send off for the necessary application forms.

Meanwhile, Niall was finding it took every ounce of self-control he had to stand back and allow Maggie to run around after the old sods. He wanted to shout at them, and tell them to think of someone else for a change. It was so ruddy unfair; he hadn't come all this way just to watch everything end up as a big fat zero.

The deadlock was finally broken when Callum's pension came through. Niall decided to go into action as soon as he heard the news. They'd had their innings, and his need was greater than theirs. It was his turn now. He was due, by God he was!

*

So it was, at precisely 11 o'clock on a wet and windy day in late March, that he found himself wobbling precariously on one knee as he knelt before Maggie in the conveniently empty lounge of the Gordon Lodge Hotel in Strathlochy. The time would stay in his memory forever, thanks to the tortuous extra minute he was compelled to suffer as eleven booming gongs resounded from the grandfather clock towering over the scene.

They were eye-to-eye as she sat smiling affectionately and expectantly at him, pitying the poor laddie for his nerves. His whole body seemed to tremble and his face glowed with perspiration at the effort he was making to steady himself. She guessed from all the signals he had been giving since she had picked him up earlier that morning that he was planning something powerfully big, and she had a fair idea what something might be! What a man of the world he looked in his chocolate brown suit and deep pink shirt with its large collar, and as for that wide pink and orange flowery tie - och, but it must be all the rage in the big towns! Although, he had overdone it a bit with the Brylcream and that smelly cologne of his. Her heart went out to him when she noticed at least three shaving cuts on his face and chin. The dear man!

At last, the endless cacophony faded away. He took a deep breath and cleared his throat before launching into his much-rehearsed speech, gratified to hear that his voice had taken on a deeper tone than usual, which, to his ears, made him sound even more dignified.

'Er, now then hen.' No, that wasn'a right. 'Lass, er ... ' more throat clearing. 'Maggie, lass, I want you to do ... er ... have the honour of being ... ye ken ... the, er, the wife.' At last, and damn it all, it was out! And he'd done a good job too because she was still smiling. So full of self-congratulation was he that he forgot to open the small blue leather box he was clutching, and offer her its contents; all his efforts going into staying upright as he remained sweating and swaying in front of her.

Maggie had heard the wonderful question, one that, until just recently, she had never dared believe would ever come her way. She stared eagerly at the corner of the box she could see peeking out of his hand, her finger almost itching with the anticipation to stop being so bare, and quickly replied, 'Och, yes, I will. *I will marry you!* And thank you very much, Niall.'

He breathed an enormous, peppermint flavoured sigh over her, then gave a high-pitched laugh. Following the direction of her eyes, he smirked at how surprised she would be when she found that the thing would fit her perfectly. He thrust the unopened box unceremoniously at her. 'Och, well then, you'd better be havin' this. It'll fit you fine; I've done my research. You know me, I leave nothin' to chance. Go on then hen, put it on!' This careful 'research' had consisted purely of comparing her ring finger with his; hers looked just as thick as his, which proved very convenient when he had tried the ring on in the shop.

Maggie opened the box and gazed gratifyingly at the unfussy diamond solitaire inside. So what if she had to put her glasses on in order to see the tiny gem, it only went to show how clever he was to know that she was not one for those big flashy things. No indeed, this was a discreet little stone. And the light was bad in here, so that was why it didn't sparkle. The nice grey band, och, but it must be silver, wasn't one of those thick, showy ones she'd seen on telly. No, this was a far more sensible and practical one. Wasn't he the canny one to choose such a ring! And to think, she - Margaret Leila MacKay - was now a betrothed woman! A woman who was going to be wed! She would be *Mrs Niall Turvey;* wife to this sophisticated, cosmopolitan man of the world; a man who knew how to succeed and survive out there in the jungle. She slipped the dear thing on. To be sure, it was a wee bit on the loose side, but no doubt her finger would soon get used to it. Confidence flared up in her as she reached over to plant a firm, no-nonsense kiss on the line of his thin, twitching mouth.

Niall blinked, and felt he should do something even more manly now. Inspiration struck, and he found himself opening his arms wide and putting them around her. This was even more uncomfortable, and necessitated him keeping his eyes open to keep his balance. He spotted the hotel receptionist staring at them through the glass doors, and gave her the prearranged, thumbs-up signal.

The smart young woman bent to retrieve the already prepared tray from below the desk. She left her post and pushed the doors unceremoniously open with her rear end, and only just remembered to smile as she placed the tray on the coffee table in front of the blushing couple. Knowing what was expected of her, for she had seen the head waiter perform many similar duties, she poured the sparkling apple juice into the glasses, thinking that this was one mean man.

'I believe congratulations are in order? May I be the first to wish you both every future happiness.' Ugh! The sooner she could escape, the better. It was difficult to maintain the forced smile as she shook the horrible little man's clammy hand. He really was quite a sight. So common! And those *awful* colours! The woman was no oil painting either, but at least she was more acceptably dressed. One could only hope that any children that came along would not take after him; he was ghastly! Voices could be heard outside and she used the excuse to hurry away, hoping that the couple would soon finish their business and vacate the premises. These were not the sort of people that the Gordon Lodge guests would feel comfortable having around.

Niall felt hot and thirsty. He quickly gulped down his drink before pouring himself another. Maggie began to twist the ring around her slightly trembling finger, it being nice and loose and all. She turned to look adoringly at him as he sat beside her now, one arm placed proprietorially around her shoulders, the other holding his already nearly empty glass. There was something she had to say, and she decided that now would be a good time. She was none too bothered, and just knew that he would be fine about it; it wasn't such a big thing to ask after all.

'Niall ... dear ... I'll need to be asking you something.'

He turned his head towards her. What was this? Demanding things already? Probably some rubbish about bridesmaids. He puffed his chest out, feeling important, powerful even; after all, now he was a man with responsibilities. Soon this woman was going to have to swear to honour and obey him. And about ruddy time too!

'Aye, aye, what's all this?'

'I'm thinking we can wait just a wee while, I mean, before we say anything to Mam and Dad. I'd like to see the house sorted for Dad. That would be fine, wouldn't it?' She went on to add cheerfully, 'Conroy's are coming to put the ramp in next week. Poor Dad, he does struggle with those steps.'

Niall's condescending smile faded as warning bells began to clang somewhere at the back of his mind. Had he heard her right? What did she just say? 'Wait ...just a wee while.' His back stiffened and he glared, unseeing, at her face, which was now starting to take on a puzzled look. She had picked on the one thing that had been driving him mad all this time - and now she'd had the nerve to ask him to do even more! All his blood seemed to rush to his head as he thought of the unfairness and injustice of the thing; second fiddle, that's what she wanted him to play. Didn't she know, wasn't she capable of understanding, that that was just what he'd been doing all this ruddy long time? How could she? How *could* she? She needed telling. Oh, and he'd tell her alright! He'd tell her loud and clear that he was not for doing any more waiting, and that *He* was more important than those ruddy stupid sods of hers!

Maggie watched in fascination at his rapidly changing expression, and was perturbed to see that the small beads of sweat on his forehead and upper lip had swelled into great blobs. What could be the matter with him? Why didn't he answer her instead of just sitting there, looking so ... so queer? Unnerved, she decided that the best course of action was to continue and try to state her case more clearly, maybe he had misunderstood. 'It would only be for a month or two, that's all.

As soon as everything's done, then we'll tell them, you know, about us, and this.' She held up her left hand and splayed out the fingers; the ring had twisted and now the stone was out of sight.

He gasped and lurched violently to his feet, breathing heavily as he glowered down at her. She sat open-handed and open-mouthed. Oh no! What had she done to ruin this most wonderful of moments? Desperate now to rescue the precious event and somehow justify her request, she raised her voice and spoke as fast as her nerves and mouth would allow. 'All I'm trying to say is that when I know they're coping fine, and the place fit - then we can tell them. What's the matter, Niall? Why are you looking at me like that? I'm only asking for a wee while longer - '

At last he spoke; his voice almost a hiss. *'Wait!* You want *me* to *wait!* What, like you've made me do all ruddy winter? Now listen, and listen to me fine, you ruddy fool, it's *me* you should be pleasin'.' He leant towards her, and began jabbing a finger hard into her chest as he spat out, 'Anyway, they already know. I told them. And they didn'a say *wait*. They don't need us to *wait*. We don't have to *wait*. *We will not wait, see! Got it now, have you? Sunk in now, has it?'* Satisfied, he stopped the jabbing and stood erect.

She had put her arms defensively across her chest, and kept them there. Obviously deeply troubled, and close to tears now, she asked, 'You ... you've already told them? But you can't have. You mustn't, no, not yet! They're in no fit state to ... not yet. Tell me you haven't, Niall, please tell me you haven't?'

'Hey! What's your ruddy problem? Listen when I tell you! I rang them yesterday.'

'You ... you phoned them?'

Breathing heavy, exasperated, and not knowing what else to say or do, he made fists, threw his hands up in the air, and started waving them about. 'Yes, and I dunna need your permission, see!'

She stared up at him in horror. What was the matter with him? Why was he so riled? She had never seen him like this before. And what a way to talk! No one had ever spoken to her like that - ever in her life! She must have said something truly terrible. Oh, why wasn't she more worldly-wise like the women he was used to? He was right about her; she was such a country bumpkin. And poor Mam and Dad. Why hadn't they said anything? They must be fretting so bad. This was horrible, horrible! Her voice quivered as she attempted to reply. 'But ... but you don't know them, they'll only fret. They've been ... they've always been aye good to me. Och, they'll pretend they're fine ... but ... but now I'm fear't they'll spend their savings on me - for a wedding, instead of getting themselves right.' She could not disguise her dismay, even a hint of disapproval in her voice, as she continued, 'Oh Niall, *why* did you do it? You know fine what they've been through, you've seen it all. I'm only asking for a month or two, and we've got the rest of our lives. We must start right. I *want* to start right, I need to. You *must* see that?'

He couldn't bear to hear any more of her whining; she was driving him mad with all this talk about those stupid old sods of hers. With the last ounce of control he was able to drag up from his furious depths, he managed to hiss, 'It's no me that's no doin' any seein'. It's you! You dunna know what you're askin'. You just dunna know what you're damn well askin'.'

The atmosphere was charged to explosive level. Aghast, Maggie felt herself sinking into some sort of chaos, but even now she managed to find enough courage to make one more valiant effort. 'Och, but *I do* know very well what I'm asking. I know they've put money by for me, but I want them to spend it on their own needs - to do the changes. If there's any left over, then I'll take it, aye ... and that willingly. But now you've gone and told them, don't you see? Now I'll never know if they left themselves short, and didn't do what was needed? Oh, Niall, if only you hadn'a told them.' She stopped, recognising that he was not listening. Rage seemed to have possessed him completely, and now he was muttering what sounded like obscenities.

He needed air, to get away from all her and all her whining. He turned and charged towards the doors, shoving and kicking any unfortunate piece of furniture that got in his way.

Desperation overtook her as she raised herself onto trembling knees, and called after him. 'Niall, come back, oh please ... *please* come back ...'

But he was gone; she heard his footsteps pound away as the well-oiled doors swung noiselessly shut behind him. Something that felt like her heart seemed to tear inside her chest. Utterly confused, and unable to take in or understand what had just happened, she grasped the arm of the couch and tried to steady herself as she stood, rooted to the spot.

A few moments later, the doors swung open again and the receptionist cautiously approached her. 'Are you alright, madam? Don't worry, he's gone. Come on now, sit down. Can I get you anything? A brandy maybe?'

Maggie could not move, her unconscious mind preventing her from moving a muscle, lest that too would tear. Emotional pain was flooding in, she did not need physical pain as well.

The receptionist saw that she had made no impact; the woman was obviously in a state of shock. 'Okay, look, tell you what, you stay here, and I'll be right back.' Thank goodness none of the residents had witnessed that vulgar scene. She hurried off to the bar, looking around her all the while and dreading the return of that nasty, ugly little man. She must try and get the woman out as well, and as quickly and discreetly as possible. The porter must be fetched and told to put her on a bus, or in a taxi - anything to get rid of her. What a nuisance! She didn't get paid enough to put up with things like this. And where was that blasted manager when you needed him anyway?

She did not hear Maggie's whispered reply. 'I only wanted to ... I couldn't live with myself if they ... mustn't have any regrets ... can't abandon them ... just a month ... or two. *Oh Niall, Niall!'*

CHAPTER 12

Yvonne looked at her watch, ten past two, and still no sign of him. She would give him a few more minutes then go back to her room and think again. Thankfully, the MacMan's were nowhere to be seen; at this time of day they were usually in their flat, relaxing after the lunchtime session. She marvelled at how trusting they were, having recognised some of the rarer malt labels amongst the more popular brands in the small cocktail bar. Partly due to her inherent honesty, and partly due to the fact that she had never developed a taste for alcohol, she was not in the least tempted to help herself to any of the precious golden liquid.

She jumped when the kitchen door flew open and a thunderous looking Niall pushed past her.

'Ten minutes!' he shouted, slamming his way out of the Inn.

Sensing that he had already gained the upper hand, and, therefore, a measure of control, she followed quickly and called, 'Slow down!'He took no notice, so she called again. *'I said, slow down! Or do you want me to get the MacMan's right now?'*

The threat had the desired effect. He stopped and snarled the word, *'Bitch!'*at the innocent ground, then shouted again, *'nine minutes.'*

'Well then, stop wasting time.' She came level with him and they set off, taking the road to the loch. Launching straight in, she asked, 'Now, would you mind telling me why you've been treating me like dirt ever since I arrived?'

'Nah.'

'No?'

'Deaf as well as stupid? That's what I said, didn't I?'

'There you go again. Can't bring yourself to give me a straight answer, but free enough with your insults. Just slow down and tell me why.'

'Nah! Can't be bothered.'

Very unwillingly, she decided to call his bluff. 'Okay, we'll play it your way, let's go back and speak to the MacMan's. Maybe you'll be *bothered* to explain your behaviour to them.' Out of the corner of her eye she noticed his head jerk and heard what sounded like a hiss escape from his mouth.

'Och! Stop your bletherin'. Hav'na I already told you? You're not wanted here. You've cheated ... someone.'

Shocked, she asked, '"Cheated someone"? Who? What do you mean?'

'That's my business.' He attempted to inch forward, hating all this walking side by side stuff.

'*Your* business!' she exclaimed. 'Well, I like that! You can't go around accusing people of cheating, and then not backing it up.'

'Och, can't I? Just you ruddy well watch me. I can do what the hell I like, and you can get stuffed.'

Yvonne felt her usually absent temper begin to flicker into life. 'Oh really? Well then, let me tell you, Niall Turvey, it *is* my business, and unless you start talking to me properly, it will soon become other people's business as well!' He was several feet ahead of her by now and showed no sign of slowing down. She stopped abruptly, banging the tip of her tall umbrella on the ground. 'And I'm *not* going to talk to your back; I've seen enough of that lately. You know what? I think you're a coward. What kind of man are you anyway? You're acting like a spoilt child, and I seriously doubt if you're even capable of talking and behaving like an adult.'

At last, he slowed his pace and turned to look at her, his breath coming in sharp, noisy bursts. 'A man? Behave like a man is it?'

'Go on then, prove it! Prove me wrong. Start behaving like one, and tell me who I'm supposed to have cheated.'

'Now look, havn'a I told you? You're not wanted here. We managed fine before, so why don't you ruddy well shove off!'

'Well then, would you care to explain to me why the MacMan's found it necessary to get me in if you all managed so well before I came?'

The dark clouds that had been ganging up for the past hour began to spill a light drizzle. He made no reply, so she continued, 'Just give me one good reason why you want me to go and what all this cheating business is about. If you can't, then I'll have to assume that you have some kind of psychological problem and need professional help. That's how crazy your behaviour's been.'

Still he remained silent, his mouth twisting into a series of ugly shapes. She considered, obviously calling his bluff and straight talking was not working; so far, they had done nothing but spark off each other. Then she remembered the list she had made earlier and searched her memory for something from it that she could use, but nothing came to mind. Maybe she should use a friendlier, chattier approach; it might help to diffuse the situation. Anything was worth a try.

The drizzle began to turn into a steady flow. She opened her umbrella, and choosing her words carefully, began again. 'Look Niall, we don't know anything about each other, but I've been moving around doing seasonal jobs for the past ten years and I want to settle down now. Do you know what I mean?' She looked at his face but could detect no noticeable change in his expression. Undaunted, she continued, 'I'm guessing you've knocked around a bit too, and maybe you've been able to settle here. The MacMan's seem to be really good bosses, and I think I'd be right in saying that, like me, you just want to do a good day's work and, well, you know, be part of it. So can't you tell me what the matter is, and maybe we can find a way of sorting things out?'

'Finished have you? Let me get a ruddy word in edgeways, will you?'

'Don't be so rude! I've given you every opportunity - '

'There you go again, yatter, yatter, yatter! Why should I bother myself tellin' you anythin'?'

'Well, you'd better - '

'Why?' he shouted, 'I don't better do anythin' for the likes of a ... a ... skivvy.'

'Okay, okay, calm down!'

'Don't you tell me to calm down! *You* don't tell me nothin'!'

'For goodness sake, what *is* the matter with you?

'Shut your ruddy mouth!'

Obviously, she was getting nowhere. Exasperated, she forced herself to try once more. 'Niall, for the last time, are you, or are you not, going to tell me what all this is about?'

'Shut up, just shut your mouth! I'm not for tellin' you nothin', so clear off, just clear off!' Large droplets of rain sat on the surface of his oily hair, some turning into rivulets that began to trickle down the upturned collar of his leather jacket. Now he was uncomfortable as well as mad as hell.

Calmly, she announced, 'Sorry, but that's not an option.'

'Not an option, *not an option!* Let me tell you, *my girl*, it ruddy well is, and the only ruddy one you've got!'

Ugh! She hated that expression; it always came with some bad memories of a previous unhappy relationship. 'Don't you call me that! I'm no one's girl, especially yours! And I've had enough of this. The MacMan's will have to ... to do something.' And with that, she turned and started walking quickly back towards the Inn.

He stood and stared disbelieving at her retreating figure. *Bitch, bitch, bitch!* Who did she think she was? No one walked away from Niall Turvey. *No one!* She needed teaching a lesson, and he was just the man to do it. Rushing after her, he knocked her umbrella to the ground and grabbed her shoulder, forcing her to stop and turn to face him. 'Oh no you damn well don't! You leave them out of it - or else.'

She needed a few moments to realise what was happening and gather her scattered wits. She stared hard at him; he was a frightening, ugly sight. She gave an involuntary shiver. Then, energized by a surge of indignation and anger that shot through her, she commanded, *'Take your hands off me!* How dare you. Or else what? Don't tell me you're actually threatening me?'

96

The look in her eyes told him that she meant business, and he instinctively knew that she was one of those bitches that wouldn't give in without a good hiding. 'Och, shut your yatter,' he said, needing time to think, and think fast. Now how was he going to get out of this fix and stop her grassing him up to the Chiefs? His mind in turmoil, and not knowing what else to do, he yelled '*Cow!*' and shoved hard at her shoulder. Then, not sticking around to see if she managed to stand her ground or fall, he turned and stalked back to the Inn. A 'coward' was he? 'Couldn't act like a man,' was it? *A man!* Stupid cow! Just let Maggie hear her say those things. Memories of the past month flooded back, especially of the tortured, sleepless night the stupid hen had put him through after he'd proposed. Then, afraid that she might think of dumping him, and all his planning and waiting would end-up going down the pan, he'd gone to meet her out of work the next day.

'Maggie, I want you to ... er ... yesterday, come on, let's forget what you made me do. I mean, not the ring ... and all. I've been thinkin', how about if I give you some time to ... er ... get things sorted your end? A month I'm thinkin'. Just a month mind! So, what d'ya say? Got a deal, have we?'

She forgave him immediately, in fact, she even begged him to 'stop his greetin'.' That was when she'd called him a man; 'It takes a big man to come back and sort things.'

But his worries were not over yet, for just a few days later the Chiefs had dropped the bombshell that they'd gone and found someone to come and help Flora. Now what was he to say to Maggie and her lot, for hadn't he already gone and told her that he'd get her sorted with a job at the Inn when they were wed? It still rankled when he remembered the look she gave him when he told her the news. 'The Chiefs've gone behind my back, hen. They've gone and given your job to someone else,' conveniently forgetting to add that he hadn't even mentioned her to them. Again, she had been quick to comfort him with some old claptrap about 'the path of true love', and she knew that 'her man would think of something to sort this too.' Yeah, he was a man alright. Only a man could stomach stuff like that.

Reaching the Inn, he felt as worried as he was wet, and knew that he would have to find a way to get this bitch off his back. But, hey, why was he panicking - he patted his chest and felt inside for his wallet. Yeah, there it was, and in it the list he'd made earlier. Rubbing his cold hands together almost gleefully, he considered what little stunt he could pull first. A little accident in her room? How careless of her to leave the wastepaper basket so close to the gas fire. Or how about planting a guest's stolen purse in there? The Chiefs wouldn't mess about and get rid of her soon enough. Yeah, that was the one. Then he'd be sitting pretty, safe, tidy-like ... settled.

Settled! That word again; it had been niggling somewhere at the back of his mind ever since she'd said it. She'd been right about one thing; he did need to settle down; wasn't that what he'd been fighting for all this ruddy time? Wasn't that what his 'Grand Plan' was all about - getting settled? Settled. *Geronimo!* Yeah, that was it! He was a ruddy genius! He'd use it - milk it for all it was worth. Somehow he'd convince the bitch that he deserved it, was desperate for it, and that his need to be *settled* was killing him. Yes sir! Let's see what the bitch would have to say about that!

*

Yvonne found him in the kitchen, making a succession of unpleasant snuffling and grunting noises as he rubbed his head vigorously with a towel.

'Right you,' he said, throwing the towel onto the draining board before turning to fill the kettle. 'Just shut your mouth and listen. And don't go blamin' me when you feel bad after what I'm tellin' you.'

She was curious. She had returned with the intention of going to her room to reconsider if, and how, to involve the MacMan's. Instead, she went to sit at the table, wondering what he could possibly say that would make her feel any worse than she already did.

He put the kettle on the hob and stood with his back against the sink, his arms folded across his chest, a mock, woeful expression on his face.

'I'm forty next year; knocked around a lot myself, never thought I'd find a place like this where I'd be treated right. Now, I'm ... settled.' He paused, hoping that she would pick up on the fateful word. After some noisy, overdramatic sighs, and aiming his next few words at his feet, he continued, 'I'm to be wed, an' you've taken the job that should have been ma hen's. And she needs it back, see?'

Yvonne sat motionless, trying to assimilate what she had just heard. What did he say? He was going to be 'wed'- get married! He had a fiancée! But no one had mentioned a thing about it - then again, why should they? And this fiancé needed the job. *Her* job!

He was well into his sob story now. 'That's all I ever hankered after, see, all my life. I'm sick of bummin' around and just want a fair crack of the whip, like every other bugger. Then I landed up here, got a roof over my head, a bit of fun - the ceilidhs like, and boss of my own kitchen,' then, almost as an afterthought, he added, 'and the chance to be wed, and ... and ... settled like.' He glanced up, and was gratified to see that she appeared to be hanging on his every word. 'She was all set to move in here ... after we got wed.' He paused, extra careful now. 'I'd ... er ... it was all sorted, tidy-like. We'd waited long enough. Too ruddy long! Then, damn me, if the Chiefs didn'a go and get *you* in - and blew it all.'

She stared at him, unable to formulate any kind of intelligent response. He began to feel his nerves kick off, and, bending his head towards her as though addressing a very young child, began to speak painfully slowly. 'You ... cheated ... her ... out ... of ... her ... job. Or are you so ruddy thick you don't get it?'

At last, she managed to put her thoughts into words. 'So that's what all this fuss is about, my job? You're saying that it had already been promised to your fiancée?'

'Aye, tha's the way of it. Fair broke ma hen's heart, so it did.' He gloated inwardly; he was good at this, especially when he used that crack in his voice. 'Got it now, have you? Sunk in now, has it?'

'And that's it?'

'Ruddy hell! Isn't that enough? Can't you see what you've done?'

'What *I've* done? she asked, incredulous. 'But how was I to know? I'm not a mind reader! And why did they change their minds, and give me the job instead of her?'

If Niall's face had been a hand, it could now be described as a tight fist. Hell! The bitch just wasn't going to give in. But he was in too deep now, and was going to have to tell her more than he wanted. The kettle came to the boil. He turned to make his drink. 'They didn'a,' he mumbled.

'Didn'a what?'

'We didn'a ... tell 'em; it wasn'a ... official like.'

'What wasn't?'

'Ruddy hell! Do I have to draw a ruddy picture? About...our plans. Things ... happened. Now we've got to get things movin'. All systems go.' He turned to face her, and shouted, *'But you're in the ruddy way!'*

'Keep your voice down! Now let me get this straight. You planned to get married, and then your fiancée would come and live-in, and work here. But you hadn't actually got around to mentioning any of this to the MacMan's. In the meantime, they got me in to fill the vacancy. Is that right?'

'Aye, sort of. You go, and we can get wed. We've hung about too long and ... er, need to get things movin'. We need to get settled like. You'd soon cause a stink if someone put the mockers on your plans. You're the type that can shovel the muck around and come up smellin' of roses.'

'Whoa there! Just you hold on. I still don't see why you're taking it all out on me, or why I'd have to leave before you can get married.'

Exasperated now to the point of distraction, he started jabbing a finger hard into the side of his head. 'Think, use your loaf! Where'd we live? In the ruddy doss-house?'

'I am "using my loaf", but I'm not telepathic. Okay, so you need accommodation. But if she's a local girl, and I assume she is, what about her family? Can't you live with them, even if it's just to begin with? Loads of newlyweds have to until they can put by a deposit.'

'NO! NO! NO!' he shouted, shaking his head furiously.

Obviously, the idea was abhorrent to him, and, for all she knew, to his future in-laws as well.

'Well, I suppose that's understandable. But can't you find a bedsit or a room somewhere till you get your own place? And anyway, I wouldn't be surprised if the MacMan's didn't offer you that big double room at the end of the corridor.'

He had heard all this before and hated hearing it again. Maggie herself had suggested that they move into her room at the croft, or rent a couple of rooms locally, but he had been quick to dismiss both notions. He would go mad living within a mile of the old woman's coughing and spluttering, never mind having to put up with the old man's creaking and grinding. And gone were the days of forking out his hard-earned cash to some snooping cow of a landlady just so that he could hole up in some pokey attic. He'd dug his heels in, and it had been harder than he'd expected, but Maggie'd decided to behave, and came around to seeing things his way in the end.

Now, with an extreme effort, he managed to calm down enough to say, 'Aye, right enough. Money's tight, and that room would have suited us grand, and then we could have started puttin' a bit by. But that's all shot to pieces - now you've got the ruddy job!'

'But surely the MacMan's won't object to her coming to live-in when you're married, even if she's not working here?' Noticing that one of his legs had begun to tremble badly, she added, 'And I'd sit down before you fall down, if I was you.'

His confidence wavered as he realised that she was right about the Chiefs; they were good people. But he wanted this bitch gone before he got Maggie in; her wages were part of his Plan - and to get hold of them, she'd have to be working here. He felt he was losing ground; a lesser man would be panicking now. He'd have to bluff his way out of this, even if it meant blackening the Chief's a bit. 'Nah, they're okay people, but they'd be needin' her to work if she's takin' up the room. And she could too, with you gone.'

'No, I can't see that. They'd probably just adjust your wages for her board and lodging. Anyway, it looks like we'll just have to agree to disagree - '

Now he did begin to panic. Slamming his empty mug down, he exclaimed, 'Agh! I'm sick of this! Why can't you get it into your thick head - she *needs* to be here. We *need* to be *SETTLED*. We *need* to get wed. Get it?'

There was something about the way he had emphasised the word 'need' that alerted her, and putting two and two together to make an incorrect five, she suddenly guessed at the reason. Of course, why hadn't she thought of it before? The fiancée was pregnant! That would explain his obvious desperation for things to happen quickly. Tentatively, she asked, 'She's not in the family way, is she?'

It took him a few seconds to remember what the expression meant, but when he did, he seized almost joyfully upon the idea. At last! Unwittingly, she had given him his final and most powerful piece of ammunition. Adopting an attitude of false modesty, he replied, 'That's my business. But … time's gettin' on. And two wage packets … save quicker. Get my drift?'

Yvonne noticed that his belligerence had turned into a very uncharacteristic bashfulness. If a baby on the way was behind all this, then no wonder he had been so agitated and defensive. It seemed that his claim to have discovered happiness and a life for himself here was genuine after all; he really had found a decent job and a woman who obviously thought enough about him to want to marry him.

'Well then, if that's the case, why on earth didn't you just have a quiet word with me when I first arrived, and explain the situation? I wish you had, instead of being so nasty and carrying-on like you have been.'

Flushed with confidence now, and rightly guessing that the baby thing had finally swung it, he decided to relax, and let the bitch have it with both barrels. She'd put him through hell; now it was her turn.

'Nasty? Your dunna know what the ruddy word means. If I'd been "nasty" you wouldn'a be sittin' here now with all your hoity-toity ways.'

'Oh, stop it, Niall! Behaving like that's what's got us off on the wrong foot already. And now that I know what the situation is - a baby on the way for goodness sake - of course I'll ... I'll think about it.'

Realising that he had gained the upper hand at last, he felt almost desperate now to secure the deal, and went on to ask, 'What's there to think about? You'll no be stayin' now, you won't. Go on, say it, say it, damn you!'

'Hey! Don't rush me. I need time to think. And anyway, when's the baby due?'

Shrugging, he replied, 'What's that got to do with anythin'? You do what's right, and keep your ruddy nose out'a my business.'

She sighed, now she knew what lay behind all the unpleasantness, she could see no reason to prolong the discussion. But still a full thirty seconds passed as she struggled to come to terms with the inevitable. When it all boiled down, it was really just a simple matter of a straight choice: her happiness or theirs - and their baby's.

At last, and with a very heavy heart, she raised herself slowly to her feet, and said, 'You know Niall, I've only been here a short while, but already I've felt ... well, never mind. Okay, you win. I'll ... remove myself. Only you'd better make it work. You'd better *be* happy. And I'll need some time to find another job - and I'll need to think about how to tell the MacMan's, so it might take a week or two.'

'Aye, that'll be fine, but ... er ... just ... er ...'

'Just what?' she asked, beginning to feel impatient.

He made a vain attempt to smile, as he replied, 'Don't tell them about me wantin' to get wed and ... all ... that's my ... for me to do. You'll just be tellin' them you're off. You'll no be changin' your mind. I've got your number; I'll no stand for it!'

She sighed again. Even now he still could not bring himself to make the slightest effort to be pleasant to her. Never one to insist upon having the last word in an argument, she felt compelled to do so now. 'When you do get married, just you make sure that you treat your wife and child right, that's all. Just you treat them right.'

*

She slept very little again that night, beset as she was by a downward spiral of second thoughts, consisting mainly of a disturbing and persistent stream of questions, chief among them the mystery as to why he hadn't confided in the MacMan's before now? And what would happen if she changed her mind and refused to leave? Would that be the end of all his plans? If so, could she really be happy staying here and taking the risk of being responsible for the possible unhappiness of two people and a child? And why couldn't she shake off this nagging feeling that he hadn't been entirely honest with her? Had she been a fool to take everything he said at face value? Who was this mysterious fiancée anyway, and was she really the only reason he wanted her out of the way? By telling him that she would leave, had she inadvertently blundered into some sort of trap, and already sacrificed her own possible future happiness too quickly?

She debated and argued with herself about the wisdom of confronting him again, knowing that it would probably only result in a repeat performance of his antics of the previous day - and she really didn't want to go through *that* again! Then there was the thorny problem of how she was going to cope between now and her departure, and how she was going to explain her sudden wish to leave to the MacMan's. What reason could she give that would sound not only acceptable, but believable too? Apart from her problems with Niall, there was no romantic type of relationship threatening to rob her of her peace here. This was a completely different scenario to what she was used to. Goodness knows what they would think of her, Flora too. She had only known them a short while, but already their hopeful good opinion of her was something she valued.

She must have dozed, because she awoke at dawn to find that, like an unexpected, timely gift, the answer had been laid quietly upon her mind. Of course, she would simply tell them the truth, and Niall must be there to hear her do so; they would tell the MacMan's together. She would give her reason for needing to leave, and he would confirm it by giving his for wanting her to leave. Relief flooded through her as she realised that there would be no need to pretend that the situation was anything other than what it actually was - a straightforward swap, a simple correction. She would go so that the fiancée could come; in that way Niall's plans could be fulfilled in an honest and transparent way. He would see and hear for himself that she had kept to her end of the bargain, and equally importantly, there would be no grounds for him to accuse her of anything underhand if the MacMan's weren't keen on the idea - and refuse to co-operate.

Niall was certainly taking a lot for granted by assuming that they would choose his fiancée over her. Or was he? Sadly, she realised that they probably already knew the woman, in which case he had every reason to be confident. It would certainly be more politic for them to let her, a stranger - a *quine* - go, than take the risk of offending a local family or clan. This was a small community and they were in business, and goodwill was a precious commodity.

She just had to accept the fact that, when the time came, it would be less inconvenient and unpleasant for everyone concerned if she made no fuss - and quietly removed herself.

CHAPTER 13

Friday morning found Alex recovering from the previous day's journey whilst soaking in one of the hotel's baths. His hair needed cutting; he grew it quite long these days, but still conservatively short compared with most other civvies. There should be time for a trip to the barbers before Charles came to pick him up.

Stretching out in the clear, hard water, his gaze rested on the thick, ugly scar that ran, snakelike, across his stomach and along his left groin and thigh, before tapering off just above the knee. He had been assured that its original angry red appearance would fade in time, and he had to admit that it had altered considerably during the past six months; now it only protruded just a quarter of an inch. There were eleven other scars of various shapes and sizes scattered indiscriminately across his abdomen, lower back and left leg. Unfortunately, the blast had also damaged a more sensitive area of his anatomy which had necessitated even more delicate and extremely painful surgery.

His altered appearance beneath his clothes had not been much of an issue throughout his recovery when he had become accustomed to being scrutinised and handled by a small army of medical professions. Thankfully, the hospital visits were becoming less frequent as he was systematically discharged from various outpatients' clinics and more into the care of his local G.P. It was a relief to return to being looked upon as having a mind as well as a body; a viable person instead of just another collection of post-operative sites.

He smiled wryly as he recalled how he had met several women who had offered him their own kind of 'therapy' during his convalescence: 'Come on, it'll do no harm to have a test run …', 'Let me help you break the ice …', 'You just lay back and let me do the rest.' But he had refused all such temptation. Initially he'd had no choice, all his energies had gone into just staying alive; the demands of the intensive treatment had proved both tortuous and numbing and had made any thought of physical intimacy utterly fatiguing. Later, as a result of discovering the Christian Faith and meeting The Boss, and, more recently, the all-absorbing challenge of the Manor, he had found it relatively easy to keep his mind off such matters. But now there was a certain young woman to be considered, and now he needed to come to terms with the fact that, sooner or later, he would have to start facing the prospect of sharing this less than perfect body.

He ran more hot water and closed his eyes, his mind active as it travelled back to the moment he had first seen Yvonne. The image of the sunlit halo of hair and her green eyes still burned vividly in his memory, and before he realised what he was doing, he began to fantasize how she would feel lying next to him: her young, healthy softness, touching his damaged, broken hardness. He had no doubt that he would be more than satisfied. But would the feeling be mutual? She was no nurse, and such a sight might make her recoil, repulsed, and unable to hide her disgust, or sensitively find some reasonably sounding excuse to remove herself from something - someone - so unnatural. And how was he to find out? He could hardly go on a recce, or walk up to her one fine day, and say, 'Hey, what do you think of this? Could you live with it? Fancy doing a little preliminary research?' He didn't need telling that it would take an exceptional woman to commit herself to sharing a bed with this almost alien looking thing that appeared to be crawling all over him.

He gave a long sigh, recognising that this could turn out to be one of those times when he wished he could take a break from being a Christian; then quickly dismissed the idea. Cherry-picking the less inconvenient, and ignoring the more challenging aspects of The Faith, was not a practice he wanted to start.

He marvelled again at how much he had changed since meeting The Boss. He had come to recognise that all his previously held opinions and beliefs had been nothing more than a mixture of comfortable excuses and conveniently held prejudices in disguise. One of these was his former attitude that sex before marriage was just a pleasurable pastime and a great way to unwind. After all, where was the harm, especially as most women were on the pill anyway? He had happily followed the crowd as it chanted, 'If it feels good, do it,' and had learned to turn a deaf ear to the niggling voice of conscience that often followed such brief liaisons. Alex Grant had not been one for wasting valuable time on looking back: the old, carnal Alex Grant.

But now it was different; now he knew that Jesus had suffered for every sin, including all acts of sexual immorality. Christian physical intimacy was for the marriage bed only, and if Jesus was to be his example, then there was to be no turning a blind-eye to, or ignoring this very unfashionable and uncomfortable doctrine. He knew that he would have to face this issue at some time, and it looked like that time was fast approaching.

Charles often quoted some words from the Bible, and they came back to him now:-

And we know that in all things God works for
the good of those who love him, who have been
called according to his purpose. (Romans 8:28).

Well, things were definitely working out for his good, he loved The Boss, and he truly believed he had been called to a new purpose. This would have to be another time when that part of his mind would have to line up with the rest of his soul, spirit and body.

He stepped out of the tepid water and found himself wondering just how many men Miss Yvonne Williams had shared her body with. A considerable amount of opportunities must have come her way, and he felt an inexplicable, momentary flash of jealousy towards these imaginary, unsubstantiated beings. But it would be unrealistic, unfair and unreasonable of him to expect that such an attractive twenty-something year old could still be a *virgo intacta* in this day and age, especially if she had worked in the holiday trade all her working life. He had heard one too many barrack-room jokes about willing chamber maids wanting to earn 'a little extra tip.' And what if she had? How dare he judge? He, who had been freely forgiven so much. Although, he had to admit that the few times he had seen and spoken to her, there had been nothing cheap or flirtatious about her behaviour. There could be a chance that her morals were as conservative as the way she dressed; if so, he probably wouldn't have too much to worry about. Like everything else about this new life of his, he would just have to trust that The Boss knew best - and would have chosen 'a good girl' for him - or at least, a fairly good girl.

He smiled ruefully as he considered just how far he had come in his thinking about her in such a short space of time: from his initial shock and incredulity at what The Boss had said, to objecting strongly, then struggling to even be willing to consider such a thing, then onto a cautious acceptance, and now, amazingly, a feeling of some excitement and anticipation at the idea. He could only assume that his spirit had been working hard in the background to get his conscious mind on-board. If that was the case, then it had done its job well.

CHAPTER 14

Tucked away down a rural Cambridgeshire lane, the Old Ferryman Public House was one of Charles and Alex's old haunts. Today, it was as quiet as it was warm, and they did not have long to wait before their basket meal arrived.

Alex commented upon how well Charles was looking, and hoped he had sounded suitably impressed when he had been shown the rings. Studying the order of service, he felt slightly ashamed for wanting these pleasantries to be over so that he could introduce the subject that was uppermost on his mind. Nevertheless, he managed to restrain himself as he repeatedly encouraged the prospective groom to continue talking about his impending nuptials, and it was to be another three quarters of an hour before Charles felt satisfied that he had emptied himself of all his news.

'Well now, that's enough about me,' said Charles at last, rubbing his hands together as though anticipating a treat, 'come on then, your turn. What's the big mystery you hinted about the other night?'

Alex studied his empty glass and held it up; now the moment had come he felt uncharacteristically shy. 'Okay, but first, another?'

'Hmm, think I've had enough fizz for one day. I'll live dangerously and mix my drinks. Coffee please.'

Alex went over to the bar and ordered two coffees. The thought had crossed his mind that he could abandon the whole idea; it would be easy enough to make-up some excuse and steer the conversation back towards the wedding. It was probably too soon to tell anyone anyway, not that there was much to tell. But then, Charles was not just anyone, and hadn't he been waiting for just this opportunity? No, he must press on, knowing that he'd be annoyed with himself later if he chickened-out now. Resolved, he returned to his seat.

Charles studied the younger man's face and thought he could detect some indecision in the usually steady eyes. 'You know you can tell me anything, don't you, Alex? Whatever the problem is.'

'Yes, I know. It's just that this…situation is rather unusual and kind of out of my safety zone, although I think I'm coming to terms with it.'

'Sounds like a quick prayer wouldn't go amiss. Shall we?'

Alex felt his courage return even before the short prayer was over. Clearing his throat, he started to speak, hesitatingly at first, but becoming more confident as he began to paint the picture of that day in the heather. The minutes passed, and their cups were empty by the time they had finished laughing over Rabbie's part in the telephone box incident. Then Alex became serious again as he described Yvonne's defensive attitude towards him in the Inn's lounge afterwards.

Charles exclaimed, 'Phew! Quite a tale. And you really believe that it was the Lord you heard?'

Alex nodded, knowing full well that that would be the first question he would have to deal with. 'It was Him alright.'

'You know, you need to be sure about that, absolutely sure, don't you? Tell me again, exactly how did He tell you; the exact words, if you can remember them.'

'Oh, I remember them alright:-

"She's to be your wife, son.
I want you to marry her."

Clear as day. Talk about shock! And that's putting it mildly. And the only way I can describe how He told me - is that it felt like an indelible message had been printed across my mind. I had a sort of overpowering awareness, or knowledge.

I just *knew*.' Even to his own ears his story had sounded fantastic. Goodness knows what Charles must have made of it; apart from when he had described Rabbie's contribution, his expression had been one of intense concentration throughout. That was a relief. Or was it? He would almost certainly have been ridiculed if he had shared this confidence with any other person, and that would have been difficult enough to deal with. But the thought that this man - who had a lifetime's knowledge and experience of The Boss behind him - could tell him that he was being foolish, or even worse, seriously deceived, would be much harder to bear. And why was he so afraid of being proved wrong? Was it pride, or fear that this crazy, mind-blowing thing could turn out to be nothing but some sort of crazy fantasy after all? Maybe he should prepare himself to receive the disappointment that a correction, albeit a sensitive one, would inevitably cause him, because he felt sure that one was coming.

'Now, let me get this straight. You were actually praying when you first saw her walking towards you and became aware of…er, let's call it the Voice?'

'Correct. Why? Is that significant?'

Charles nodded slowly, deliberating how to frame his reply. There was a possibility that this had been a genuine experience and that Alex had indeed heard the Lord's voice. The Bible itself was full of such accounts, and Christian bookshops had plenty of books on their shelves describing how God had spoken in various ways to people throughout the ages. And Charles Harmer, for one, was not about to denounce or set limits to any of God's methods, *super*-natural though they may often be. As for Alex, he was a man he had come to know, like and respect, and considered him to be an exceptionally self-disciplined and level-headed individual. It was true that he had not known him before he had been wounded, but the records had revealed that Major Alexander Grant possessed a particularly cool and calculating character; there had been no hint of any unusual, problematic or erratic behaviour throughout his exemplary eighteen-year military service.

Alex broke the silence. 'Actually, I'm kind of warming to the idea, even though I've only just met her, or to be more accurate, bumped into her a few times.'

'And is that it? No more ... instructions since then?'

Alex gave a small laugh. 'No, no more. And I can guess what you're thinking, "Poor Alex, he's swallowed one too many pills and been stuck up there in the wilds for too long, and now he's hearing voices, or, at least, the wrong voice."'

'Well, I don't need to tell you that we can all be deceived. Remember that's one of the Devil's names, the Deceiver? He knows when we've been hankering after something, and has ways of fooling us into thinking that it's God's will for us to go out and get it. I don't want to rain on your parade son, but I think you need to go very carefully with this.'

'But, don't you see, that's just it Charles! That's the whole point. I wasn't "hankering after" anything. But there it was, out of the blue. Bang! Here she is - marry her!'

Charles inhaled slowly. 'I see. Just give me a moment here, will you.' He closed his eyes and prayed again, silently this time, asking God for a special dose of wisdom and discernment. At last, he spoke, carefully and deliberately. 'For now, let's just assume that it was the Lord speaking to you; let's try to apply the usual guidelines over relationships. First things first, I'm assuming that you don't know if she's a Christian?'

'Haven't been able to find out.'

'Hmm. Well now, you know that's all the more reason to proceed with care. Remember what it says in *Corinthians*: *Do not be unequally yoked together with unbelievers.* And the Lord had good reason to say that. In your case, it's even more important, bearing in mind the type of work you'll be doing at the Manor. Any woman you marry should ideally be your partner in the venture, like Izzy will be for me. A non-Christian could prove disastrous in more ways than one. I've seen too much unhappy proof of the old saying, "Marry in haste, repent at leisure".' He almost cringed at using the old hackneyed expression, but, for the life of him, could not think of anything more appropriate to offer.

Alex nodded slowly. 'Yes, I know. And the very last thing I want to do is to cause any complications for the Manor. Guess that's why I was so shocked when He told me, especially the timing of it. Why now? Why not later - when the place is up and running?'

'Yes, a bit of a mystery. Okay, moving on. How about Scripture? Anything been given to you? Any kind of confirmation? And I don't mean any of that poking around with a pin, lucky-dip type of nonsense, but something that speaks directly into the situation. You need words that are relevant, that make sense.'

'Oh yes!'

'Really?'

'Well, how about this? My daily readings have all been based on *The Song of Solomon*, and just this morning's was ... I've forgotten the actual words, but something from *Ecclesiastes,* something about two being better than one, and lying down together to keep warm. I've actually gone over them all and made a list, and it's quite a long one I can tell you!'

Charles smiled knowingly. *The Song of Solomon* was considered to be the most physically passionate book in the Bible. As well as the romantic and physical love between a man and a woman, it was often used to describe the love the Lord has for His Bride - the Church.

'Interesting. There could be something there. But what about circumstances? Remember how the doors just seemed to fly open when we were thinking and praying about the Manor? Anything significant - in this case?'

'Circumstances? I'll have to think about that, unless you take into account the coincidence, or God-incidence as you like to call them, that of all the people on earth it was she who walked past me that day. And why she should come to work at the Inn of all places, one of the remotest parts of the British Isles, to do a job she could do anywhere?'

'Hmm, that's something else you'll have to find out. But I think you're going to need more than that to go on. How about feelings? Do you sense any kind of unease, or hear any warning bells going off? Be truthful now. If things do develop, and your feelings are in-line with God's will, you'll need to feel real confidence and have the peace to go ahead. It would be foolhardy to deliberately try and force your feelings, or manipulate circumstances to fit.'

114

'I know what you're trying to say. Here we are, just months away from opening the Manor, and suddenly I'm told to marry a complete stranger! All I can assume is that The Boss knows what He's doing. Okay, my feelings might be a bit up in the air right now, but I'm not sensing any kind of foreboding at the idea. I'll admit that it's all a bit beyond me, and that's why I'm determined to play it cool and keep the whole thing under wraps. You're the only person I've told, and I've no intention of telling anyone else.'

'Good. And you'd be wise to keep it that way for the time being. If it is the Lord at work, then you'd be advised to let Him bring it about. Everything in good order and in His time. He'll send the woman of His choice your way at just the right time, whether it's this one or not. Your part is to keep walking with Him, and trusting Him.'

Throughout the conversation Charles had noticed that Alex's expression had changed from one of controlled enthusiasm to growing concern. Now he wondered if he had been a bit too negative about the whole thing, and felt a sudden desire to be more positive. Tempering this with the need to remain cautious, he added, 'And there's absolutely nothing else you know about her then, apart from what you've already told me?'

'No. Nothing.'

'That must be frustrating. Is she attractive, and how old would you say?'

'Possibly in her mid-twenties. And not what you'd call beautiful, but certainly nice-looking.'

'I see.' He leaned forward to look intently into Alex's eyes, then patted his arm, just like an anxious father would do to a son who was set on a reckless course of action. 'Alex, you know that the most straightforward and effective way of discovering if something is God's will or not, is to discern if He will be honoured as a result of taking that action. If He won't be, then you can bet it's not His will. It might sound egotistical of Him, but actually the principle serves as a safety net for us. And if you find yourself having to go against His written word, or compromising your conscience in some way, then that's also a strong indication that you're on the wrong track.'

Alex nodded, but remained silent.

'And you have to promise me that you won't get carried away when you do get to know her. Promise me that you won't take matters into your own hands, and be tempted to run off to Gretna Green, or do anything foolish like that?'

Alex laughed. 'Thanks for putting the idea in my head. But I promise. I won't even hobble off.'

Charles grinned and sat back. It seemed natural now for them both to remain silent for a while. One began to pray quietly; the other feeling some relief that, at last, he had been able to share this strange and remarkable thing that was happening in his life.

Charles knew that something like this was bound to happen sooner or later to Alex, only he had not bargained on it happening just now. He was a good-looking man, and certainly fitted into that needy category that some women find irresistible. How many times had he told Izzy that he wished his young friend could be given what they had been given, the companionship, comfort and real happiness of being in a genuine, loving relationship. If this was indeed an answer to that prayer, then the timing of it was puzzling. Alex was still recovering from his injuries, and getting the Manor up and running would take most of his time and energy for the foreseeable future. The added demands of entering into a romantic relationship, might, at best, turn out to be a temporary but pleasant distraction, or, at worst, a painful experience which could seriously compromise his recovery. He could be left with his precious, new-found faith badly shaken, as well as having to deal with a broken heart. If the Devil was behind all this, and he was being deceived, then he might need some very careful counselling to help him rebuild his confidence in himself and his faith. This young woman could either turn out to be a disaster, or, and please God, let this be the case, a great and unexpected blessing.

At last, he asked, 'Would you have any objection to me sharing this with Izzy? Or do you want it kept just between ourselves for the time-being?'

'I was hoping you'd want to tell her. It might be helpful that she knew about it right from the start, especially when things do start to develop.'

'Okay, good. And we'll be praying about it, of course,' replied Charles, noting that Alex had used the word 'when', and not 'if'.

CHAPTER 15

Charles and Izzy's wedding was a relaxed and dignified affair. Alex had never had much interest in the marriage service before, but now found himself paying close attention to every word and action involved in the ceremony. Afterwards, and during a particularly lengthy and rather uninspiring speech at the reception, he became aware that he was being pestered by some very unpleasant and disturbing thoughts:-

You're a fool, and in danger of making the biggest mistake of your life if you carry on fantasising about that woman. You're behaving like a thirteen-year old schoolboy, clumsily trying to deal with the onset of puberty. You should take a long, hard look at yourself. You're nothing but damaged goods, a feeble half-man. Who do you think you're kidding? Why would such a lovely, healthy young woman want to hitch her wagon to something so pathetic? How much more proof do you need that you're not the right type to be involved with the Manor? They're going to need professional, level-headed people on the staff, not someone as inexperienced and immature as you. You know you'd be doing everyone a favour if you went off and found something else to do with your pitiable life.

More annoyed than alarmed, he recognised that he had been allowing Satan to interfere with, and threaten to ruin, the happy occasion. He mentally shook himself, and decided to go on the attack. No one would have known that the distinguished looking Best Man, sitting next to bride on the head table, was taking authority over the Devil, and silently ordering him to be silent.

*

The next day was Sunday and he was delighted to receive an invitation to spend the evening with the newlyweds. The three spent some time going over the events of the previous day before moving on to study the Manor's revised plans. Alex was pleasantly surprised when Izzy dropped Yvonne Williams' name in several times throughout the discussion, and hoped that this was yet another one of those circumstances pointing in the right direction.

They were interrupted when the telephone rang. Izzy went into the hallway to answer it, leaving the two men alone in the sitting room. Although reluctant to introduce anything negative into such a convivial time, Alex felt he should mention something about the thoughts he had been pestered with during the reception. 'I hope you don't mind if I tell you something that happened recently, to do with the Manor ... and Yvonne Williams.'

'The Manor? Go on,' said Charles, immediately curious.

'I've had the idea that I'm not spiritually mature enough to be of any use, that I'll only be a hindrance to you, and kidding myself about being needed there. And that I'm wasting my time thinking I'll be able to get anywhere with Yvonne.'

Charles felt that this was not the right time or place to begin an in-depth counselling session about the whiles and ways of the Deceiver, but also knew that he should not ignore this disturbing new development. It could have serious consequences if not nipped in the bud, and in more ways than one.

There was a ping as Izzy replaced the receiver. 'That was Jackie, just to say she got home okay. Another cuppa for anyone? I'm going to have one.'

'Yes pet, one for Alex too,' replied Charles. Turning his attention back to Alex, he said quietly, 'Listen son, I'm not surprised that you're on the receiving end of such thoughts. There's something that Martin Luther said, and something we all need to be on our guard against, about when God's building His Church, and how the Devil can be busily working on the inside. We can all expect to take some flak; it can come from any direction, and just when we least expect it. But he'll be the influence - the mischief-maker - behind it, behind those thoughts. We know the Lord's definitely at work with the Manor, and it remains to be seen about you and this young woman. My advice is to stay on full alert; be on your guard at all times. Do some work on your armour, and don't give him a chink to sneak through. Remember everything the Lord's already done for you. He definitely hasn't led you all this way just to leave you high and dry now. He'll never, never do that. You're needed, you can be sure of that. You're the right man for the job, and don't let Satan - or anyone else he'll try to use - tell you otherwise.'

Alex grinned and gave a mock salute. *'Yes Sir!* I'll see to it. You go and have a great honeymoon, you know, experience some of that *Song of Solomon!'*

'And remember,' added Charles, smiling, 'of ourselves, none of us can do anything really worthwhile for God, but in Him, we can do everything He asks of us. He equips those He calls. Just keep your focus on Jesus. He's your purpose and reason now, your justification, your righteousness. Just you tell Satan that, and we'll talk more about this when I get back. Amen?'

'Amen!'

Izzy came back into the room, 'Tea's brewing.' She handed Alex a Tupperware container. 'Wedding cake, extra rations. There should be enough for the Tweedie's and for you to have a few nibbles at.'

'That's extraordinarily kind of you, Mrs Harmer!'

Izzy liked the sound of her new title. She gave Charles a knowing look as she went to sit beside him, and they shared a pleasurable moment as they both remembered how he had used her new title so effectively on several occasions throughout the previous, glorious night. She was still trying to come to terms with the level of passion he had been able to arouse in her; and to think that before she had met him, she had been so calm and peaceful in that area. She could not deny that, as a young woman, and before she had met the Lord, she had indulged in a few foolish dalliances. But she had not shared her bed with another soul for many years, and it had come as a marvellous surprise that this wonderful man had known exactly how to spark her mind and body back into life. Miracles did happen! Flushed with all these delicious new emotions, she could not help herself from doing a little teasing, as she added, 'Miss Williams might like some too.'

Charles patted her hand. 'Down girl, down! I'm sure Cupid doesn't need a helping hand from you!'

He took her hand and kissed her palm, feeling that they really should be thinking about retiring to bed - and very soon.

She chuckled. 'Oh, I don't know; he had to aim a few discreet arrows in your direction before you got the message.'

'Did he indeed?'

Smiling, she withdrew her hand and sat back. 'Maybe I'll tell you about it one day. But if Cupid and the Lord have teamed up over Alex, then I'm guessing it won't be too long before we're eating more wedding cake!'

Alex smiled broadly; somehow, he liked the sound of that.

CHAPTER 16

Yvonne felt as though a heavy grey dustbin lid had been placed over her life. No longer did she revel in the newness and beauty of the environment or eagerly soak-up any new experience. Instead, she gazed upon the place and people with a resigned sadness. The one good thing about this time was that Niall appeared to be containing his angry and impatient outbursts, and a sort of uneasy truce had formed between the two of them. Now, depending upon his mood, he treated her with a cool indifference or a disagreeable sycophancy. Sometimes she would catch him giving her sly, curious glances, and guessed that he was trying to spot any clues that she might have changed her mind about leaving.

It was not long before the MacMan's noticed the change of atmosphere and became curious. When neither party offered any meaningful explanation after being gently quizzed, Georgina thought it expedient to believe that the pair had been successful in settling their differences. Donald, however, preferred to reserve judgement.

*

Yvonne flagged down the morning bus to Strathlochy on her next day off and made her way to the smallest labour exchange she had ever seen. There were over a dozen vacancies for hotel live-in staff, most of them in places she had never heard of. Armed with the contact details of several possibilities and a purse full of change, she headed for the nearest public telephone box and started the laborious task of ringing around. Asked, 'Where was she working now? And why was she leaving?' she simply answered, 'Apparently, I'm going to be surplus to requirements soon,' and did not blame the few who lost interest in her at this point, she would have done so as well. However, the manager of a three-star hotel in Beaulane did not sound too concerned, stating, 'As long as you're prepared to work hard and keep your nose clean...' She had not liked the sound of the man, and felt instinctively that this was going to be another of those miserable mistakes, but the fight had gone out of her; it would have to do for now. At least she had accomplished what she had set out to achieve that morning: another job to go to with another roof over her head.

Although required to give just one week's notice, she thought it only fair to give the MacMan's two, which meant that she would have to tell them the following week. Hopefully, they wouldn't be too put out, especially now that there was this fiancée waiting in the wings.

*

Niall called after her as she was leaving the kitchen after lunch the next day. 'Hey, you'll be at the ceilidh tonight? It's a good crack.'

Puzzled, she turned to look at him, wondering why he should care whether she was there or not. 'No, I don't think so.'

'Och, but you'll no sleep till it's over.'

'Well then, I'll just stick some cotton wool in my ears!' she replied, feeling that, in her present state of mind, it would be unbearable to have to spend the evening pretending that everything was fine and dandy when everyone around her was enjoying themselves.

'But you'll have the Chief after you; she'll smell a rat.'

So, that was the reason for his unusual show of concern. By all means they must both be seen to be having a good time. The MacMan's had been successfully hoodwinked so far, and he was obviously concerned that her absence from the event might arouse suspicion. The pretense must go on and not be compromised in any way. Well, that was a risk she would have to take. 'In that case, I'll just say I've got a headache.'

'Och, away with you! That's stupid. Just you take yourself there. Anyway ...' he hesitated, inwardly cursing her for her obstinacy; now he would have to reveal his real motive. 'Ma hen's comin''. He paused and gave her a stony, penetrating glare. 'And you'll no be wantin' to let *her* down now, will you?'

Yvonne was indignant. Let her down! That was rich. If anyone was being let down here, it was certainly not this ... this 'hen'! And how many more hoops did he expect her to jump through before she left? 'Well, I'm sure I can live without *that* honour,' she replied smartly.

A sudden commotion of voices and thumps could be heard coming from the reception area, effectively putting an end to their discussion. 'Och, to hell with you then!' he snarled, rushing past her to beat a hasty retreat to his room. 'That'll be the Glasgow lot. I'm off!'

'The Glasgow lot', otherwise known as the Maxwell family, consisting of seven adults and nine children, had indeed arrived. Yvonne went through to reception, all thoughts of the ceilidh temporarily forgotten as she helped Georgina with the welcoming and registration process. Donald was despatched to find a truculent Niall, who was then ordered to help carry a small mountain of luggage and hiking paraphernalia through to the guest rooms. The younger members of the party began to squabble and jostle each other as they attempted to negotiate the safe passage of several cumbersome musical instrument cases and record players along the corridor. No one could help but notice Niall's glowering face as he pushed and shoved his way rudely between them all, carelessly hitting several shins en route. Looks were exchanged as they wondered who the angry little man was, and Georgina found herself having to talk sharply to him on more than one occasion.

And so the Inn burst into life. From all directions came the sounds of much running-about, door-slamming, shouting, laughter, snatches of song, and the strangled sounds of various instruments being tuned. By dinner time most of the noise was contained within the dining room. Yvonne had just finished serving coffee when she noticed Georgina, looking resplendent in a full-length skirt in the MacMan tartan and an elaborate, frilly white blouse, walking through reception. Georgina called her over, and casting a wary eye over her plain blouse and skirt, said, 'Off you pop, and get yourself ready. We're expecting a full house tonight.' She stroked the back of her head, appreciating the silky feel of her freshly *Hint of a Tint* coloured hair. 'And Donald will be glad of some help. You won't mind, will you?' - giving Yvonne no time to reply as she swept majestically through into the lounge.

Bother! Now why hadn't she thought of that? How was Georgina to know that she was in anything but a party mood? And from what she had heard, these ceilidhs were always well attended by the locals; of course she would be expected to help.

She made her way up to her room and stood disconsolately in front of her open wardrobe. Unlike Georgina's elaborate blouse, all hers were plain, and she would probably get too hot if she wore a jumper. It would have to be a dress; the brown one would do; beer spills always washed out well. She quickly bathed, re-plaited her hair, applied a few strokes of face powder and lipstick, dabbed a few drops of vanilla scented cologne behind her ears, and decided she would do.

*

Alex and his party had arrived early. He had taken extra care over his appearance and was wearing one of the new shirts and casual slacks he had bought on his recent trip down south. He looked up expectantly each time someone entered the lounge. And now, at last, here she was. He studied her analytically; she was certainly more plainly dressed than the other women, but he liked the unfussy, almost severe look of her. She looked a decent enough girl.

Unaware that she was being so carefully scrutinised, Yvonne had walked into the already crowded lounge, and was attempting to make her way towards the bar when she heard someone call her name. The large dividing doors between the lounge and dining room had been opened and the tables and chairs had been pushed to the sides, creating a large, open space where the dancing would take place later. She looked for the disembodied voice and spotted Niall waving at her from the far corner, and assumed that the bemused looking woman sitting bolt upright next to him was the mysterious fiancée.

'Hey, wake up girl! Someone to see you.' he called. He had also been looking out for her, and was more than a little keen to get this bit over and done with. He'd been on tenterhooks for days, and felt that the sooner the bitch saw him and Maggie together, the harder she would find it to do the dirty on him and change her mind. He'd been promising Maggie that she'd meet the girl who was the cause of all the trouble this very night. Now she'd see for herself how well he'd sorted her problem out.

His eyes narrowed as Yvonne drew near. Yvonne watched as the woman began to get to her feet, only to be pushed unceremoniously back down by Niall.

Maggie had been dreading this moment and was at a loss as to what to do next. Should she hold out her hand, nod, or what? She could hardly come out with what she was actually thinking: 'Hello I'm right pleased to hear you'll be gone soon. It's a great shame that you came all this way just to be having to turn around and go back.' Oh dear! What did Niall expect of her now? She must make sure she didn't embarrass him; he was right, she did have such a lot to learn.

Yvonne took the initiative and held her hand out to the nervous looking woman. Unsmiling, she said a plain, 'Good evening,' and received a weak echo back.

Niall's chest expanded several inches. Being a man with so much power over these two women was a heady responsibility, and he sounded boastful as he announced, poking a finger into Maggie's arm, 'Aye, so it is, especially for this one, 'cos she'll be Mrs Turvey - Mrs *Niall* Turvey - soon enough. So, what d'ya say to that?'

Yvonne wondered at the man's conceit, and did her best to remain polite as she stood in front of the object of his desire. The heavy-set woman grinning sheepishly back at her could easily have been taken for a maiden aunt rather than a soon-to-be-bride and expectant mother, and being seated, it was difficult to tell how much of her rotund shape was due to overweight, or how much to the baby growing inside her. Ignoring Niall, she gave Maggie a fleeting smile, and asked, 'It sounds like your big day will be soon then?'

Once again, Niall took charge as he quickly replied, 'Aye, aye, that it'll be, but that's our business.' There, he thought, it's done; she wouldn'a have the nerve to change her mind now that they've met. He placed a proprietorial arm around Maggie's shoulders and drew her none too gently to him. 'So, you've seen ma hen now, you'll be behavin' yourself'.'

Maggie wasn't too sure what to make of all this; she felt strangely out of sorts, having been expecting something different from this pleasant looking young woman standing in front of her. However, she soon rallied when she felt Niall's body heat warming her skin through that lovely pink shirt of his.

'Off you go and do your bit,' he said, 'you'll be wantin' to get your claws into the local talent. And I've got important things to sort here.'

Yvonne stood her ground. Was there no end to the man's rudeness? Fiancée or no fiancée, she was not going to be spoken to like that! '"Do my bit"? And what would that be then, Niall? Do tell me!'

Maggie's heart had started to pound. 'Important things' he'd said. He could only be talking about getting wed. At last! And he was wanting to get things sorted *this very night!* Oh, things were *wonderful!* And soon everything would fit together just fine. Conroy's were getting on well with the alterations, and Dad had promised her a tidy bit for their big day. Now they could have a nice sort of wedding, and even a bit of a honeymoon. But hush now, Niall was speaking to the English girl again.

'Och, stop your bletherin' and look sharp. Your needed over there,' he said, waving his hand dismissively towards the other end of the room.

Yvonne turned and spotted Donald peering in her direction. She nodded and waved, before turning back and looking hard at Niall. 'For your information, Niall, I'm not in the least bit interested in getting "my claws into the local talent", as you so delicately put it, especially if they're anything like you!' Shifting her focus onto Maggie, and in a softer tone, she added, 'Well, all the best, and I hope that everything works out for you when your …'

Just at that moment, Niall decided to have a coughing fit, thereby preventing Maggie from hearing what the English girl had said, but it had sounded almost like 'baby'. Baby! Och, but she must have misheard, or the silly girl must be getting her confused with someone else. Fancy making a mistake like that! It was a good job she wasn't one to get upset about such things, or it would have been bad luck indeed.

Yvonne turned and walked away, something in her wanted to shake the woman and tell her to wake up and come to her senses before it was too late. Someone really should warn her. Couldn't she see what she was letting herself in for? Talk about love being blind! But it was the unborn child that she felt really sorry for; poor little thing; she knew all about having a father like that: arrogant, brutish and dominant.

Donald was looking flustered, an unusual frown creasing his normally unfurrowed brow. 'I'm sorry to do this to you, lass, your first ceilidh and all,' he said as she reached the small bar. 'There's a lot more in than usual…and what with the Maxwell crowd. Do you think you could give me a hand, and go round and take orders? Stop them queuing, and blocking the doorway?'

'Yes, of course, I'd be happy to,' she replied, and she meant it. If she wasn't going to be allowed to find a dark corner to sit this thing out, then she might as well be kept busy. She had spotted the fair hair and rangy figure of Alexander Grant out of the corner of her eye as soon as she had entered, and just knew that nothing about this night was going to be easy.

*

Alex smiled as she approached his table. 'Ah, here she is at last. Hello Yvonne.'

She looked at him. There it was again, that searching, questioning look in those grey eyes of his.

'Settled in yet? Any more run-ins with Rabbie?' he asked, then immediately felt that that had not been the most tactful thing to say.

Unable to raise even a polite smile, she answered, 'Yes thank you, Mr Grant. Rabbie and I are quite good friends now; we just needed a proper introduction. Are you ready to order?'

Feeling suitably chastised, he replied, 'Er, right. Oh, by the way, this is Angus and Dot Tweedie. Dot and Angus, this is Yvonne Williams, the young lady Flora's been telling you about.' The elderly man stood and gave Yvonne a firm handshake as he greeted her. The woman remained seated, and said a cheerful, 'Helloo, Helloo!' as she offered her hand. She liked the look of the quine, nothing fancy to be sure, and Flora had been right, my, she was a pale one!

Alex spoke again. 'My round, I think. Same again for you folks?' The couple nodded their agreement. 'Right, so that's a whisky chaser, a port and lemon and ...' he paused, waiting for Yvonne to look at him instead of the empty glasses on the table, 'I'll have another blackcurrant squash, on the rocks. And one for yourself. And you can call me Alex.'

She ignored him and lowered her eyes to write the order down, wondering at the fact that he drank squash. But wasn't he supposed to be ex-Army? Most of the ex-servicemen she had come across were drinkers; squash would have been anathema to them. Then she remembered that he was supposed to be very religious. Maybe he had taken the pledge; apparently people still did, even in this day and age - although she had never met one yet.

She returned a few minutes later and placed the drinks on the table. Alex took out his wallet as he glanced at the bill and noticed that she had not bought one for herself.

Donald was content to remain safely ensconced behind the bar. He beamed widely at one and all, congratulating himself at having found such an efficient helper. Everyone had a drink and appeared to be enjoying themselves. Even Niall looked happy enough, and there he was with Maggie MacKay again. Now what was going on there? Georgy was in full flow, doing the rounds, nodding, smiling and chatting. He was relieved when he saw her open another window, the room was already thick with smoke. The plates of complimentary sandwiches, rolls, scones and cakes were almost empty, and the small baskets of peanuts and crisps that had been dotted around the place would soon need replenishing. But what particularly pleased him was that people were drinking plenty; the bar takings would get a much-needed boost.

This was Yvonne's first experience of a ceilidh, and she was impressed. Energetic reels were danced: some graceful, others not quite so; impossibly fast tunes were played on bagpipes, violins and accordion. The crowd joined in enthusiastically: thumping tables, clapping hands and stomping their feet whenever a catchy, toe-tapping melody was played. She almost expected another Jacobite rebellion to break out when the whole place erupted to the rousing words of *Flower of Scotland*. Flora, Hamish, Dot and Angus Tweedie, along with most of the other, more senior guests, remained seated throughout. Occasionally, one of them would stand to recite an obviously much-loved poem, or sing, unaccompanied, a haunting Gaelic chant, after which the applause could only be described as being thunderous.

Alex did not ask anyone to dance, and had himself refused several offers. Nevertheless, he found himself wondering what it would be like to do one of those slow, close numbers with Yvonne, but instinctively knew that she would turn him down, just as he had seen her do to a few other men.

Since their first ceilidh, Maggie had known that Niall was not one for the dancing; neither would he let her dance with anyone else, although sometimes he did allow her to join in a reel. But this was a small price to pay for who she was soon going to be.

An hour had gone by when Georgina clapped her hands and raised her arms in the air in an attempt to catch the crowd's attention. After much hushing and shushing she was finally able to make herself heard. 'Thank you, thank you everyone. If I could just have a minute of your time. I have some rather … er, it seems that we have some good news to announce.' Her voice became almost a shrill as she continued, 'I have just been informed by Niall, who is, as you know, our Chef, that he and Maggie have just become engaged!' She waited for the resultant gasps and exclamations to die down. 'Yes, I can see you're as surprised as me. Talk about a dark horse! But, come on now, please join me in raising your glasses and wishing them a very long and happy life together.' She raised her glass towards the couple, 'To Maggie and Niall.'

Toasts were drunk and loud cheers followed. The accordionist struck up with *Mairi's Wedding* as a small crowd gathered around the couple, asking the usual questions at a time like this and demanding to see the ring. No one commented on the meagre looking stone; that would be cause for much discussion later on.

Alex's attention was elsewhere, he was studying Yvonne's face as she stood apart and leaning against a wall. Although she had toasted the couple with the rest of them, it was obvious to him that she was feeling anything but joyful at the announcement. On several occasions he had noticed her stop and lean against the same wall when no one had required her waitressing services, a preoccupied, almost sad look on her face. The more melancholic ballads could often have that effect on sensitive people, but her cheerless expression had taken time to fade, even during the more up-tempo songs. It appeared that Miss Yvonne Williams was a young woman with something very much on her mind, and he found himself starting to become not only curious, but quite concerned, as to what that something, or someone, might be. And at the moment, that chef was suspect number one.

Dot broke into his reverie. 'Alex, we're after going laddie; we're needing our beds.'

'Right, no problem. Ready whenever you are,' he replied, feeling some disappointment at having to go so soon, but the old folk looked tired and had obviously had enough, and he was the driver. Given the choice, and despite the nagging pain in his hip and leg, he would have preferred to have stayed till the end. If this sad-eyed young woman was going to become his partner in life, he was going to need more opportunities like this to be able to observe and assess her.

Yvonne noticed that he was limping badly when the small party made their slow progress through the room.

'Goodnight Yvonne,' he said, passing her.

'Goodnight Mr Grant.'

'Yvonne.' He stopped directly in front of her, forcing her to look up into his now customary penetrating gaze.

'Yes?'

'It's Alex, remember. Well, goodnight again, and take very good care of yourself, won't you.'

'Oh! Okay.' What an odd thing to say, she thought, and what was it to do with him what kind of care she took of herself? She was no concern of his. And the way he had looked at her, almost as though he knew how rotten she had been feeling all night. But how could he? And those eyes of his, there was something very disturbing about them. She thought she had caught him looking at her a few times, but then, what else could he do with that bad leg of his but look around him; she could hardly blame him for that. How tired she was, but it would be a while before she could escape to bed. Donald would need a hand to clear up and get the place ready for breakfast, and then she would have to be up and dressed in time to do the early morning teas. She had better stop all this thinking about Alexander Grant … or Alex as he seemed to want to be called; it was such a waste of time and energy. The man could be as handsome and as disturbing as he liked; he was nothing to do with her; nothing to do with her at all.

CHAPTER 17

Three days later, Yvonne began to wonder if she had been transported back into the frenetic environment of the holiday camp world. Her busyness meant that she was able to forget about her impending departure for hours at a time, and for this, she was very grateful. In her opinion, many a camp's entertainment manager could have learned a thing or two from Sonia Maxwell, the matriarchal head of this branch of the clan. That lady's skill at organising a challenging itinerary of indoor and outdoor activities to suit all age groups was impressive. Nature rambles, hikes, bird-spotting, sketching and photography field trips, as well as outings to Strathlochy, Invermaden and Beaulane, were fitted snugly around an inexhaustible list of indoor competitions, quizzes, slide shows, talks, games and treasure hunts. The family fascinated Yvonne and she found herself closely observing the way they talked, played and worked together, and came to the conclusion that the advantages of belonging to such a tight-knit group would probably outweigh any disadvantages.

The lunchtime rush was nearly over when she spotted Alex's car pulling up outside. She glanced over at the MacMan's, they were still preoccupied with the conversation they had been having with Sonia and her husband for some time; she would have to deal with him. She went to stand behind the reception desk and watched him approach, greeting him with a hopefully cheerful sounding, 'Hello … Alex. How are you?' when he entered.

'Hi Yvonne. Blessed thanks. And you?' he replied, as a burst of laughter erupted from the lounge. 'Sounds as though things are going with a swing here?'

'You can say that again! Are you after Mr and Mrs MacMan?'

'No, it's you I came to see.'

'Me?'

'Affirmative. I'm after a bit of help at the Manor. There's a problem with some of the staff accommodation, the decorating side of things.' He pointed outside. 'There's a small mountain of wallpaper and curtain samples out there, and I was kind of hoping that you'd see your way clear to giving me the benefit of your vastly superior feminine knowledge, and go through them with me? That is, if you've got an hour or two to spare sometime?' Good, he thought, that sounded casual enough. Since the ceilidh he had been unable to shake the image of her downcast face from his mind, and had spent a considerable amount of prayer time on her. When this latest difficulty had occurred, he seized upon it as a reasonable sounding excuse to see her again. She was looking shocked - no, stunned - so he hurriedly went on to explain, 'One of my partners was meant to be handling this kind of thing, but she's gone down with a bad attack of shingles, and won't be able to travel for a while. She's advised me to get the rooms painted off-white, but I thought I'd see what I could do myself. But I really could do with another pair of eyes.'

Just then Georgina came bustling through. 'Oh! Hello Alex. I thought it was you. Have you come for lunch? Only you're a bit late, you know.'

'No, not today thank you Georgina. Actually, it's Yvonne I've come to see.'

'Yvonne?'

'That's right.'

Georgina looked from one to the other, making it obvious that she expected to be given an explanation. Reluctantly, and mildly irritated at the woman's unwelcome interference, Alex repeated his request, adding, 'The staff will be the first to arrive, and we need to be making a start if we're to be ready on time; so you can see my predicament.'

Georgina looked thoughtful. 'I see. How very unfortunate.' There was another burst of laughter, and she pointed towards the lounge. 'But, as you can hear, we've got rather a full house, and it's our chef's half-day, so it's all hands on deck I'm afraid.'

Now Donald came ambling through. 'Alex! How's tricks? Fancy joining-in the quiz? Chance to win the biggest box of chocolates you've ever seen!'

'Hello Donald, thanks for the invite; sounds tempting, but-'

Georgina interrupted him. 'He's wanting to take Yvonne off to help him choose things for the Manor. Got a bit of a panic on by the sound of it. Remember Niall's not here, and we're needing her to do the teas.'

'Really? Choose things? What type of things?' Donald asked, obviously keen to hear more.

'I'm needing inspiration with some of the staff rooms: wall colours, curtains, stuff like that,' replied Alex. 'There's been a change of plan over them and we'd like to get the ball rolling. I just need someone else to bounce ideas off.'

Donald turned to Yvonne. 'Well, sounds fair enough to me. What do you say, Yvonne? Reckon you can help?'

'But Donald - ' exclaimed Georgina.

'Come on Georgy! A neighbour in need and all that. Anyway, we owe her some time off for helping at the ceilidh. What do you say, Yvonne, okay with you?'

'Well, yes, I suppose there is that,' said Georgina, reluctantly deciding to capitulate, and giving Yvonne no time to reply. 'But I must insist that she's back in time to help with dinner.'

It appeared to Yvonne that, despite her own feelings on the matter, her mind had been made up for her. Trying to sound gracious, she said, 'Alright then. But I honestly don't think I can be of much help.'

Georgina flicked an imaginary fleck of dust off her sleeve. 'Oh, you won't go far wrong if you keep to mute shades for the walls, and patterned carpets; far more practical, doesn't show the dirt.'

'Thanks, we'll bear that in mind,' said Alex, privately congratulating himself that the first part of his mission had been accomplished relatively easily. Hopefully, the second part would be just as straightforward.

Still not too sure how she felt about having been volunteered in this way, Yvonne excused herself, and went off to change.

*

Ten minutes later, she was in Alex's car and on her way to the Manor. He glanced over and noticed how stiffly she was holding herself, which could mean that either she was painfully shy, which he doubted, or annoyed at having been coerced into coming along, which was more likely. 'This is very good of you, Yvonne; I hope you don't mind. You were put on the spot back there.'

Yvonne was intensely aware of the man sitting just inches away from her; he was far too attractive, far too close. Now she began to feel embarrassed that he had obviously picked up on her mood, and not being spiteful or sulky by nature, she made an effort to snap out of her pique. 'It's like I said, I really don't know how much help I can be.'

'Any help would be greatly appreciated. We've had interior decorators in, and they've done a great job with the rest of the place, but they seem to have lost interest when it came to the staff wing. Wanted to do it a bit too plain for my liking. We're after something a bit less utilitarian, more comfortable. Am I making sense?'

She felt her confidence dip even lower as he spoke. She was institutionalised, and she knew it. What she knew about choosing a comfortable and non-utilitarian type of décor could have fitted onto a postage stamp. 'I think so. But wasn't there really anyone else you could have asked?'

'Down south, yes, plenty. But you and the MacMan's are the only ones I know around here who've got any experience of living in a similar type of environment.'

'Oh, I see. It's just that I'm sure Georgina would have helped you out; you just caught her at a bad time. Maybe you could try asking her again when she's not so busy?'

Changing gear, he said matter-of-factly, 'You know, I've got a feeling she wouldn't be all that helpful. And anyway, she's not too thrilled at the idea of the Manor.'

They drove on in silence as she digested this piece of information. It certainly sounded as though he had given the matter some thought. 'So, I really am your last resort then?'

He turned to look at her, a strange, knowing look in his eyes. 'Well now, I wouldn't put it *quite* like that. I've got a feeling you'll turn out to be just the right person for the job.'

Slightly perplexed as to what he could mean, she decided to become fascinated with the view. This man really was a bit of mystery; it almost sounded as though he knew something about her that she did not know herself. She told herself to stop being so fanciful, and replied, 'Er, well, I'll do my best. As long as you're not expecting much.'

'Don't worry, my partners will have the final say on anything we can come up with, but I'm sure that between us we'll find something useful.'

*

It was raining by the time they turned into a pleasant tree-lined avenue and approached an imposing, two-story, granite-faced building. A small, pinnacled turret projected from one of the corners, giving it a fairy tale like appearance.

'Here we are Yvonne, welcome to Braegarroch Manor,' he announced, pulling up behind a builder's wagon. He opened his door and began walking around the car. Realising that he was coming to open her door for her, she quickly stepped out. He liked that, and turned to open one of the back doors instead. 'Right, down to business. Can you manage one of these?' he asked, retrieving one of the heavy books of wallpaper samples from the back seat. Without hesitation, she leant in and took one in each hand.

'Atta girl! Careful on the steps now, this old slate's deadly when it's wet. There'll be handrails and a ramp here soon.'

He led her into an impressively large room. The sound of falling masonry could be heard coming from somewhere above. 'That'll be the builders. We're installing a lift. I'm afraid the place is in a bit of a mess and none too warm, but at least we can do something about that.' He stooped to switch on a large, electric fire. 'Do you mind giving me a hand with the rest? We'll have a drink once they're all in.'

The rain persisted as they collected the remaining books, and they were both considerably wet by the time the job was done.

'Right, you stay here and make yourself comfortable while and I go and rustle-up some drinks. Tea, coffee?'

'Coffee, milk with one sugar thanks,' she replied, taking off her coat and spreading it over the front of one of the dust-covered armchairs near the fire before looking around her. The room's high walls were covered, in her opinion, with an extremely unattractive wallpaper, made up of a large, geometric design of interlocking rectangles and squares in various shades of orange and brown. Curious, she lifted the cover from under her arm, and was confronted with a bright orange material which clashed appallingly with the lime green, shag pile carpet. Heavy, dark brown and orange striped curtains hung from the two large bay windows. The only part of the room where her eye could rest without being challenged was the dingy, artexed ceiling. A dark wooden light fixture, consisting of eight, lightening-shaped, jagged arms with small candle shaped light bulbs at each end, hung from a faded gold painted ceiling rose. The whole effect made her shudder, and she told herself to be careful, for all she knew this might be to Alex's taste. If so, she would have nothing but sympathy for his poor guests.

The rain came to an abrupt stop and a shaft of sunlight came from behind the clouds, casting a cheerful, golden glow across the room. A ray fell across her face. She closed her eyes and sat back, trying to sense and imagine what the room could look like if freed from all the clashing colours and designs.

Alex reappeared a few moments later and stood in the doorway, holding two mugs and with a towel draped over one shoulder. She did not appear to have noticed him and remained as she was. Now that he did not have the distraction of her eyes, he was free to concentrate on the rest of her. The light made her pale skin look almost translucent against her dark hair, and he found himself imagining what it would be like to twist some of those loose tendrils around his fingers. She was pursing her lips together in concentration and he felt a sudden urge to experience their movement against his own. Her breathing was steady and his eyes moved slowly down her neck before settling on her full breasts. He felt himself becoming aroused, and it was with some effort that he managed to calm down; this was not the idea at all. It was too soon, much too soon.

'Here we are then,' he said, stepping into the room and placing the mugs on a nearby coffee table. He handed her the towel, then threw his wet jacket off before going to sit on the opposite armchair. Sighing deeply, he looked around him. 'Fabulous isn't it?'

Patting her damp hair with the towel, and noticing an expression of mock-horror on his face, she felt confident enough to reply, 'You should have warned me to bring my sunglasses! I can't remember when I last had the privilege of being surrounded by such brilliant taste and refinement.'

He threw back his head and laughed. 'Good one! I did think about changing the name to Cringeworthy Court, but my partners weren't too keen. Can't think why. But hey, I like a challenge!'

'Well, you've certainly got one here. What were the previous owners like?'

'Never met them. The place had been empty for nearly three years before we saw it. All I know is that a couple from London used it as a holiday home, but apparently got fed-up with all the travelling. Rumour has it that they got divorced, and neither party wanted anything to do with the place after that. They must have had a few bob to be able to leave all this furniture behind. Still, I'm not complaining, we managed to get it for a very reasonable price, and the structure's sound. It's just the ... er ... décor.'

'Hmm, it is rather shocking. What'll you do? Get rid of the whole lot, even the carpets?'

'That's the general idea. Pity, this one's in good nick.' He dug and twisted his heel into the deep pile. 'Although we may keep some of the furniture, it's good, solid stuff and just needs re-covering. Well, now you've been exposed to this room's unique blend of chemical and biological warfare for a while, have you managed to come up with anything?'

'Maybe. It was when the sun came out just now; I could almost see the walls in a very pale shade of lemon. Nothing brash, but subdued.'

He looked thoughtfully at her. 'Really? Okay. Any other ideas?'

She pointed upwards. 'Those cornices would look lovely with a fresh coat of paint, it's all so dingy. Were they heavy smokers or something? And the carpet could be in a sort of oatmeal colour. The curtains could be in a … a dusty shade of blue; that would provide some contrast. I think it could be a lovely room, welcoming, you know, light and cheerful, but calm and peaceful at the same time.'

'Sounds good! What about the furniture?'

She considered, looking around her again, before replying, 'Maybe some kind of beech, but not pine; that would make it look too…yellowy.'

Obviously impressed, he remarked, 'You know, that's not a hundred miles away from what the professionals have come up with. Maybe you've got a flair for this kind of thing after all. Right, come on, we'd better make the most of the time we've got. Bring your drink, and let me show you why I'm seriously in need of your help.'

*

There were nine rooms in the staff wing, none of them modernized, and all in a sad state of repair. He explained that two of the largest were to be divided into a lounge and kitchenette; each would have an adjoining bedroom. His partners would have one and he the other. The partners would choose their own colour scheme when they arrived. In the meantime, their rooms would be re-plastered and painted in an inoffensive magnolia. The two rooms nearby would be converted into bathrooms. The smallest room had been earmarked to become an area where drinks and light snacks could be made, and the remaining two would remain as bedrooms.

They made slow but steady progress. The effect his physical presence was having upon Yvonne was alarming, and she had to exercise a considerable amount of self-discipline in order to stay focused upon her task. He was at least six feet tall, a good seven inches taller than her, and there did not appear to be any spare flesh on his very obvious masculine body. But, more often than not, it was his hands that would hold her attention. Unlike hers, which were in constant motion, his were calm and steady, and somehow reassuringly strong. She tried to look away as he made detailed notes of her ideas, but invariably found herself staring back at them, finding their action soothing almost hypnotic. She liked his smile too, and his neat, trim beard. Then there was the way his fair hair tapered into the back of his neck. With some annoyance, she had to acknowledge that she was definitely attracted to him, and found it necessary to remind herself on more than one occasion why she had made that decision to leave all such nonsense well and truly behind her.

*

An hour later they returned to the lounge. Alex reached over and lifted the first of the sample wallpaper books onto the coffee table between them.

'Right. Let's make a start on my quarters and see if there's something I could live with in these.' He began flicking through the pages. Success came towards the end of the second book, when they found one in a subtle pattern of pale blue and silver panels.

'Perfect!' She exclaimed. 'That's exactly the shade I imagined, and it's a quiet sort of pattern, restful, but not dull.'

He agreed enthusiastically. 'You know, I like it! I think it'll work.' He made a note of the make and pattern number. 'Come on, van Gogh, you're on a roll. What about the curtains?'

Once again, success was achieved when they found a heavy velveteen in a midnight shade of blue. Thereafter, the procedure was much the same for each room. Tartan did not figure at all in the plan, however, feeling that it would be churlish to avoid it altogether, she suggested it could be used for some of the bedspreads and cushion covers, stating that it

141

would be easier to select these at a later date, especially when all the decorating was done.

Another hour was to pass before Alex slammed the last book shut. He leaned heavily back into his chair, and exclaimed, 'Phew! What a relief. I can't thank you enough. You've saved my bacon. If it'd been down to me, they'd have all ended up with khaki walls and brown lino floors! Anyway, that was thirsty work; ready for another drink?'

She glanced at her watch. The mental exertion had tired her, but she had really enjoyed herself, and it had been good to be able to forget her troubles for a while.

'Okay, tea this time, but only if you let me help. And if you really can't live without khaki, you could always have it on the corridor walls!'

'Oh no, young lady! Those days are well and truly behind me. We'll stick to that pale peach - or whatever it was you came up with.' He led her through several rooms, all equally hideous, until they reached a long hallway with a door at the end. This turned out to be a large kitchen, which, he assured her, only needed some cosmetic work doing to make it fit for purpose. Even so, she guessed it would take someone a considerable amount of time and labour to strip the orange paint off the units and replace the rows of gaudy green and orange tiles.

He filled the kettle, put three teaspoons of tea into a large earthenware teapot, then began searching through the cupboards. 'You know, Yvonne, I'm thinking we make a good team. Biscuit?'

She fetched the milk from the fridge and looked around for some clean mugs, before giving up and rinsing the ones they had already used. 'Yes please, but I expect you'd have found someone else, sooner or later.'

'Possibly, although what you've come up with has been just that bit special; you've got real flair. And apologies, it looks like the builders have taken all the biscuits.' He turned and crossed his arms as he leant against one of the units, deciding that now was as good a time as any to embark upon the second part of the mission. Tilting his head to the side, he looked at her quizzically. 'I'm curious about you, Yvonne. Tell me about yourself. What brought you all the way up here to work? You're a long way from home, aren't you?'

She had been asked the same question several times recently, and decided to give her usual reply. 'Oh, you know how it is, I fancied a change. I'd never been to Scotland, and when I saw the advert, I thought, well, why not?'

'What about your family? What did they think?'

She shrugged. 'Haven't got any.'

He stared at her for a few seconds, before saying, 'I'm sorry, that was rude of me.'

'That's okay. Don't worry about it.'

The tea made, they settled themselves back down in front of the lounge fire. She felt it only polite to ask him how he had ended up here as well, but he was as evasive as she had been as he glossed over his Army career and how he had come by his injuries. She appeared to be satisfied and relaxed, so he went on to comment, 'I should imagine Flora's mighty glad of the help. Dot tells me she's been battling on for some time with that back of hers.'

'Apparently so. It's all the bed-making and hoovering that she seems to find difficult. I try to do as much of it as I can.'

'Then it would make sense if the MacMan's asked you stay on at the end of the season, and take you on permanently.' He hesitated when he saw her frown. 'What's the matter? You don't look too keen on the idea.'

She felt annoyed with herself for allowing him see her negative reaction, and knew that she would have to be more careful from now on. The last thing she needed was for him to somehow tease the truth out of her, and alert the MacMan's that all was not as peaceful as they were being led to believe. Trying to sound casual, she said, 'Oh well, you know how it is, nothing lasts forever. And anyway, I'm used to moving around.'

He persisted, 'But you would stay, wouldn't you - if they asked? Anyone can see that they think highly of you.'

'As I do them. But who knows what will happen when their son takes over? He might have other ideas.'

'From what I've heard of it, he'll be needing experienced staff, especially good all-rounders like you.'

By now she was feeling decidedly uncomfortable and just wanted him to drop the subject. 'Well, that's enough about me. I'm more interested in what's going on here. When do you plan on opening?'

'Right, well, if all goes according to plan, towards the end of summer. But, no, let's not change the subject. Now look Yvonne, you'll have to forgive me if I'm speaking out of turn, but I couldn't help noticing that you weren't particularly enjoying the ceilidh the other night.'

Her eyes opened wide. He continued. 'Don't look so surprised! Fortunately, or unfortunately for you, you've got the type of face that can be easily read.'

This was getting far too personal for her now. What right had he to question her like this? Then, for a split second, she played with the idea of telling him about her problem with Niall. She could be vague and generalise; it might even be a relief to be able to confide in someone outside of the situation. After all, he had used her to help solve his problem, 'to bounce ideas off', why shouldn't she ask the same of him? He was obviously interested and willing. But then her head took over from her heart, and warned her to be careful. What was she doing allowing herself to think and feel like this? She looked across at the grey, questioning eyes, and knew that, somehow, she would have to put a stop to this - and quickly.

'Alex, please don't think me rude, but I really don't want to talk about it. Anyway, everything's been sorted out.' She glanced at her watch. 'And I really need to be making a move. There's a few things I want to do before I go back on duty.'

It was clear to him that he had touched a sore nerve, which he felt was a shame, they had been getting on so well. And he had been right to think that there had been some sort of a problem, although he was not convinced that it had been satisfactorily 'sorted out'. 'Sure, and I'm sorry. Come on then, drink up, and I'll drive you back.' Draining his mug, he reached over to retrieve his coat, which had been draped over the front of a chair, near the fire, and was almost dry. He liked that about her too.

*

He knew that he had to see her again, and soon. 'I don't need to tell you how grateful I am to you,' he said, turning the car's heater on full. 'But I am. And by the way, I don't suppose you're free again in a day or two, are you? Only I'll have to take the samples back to Strathlochy, and I'd like to buy you lunch; it's the least I can do to repay you for all your help. It's not a bad little place. Have you been?'

Yvonne's immediate reaction was to decline, even though she was off the next day. Then she remembered that Sandra had been dropping hints about her and Tom getting married, and she had thought about crocheting a blanket as an engagement present. Maybe she could use this as an opportunity to get some wool and make a start. The buses were inconvenient, with just one in the morning and one back in the early evening, so the offer was very tempting, although the thought of spending more time alone with him was disconcerting. But then again, why not? She was leaving soon anyway, and what harm could it do? He was only suggesting that they return the samples and have lunch. That was all. Why did she have to go making a mountain out of a molehill? Blow it! Yes, she would go.

'No, not yet,' she replied. 'Okay then, as long as you won't mind if I can have some time to do some shopping as well.'

*

Whistling tunelessly as he drove back to the Tweedie's, Alex promised himself that he would make sure to give her a pleasant sort of outing. There would be no intrusive questioning, just easy chat over a good meal in convivial surroundings. It was not a date as such, hopefully that would come later - but not too much later. He was still curious about the problem that she claimed had already 'been sorted out'; and she had definitely fobbed him off when he had mentioned about the MacMan's taking her on permanently. Now he had no doubt that she was definitely hiding something.

He experienced an uncomfortable few moments as he wondered if he would have felt just as drawn to her if she had been just another pretty woman, and not the one The Boss had chosen for him. But no, now he had spent some time alone in her company, he knew the answer to that. The old, non-Christian Alex would definitely have been interested in her, just as much as the new, Christian one was; and not because of the shortage of fanciable females around the place either. He could truthfully say now that he was more than a little attracted to her, and not only for her looks. She had proved to be an agreeable and interesting companion that afternoon. They had worked well together, and it had felt so natural, so right; there had been nothing forced or heavy about it. She appeared to possess a mature, sensible character, and an unassuming dignity which he found very appealing. She had impressed him in more ways than one.

*

Yvonne congratulated herself as she changed into her waitressing outfit. Her eyes were wide open; she knew what she was doing, but it was just as well that she was leaving soon. Even if she was staying, and assuming that Alex Grant ever became interested in *that* way, she would make very sure not to allow herself to become romantically involved with him. Oh yes, she would make doubly sure not to stumble into the very trap that she had promised herself she would do everything in her power to avoid! Tomorrow would come and go; it would be a nice change, just a day out. That was all. What harm was there in that?

CHAPTER 18

Yvonne was ready when Alex came to pick her up the next day. The intermittent spring showers that had been bursting upon the already drenched land all morning had ganged up to form one continuous heavy downpour. Her black corduroy trousers and cream Aran jumper would do, not very feminine, but that was not one of her priorities for this particular outing. She put on her duffle coat, jammed her beret unceremoniously on her head, grabbed her umbrella, and went to wait by the telephone box.

He arrived promptly at twelve noon. They exchanged the usual pleasantries for the first few miles, but were then forced to crawl for some time behind a Highland cow as it ambled along the road in front of them. Alex relaxed back into his seat and decided that now might be as good a time as any to ask a few of his less intrusive questions. 'Do you drive Yvonne?'

'Yes, but I've never owned a car,' she replied, feeling reluctant to tell him that she had never been able to earn enough to make such a large purchase, never mind keep one on the road.

'You have to rely on the buses?'

'Such as they are, I mean, such as it is.'

'Not had much chance to look around the area then?'

'No, and my shifts make it difficult too.'

'Double blow. That's a shame. Well, we'll just have to see what we can do about that.'

Now what can he mean, she thought, as the cow came to a dead halt.

He switched the engine off. 'Fancy taking the wheel for a bit on the way back?'

'Er, well, okay.'

Resigned to their enforced stationary state, he commented, 'There's some pleasant countryside around Cambridge; that's where I'm from by the way. Bit flat in some places, like your neck of the woods too.'

She wondered what else the MacMan's had told him about her, not that they knew that much to tell, and said, 'Some people like it, you know, big skies, open spaces.'

'Your kind of thing then?'

She considered before replying, 'Not really. I'm still trying to get over the shock I had when I arrived here. It's so beautiful, even in this weather.'

'Yes, I know what you mean. It has a way of getting into your blood.'

'Are you Scottish?'

'Partly. Apparently one of my great grandfathers came from somewhere around Kingussie. How about you? Williams is a Welsh name, isn't it?'

'I think so.'

'Ah, now then, that would account for your Celtic colouring.'

There was a natural pause in the conversation, then Alex picked up the thread again, as he said, 'I don't go home very often, but I'm hoping to see a lot more of the family once I've got a permanent roof over my head. They want to come up for holidays, and that'll be fine, as long as they take it in turns.'

'Why, are there a lot of them?'

'Enough. Two brothers, both married with kids. You mentioned yesterday that you don't have any family. Does that mean no relations? No uncles ... aunts?'

'None that I'm aware of. And, actually, I think I misled you slightly, I do have a father, but he went to live in Wales years ago.'

'And you don't see much of him?'

'No.'

He had to think about that. It sounded as though she had no fixed home, no base camp. She's wasn't giving much away; why this reluctance? But that was enough for now. If only he could control this burning curiosity about her and everything to do with her. Life could be so unfair. Here he was, the result of a happy childhood, with great parents and both sets of grandparents still alive and well. He got on well with his brothers and their wives, and was uncle to four nephews and three nieces at the last roll call. As if that had not been enough, he was now part of the extensive Christian family. Charles and Izzy often joked about not just being his friends and business partners, but his spiritual uncle and aunt as well. Now he felt genuinely sorry that this young woman had not been similarly blessed. Even in the forces the women were better off; they had companionship, security and a decent standard of living, no matter how much they complained.

'Never thought of joining-up?' he asked, 'a girl like you could have gone far in the forces.'

The cow moved to inspect some vegetation at the side of the road, and they were able to set off again.

'I did try and join the Wrens once, when I was seventeen, but my father refused to give his consent, and I'd gone off the idea by the time I was old enough not to need his permission.'

'Why did he refuse?'

She shrugged. 'Who knows?' Then, for the first time in years, she remembered her acute embarrassment when the Recruiting Officer had informed her that her father had 'paid them a visit,' and that, as a result, 'her application could not proceed'. She never did find out what had really happened.

'And your mother wouldn't sign?'

'She was dead.'

Alex felt a sudden flash of animosity towards this unknown father of hers, and said, 'Someone should have told him that most fathers would be as proud as punch to have a daughter in the Wrens.'

'Ah well, that's life!' she exclaimed, effectively putting an end to the subject, then went on to remark how colourful the gardens were looking in the small hamlet they were passing.

They drove on in thoughtful silence: Alex concentrating on the narrow road as it skirted around the shores of several lochs; Yvonne preoccupied with the view, and marvelling at how the wind had separated the clouds to reveal that the sun had been shining in a watery blue sky above them all the time. Unknown to her, her companion was fighting the urge to reassure her that her solitary state was not destined to last for ever. Eventually, he found himself saying, 'Life's full of surprises, Yvonne, and you know, don't you, that after your help at the Manor yesterday, you're part of the team now.' As far as he was concerned, this was not a question, but a fact.

She chewed her lip, trying hard to think how she could reply without alerting him to the fact that she would not be around long enough to be part of anyone's team. Then, as she had done yesterday, she decided to use the subject of the Manor as a diversionary talking point. 'Can anyone stay at the Manor, even if they aren't religious?'

He realised that she had just provided him with the opening he needed to broach the all-important subject of faith, and replied, 'Actually, we don't think of ourselves as being "religious", just people who have a relationship with God. And we're hoping that the kind of people who'll want to come will want that for themselves. It won't matter what their faith, or none-faith background, is, as long as they're open-minded about the actual existence of God. I don't suppose we'd shut our doors to agnostics, or even atheists, providing they're not aggressive about things, and prepared to listen to another point of view. How about you Yvonne, do you go to church?'

'Church? No, that is, I haven't been for ages.'

'Just for hatches, matches and despatches then?'

'Pardon?'

'You know, the usual. Christenings, weddings and funerals. Nothing wrong with that, all part of the Church's work.' He must be careful here, the last thing he wanted to do was to come across as being holier-than-thou. *Please help me out here, Boss. Help me to go steady and not frighten her off.*

'Oh, I see. I've not heard that before. Well, I suppose you could say that, although I do sometimes try and go at Christmas.'

'And where do you go, when you do go?'

'Church of England.'

'Been confirmed?'

'No, my parents weren't churchgoers; suppose they never saw the point. And I'm afraid I'm not very religious either.'

Now he had his answer; she had no faith and was not a Christian. What was it he had read not so long ago, something about it being better to deal with a blank page than one that had been filled-in incorrectly? If he was reading her right, then she might be a very blank page indeed.

*

The small market town of Strathlochy was busy when they arrived. With some difficulty, they managed to find a parking spot near the hotel where Alex had booked a table for lunch. They were in the process of studying the menu when a loud crash came from the opposite end of the dining room. An instant hush descended as all eyes turned to watch a waiter lurch towards a wall and slide slowly to the floor before coming to rest in a sitting position, his eyes and mouth wide open.

The waitress nearest the scene noticed a pool of blood beginning to form around his feet, and began to shriek, *'Oh my God! Blood!* Oh Jock, Jock, you're bleeding. *Oh My God! Help, somebody ... help!'*

Alex was on his feet in an instant and manoeuvring his way through the tables and chairs. A man, looking like the archetypal hotel manager, burst through the dining room doors and began looking around for the cause of the commotion. He spotted the crumpled figure propped-up against the wall, and rushed over to reach the fallen waiter at the same time as Alex. The two men stood watching the fast-growing pool of blood, and it was Alex who was the first to react as he lowered himself awkwardly to kneel beside the beleaguered man.

The probable manager, who was indeed the manager, asked in a hopeful voice, 'Are you a doctor?'

'No, but I've had some training,' replied Alex, producing a Swiss Army knife from his jacket pocket. He began to cut the relevant trouser leg in order to reveal the site from which the blood was pumping unchecked. 'Right, you'd better call an ambulance,' he instructed.

The manager found that he was unable to speak or move, fascinated as he was by the awful sight.

151

Alex began to undo his belt, and said impatiently, 'Come on man, ambulance - now!' then quickly tied it around the affected thigh to form a tourniquet.

At last the manager found he was able to move, and turned his body, zombie like, towards the dining room doors. It took him a full ten seconds to remember that they pulled inwards and not pushed outwards.

Unable to sit there and do nothing, Yvonne went over to see if she could be of some use. Taking in the scene, she went into the kitchen and emerged seconds later holding several large wads of kitchen paper and a bowl. She knelt down opposite Alex and offered him a wad.

'Yvonne. Good, well done.' He pressed and held the wad firmly over the ruptured vein, which was situated awkwardly behind the man's knee. 'Undo his collar and tie, his belt too, would you.'

She started to loosen the items, all the while explaining what she was doing in a calm, quiet voice. By now, some of the kitchen staff had left their posts and were standing in a small group nearby, muttering and staring with horror at their fallen colleague.

Alex called over his shoulder, 'One of you go and get a blanket, and what's his name?'

A quartet of shocked voices replied raggedly, 'Jock … Jock … Jock Loranzo.'

Alex discarded the now sodden wad and replaced it with another. 'Atta girl, Yvonne. Try to get him talking, would you.'

Yvonne's mind went blank, but she forced herself to think of something - anything that could possibly be appropriate to say to someone going through such an ordeal. Then she remembered that the most interesting thing a woman could talk about to a man was himself, so she started to ask a series of questions. Although hesitant, the waiter managed to make a few coherent replies. Alex sent up a silent arrow prayer, and was relieved when the haemorrhage began to turn into a slow trickle.

Having at last regained some composure, the manager reappeared and told the kitchen staff to return to their duties. He addressed the diners, a few of whom had already left, and announced that an ambulance was on the way, and asked for their forbearance. The blanket arrived and was placed over the waiter's chest and abdomen. Tense minutes passed. Those who had remained chatted quietly, unable to drag themselves away from the scene, and keen to see how all this was going to end. Worryingly, the waiter's speech was becoming noticeably slower and Alex suspected that he was going into shock.

At last, the welcome sound of an approaching ambulance siren could be heard. Two ambulance men entered the room a few minutes later. Alex gave a brief report as one of them took over applying pressure to the wound, whilst the other went off to fetch a stretcher. Yvonne went into the kitchen again and returned with a plastic bin bag and more kitchen paper. She knelt down and busied herself with soaking up as much blood off the floor as she could without tripping everyone up.

Their on-the-spot ministrations complete, the ambulance men lifted the waiter onto the stretcher and began making their way out of the hotel. Yvonne pushed the plastic bag containing the blood-soaked items into the manager's hands, explaining, 'Here, take these. They might need to know how much blood he's lost. Tell them there's a lot soaked into the carpet too.'

He nodded, holding the bag at arm's length as he hurried out.

'Good thinking,' Alex remarked, rubbing his thigh, and hoping that his own blood supply would start to flow again soon.

They stood looking down at the enormous dark stain on the green, nondescript patterned carpet, the practicality of which Yvonne could not help thinking Georgina would have approved. Alex suggested to a waitress that it might be a good idea to cover it with something. Then, deciding that their part in the drama was over, he placed a hand under Yvonne's elbow, and limping badly, began to escort her back to their table. The remaining diners watched his awkward progress, some saying, 'Well done' and 'Good chap' as they passed by.

Despite his clumsy gait, Yvonne felt no sympathy for the man by her side, only an overpowering sense of admiration for him. Of all the people in the room, it was he who had not hesitated to help. How could she feel sorry for anyone who was able to take control of such a situation and handle themselves with such confidence and dignity?

The diners' attention turned once more to their own circumstances; by now the food had gone cold and some had lost their appetite.

Picking up her handbag, Yvonne said, 'We'd better go and wash our hands.'

They passed the manager in reception; obviously he had not accompanied his stricken member of staff to the hospital. They returned to their table a few minutes later. The manager reappeared; his face still very flushed as he cleared his throat to make another announcement.

'Ladies and gentlemen. I can only apologise for the inconvenience this unfortunate ... incident has caused. You will, of course, understand that we need to tidy up a bit in here, and would appreciate your co-operation by finishing the course you are on and ... er ... leaving fairly quickly. Complimentary coffee will be served in the lounge for any who wish to take it.'

Satisfied, he made his way over to Alex and Yvonne's table. 'They didn't need me to go after all. And I'd just like to say a very special thank you to you both for your help. I'm sure Jock would too, if he was able. He'll be okay by the way, apparently, they've seen this kind of thing before. They think it's a varicose vein that burst, and reckon he'll live to fight another day.' Then, noticing their unused cutlery, went on to ask, 'You hadn't started your meal?'

'We'd only just arrived when the balloon went up,' replied Alex.

'Well, in that case, maybe you'd like to be our guests at another time? It's the least we can do.'

Looking at Yvonne, Alex considered the proposal for all of two seconds, before replying, 'That's very good of you. Maybe we'll take you up on that.'

Yvonne wondered if she should speak up, but what could she say? 'Sorry, thank you, but I won't be here,' or, 'I'm afraid I won't be available.' It all sounded so weak and ungrateful, even if it was true. She decided that there was nothing for it but to play along, and offered a half-hearted, 'Yes. Lovely, thank you.'

*

They left the hotel a few minutes later. Once again, Alex placed his hand under her elbow, and began to guide her along the puddle-strewn pavement, insisting that she walk on the inside to avoid being splashed by the passing traffic. 'Pity, I was looking forward to that. Tell you what, there's quite a good café around the corner. By the way, I meant to ask if you wouldn't mind doing the shops by yourself? I'll drop the sample books back, and we could meet up somewhere after an hour or so. How does that sound to you?'

She readily agreed, thinking how comforting his hand felt. She noticed that he was still limping badly, but he reassured her that he would be fine, just as soon as he'd had something to eat and could take a pain-killer.

The café was warm and welcoming, although glaringly decorated in a multiplicity of tartans. They placed their order, and gave each other knowing smiles as they found themselves studying the back of the waitress's calves as she walked away.

'You know, I was very glad of your help back there,' said Alex, 'and the way you kept him talking was inspired. Told you we make a good team.'

Since leaving the hotel, it had been all she could do to stop herself from blurting out that she would be leaving soon, and he would have to find someone else to go back with. She was wondering how to reply when a young woman with a noisy toddler came to sit on the nearby table, and the moment passed.

Soon, they were tucking into a substantial meal of steak pie, chips and mushy peas. Alex found several natural openings to introduce the subject of the ceilidh, but all she would reveal about the event was how much she had enjoyed it. He gave up in the end, and resolved to put this particular thorny subject on the back-burner, deciding to tackle it another day. But get to the bottom of it, he would.

They separated after the meal, and she spent a pleasant hour looking around the shops before returning to the car at the prearranged time. Alex invited her to take the wheel once they reached the open road, but it soon became obvious that she was very rusty. As a result, conversation was kept to a bare minimum, which gave him plenty of time to consider if he had gone against Charles' advice and had been deliberately manipulating circumstances, and had to admit that he probably had. But after the way she had helped him at the Manor, and during the incident with the stricken waiter, he decided that it looked as though The Boss didn't mind; in fact, it appeared as though He had actually been blessing his efforts.

*

It was no surprise to Yvonne that she had trouble trying to get to sleep again that night, and without realising what she was doing, found herself mentally compiling another type of list. This one could have been entitled 'The Things I like About Alexander Grant'. It began with the telephone-box incident, and how he had come to her rescue, although, as it had turned out, she had not really needed rescuing - but she had no doubt now that he would still have come to her aid even if Rabbie had been some kind of dangerous beast. Then she recalled how calm and capable he had been throughout the incident at the hotel, and decided that he was the type of person who people could lean on, especially during times of crisis. Then, too, she had liked the way he had held her elbow and guided her; somehow it had felt so comforting, so right.

Breathing slowly, and beginning to feel more peaceful now, she came to the conclusion that Alex Grant was a truly special type of man. No wonder he was going to be working at the Manor; a place dedicated to the needs and care of others. They were lucky to have found someone like him. He was a rare person indeed.

Very sleepy at last, she thought how strange it was that he was still single. No doubt, he had been too involved with his army career to settle down. But now he was a civilian and, therefore, more available, and probably more accessible; it was just a question of time before some lucky woman would discover his qualities and snap him up. One day they would meet, he would take her arm, and guide and protect her along life's twists and turns. Some lucky woman ... bound to happen, a man like that. She began to doze ...

You're right there Doley! You'll be off soon and he'll be thanking his lucky stars that he didn't get involved with the likes of you. He'd have avoided you like the plague as soon as he realised what a waste of time you are. He wouldn't want a millstone like you around his neck. You're good for nothing; never were, never will be. Sneaking in through a hole like that. You shouldn't be here, taking up someone else's space. Remember, Doley, always remember what you are ... remember ...

CHAPTER 19

All but three members of the Maxwell family left straight after breakfast the next day for a shopping trip to Beaulane. Two of the men, Reg and Mark, were looking forward doing some fishing, and Matilda, the oldest member, planned to spend the day quietly in her room nursing a painfully arthritic knee.

Donald and Georgina took the opportunity to have an outing themselves and go into Strathlochy. She had booked an eleven o'clock appointment at the hairdressers and was looking forward to her biannual perm. Donald planned to spend some time in the poetry section of the library before going on to the Cash & Carry.

Georgina sat back to enjoy the ride. For the past week she was feeling more relaxed about things. The Maxwell's visit was going well, and it had been such a relief when Niall and Yvonne had obviously found a way of sorting out their differences. Donald was thinking along the same lines, and could only assume that the prospect of marriage was having a sobering effect on the lad. Maggie was sounding cheerful enough as she went around announcing to one and all that her trousseau was like her, 'fine and ready'.

'Good to see that Niall's calmed down a bit since he's got engaged,' he said.

'And not before time too,' agreed Georgina. 'But don't you think he's being very cagey about what they plan to do afterwards? I keep asking, but I just can't seem to get a straight answer out of him.'

'Aye, the lad's one for keeping things close to his chest.'

'I can't see them living with her parents; there's not enough room to swing a cat in that old place. Apparently Callum's had to give up driving, and they've given Maggie the car as part of her dowry. Dowry! How quaint is that?' She sighed heavily. 'I'm half expecting them to ask if she can come and live-in. She'll need the car to get her to the school. I know for a fact that Dorothy wants to keep her on. She says she's the best cleaner she's ever had.' She made a few dramatic tut-tuts. 'He really ought to let us know about things; all this guesswork is so tiresome.'

'Aye, her folks'll miss her around the place. Niall's landed on his feet there. Let's hope he's found what he's been looking for and carries on behaving himself. But … I honestly don't know.' He shook his head, and sounded forlorn as he posed the question to which he knew there was no answer. 'Can a leopard change its spots *that* much? I don't mind telling you, I was getting a bit fed-up with all those tantrums.'

'You're not the only one, dear. I was on tenterhooks for days after the Maxwell's landed. Look how tetchy he was when they arrived? So rude. I was quite ashamed of him.'

Donald nodded slowly. 'I've been watching points too. You know, we were damn lucky that Yvonne didn't up-sticks and leave after the way he carried on that first week she was with us.'

'And thank goodness she didn't! I can't be doing with finding someone new again. But I just hope that Maggie knows what she's letting herself in for.'

'How'd you mean?'

'Well, if they do live-in, and then, you know, he starts his antics again … and they start rowing. We couldn't leave Robert with a thing like that to deal with. It wouldn't be fair. I'd never forgive myself.'

Donald wriggled impatiently, finding his seat suddenly uncomfortable; he didn't like the sound of that at all. The very thought of Niall behaving badly towards the pleasant, docile Maggie was deeply disturbing. She was the stay-at-home type and used to the quiet life; somehow, he couldn't imagine her fighting her own corner. Yvonne was a different kettle of fish altogether and had obviously found a way of handling him.

'I can't see Maggie coping with that,' he said, 'she's not the rowing type, and more likely to be the one doing all the giving-in.'

Now, and not for the first time, Georgina began to question her decision to ignore her first instinct and give Niall his marching orders soon after he had arrived. But kind, patient Donald had persuaded her otherwise, telling her that she was being too hasty, too unreasonable. 'Give the lad a chance,' he'd said, 'at least let him see the month out.' Had giving in then been her first mistake? Had she actually allowed herself to be seduced - and there really was no other word for it - by the consistently high standard of food he was able to produce? Now look at them both, fretting about what this forthcoming marriage could mean, and not only for themselves, but for Robert too. It really was too bad, and so very unfair, that just one person could cast such a gloomy shadow over all their lives.

*

Meanwhile, back at the Inn, Yvonne was making a start on the bedrooms when she thought she could hear what sounded like someone shouting near the reception area. Hurrying through to investigate, she found Niall involved with some sort of altercation with the three Maxwell's who had remained behind. His face was an angry red mask as he held his body erect and stiff. Reg and Mark were standing nearby and looking concerned at Matilda, who was leaning heavily against the counter, and obviously in some pain.

'Is there a problem?' she asked, stating the obvious.

Reg quickly explained that he and Mark had gone to collect their packed lunches, and had been told by a none too diplomatic Niall that there was none to be had, and he 'wasn'a going to waste his time makin' up any for anybody!'

Having just finished a leisurely breakfast nearby, and having witnessed the scene, Matilda felt that she should intervene. Putting on her most authoritarian, retired schoolmistress voice, she informed the truculent chef that 'He was one of the rudest people she had ever had the misfortune to meet', and instructed him 'to behave himself and get on with the job.' He had reacted with such ferocity that she had been forced to step back, and in so doing, had lost her balance, and would have fallen if Reg and Mark had not managed to grab her in time.

What these three good people were unaware of was that Niall was already in a heightened state of anxiety, and had been since leaving Maggie the night before when she had made him lose his temper with her again. The last thing he needed were these old sods getting on at him and bossing him around now. And anyway, how was he to know the decrepit old cow was so ruddy doddery? Unfortunately, Yvonne's arrival on the scene seemed to infuriate him even more. He glowered at her. 'And you can keep your ruddy nose out of it, or there'll be no ruddy food for anyone.'

But Matilda had not finished with him yet. 'Dear, dear! There's no need for this. Stop this nonsense at once! Just you do as you're told young man, and keep a civil tongue in your head.'

'Hey! What … who d'ya think you are? Tellin' me what to do! No one tells me - '

'Well then, it's about time somebody did,' interrupted Matilda, pointing her walking stick in the direction of the kitchen door. 'Go on! Just get yourself in there, and do as you're told. And be quick about it!'

Niall snapped. He caught the end of the stick and hurled it furiously away. It all happened so quickly that Matilda lost her balance again, and this time she did fall. Yvonne and Reg quickly went to her aid as Mark leaped forward, and put his face as close to Niall's as he could bear to. *'What's the matter with you?'* he shouted. *'We're only asking for a few sandwiches, not a damn three course meal!'*

Yvonne and Reg were struggling to get Matilda back on her feet again, and despite the pain in her knee, and her extreme annoyance at the indignity of it all, she managed to say, 'This is appalling! I'm going to report this. What the MacMan's think they're doing employing such a … a brainless oaf like you is beyond me. Oh yes! Your days are numbered here my boy. I'll see to that!'

This was all far, far too much for Niall, who yelled, *'Don't you call me brainless, you ugly old bag!'* He began to jab his finger into his temple with such force that Yvonne felt sure he was in danger of fracturing his skull. 'There's nothin' wrong with my brain. You're the one who's not usin' your ... your ruddy loaf.' His words were accompanied by a shower of spittle that would have reached anyone who was unfortunate enough to be standing within three feet of him.

Matilda was erect again, and knowing that she should intervene, Yvonne said firmly, 'That's enough Niall. Be quiet! It's obvious that Mrs MacMan just forgot to tell you.'

However, either Niall had not heard, or decided to take no notice, and continued his tirade and head-poking, increasing his vocabulary to include such unpleasantries as 'ugly fat cow' and 'nasty old bitch'.

Eventually, he had to stop to catch his breath. Yvonne instantly took advantage of the brief respite to repeat her demand. 'Niall, will you please be quiet and calm down!' She pointed towards the kitchen door, 'And for goodness sake, just go and make up the sandwiches, and stop all this fuss.'

However, Niall was far from finished. He'd burn in hell before he'd let himself be ordered about by that bitch. His temper had reached boiling point, and despite the strange throbbing on the side of his head, he started to bellow even louder now. He waved his fists around, mainly in Yvonne's direction, as a string of obscenities poured unrestrained from his snarling, twisting mouth.

Reg and Mark had heard enough. They looked at each other and nodded, and then, as one man, stepped purposefully in front of him. Niall's roaring mysteriously started to lose some of its force and was replaced with a succession of noisy, nasal-blowing breaths. In a steady, controlled voice, Mark asked, 'Finished now, have you laddie? Had your say now, have you? Or shall we be stepping outside?'

The threat in his voice was unmistakable, and somehow Niall recognised that his life could get very difficult if he chose to ignore it. Even then it took him several seconds to reign in his fury as he continued to glare malevolently at them. Such was the effort he was exerting to calm down, that his body started to sway, back and forth, back and forth. At last, he managed to steady himself, but even now he was reluctant to leave. He was damned if he was going to let them get away with speaking to *him* like that. No one threatened Niall Turvey. *No one!* He'd have sorted this lot out sharpish if that bitch hadn't come and poked her ruddy nose in. Well, he'd show her! Quick as a flash, he turned his head and fired off a globule of yellow-streaked spit in Yvonne's direction. Thankfully, the foul liquid fell short, to land just inches from her feet. Almost satisfied, he turned on his heel and headed for the kitchen. Just let those devils try to follow him. This was *his* kitchen, *his* territory, *his* kingdom! They'd be sorry - he'd scald the lot of them alive!

Yvonne managed to control her revulsion as she turned her attention back to Matilda, who was now attempting to knead a seriously swollen knee. 'I'm so sorry Matilda. Are you alright? Can I do anything to help?'

Reg replied, 'It's alright lassie, we know the routine. Maybe you could put some ice in a towel and, er, we shan't be wanting those pack-ups now. I'm thinking we'd do better to stick around for a while.'

Although relieved that the incident was over, Yvonne found herself becoming both angry and apprehensive at the prospect of having to go into the kitchen and face Niall again so soon, but do it she must. 'Of course, and I really can't apologise enough.'

Reg's reply was short and determined. 'No lass, don't you be worrying yourself. It's not you who needs to be doing any apologising. Now I think we'd better get Matty back to her room, and maybe you'll be good enough to bring along some ice?'

And with that, the two men took hold of Matilda's arms, and began to lead her slowly away.

Yvonne entered the kitchen and was greatly relieved to see no sign of Niall. She made the ice pack and took it along to Matilda's room. Reg was still with her. Taking it, he gently laid it over the swollen knee as the old lady lay back on her bed, a stiff letter of complaint already beginning to take shape in her mind.

*

The Inn was calm when the rest of the Maxwell's returned later that afternoon. They had obviously had a good day and now they were hungry and tired. Niall was back in the kitchen, preparing the evening meal. It was a good thing that no one was aware of what was going on in his troubled mind as he poured milk into a large pan. He knew he had gone too far with that old bag, and would probably have to face the music when the Chiefs got back. Still, that would come right; a few 'specials' on the menu would soon bring them round. It always had. Now he had more important things to deal with, namely how to stop Maggie giving him any more gyp about wanting a whole wardrobe just for her stuff. He'd told her over and over that the double room wasn't big enough for two wardrobes. Oh hell! This marrying business was starting to get on his nerves alright.

Unlocking the cold store, he stepped in, and spent the next few minutes contemplating the shelves lined with his own pre-prepared tarts. The cold must have sharpened his wits for he let out a loud, triumphant *'Hah!'* as inspiration struck. Damn it! Two staff meant two rooms. Why shouldn't they have two - or even three if they needed them? There were plenty of empty ones up there, and there'll be one more when that bitch was gone. Yeah! Then the hen could bring as much stuff as she liked. Damn, he was good!

There was a hiss behind him as the milk for the custard boiled over.

*

Yvonne was not looking forward to the MacMan's return; knowing there was bound to be trouble. She was handing out keys when she became aware of an unpleasant, burnt smell coming from the kitchen behind her. She sighed, guessing that whatever had happened in there would not help Niall's mood. After today's incident she would have to watch her every word even more carefully whenever he was around. But why should she? Why should anybody have to? It had been like that with her father, and her poor mother had learned how to become an expert at the art of compromise. Her father and Niall, two of a kind; both seemed incapable of understanding, or even caring, that their behaviour was making other peoples' lives a misery. And this problem with Alexander Grant wasn't helping. But why was she thinking of him again? For some reason, it was really starting to bother her about what would he think of her when he learned that she was leaving. Oh, blow it! There, she was at it again!

She jumped when the telephone rang. 'Good evening. The Tananeach Inn. Can I help you?'

'Hi Yvonne, Alex here.'

'Alex!'

'You sound surprised?'

'Do I? Er, what can I do for you?'

'Several things to report. First off, thought you'd like to know that Jock, you know, the waiter, is doing okay. Although they've discovered he's mildly diabetic. He's being kept in for a few more days to get him stabilised.'

'Oh no! Poor man. As if he hasn't got enough to worry about. I hope he won't lose his job.'

'I shouldn't think so, and it's a good thing it came to light now, apparently he didn't have a clue. Should prevent anything more serious happening further down the line.'

'Sounds like a case of God working in mysterious ways,' she said, flippantly, thinking how she could do with some divine intervention in her own life right now.

'Actually, you know, the more I get to know Him, the more I've come to realise that His ways aren't that mysterious. He has rules ... order. It's us who break them and help chaos along.'

'Er, well, it's just a saying, you know - '

'That's alright, Yvonne. Sorry if I came on a bit preachy. Anyway, changing the subject, I've just a call from that curtain shop. Apparently, they can't get hold of one of the fabrics; the dark blue one. Looks like I'll have to go in and choose an alternative. Don't suppose I can persuade you to come as well?'

She had to think quickly. On the one hand, she liked the idea of another outing, especially after that morning's upset; on the other, the invitation had come from someone she knew she should avoid. No, she could not go. She should not go. She *must* not go. She must control her fickle feelings and be sensible. 'I'm sure you won't need me, and it should be easy enough to choose something else.'

'Well, I don't know about that. You've got a keener eye than me for this sort of thing. And now you've been to the Manor, I really think you've got a feel of the place.'

He had a point, but she must stick to her guns. 'Why don't you choose that other one we liked, you know, it was almost the same? I know you made a note of it. And anyway, someone at the shop's bound to help you if you get really stuck.'

'Possibly, but ... look, I need *you*, Yvonne, and the Manor needs you. What's the matter? Don't you fancy another outing? What can I do to persuade you?'

Two of the younger members of the family approached the desk, giving her the perfect excuse to end the conversation. 'Oh, I'm sorry, I've got to go.'

'Have I got caught you at a bad time?'

'You could say that.'

'Where is everyone?'

'Niall's in the kitchen, and the MacMan's are out. I'm expecting them back any time now.'

'You mean you're holding the fort alone?' He thought, she's only been there five minutes, what were they thinking of, going away and leaving her in charge! If that was the case, then the last thing he should be doing now was to put her under even more pressure; that could prove counter-productive.

'Right. Look, I'm sorry. I'd better let you go.'

Someone shouted for the youngsters and they moved away, leaving Yvonne alone again. She suddenly felt very tired and badly wanted to sit down. It had been a difficult day. If only she could escape to her room and have some peace.

'You can always give me a ring. You've got the Tweedie's number there, haven't you?' he asked.

'Yes, it's around somewhere.' Actually, now she thought about it, what real harm could it do - now that she was leaving? And, to be fair, she couldn't argue with his logic; his request had been a reasonable one, and it was for a worthwhile cause after all. And, anyway, she was needing more wool for Sandra's blanket.

'Okay. Well, goodnight then,' he said.

She heard the disappointment in his voice, and then, without any warning, heard her own voice say, 'Oh, alright! I'll go.'

'You will! Great! You know I'd get punch drunk if I had to look through all those books again.'

'Only my next day off's not till next week, and I'm not sure what day.'

'That's fine. I can wait. You're worth waiting for.'

Momentarily nonplussed, she hesitated, unsure how to respond to such a statement.

'You'll give me a ring then? And leave a message if I'm out?'

'Alright.'

'Wonderful! I'll wait to hear from you. Now just you take very good care of yourself in the meantime, and may God really bless you in every way you need.'

'Okay, thanks. Bye.' She replaced the receiver slowly. How relieved he had sounded, happy too, almost like a little boy who'd just been given an enormous Meccano set for Christmas. And as for all that, 'You're worth waiting for,' and, 'may God really bless you,' business - kind sentiments to be sure, but what did The Almighty have to do with anything to do with her anyway?

*

The MacMan's returned soon after and the evening routine went ahead as usual. After dinner Reg and Mark asked to have a quiet word with them in the office. There was much discussion, after which it was unanimously decided that the best course of action would be to maintain the status quo, and do nothing until the family left in just two days' time.

Despite being kept busy for the rest of the evening, Yvonne could not prevent frequent thoughts of Alex from crossing her mind. It seemed that the more determined she was to have nothing to do with him, the more fate was determined that she would. Why had she given-in? And why, oh why, had this man come along just now? Wasn't her life complicated enough already? Maybe, at any other time, at any other place ... but no, she must stop thinking like that, it was dangerous. *He* was dangerous. It was just as well she was leaving. If she stayed, and somehow they did become involved, then she knew it would just be a matter of time before she ran true to form and invent some spurious excuse as to why it was absolutely essential that she had to leave. Now she had come to realise what a really worthwhile person he was, the last thing he needed was someone like her coming along to sap his time and energy. God must indeed be looking out for him by getting her out of the way before anything could develop between them. Which only went to prove that her father had been right all along - she really was a complete waste of time and space.

CHAPTER 20

For the past week the weather had been kind, and Yvonne found it hard to believe the radio's insistent warnings that a light to medium snowfall was expected, so it was with some surprise that she opened her curtains on the morning of the Maxwell's departure to discover that the ground had been covered with a silent, white mantle. However, much to the family's relief, a steady rainfall began an hour before they left and obligingly washed all but a few sheltered patches away.

Georgina, Flora and Yvonne stood outside the vestibule making their goodbyes and reassuring the ever-efficient Sonia that next year's Easter visit had definitely been provisionally booked. Finally, amidst much arm waving and horn tooting, the small convoy set off and disappeared over the skyline a few minutes later.

Georgina sighed with relief. She patted the small tuft of frizzy hair just above her right ear that had obstinately refused to wave and blend with the rest of her perm. 'Well, that's that. I don't know why, but I found them much more … ah well, never mind.' Turning and rubbing her cold hands together, she exclaimed, 'Brrr, let's get in! You go and make a start Flora, and Yvonne, you go and wait for me in the office; there's something we need to discuss. I'll just pop up and see how Donald's doing.'

Yvonne made her way to the office with a heavy heart. Since Niall's outburst she had been watching and waiting for any repercussions, unaware that the decision had been made to wait until the family left before any disciplinary action was taken. Now she wondered if this was what Georgina wanted to discuss, which was unfortunate, for this was the very morning she had decided to hand in her notice.

Safely ensconced in the kitchen, or so he thought, Niall was emptying the dishwasher and feeling smug. For the past two days he had been only too willing, and did not need telling, to keep a low profile. The Chiefs must have been told about the row with the interfering old cow, and come down on his side. Bully for them! Still, just to be on the safe side, he might as well turn out a few more of his 'specials'. Tonight's crushed nut and chocolate pavlova should keep them sweet.

Georgina found Donald standing by the window, peering through his binoculars and making one of his regular scans of the surrounding countryside. His head jerked as he caught sight of something big and brown moving slowly in the distance. All thoughts about the unpleasant task ahead vanished from his mind as he strained hard to recognise the form of his old pal. She went to stand beside him and looked in the same direction; she had excellent long vision and recognised a cow when she saw one.

'Come on Donald, that's a cow!' she said, exasperated. 'I wish you'd stop all this fretting. You know he's off somewhere enjoying himself.'

The brown object wandered out of sight. He could have sworn it was Rabbie. He felt a stab of disappointment, and reluctantly admitted to himself that she was probably right. She always was. Now he was forced to think again about Niall, which was the last thing he felt like doing, having woken up that morning with what threatened to become one of his periodic head colds. The aspirin had started to work and the nose blowing had eased, but he still felt washed out. Sighing heavily, he said unenthusiastically, 'Okay. Let's get the thing over and done with. You go and get Yvonne, and I'll round Niall up.'

'She already there, but are you sure you're up to it?'

'I'll be fine. United front and all that.'

*

Georgina took her seat and patted the frizzy bit of hair again as she studied the young woman opposite. Was it her imagination, or was she looking paler than ever? 'You aren't coming down with a cold as well, are you? You're looking very pale.'

'No, I'm fine thanks. It's just that I was hoping to have a few minutes of your time this morning. Actually, it concerns

Niall as well, but I'd rather he was …' she stopped, surprised to hear Donald's raised voice approaching the office.

Niall appeared in the doorway a second later; his head bowed low, hiding his deep sulk. Donald followed close behind.

'Go on, man. In!' he ordered. Niall shuffled in. 'Sit there!' commanded Donald, pointing at the empty chair next to Yvonne. Niall did as he was told with obvious bad grace. Donald crossed the room and perched on the safe.

Georgina sat bolt upright, momentarily nonplussed by such a show of assertive behaviour from her normally even-tempered and easy-going husband. She looked disapprovingly at Niall, who was balancing awkwardly on the edge of his chair and looked ready to bolt.

'Goodness me! What's all this?' she asked.

'Sorry about that love. Had a bit of trouble persuading him to come,' explained Donald.

'Really?' said Georgina, opening a drawer and taking out an envelope. 'Well Niall, I should have thought you'd be only too glad to have the opportunity to explain your recent atrocious behavior. We've let the matter rest for the Maxwell's sake, and you can thank your lucky stars that they were so good about it. But from what we've heard about the affair - '

'Couldn'a help yourself then?' interrupted Niall, shooting Yvonne a furious look, 'couldn'a wait to stick the knife in?'

'Be careful now, Niall,' Donald warned, shifting uncomfortably, and wondering how long his haemorrhoids could cope with the cold iron surface beneath him. 'For your information, it wasn't Yvonne who told us. And I'd calm down if I was you.'

Georgina glared at Niall. 'I'm *very* upset! Don't you realise that even the whisper of a thing like this getting out can ruin a reputation?'

Niall winced; this was sounding bad. Trouble ahead alright.

'Well? Come on! We haven't got all day. Out with it, and none of your mumbling,' said Georgina, beginning to feel slightly more than impatient.

Niall's head sunk again, and he did indeed mumble. 'Wasn'a told, was I? Wasn'a my fault!'

'What, about the packed lunches?' asked Donald.

'Aye.'

'And that was it, that's what upset you?' Georgina enquired, a sharp edge to her voice now.

'Aye.'

She made a great show of rolling her eyes. 'Oh, for Heaven's sake! Two - just two - that was all. It wouldn't have taken you a jiffy. Instead … instead we get all this fuss.' She tapped the envelope, 'Insulting and upsetting poor old Matty. It's a wonder she hasn't tried to sue us!'

They sat and waited for Niall to make some response, but all he could manage was a succession of rasping noises. When it became obvious that he was incapable of uttering anything coherent, Donald turned to Yvonne. 'We'll be here all day at this rate. Looks like you'll have to do the talking, Yvonne. We've already got a fair idea of what happened, but we'd like to hear your take on it.'

However, Yvonne was beginning to feel deeply uncomfortable, and was reluctant to repeat the sad tale again. Looking at the envelope, she replied, 'I'm sure the account you've been given is accurate.'

Donald sighed heavily. 'I see. Right'o. You know, Niall, things aren't looking too good for you just now, so I strongly suggest that if you've got anything to say, you say it, and be darned quick about it!'

The threat was not lost on Yvonne, and now she felt herself becoming concerned, although not for her own sake, but for Niall's. She had known people to get the sack for less, and the repercussions for him would be extremely bad. With no job, he would lose his room, and would probably end up having to move in with Maggie's parents after all - and she already knew what he thought about that idea! He'd be as miserable as sin, and would make everyone else's life a misery too. What a depressing start to married life, and certainly not a good situation to bring a child into. But maybe she had the means to prevent such a catastrophe. Bracing herself, she announced,

'Actually, before anything else is said, there's something I need to say. I … I'm afraid I'm going to have to hand in my notice. Certain circumstances have arisen, and I think … for everyone's sake, that it would be better if I left.'

The ensuing silence - which seemed to last far too long, but was only a matter of seconds, was broken when Niall's leg started to tremble uncontrollably and thud against the wall. Georgina was the first to respond. Making no effort to disguise her incredulity, she exclaimed, 'Good Heavens! Leave us … so soon! But why?'

Donald spoke up quickly. 'Calm yourself, love. Give the girl a chance. And stop that racket Niall! Go on Yvonne, what do you mean, what are these "circumstances"?'

Yvonne glanced at Niall, who's chin was now tightly tucked into his chest, and unexpectedly found herself feeling some sympathy for him. At least she had been prepared for the discussion, but he had been unaware that she had planned on having him present when she handed in her notice. Could it be that he had learned his lesson? And didn't everyone deserve a second chance? The rasping noises were becoming more forced, and it was obvious that he was having trouble trying to breath, never mind speak. Maybe she should break the ice for him. Hesitantly, she began, 'Well, it really concerns Niall … and his plans. I know he's been wanting to ask you about a job for Maggie, and about some accommodation for when they get married.' There, it was out. She looked encouragingly at him, willing him to champion his own cause. But still he refused to say anything or look up.

Georgina looked at Donald as she assimilated this unpleasant piece of information. Then, staring hard again at Niall's bent head, asked, 'Oh really? Is that so?'

Yvonne waited expectantly. Why wasn't Niall jumping in and grabbing the opportunity to try and secure everything he claimed he had ever wanted in life? Why was he being so slow about it? Apart from the leg trembling, which was gathering apace, he had started to make a series of unpleasant choking noises between the rasping. It was becoming obvious to everyone that he could not, or would not, say anything in his own defence.

'Well now, we don't know about that!' said Donald, before turning to Yvonne, and asking, 'and are you saying that that's got something to do with you wanting to leave?'

Yvonne knew that she would have to speak up yet again if they were to get anywhere. Weighing each word carefully, she went on to explain. 'It's like I said, Niall would like Maggie to come and work here when they're married. I believe they want to start saving for a home of their own, and they'll be able to do that sooner if they're both living-in. They'd have less expense. At least, I think that's the plan, isn't it, Niall?' She stopped there. It was not her place to announce the fact that Maggie was pregnant, but she had no idea how to continue without revealing this pivotal piece of information. Her face must have shown her resolve because the MacMan's now transferred their full attention back onto Niall.

Georgina said testily, 'For goodness sake Niall, how many times have I asked you to tell us where you're planning to live after you're married? But no, you just couldn't bring yourself to give me a straight answer, could you? All that mumbling. We naturally assumed that you'd be moving in with the MacKay's. Now we learn, and not through *you* I might add, that all the time you were having other ideas! And what's all this about wanting Maggie to work here? What's happened? Doesn't she want to stay on at the school?'

A strangled, sob-like noise emanated from somewhere near Niall's mouth and throat area, to be followed by his first stuttering response. 'I ... I ... I ...' the effort causing beads of sweat to begin forming on his very red brow.

Donald felt his own patience being tested now, and asked sharply, 'You what? Come on man, out with it!'

Niall raised his head a few inches, and darting a fleeting, nervous look towards the desk, ventured, 'I ... that's right. Move in here, wed, it's only right. That big bedroom, empty ... an' all. If ... if ... you like.'

Georgina raised her already supremely arched eyebrows, and exclaimed, 'If I like! If I like! *No, I do not like!* And you still haven't answered my question about Maggie's job.'

Niall managed to find another scrap of courage from somewhere, and replied, 'Och, she's doesn'a have enough hours. We can'a save on that!'

Donald's eyes narrowed as he felt he was gaining a clearer picture. 'Ah, I see. And you think that you'll be able to put more by for a place of your own maybe if she's holding down another ... what ...another part-time job?'

Georgina shot him a look of alarm. He knew as well as she did that they could not afford another member of staff just yet. Naturally, the couple would want to live together, but to expect them to accommodate *and* employ the woman as well - now that was a downright cheek - especially after all this recent upset with the Maxwell's. She would have to nip that idea in the bud, and straight away! 'No-o. I don't think we can help you there Niall. You know we're fully staffed ...' She paused as understanding dawned - was *that* what all this was about? Yvonne had said, how had she put it, 'Certain circumstances have arisen ... better for everyone's sake if I left.' Could it really be that the silly girl was actually willing to give up a job that she obviously enjoyed, and for which she was so well suited, a job that had prospects - just to make way for Maggie? She was aghast at the very idea.

Niall's head jerked up violently. 'But the job was hers before ...' he turned to look at Yvonne with such an undisguised look of hatred that both Georgina and Donald found themselves becoming alarmed.

'Before what?' prompted Donald.

Niall shot his hand out in a throwaway gesture, narrowly missing Yvonne's face. '*She* came, an' spoilt everythin' for ma poor Maggie.'

Convinced now that she had been right, Georgina speculated, 'Now, let me get this straight. You're claiming that the job was Maggie's? I assume you mean Yvonne's job? If that's the case, then let me tell you, Niall Turvey, you've got your wires badly crossed somewhere. *The* job most certainly was *not* Maggie's! Whatever gave you that impression? Good gracious! She's never even asked about working here. She'll just have to try and get more hours at the school, or somewhere else. I expect the Manor'll be taking on later; she could try there. But let me assure you, here and now, that Yvonne's job is not on offer, not now, nor at any time in the foreseeable future. Do I make myself clear?' She turned to Yvonne. 'And *you,* young lady, if you've had the misguided notion that we'd get Maggie in to replace you, then you're very much mistaken. And we certainly will *not* accept your resignation on *those* grounds. Goodness me! We have plans for you; Robert wants you to handle all the coach side of things when he comes, and Maggie certainly wouldn't be up to that!'

Donald tried to force the notion of rabbits and headlights out of his thinking as he looked at Niall's horrified gape.

Now all Niall could hear was that there was no job here for Maggie. Now all he could think of was that he would have to face her and those ruddy old sods of hers and tell them that it was no-go -.*again!* And all because of this English bitch! Such powerful emotions required an outlet, and unable to control himself, he lurched to his feet and let out a stream of vulgar expletives as he kicked out savagely at the nearest object to hand, which was, fortunately, an empty waste paper basket.

Donald sprang up. 'That's enough! Control yourself man! You're making a spectacle of yourself. And if you carry on like that, you'll be out of the front door and out of a job. Is that how you want to start married life?'

It worked. Niall froze. All he wanted to do now was to escape and get well clear of all this business, but somehow he managed to make a superhuman effort, and forced himself to sit down again.

Yvonne was dismayed, what a fool he had been! He had totally mishandled the situation, and now he could very well lose his job, and so much more. And *still* he had not mentioned the baby. Despite everything, and forcing her own feelings to the back of her mind, she willed him to find the courage to speak up, as she said, in what she hoped was a suitably calming and encouraging tone, 'Go on Niall. You can tell them about ... you know. They'll understand.'

Unblinking, Niall glowered at her, a series of mystified and ugly expressions contorting his beetroot red countenance. What was the bitch talking about now? Tell them what? Understand what? Hadn't she already spilled the beans and stuck her nose in where it didn't belong? Why couldn't she shut her big mouth? Incredibly, his crazed and chaotic mind had completely forgotten how he had misled her to believe that Maggie was pregnant with his child.

Georgina could not stand the sight of his sweating and distorted face any longer. 'Oh! I've had enough of this. Niall, you will tell us immediately what Yvonne's talking about - or else. You'll be a married man soon, and this type of juvenile behaviour won't go down too well with Maggie's parents, I can tell you!'

By now the tension in the small office was unbearable for all its occupants. Georgina glanced up at the wall-mounted electric fire. The element was black, but the temperature in the room was far too hot for comfort, and now there was a most unpleasant body odour around the place. The three looked expectantly at Niall, but were to be disappointed, for now the continuous leg trembling and rasped breathing were accompanied by a series of unnatural squirming motions. And he appeared to have clammed-up again.

Yvonne's own patience finally snapped. 'Okay Niall, I'll tell them. But you've forced me into it, so just you remember that.' She looked straight at Georgina, and made the shocking announcement. 'Maggie's pregnant. And I think that's why they want her to come and work here. It's like you said Donald, to put as much by as they can ... before the baby comes, you know, for a place of their own.'

Georgina gasped as Donald bent slowly in the middle and lowered himself back down onto the safe. Several agonizingly long and silent seconds passed as the couple stared incredulously at each other. Eventually, Donald found he was able to ask, 'And is that one of those "circumstances" why you feel you should be leaving us, Yvonne?'

She nodded, feeling a mixture of sadness and relief that everything was out in the open at last.

A shadow fell across the room, and aware that someone was standing behind her now, Yvonne turned to see Flora's erect, willowy frame in the doorway. She had heard the whole thing; indeed, it was hard not to, what with the door being open and all. And hadn't she stood by and kept quiet for as long as a body could take? The time had come to bring some wisdom into the matter, and she was just the one to do it. Now it was to be her calm, wise voice that bathed, even soothed, their ears, as she imparted her own shocking, yet vital, piece of information. 'Och no! That's no right, no right at all. Maggie's no pregnant. No, no, no! And that's a fact.'

Georgina managed to rally sufficiently to ask, 'Flora! Oh, my goodness! Maggie's not … but … how do you know?'

Taking a step in, Flora tried hard not to look accusingly at the nasty wee chef as she revealed how she had come to possess such an intimate piece of knowledge. 'I was in McGregor's this last Thursday, and wasn't Maggie there, fretting that Doreen was out of those extra-large Dr. White's again, and weren't they the only ones that suited her? And, och, I'm no believing that Maggie would tell Niall such a thing to trap him like. She's always been a decent girl, and I'm guessing she's no part of this foolishness. No, no, I'm telling you straight, that lassie's no in the family way at all!'

Donald covered his mouth with one hand and began to stroke his beard slowly with the tip of his fingers; this was a fine kettle of fish if ever there was one, and damned embarrassing at that.

By now, Niall was bent almost double in his chair, and busily massaging his head with sweat-soaked hands. If ever a man felt ill-done by, then he was that man.

When Yvonne had managed to take in what Flora had said, a surge of anger shot through her, and like a line of dominoes, the implications of Niall's deceit began to come crashing down: Maggie was not pregnant; *there was no baby!* There was no real urgency for them to save for a deposit towards a place of their own. Niall had tricked her, and she would not help them by leaving after all. Fair enough, she had to admit that he had not used the actual words, 'Maggie's pregnant,' but he had definitely led her to believe that there was a baby on the way. What kind of a man would conjure up the excuse of an imaginary baby, and for what? Just to get rid of her - and get Maggie in? Was that *really* all that this was about?

Patting the troublesome frizz, and with a tight smile on her compressed lips, Georgina felt her mind becoming razor sharp again. 'Thank you, Flora. That was *most* illuminating.' She turned her gaze onto Niall's still stooped and squirming body, and said caustically, 'Well now, Niall, what have you to say to *that?* Is Maggie pregnant, or is she not? And before you answer, just know that I fully intend to make it my business to find out for myself, so you had better be giving us the truth.'

However, like a trapped animal, all the emotionally and physically shriveled form that was Niall could manage was a long, low, menacing growl.

Yvonne could not help herself, as she asked, 'And *why* did you lie? What a thing to lie about! What on earth were you thinking of? Surely it couldn't have been just to get rid of me?'

Now Flora had a question of her own that needed asking. 'And what will the lass do when she's told about this ...' she paused to flip her hand in his direction, '... this ... foolishness. And Callum, aye, and Ailsa? My, my! I daren't think on it!'

The growl grew in volume and erupted to make one solid, stentorian roar as Niall twisted around to face Flora. 'What d'ya mean? What'll she do? What's it to do with you, you nosey old cow? You won't be tellin' her, that's what! And *you* ...' he spun back to face Yvonne, '*You!* You've always been in the ruddy way.' Now, as was his habit in times of extreme stress and anger, he began jabbing his finger forcefully into the side of his head. 'Only can't use your loaf, can you? Too ruddy thick in the head to see it. Bloody English bitch!'

He turned to Donald, 'Och, man, man! This is load of tosh. Anyone can make a wee mistake. Ye ken how it is with hens; one minute they're killin' themselves with dietin's, and the next they're fat with bairns. It's us men have to live with all their fancyin's. And then *we're* the bad guys!'

Now it was Georgina's turn to be given the benefit of his own particular brand of ancient wisdom, as, with a succession of knowing winks, he looked in her direction, and said in his most manly tone, 'Och, Mrs Mac, dunna you go frettin' yourself'. I'll get her pregnant soon enough, and then all you hens'll be quick enough to come cluckin'' - which was an outright lie, for he had no intention of doing any such thing.

Donald found himself almost physically recoiling from the younger man's coarse remarks to his wife, and could hardly keep the disgust from his voice as he said, 'Er, no. I think you've made a grave error there Niall. A very grave error of judgement indeed. I think I get the picture. And I, for one, have heard enough. Right'o, I think the best thing for us to do now is for Mrs MacMan and myself to have a chat about all this … and decide what's to be done.'

But Georgina needed no time to know exactly what was to be done 'about all this', and quickly came in with, 'And shame on you Niall! This really is the last straw. You've let yourself down badly, and involved Maggie in goodness knows what. And on top of that, you've insulted our guests and upset other members of staff.' She pointed at the upturned waste paper basket. 'And after this little display, I feel we would be foolish in the extreme to continue employing someone who is capable of such … such deceit and childish behaviour.' She looked at Donald. 'And apart from anything else, we do have our son to consider.'

Donald nodded. She was right; they wouldn't be doing Robert any favours by having someone so conniving and unpredictable around the place. Things had gone too far. Way, way too far, and as the man of the house, the buck would have to stop with him. Sighing heavily, he raised himself slowly to his feet, and declared, 'Okay, that's it! You know, Niall, we've done our darndest to make all sorts of allowances for you since you came, but enough's enough. Time's up. I'm sorry, we can't overlook your tantrums any more, and this last stunt of yours shows just how unpredictable you can be, downright devious too. Well, my lad, it's cost you your job!' Yvonne gasped. Undeterred, he continued, 'Go on now, off with you, and pack your things.' He paused to look at Georgina, who was nodding in agreement. 'One week's pay would be fair, I think. Then I'll run you somewhere. Maggie's ... or wherever.'

But the ordeal was not over yet. Niall's whole body convulsed as he gave a noisy sob, tears ran down his face and two lines of mucus began to stream from his nose. He was a messy, pathetic sight. He jumped to his feet and spun around to face Yvonne, giving her shin a series of rapid, savage kicks, yelling, *'Bitch, bitch, bitch! You ruddy English bitch!'* She let out a cry and recoiled instinctively as he towered over her, his face contorting with pure rage as he grabbed her shoulders, and pushing her hard back into her chair, spat with full force into her face.

'Enough!' shouted Donald, lunging forward and attempting to seize Niall's arms. 'I said, *enough!'* Succeeding, he managed to pin both arms tightly against the squirming body, and exclaimed, 'For God's sake, man! What the hell's the matter with you?' as he began to propel the struggling body towards the door.

Working up one last mouthful of spit as he was pushed unceremoniously past Flora, Niall shot it in her direction. Despite her bad back, she could be surprisingly nimble when the need arose, and just managed to dodge the repulsive globule, which landed on the doorframe instead. Disgusted, and staring at its slow, slimy progress, she remarked, 'And you're for wanting to be wed? Och no! No, no, no laddie! No wise at all.'

'Shut your face, you stupid old cow! Or I'll be shuttin' it for you,' roared Niall, now finding himself being frogmarched through into reception.

'Control yourself man!' ordered Donald, 'or it's the law for you. And don't think I wouldn't.' Reception successfully negotiated, the pair entered the kitchen, as Donald called back, 'Get his cards ready love, and bring the car round if ...' but his words were lost amongst the continuous torrent of Niall's furious obscenities.

Several boxes of crisps had been stacked against the table leg, effectively blocking their passage, and it was necessary for

Donald to release him for a split second. This was all the time Niall needed. So enraged was he by the injustice he had been forced to endure, that he lost no time in kicking everything in his path, before lashing out at the innocent radio, which he would have hurled through the window, had not Donald regained control of his flailing limbs, and threatened him with the law again.

Freed at last, he took the staff stairs two at a time and burst into his room. No one, but *no one* got rid of Niall Turvey! They could shove their ruddy job somewhere where the sun didn't shine! He'd go when it suited him, which so happened to be right now. He dragged a battered leather suitcase out from under the bed and began throwing his belongings into it. Oh yeah! He could do without this pokey old hole alright. There were plenty of other places out there that were breakin' their necks to get hold of a chef like him; weren't they cryin' out for them at this time of the year? To hell with the lot of them; he'd find somewhere where he'd be appreciated, and where no ruddy English bitch would spoil things for him again. Hell, he might even give the Merchant Navy a try! Yeah, they'd be glad of him alright; he'd thought about giving them a go before he'd got trapped in this pokey old dive.

As for Maggie, och, she'd just have to find a way of gettin' over him. He couldn't hang around for her. She wasn't much of a catch anyway. Frigid, that's what she was, a frigid, stupid, fat old maid. Well, she could bury herself alive here with those ruddy old sods of hers, and they could all rot in this hellhole together. From now on he was going to take care of himself. Number One - that was him. Yeah! He'll be takin' care of Number One from now on alright. He'll do okay. He'll show them; them and their fancy reputation. They'll be sorry. He'll see to that. Oh yeah, he'll see to that alright!

Finished, he felt an overpowering urge to upturn the bed, then thought better of it knowing that Donald was standing guard outside; the stupid, hen-pecked old sod! Swinging his rucksack over one shoulder and keeping his focus determinately on the floor, he flung open the door and proceeded to crash and bang his way along the corridor.

Donald did a quick check of the vacated room before hurrying after him, and asking, 'Where do you want to be taken? Maggie's ... or somewhere else?'

'Na-a, I've got other places to go.'

'I see. But you'll need to put things straight with her first.'

Niall ignored him as he entered the kitchen, *his* kitchen, for the last time. He opened several draws and selected a few items before shoving his knife block into the rucksack.

'Is that it?' asked Donald.

'Aye.'

'Then let's get going.' Leading the way into reception, he instructed, 'Wait here.'

But Niall was not for waiting. As soon as Donald was out of sight, he set off, and began walking as fast as his legs and breath could carry him. He had a tidy sum put by; they could shove their guilt money where it hurt! A lift would have been useful, but not to Maggie's. He'd have to hitch, and then he'd keep goin' till this dump was way behind him. He was a free man again - and it felt good, *ruddy* good. Oh yeah! Watch out boys, Number One was on his way!

CHAPTER 21

Yvonne watched the car approach the Inn. One problem had disappeared over the horizon with Niall's departure, but now here was the other one. Somehow, today, she must find out exactly what Alex's interest in her really was. She found it hard to believe that he was one of those men who always had to have a woman hanging around and dancing to attendance, and even harder to believe that he might want her for her own sake. It must simply be a case of him wanting help to choose things for the Manor. Whatever it was, she would need to put an end to it, and as quickly and as tactfully as possible. She was pragmatic enough to realise that it would be difficult to avoid him; he would probably be calling frequently at the Inn for all sorts of reasons in the future. Flora had told her that there were times when folk up here had to rely upon each other to be good neighbours, and the Manor was one of the Inn's closest.

Georgina had started to hint that she and Donald might want her to stay on when the season was over, and she was beginning to allow herself to believe that somehow, unbelievably, and at long, long last, she might have actually wandered onto the right path. If so, maybe now she could begin to settle, and she must not allow anything, or anyone, to cause her to stray off it - especially any habitually self-destructive pattern, or any man - no matter how decent and honourable he may be. If only she felt a bit sharper; once again, her sleep was being affected by the old familiar menacing voice making a nuisance of itself. She could sense its tentacles pushing and forcing its way through her happiness, determined to make its presence felt. But no! She would not allow it to control her this time. Whatever it took, she must learn to conquer it, to banish it, to live her life free from its malevolent, tyrannical grip. She would not - *must not* - throw away this wonderful new opportunity that fate had kindly sent her way. Now there was a chance that she could really unpack, and not just her earthly belongings, but her travel-weary heart as well.

The car drew up. 'Hi there,' called Alex, leaning over to push open the passenger door. 'Good to see you again.'

She climbed in. 'Morning Alex.' The interior of the car was comfortably warm. She stifled a yawn and began undoing her coat as they pulled away.

'That family still keeping you busy?'

'No, they've gone now. We're quiet again.'

'Chance to catch your breath then?'

'If only! We're going to start doing refreshment stops for coaches next week.'

'Really? How will you manage? I did hear something about you losing your chef.'

She tried to sound matter-of-fact, as she replied, 'We'll be alright. Donald's covering the kitchen till we get someone else'

Remembering her reaction at the ceilidh, he decided to pursue the subject of the chef. 'Odd time for a chef to leave, isn't it? Just before the season starts?'

She chose her words carefully. 'Well, it was a bit sudden, but there'd been some problems for a while, you know, differences of opinion.'

'Must have been pretty serious for him to desert his post. Still, you're probably well shot of him if he was that unreliable. I hear Maggie's taking it very badly.'

'Yes, but it's probably for the best. Hopefully, she'll see it that way one day.'

'Must have been a strain, keeping up a cheerful front if there was a bit of an atmosphere going on behind the scenes?'

She nodded but did not elaborate. 'Anyway, it's over now.' A change of topic was needed, so she asked, 'What about you? What was your Easter like?'

'Quiet. Got involved in some research, and went to church a few times.'

'Which one?'

'The local one in Braegarroch. The Minister's a decent enough bloke. And you can wander in and sit on the back pew without causing much of a stir. All very ... restful.'

He had not sounded very enthusiastic. 'You don't sound all that keen,' she commented.'

He smiled. 'Let's just say that it doesn't scratch where I itch. I'd prefer to go to a Baptist or Methodist church, or an A.O.G., or a Pentecostal if I feel the need for a boost.'

'What's an A.O.G?'

'Assemblies of God, like the Pentecostals. They're usually a bit more lively; more Bible-centred.'

'Aren't they the ones that clap their hands and have guitars in their services?'

'Amongst other things, and there's no sin in enjoying yourself when you're worshipping God, it's scriptural. But I'm talking more about what they teach from the pulpit, although, to be fair, there's good and bad in every denomination.'

She moved her handbag away from the warm current of air bathing her feet, and remarked, 'It must be comforting to have a faith, something to lean on.'

'Comforting, yes, but no crutch.'

'But isn't that what religion is, just a ... a coping mechanism? And you sound like you expect more from a church?'

'I do! A lot more. For example, I heard a thirty-minute sermon ... lecture ... on how to make the perfect loaf of bread in a Methodist chapel once. Can you believe that? When I asked the minister what the point of it was, all he could do was give me a load of old waffle; couldn't look me in the eye and give me a straight answer. A complete waste of time. Talk about the blind leading the blind!'

Genuinely curious now, she went on to ask, 'But what else is there? I mean, what can ... what does it give you?'

He was quiet for a while, then said, 'So much. Peace, hope, a real sense of purpose and happiness, companionship, challenge, fulfilment.' He paused, then went on, 'Don't get me wrong, I enjoyed my life before; in many ways it was very fulfilling. But now I look back, there were gaps, you know, something missing. I suppose you could say that then I was living on almost full batteries, and now I feel as though I'm connected to the power source ... permanently! To put it another way, it was like I was always looking downwards, straining my neck to look at a dim forty-watt light bulb, unaware that the Son - that's S-o-n - was shining above me all the time. I'd have seen Him sooner if I hadn't been so stiff-necked and looked up. And another thing about crutches, non-Christians are always quick to point the finger. But what are they leaning on? What coping mechanisms do they use? I'm not judging them; I used to be like them before I became a committed Christian.' He shook his head, remembering, 'Oh yes, I know all the arguments, all the angles.'

She looked preoccupied and made no reply. He wondered if he had been a bit too heavy, then went on to say, 'By the way, there should be plenty of time to do the shops after we've chosen the material. I've booked lunch for one o'clock.'

'Okay.' And then, having picked up on something he said, and because she knew she would always be curious, went on to ask, 'Why do you call yourself a *committed* Christian, why not just a Christian? I mean, this is a Christian country, and we're all supposed to be Christians anyway.'

Alex was pleased that she had voluntarily returned to the subject, and prepared to answer the question that he had often been asked since meeting The Boss. He began thoughtfully, 'Well, this is how I see it. My family are good old C.of E., and I was christened into that august organisation as a baby. But, in a way, that was nothing to do with me. I was too young to say anything about it at the time. It was done *to* me, and *for* me, but not *by* me, nor as a result of any conscious decision that I'd made.'

She frowned. 'But that's the same for everyone isn't it? What's wrong with that?'

'Let me put it another way. Just because your parents are married, doesn't mean to say that you are. You have to make your own choice, and it's good to have a definite time and place that you can look back on, and say, "I know I'm married; I remember taking my vows in such-and-such a place, and on such-and-such a day. No one else took them for me; it was my decision, my choice." And as far as christenings go, I'm sure that God's pleased when people bring their babies along to a church to be...sprinkled. Jesus reprimanded the disciples for trying to keep the children away from Him, and told them to bring them back so that He could bless them. But that didn't make them His followers. It was just a blessing, which, in my opinion, is all a christening is. We make our own minds up about all sorts of things when we become adults, and part of the Church's work is to explain the choice all of us need to make about God.'

'Choice? What choice?'

'The big one. Whether or not we want Him in our lives; whether we want to fully accept and embrace His love for us - or not. We're all free to believe in what Jesus did for us on the Cross - or just ignore it.'

'And you...chose to believe?'

He was amazed that she had not tried to change the subject, like so many other people would have by now. 'That's right. Although I came in through the crisis faith door. There's nothing wrong with that, as long as you don't go back to ignoring Him again when everything's back on an even keel. I guess He'd been trying to reach me before, but I couldn't, or wouldn't, acknowledge Him. He's a gentleman and waits to be invited in into our lives.'

'How had He been trying to reach you?'

He thought for a moment, looking back and trying to remember, before saying, 'Through circumstances, people, but mainly my conscience.'

'And after you invited Him into your life, that's when you started calling yourself a committed Christian?'

He nodded. That's right. I responded, and committed myself to Him, into His care, and started living a new kind of life. That's what being *Born Again* means: believing in what Jesus did for us by dying on the Cross. We need to repent and ask for His forgiveness, then invite Him into our hearts - into our lives. We believe in Him, and receive Him. It's only then that we can call ourselves true Christians - Committed Christians. Am I making sense?'

'I think so.' Privately, she thought that it was unrealistic to expect people to commit themselves to someone long dead, and went on to say, 'I've never heard anything like this before, and frankly I find it ... disturbing ... to think that people are walking around with no idea of what you've just said.'

'Hmm, and therein lies the problem; and I lay the blame squarely at the door of the Church. But, thank God, there are some that are doing the job properly by preaching a clear Gospel message and telling the truth about Him.'

She remained silent, deep in thought, wondering what churches had been doing all this time if they hadn't been doing their job properly and telling the truth.

They journeyed on. Alex endeavoured to keep all their talk light as he introduced other subjects, all the while silently hoping and praying that a seed had been sown in her heart.

*

They arrived in the busy market town of Strathlochy soon after eleven o'clock and elected to have coffee in the same café they had visited before. Yvonne felt a pleasurable sense of wellbeing as she sat back, trying hard not to stare at the sight of Alex's fine, strong hands, wrapped around a hot mug of coffee. By now, several questions had formed in her mind about their earlier conversation, and she decided to take this opportunity to quiz him about them. 'Can I ask you something about what you said earlier?'

Alex took a sip; the coffee was strong. 'Fire away.'

'It's about that decision you spoke about. I've been thinking, what about children who die, or the mentally handicapped? You know, those who can't ... aren't capable of making their own decisions?'

He sipped again. 'Good question. A lot of people stumble over that one, but I've come to realise that the suffering of others doesn't lessen God's love for me. And they're innocents; they don't need forgiveness. For them there's no problem - they go straight to Heaven.'

'But why would God allow them to die so young, or be born like that in the first place? It doesn't make sense.'

'He didn't, I mean He doesn't. It's not God who makes bad things happen. Everything He does is for our good. When He created the Earth, He made it good, but the Devil came along and tempted, or, to put it another way, influenced humans to doubt God's love for them. When they rebelled, all the ... badness entered into the human existence, and has been part of our makeup ever since.'

'Are you talking about Adam and Eve?'

'Correct. You could say they've got a lot to answer for. But God gave them freewill; they were free to choose to maintain their relationship with Him, their Creator, and obey Him, or not. Unfortunately, they allowed themselves to be tempted and led astray. It's been the same for mankind ever since. Actually, we don't realise it, but what we're doing is listening to, and following, other voices; the Devil being one of them.'

'You believe in the Devil too?'

'No!' he replied emphatically.

'No?'

'I don't believe *in* him. It would be more accurate to say that I believe he exists. We don't have to look very far to see his handiwork, in us and around us.'

'But, if that's true, why doesn't God stop him?'

'Well, in a sense, He does. By giving us free will. The offer's always there. The shop's always open, and everything in it's free. We can't blame Him if we refuse to go in.'

'But why didn't He ... programme us to have nothing to do with him, I mean, the Devil.'

He laughed. 'Nice idea! But if He'd have done that, then He could have programmed us to just believe in Him. But God doesn't want automatons; unthinking beings, mindlessly bowing and scraping to Him. He wants people to know they are free - free to choose. Afraid it's back to that free will thing again.'

Things were going far better than he could have hoped, and he decided to keep going until she showed signs of losing interest. 'When we allow ourselves to be drawn away from the

One who really loves us, we can end up opening ourselves to some unhelpful, and unpleasant things, like fear, greed, pride, selfishness, stupidity, ignorance, foolish choices, and so on - all forms of rebellion against God - Who we then go on to blame! For instance, I could use my freedom to drive like a maniac and kill someone, and then blame Him!'

She felt he was beginning to make some kind of sense, and said, 'I've honestly never heard anything like this before.'

'And you won't, not unless you make a conscious effort to discover the truth about Him for yourself. And what I've told you about Jesus dying on the Cross for everyone is the Gospel. It means *The Good News*. Like I said before, if only more churches were doing their job properly, and telling their people the truth. Hearing how to make the perfect loaf of bread won't get anyone into Heaven! We could do with a dozen Billy Graham's to get the message out there.'

'Billy Graham! But he uses emotionalism, doesn't he? They say he gets people into such a state that they get carried away and make a lot of promises they don't mean, and can't keep.'

'In a sense, you're right. I've watched some of his crusades on tape, and there can be a lot of emotionalism, but ...' He lowered his head and clasped his hands together on the table in front of him. Yvonne thought for all the world that he looked like a man in prayer. His voice was low when he spoke again, 'I was emotional myself when I first understood what Jesus had done for me.'

She looked intently at him. She had never met anyone who talked so candidly and affectionately about God before; it was as though he really knew Him. Suddenly she felt guilty. What was she thinking of? Here was someone who had obviously had a deeply religious experience, something she had never really thought too much about, and certainly never expected to have herself. What made her think she had the right to question him about his private beliefs?

'I'm sorry, Alex. I've got no right to question you like this. But I think it's wonderful, I mean, that you feel so certain. Actually, you've taken my breath away, and I honestly don't know what to say.' She peered down into her mug. 'But I'll confess to you now that there have been times when I've wondered what the Baby in the manger was all about, and what the story's got to do with me. And, to tell you the truth, I've never really given any serious thought about why Jesus Christ was crucified. I suppose the closest thing I've ever experienced to anything religious was the odd time I've been to church, or singing hymns in school assemblies.'

He smiled. 'You know, they begin to make sense once He's in your heart. I suppose you could say that we can't really grasp what marriage, or parenthood, really means, until we are married and become parents ourselves. We have to enter in, to live the life, and experience these things firsthand before we get our questions answered. Even then, do we ever stop learning?' He knew that this would probably be a good place to stop, but realising that it might be some time before he was given such a good opportunity again, decided to press on. 'And about that Baby in the manger, the Bible's full of accounts of how God tried to reach mankind and bring us to our senses. But it was only when His Son became like one of us, and joined us, that more people sat up and began to take notice.'

She nodded, feeling that that had sounded logical enough.

He continued, 'And there are several reasons why He was crucified, partly to do with the religious leaders and politics of the day, but the *real* reason was to bring mankind back to God and restore our relationship with Him. It's a journey we all need to make; every one of us is a sinner. We all fail to meet God's standards. How many people do you know who've never thought, said or done anything wrong?'

She had to think about that. Did she know anyone who might fit the bill? *She* certainly didn't.

He leant forward and rested his elbows on the table, a softer, more thoughtful expression on his face. 'Try thinking of the Cross as being a sort of bridge between God and mankind. That includes you. One arm touching you, the other touching God. Jesus is the meeting place. He allowed Himself to be sacrificed in our ... your ... place; on your behalf. In that way God's justice was satisfied - by allowing His own Son to pay the price for our sin - and redeem us. He was the perfect, final sacrifice. Unless we take the time to understand what was really going on, and come and kneel at the foot of His Cross, we'll never know real peace with ourselves, with each other, and with God.'

She was staring at him now; her eyes enormous, green and searching. What was happening to her? She had begun this day determined to discover what lay behind this man's interest in her, and, if necessary, to deal with it. Yet, here she was, becoming more drawn to him by the second! He was the first genuinely religious person she had ever met, and she marvelled at how he could talk so openly about something so personal. But maybe he was able to talk like this to everyone? She was both disturbed and fascinated by him at the same time, and knew that she would have to be even more careful from now on. Very careful. This man represented a different type of danger, and one that she had not encountered before - or had any idea how to handle.

Alex went on to say, matter-of-factly, 'But you don't have to take my word for it, in fact, I'd rather you heard it from Someone else. If you are interested, then take a look in the Bible, especially the New Testament. Best to start there. Read all about it for yourself.'

She had often dipped into the mysterious book's flimsy pages, but had always come away frustrated and puzzled at its antiquated language, having found no relevance to her own life. 'Er, not sure I want to. I can't get on with all that talk about begetting and begotting.'

He smiled and nodded. 'There are more up-to-date versions around.' An idea struck him, and he looked down at his watch. 'Anyway, it's probably time we got this show on the road. Are you ready?'

She reached down and retrieved her purse from her handbag.

'Er, you won't be needing that when you're with me,' he remarked.

'But you insisted on paying last time!'

He shook his head vigorously. 'That was my pleasure. I owed you. And you're only here now because I still need your help. And, as far as I'm concerned, any bloke that invites his lady out, and then lets her pay, deserves to be put on a charge.'

She stared at him, wondering if she had heard right. What had he called her? 'His lady'? No! He must have been generalising. She held her hands up in an attitude of surrender. 'Okay, okay! But just so you know, I'm not one for expecting and taking without doing some giving.'

He looked at her, his eyes narrowing as he considered how to handle this new difficulty. Everyone knew that live-in hotel staff were notoriously low paid. But she had her pride, and was obviously used to fending for herself and paying her own way. Refreshing, but unnecessary. Standing, he said, 'Tell you what, let's make a deal. How about you cover a coffee break, say, once a week, and let me take charge of the rest?'

Satisfied that he had handled the matter with tact and diplomacy, he turned and walked over to the counter, thereby missing the look on her face, which, if he had turned around, might have made him think again.

Without a word, Yvonne stood and put on her coat. How many more clues did she need? The other week he said that he would show her around the area, and that she was 'part of the team,' and now he had announced - decided - that she could pay for a weekly coffee break! But the most alarming one of all was this 'his lady' business. Well, now she had her answer; it wasn't just help with the Manor he was after, but for some inexplicable, unaccountable reason, he wanted her too! This was bad. What a fool she had been. Why had she asked him all those questions? She should have kept things impersonal. And why hadn't she taken action before it had come to this? Now she really would have to - and in such a way that they could still be civil towards each other. Then again, it might be interesting to see how far she could go with him before the old panic set in. But no, she must do the right thing; he was too good a person to be messed about. She must stick to her decision, and find a really effective way of putting him off - and for good.

CHAPTER 22

It did not take long to choose the alternative curtain fabric, and Alex managed to acquire a substantial pile of brochures and leaflets on various forms of lighting before they left the shop. Their next stop was the library. However, she was reluctant to join, stating, 'I don't know how often I'll be able to get here, and I don't fancy paying loads of fines for late returns.'

'No problem there,' he replied, 'I come in pretty regularly and can bring you in, or bring your books back for you.'

'That's kind of you to offer, but I'd rather not,' she said, not wanting to be beholden to him in any way, and was glad when he let the matter drop.

Soon, it was time to make their way to the hotel, which they found humming with life thanks to a North of Scotland Hydro-Electric Board Convention. She was relieved when they were obliged to share a table in the busy dining room.

'Phew! That's better,' Alex exclaimed, stepping out onto the quieter street after their meal. 'Trust me to choose the wrong day. Still, it was interesting to hear what those guys actually get up to. Good to hear how well Jock's doing too.' He rubbed his hands together. 'Fresh isn't it? Right, down to business. I've got some things to take care of. Mind if I leave you here, and we could meet up, say around three thirty?'

She readily agreed. He watched her walk away before going down one of the side streets, and enter a small, but well stocked, bookshop. Minutes later, whistling and barely limping, he crossed over to the Post Office. Finally, he made his way to a small Methodist Chapel, where he spent the remainder of the time in quiet prayer and reflection.

Yvonne's first task was to find a public telephone box and call the hotel in Beaulane. The shrill voice that eventually answered sounded stressed, and informed her that the manager was, 'Not around, as usual.'

'Can I leave a message then? Can you tell him that Miss Williams will not be coming to start work next week?

Circumstances have changed, and she will not be requiring the job after all. Have you got that?'

The voice replied testily, 'Humph! Okay for some.'

'Er, yes. And there's a letter in the post confirming it, but you will pass the message on, won't you?'

'Alright,' came the weary reply as the line went dead.

Yvonne replaced the receiver, feeling that she'd had a narrow escape if the tone of that obviously discontented receptionist had been anything to go by.

She managed to find everything on her list before hurrying back to the car with just a few minutes to spare. Alex saw her struggling with several bulging bags, and could not resist asking, 'Anything left in the shops?'

'Oh, a few bits,' she replied, piling her haul onto the car's back seat. 'Mostly books and wool. I like to keep busy when I'm watching telly.' She was not going to tell him that she had spent most of the time in the Spastics Society Shop. Years of poor wages meant that she had never been able to afford some of the good quality clothes she now possessed, and today she had managed to find more - all in good condition and only requiring some minor alteration. She had also found an enormous bag of odd balls of wool, stuffed under one of the tables. Finally, she had come across several paperbacks by her favourite authors. Who needed a library!

'You're a knitter then?' he asked.

'More of a crocheter.'

'Really! You're full of surprises.' He glanced up at the sky. 'Now, why don't I give you one? How about a spot of sightseeing? We could take the scenic route back. There are some great views of Ben Laith and the lochs from the back road. Looks like we'll have enough light. Are you up for it?'

Yvonne considered. When out walking, she had often been tempted to see how far she could go before losing her nerve or getting lost, and had never dared attempt any of the narrow, uphill off-road tracks. Now, here was an opportunity to satisfy her curiosity. 'Okay, I'd like that,' she replied.

*

Fifty minutes later, they pulled over onto a small flat grassy area on the western slope of Ben An-t-Earrach. A strong gust of wind wrenched the door from her hand as she stepped out. It was exceptionally cold, and she crossed her arms tightly across her chest as she stood peering down at Braegarroch, nestling peacefully, well over a thousand feet below. She shifted her focus onto a straight, tree-lined cut in the landscape, and guessed that it hid the railway line that had brought her here just over a month ago.

Alex came and stood beside her, pointing down and to the left. 'Look, over there. Ardgealish. Can you see? Follow the road around the loch edge.'

She turned, and her eye was caught by the movement of a miniature sized lorry as it moved slowly along a thin grey ribbon of road, hugging the edge of Loch Laith. It disappeared into an area of dense woodland, before emerging again between the small line of Monopoly-sized cottages of Ardgealish, streamers of white smoke rising silently from the chimneys. Looking up and over to the horizon, she gazed with wonder at the snow-peaked range of sombre, green and grey shaded mountains, standing like majestic chieftains, owning and guarding the panoramic beauty around them, their slopes gashed with cascading streams, and dotted with the tiny white figures of grazing sheep.

'Down there!' He pointed to a pair of birds of prey, gliding silently and effortlessly below, and hovering menacingly over their unsuspecting quarry. He took his eyes off the scene he had witnessed many times before and fixed them onto her. They stood, just inches apart now, and he watched as she snatched impatiently at the fine tendrils of hair whipping across her face. As though obeying an impulse, his arm began to raise, and it was with some effort that he managed to control the urge to touch them for himself - and place it around her shoulders instead.

'Here, it's a bit blustery, I don't want you getting blown away.' He felt her stiffen under his protective hold. She quickly shrugged him off and stepped away, feigning interest over a rocky outcrop to her left. He went and stood next to her again, and instinctively grabbed hold of her arm when they were buffeted by an exceptionally strong series of gusts.

She shuddered, and exclaimed, 'It's lovely, but this wind's a bit too wild for me.'

'There's another good view further on; might be calmer there. Come on, let's take a look.'

There was no sign of wind when they stepped out of the car a few minutes later, just a kinder, gentler breeze. This time, he made no effort to put his arm around her as he pointed to the various features and landmarks laid out below them. They had a clear view of the Inn from this side, and it was hard for her to believe that now her whole life depended upon what happened in the miniature sized building. And there, with its dark waters, Loch Nan Solas, looking more like a shallow duck pond than the deep, impressive loch that it was. She could only see two farmhouses from this view, their cattle and sheep with their newborn feasting on the long, green sweep of fertile land running down to the estuary.

She felt moved to put into words the wonder she was feeling. 'It's really, really lovely. You know, it was the colours that I first noticed when I arrived, they're so vivid. You can almost feel the life force radiating out of them. This would make a wonderful painting, although I don't know which view I would choose; you're spoilt for choice up here.'

'I know what you mean. Makes you feel small and insignificant, doesn't it? There's something glorious about it; stirs the soul. Often wish I was poetic, or artistic.' He remembered something. 'That reminds me, hang on a minute.' He walked over to the car and returned a minute later with a camera strapped around his neck. Positioning himself several feet behind her, he started to focus and click, before inclining his head towards the view of the estuary, and asking, 'Look that way, will you.'

She obeyed without thinking too much about it. Several clicks later, he said, 'Thanks, that'll add perspective. Now look over that way.' Again, she obeyed, feeling it would have been churlish to refuse, but now beginning to speculate what fate had in store for those particular photographs.

Satisfied, he came to stand beside her again, and remarked, 'Hard to believe that there's nearly fifty-four million people out there, and well over five million of them in Scotland.'

'Well, they're certainly not around here! It sounds like the country's bottom heavy. I came across an old lady once who reckoned we'd sink one day; she'd panic every time she heard of another tower block going up!'

'Yes, fear's a strange beast. How about you? What are you frightened of Yvonne?'

'Oh, I don't know, spiders, things that go bump in the night.' How could she say, 'And you, and what effect you could have on my life'?

He laughed. 'I've met a few of those in my time; great big hairy ones, and I've heard a whole variety of bumps in the night.'

'But there must be something you're afraid of? Or at least, a bit wary of?'

He considered before replying. 'Well then, I'd have to say loneliness, going it alone, especially for any length of time. I've always been used to teamwork.'

'You…get used to it,' she said reflectively.

There was a long pause. Then he said, 'The forces are full of people trying to fit in and belong, as well as the odd loner. But I'm convinced that no matter how independent a person is, we all end up needing, someone sooner or later. "No man's an island …," and all that. I saw a film the other day about a man who survived a nuclear war and found himself completely alone. Not a situation I'd like to find myself in.'

'But if you'd managed to survive, maybe others would have too?'

'No doubt. Hey! How about it, fancy joining my clan?'

Clan meant other people, no problem there. She played along. 'Suppose so. You'd be a handy person to have around.'

'Oh yes, and why's that?'

'Now you're fishing for compliments. You know why, you being ex-Army and all. You'd be good at all that survival stuff.'

'Hmm, you and me. Sounds cosy.'

Nonplussed at this sudden leap from clan to pair, she exclaimed, 'Sorry to disappoint you, but I think I'd be desperate to find other survivors.'

He laughed. 'What, doesn't the idea appeal? No Adam and Eve situation? No begetting and begotting?' She looked shocked. But he had the bit between the teeth now, and went on to say, 'I reckon we'd make a good team then too. I'd be the hunter-gatherer, and with your flair for interior design, reckon we'd end up with the best stocked, classiest cave on the planet!'

'Don't be daft!' she retorted, 'and why do you assume we'd team up anyway? How'd you know I wouldn't want my own cave?'

'Oh yeah! And do all your own hunting and fishing? I reckon you'd last about a week - no, three days - before hunger set in. You'd soon come a-knocking.'

She thought that he was probably right, but the arrogance of the man! 'Sorry to disappoint you again, Tarzan,' she retorted, 'but you'd have to hunt around for another Jane to mop your fevered brow and boost your inflated ego!'

He turned his head to look directly at her. 'Hey! Don't tell me you're one of those bra-burning Women's Libbers?'

'No! But so what if I was? And what's wrong with me wanting to have my own place anyway? I wouldn't have accused you of being a male chauvinist pig if you'd have said you wanted to be alone.'

He pulled a knowing face. 'Take it from me, my girl, you wouldn't last long. You'd soon come to your senses.'

My girl! Ugh! She hated being called that; the gloves were off now. 'What's the matter, *little man?* Afraid of tidying your own cave?'

He tossed his head back and laughed. She had spunk alright, and he liked that. 'Aren't you forgetting something?'

'What?'

'Well now, let's just hope that there's still a few telephone boxes still standing!'

It took her a few seconds to realise that he was referring to the acutely embarrassing Rabbie incident. How dare he! What an infuriating, superior beast of a male he was. 'Well, of all the nerve! In that case, you'd definitely be in trouble. I can't imagine there'd be any heather left for you to go shouting around in!'

He nodded, fair enough, he deserved that. But why such a strong reaction? A bit of sparring was entertaining, but this was different, somehow more serious - and she did not appear to be enjoying it. 'Whoa! Down girl, down! A bit touchy, aren't we?'

Unfortunately, this did not help, and she found herself becoming even more indignant. The pent-up pressure of the past month finally weakened her normal self-control, and she was unable to prevent herself from holding back the torrent of angry words that now came pouring out.

'Touchy? Touchy? Ah, but I forgot, silly me! Men can go around doing all sorts of stupid things and get away with them, but just let a woman do something … unusual … and, my goodness, let the whole world know about it! Honestly! What's the matter with you men? I hadn't been here five minutes when that ... that Niall started treating me like dirt and making my life a misery, and now you're making me sound like some sort of freak … just because I don't fancy the idea of shacking up with you in some stupid cave!'

He looked into her flushed face, and tried to read what was really going on behind those flashing green eyes. My, she was a live one! Exciting, and quite, quite lovely. And now he was finding it hard to control an almost overpowering urge to grab her and kiss the tantrum out of her.

Seconds passed as they stood looking at each other, he with admiration, she, cooling now, and with a growing sense of dismay at the realisation that she had overreacted; he had only been making conversation after all.

At last, she said contritely, 'I'm sorry, Alex. You didn't deserve that. Guess I'm a bit out of sorts. But that's no excuse. I should be thanking you for bringing me here, not yelling at you.'

Now he really, badly, wanted to hug her. At least, to begin with. 'Hey, that's okay. Sounds like you've been having a rough time of it lately?'

She sighed. 'A bit. Look, can we go now? Before I feel the need to push you over the edge ... or something.'

'Reckon I'd deserve it. I shouldn't have goaded you like that, and I'm sorry too. Guess I got carried away. Let's agree that it's the thin air up here to blame.' Cautiously, he placed his hand on her arm. 'Come on then. I need to call in at the Manor on the way, do you mind? We can have a quick brew before I run you back. And I think it's your turn to drive.'

Torn between the desire to get back to the privacy of her room to hide and think about all this, or an almost overpowering urge to show him that she really was not the oversensitive harridan that he must think her to be, she agreed.

CHAPTER 23

Yvonne thought it best to leave Alex alone to make the drinks, and relaxed back on one of the settees to wait. There was no sign of the builders, and the Manor felt colder than ever. She watched the fire's elements turning red, and wondered when, and under what circumstances, she would sit here again - if ever, then felt perturbed at the sense of regret that accompanied the thought. She knew that she would always be curious about how the place would look when all the work was completed, and how well the venture succeeded. Or was it *just* the venture she would want to know about?

He came in holding two mugs of tea, and she lost no time in asking him about the alterations, a safe subject. 'How's the work coming along?'

'Steady. I'm hoping that my partners will be joining me in a few weeks. Our rooms look to be a fair size now that some of the interior walls have been taken out.'

'Will it be just you and them on the staff?'

'No, two more, that'll make five, that is, officially. Unofficially, I'd have to include you; you've been a fantastic help.'

'Pleased to have been of service.'

'*Been* of service?'

'Well, yes. There's nothing else I can do.'

'Hey, I don't want you to get the idea that you've only been - '

'And when do you expect to move in?' she interrupted him quickly, suspecting that he was going to say something that she would probably have trouble trying to forget.

'Some time soon, but I was going to say - '

'And you're still on course for opening in the summer?'

'If all goes well.' Then, determined to tell her what he wanted her to know, added, 'You know Yvonne, I'm not interested in you just for what you can do for the place, but - '

Once again, she found it necessary to interrupt him. 'But what about things you haven't planned for, you know, like the weather? Apparently, there's more snow on the way. Won't that hold things up a bit?'

He recognised a rebuff when he saw one, and replied, 'All taken into account and built into the timetable. Everything's progressing according to plan. Most of the outside work's been done anyway; just the ramp to do.' Then, without any warning, he changed the subject to the other matter that had been exercising his mind. 'By the way, you mentioned something about Niall earlier, something about him making your life a misery?'

She reached for her mug, once again regretting her earlier outburst. 'That? Oh well, that's all done and dusted now.'

'Sounds like life's not exactly been a bed of roses for you lately?'

'You could say that.'

Obviously she was not going to give much away. Nevertheless, he pressed on. 'What about the MacMan's? What did they have to say about it?'

'They ... didn't know.'

'Didn't know?' This surprised him; Flora had told Dot otherwise. 'But he left under a bit of a cloud, didn't he? I assume they must have found out?'

It seemed that he was not going to let the matter drop, so she decided to give him a few details, and hope that he would be satisfied. She began, glossing over Niall's plan to get her out and Maggie in, ending with a brief description of the final showdown.

His face hardened as she spoke. When she finished, he said, 'They should have been more on the alert. Insubordination like that needs to be dealt with right from the start. He'd obviously got away with it once too often; stands to reason he'd have no qualms about firing-off elsewhere.' He shook his head, frowning heavily. 'No. No excuse. Very remiss of them.'

'But you can't blame them! I've known quite a few other temperamental chefs, and I suppose they just got used to his moods. But I was a direct threat to his plans, so he took it to another level with me, especially when they weren't around.'

'The b......!'

Coming from him, she found the word doubly shocking. 'Anyway, like I said, it's all done and dusted now.'

'Hmm, wish I'd have known what he was up to.'

'Why? What could you have done? It was my problem. And they did sort it out anyway.'

'Your loyalty is commendable, but the bottom line stops with them. They should be a lot more careful about who they take on.'

'Well, from what I've seen of it, it's not that easy to get staff up here. Even I was interviewed over the phone, and they didn't get to see my references until after I'd arrived. I suppose they turned a blind eye to some of his antics, especially because he was such a good cook.'

'That's no excuse. Other places manage it. And look at the mess he's left behind: left you all in the lurch, probably deserted Maggie, not to mention upsetting you.' He shook his head again slowly. 'No, I'm not impressed.'

'Ah well, that's men for you.'

'Oh yes?'

'Yes.'

'All men?'

She shrugged.

'Me included?'

'How do I know? You've been a perfect gentleman so far, but ...' She paused, shrugging again. 'Who knows?' Allowing him to reach his own conclusion.

He drained his mug before putting it down slowly on the table. 'I might turn out to be a b...... too?' He was dismayed to realise how easily the word had slipped out. Swearing had once been second nature to him, although one of things he had found relatively easy to control since day one of his new life. Now his mouth seemed to have taken on a life of its own.

'No need to swear,' she said, calmly.

'*Every* need to swear!' he retorted, indignant that she could even think that he was capable of treating her like that damn cook.

Realising that she may have gone too far, she said in a conciliatory tone, 'I've offended you. I'm sorry. That wasn't my intention.'

He stood and went over to the window, his back to her, praying silently. A minute passed before he turned around, and said, 'No need to apologise, Yvonne. I was a bit touchy, and I'm sorry too.'

Resolved to see this thing through, and deciding that it was now or never, she braced herself, and began to deliver her all-important message. 'Actually Alex, there's something I need to say. And you'll have to forgive me if I'm jumping to conclusions, but ... look ... I don't play games, so I'll just tell you straight. The thing is, I'm not sure if you like me, I mean, in a relationship sort of way. If that is the case, then I'd much rather you didn't.'

He remained still and unresponsive, looking intently at her. The seconds ticked by.

'Do say something Alex! You're making me nervous.'

At last, he spoke. 'You're not tarring me with the same brush as that chef, are you? You must know that we're not all like that?'

Shocked, she exclaimed, 'What? No! You're *completely* different from him.'

'Then it's what I told you about becoming a committed Christian, isn't it? I put you off?'

'*No!* Please don't even think that. Actually, if anything, I found myself ...' she stopped abruptly.

'Yes?' he prompted, keen to hear what she had thought about their earlier conversation. 'Found yourself what?'

'I ... I liked that in you. Honestly, that's got nothing to do with it. I told you I thought it was wonderful, and I meant it. The plain truth is that I just don't want a relationship.'

He studied her for a while. Then, almost smiling, he rubbed his hands together; it was cold by the window. 'Why?'

'Why don't I want a relationship?'

'That's right.'

'Well I … I don't see why I should tell you. It's personal.'

'Well now, I happen to be taking this *very* personally, so I really do think that you should tell me.'

'No, I won't! And stop probing. It's got nothing to do with you anyway. I decided before I came here and … met you.'

An awful thought crossed his mind as he recalled her cool, abrasive manner on the mountain. He didn't want to ask the question, but he had to know. Returning to his chair, he asked cautiously, 'Yvonne, you're not a lesbian, are you?'

She didn't know whether to laugh or slap his face. In the end she did neither, and just stared hard at him, as she replied coolly, 'No, I am *not* a lesbian, thank you very much! I simply do not want to have a relationship. Can't you understand that?'

'I would, if you'd care to tell me why. No one makes a decision like that lightly. And I'm not asking for the sake of it; I do have my reasons.'

'I'd rather not,' she replied impatiently, wondering what those reasons could possibly be.

He pursed his lips together and leant forward. 'I see. Well then, I think we've got a bit of problem here. I'll tell you now that I'm disappointed. You must have guessed that I like you; I like you a lot.'

She stared at him, the dismay evident in her voice as she replied, hesitatingly, 'I … had wondered … and that's why I've spoken up. I wasn't sure before.'

'I enjoy being with you Yvonne. You're good company, and, well, damn it, I don't want it to end.'

Her heart missed a beat, but she told herself to ignore it, to stand firm. 'And I've enjoyed your company too, and please believe me when I say that it's got nothing at all to do with what you told me about your faith.'

'So, what is it then? Do you think I'm too old and doddery for you? I think there's only, what, thirteen, fourteen years between us, isn't there?'

Again, she became alarmed that he could even think something like that, and replied with an emphatic, *'No!* It's got nothing to do with your age, and I happen to think you're ... you're very attractive.'

He gave a wry laugh, remembering how forcefully she had shrugged him off earlier. 'Attractive? You do surprise me. But not attractive enough, is that it?'

She was starting to become impatient. 'Look, the problem's not with you, you're fine. It's me. Now can't we just drop the subject?'

'I can't see how.'

'Why? Why not?'

'Well, what's on offer? Friendship ... or what?'

'Friendship! No, I ... don't think that would be a good idea.'

'Care to tell me why?'

'Things could get ... you know ... complicated.'

'Hmm. You're probably right,' he agreed reluctantly.

Encouraged, she went on. 'And you know that we're bound to see each other around, so can't we just agree to be civilized about it?'

'Well, I suppose it wouldn't be very practical, and rather awkward, if we begin taking evasive manoeuvres. But I get the message. You don't want me to ... how can I put it ... pursue you?'

She gave a small laugh, feeling some relief. 'That's right, and anyway, you'll probably be too busy for anything ... like that ... once this place opens.'

'Don't you be so sure about that! Believe me, I don't think I'll ever be too busy for you.'

Her heart missed another beat, and now her face began to grow unbearably hot, as she exclaimed, 'Alex, please!'

'The trouble is, Yvonne, that I've already got used to having you around.'

She decided to concentrate for all she was worth on the fire's glowing elements. This was much harder than she had anticipated, and she had no idea where to go from here. 'I ... I don't know what else I can say.'

He sent up an arrow prayer, then said, 'Can I suggest something? You don't have to go along with it, but it might prove to be a mutually acceptable solution.'

Intrigued, and knowing she should not be, she said, 'Go on.'

'Try this for size. We carry on just as we are, seeing each other, maybe once a week - for days out, lunch, that kind of thing, a sort of casual but fixed arrangement. No demands on each other, no expectations, and nothing physical. I'll do my best to keep the pressure off. Then we can review the situation in, say, a few months? See how we both feel? How does that sound to you? Do you think you could cope with that?'

'That sounds more like a friendship to me, and you agreed that things could get complicated if we ... did go that way.'

'Yes, but we can't very well draw up a legal document guaranteeing that that wouldn't happen. We're both adults here and know the score, and I'm prepared to take the risk if you are.'

Even she had to agree that this option sounded reasonable, until the idea of playing with fire came into her mind. No, she must not give in. Now she decided to study the view out of the window, and replied as casually as she could, 'I don't know. I just can't imagine it working. I don't think it could.'

'And you wouldn't even be prepared to give it a go? I don't think I'd be wrong in saying that you've enjoyed our outings as much as I have. And I, for one, don't want them to end.'

The view lost its fascination, and she lowered her head to study her feet, her silence speaking for her.

'Or, are you already in too deep?' He held his breath and waited, fully expecting her to jump up and demand to be taken back to the Inn there and then. But she remained motionless, and when she eventually spoke, he had to strain hard to hear her.

'Maybe I am. And that's why I'm speaking up.' She raised her head and looked him straight in the eye. 'I'm telling you, Alex, it *won't* work.'

'But what makes you so sure?' How he wanted to add, 'But it *will* work. I know for a fact it will.'

'It never has, I mean, every time I get close to someone, something happens and ... things get difficult. And I really can't face going through all that again.'

He studied her unhappy face. 'Sounds like you're an old campaigner? Just how many times have you been "close" to someone?'

She tutted impatiently. 'There you go again! Why is it that men can carry on as much as they like, but a woman's thought of as cheap, or a tart, if she so much as - '

'Whoa! Point taken. Sorry!' he exclaimed, holding his hands up in surrender. 'You're right, and I didn't mean it to come out that way. But I need to know. Like I said, I do have my reasons. So what happens? Are you the one who gets hurt? Is that why you're afraid of trying again?'

'No, not really. And why do you need to know? What are these "reasons" you keep going on about?'

Ignoring her questions, he speculated, 'Then it's the other person, all the men you've been ... involved with.'

'*All the men!* Honestly! You're making me sound like some kind of Mata Hari! And if you must know, for your information, there haven't been that many. And I wouldn't say exactly hurt. The few relationships I've had never really got that serious. I made sure of that.'

'You made sure?'

'Yes. *Now* are you satisfied?'

'Afraid not. You'll have to explain it to me a bit more. It sounds like you've got a problem with getting close to someone. Am I right? I need to know, Yvonne.'

'I'm not going to answer that. And will you *please* tell me what all this needing to know business is all about?'

'Well, let's put it like this.' He stood, walked around the coffee table, and came to sit next to her, his face so close to hers that she was surprised to notice what looked like tiny flecks of gold in the grey part of his eyes. Coming to her senses, she pushed herself further back and crossed her arms, shield-like, across her chest. He leant forward and gently but firmly uncrossed them. Taking both her hands in his, he looked straight into her anxious eyes, and said softly, 'Because, like you, I don't play games either. And I'll tell you right now that *I'm* already in too deep.'

He was much, much too close to her - in every way. Sounding almost desperate, she replied, 'But this is awful! You can't be. We've only known each other five minutes!'

'Long enough for me. And what's so awful about it?'

'You don't know me and … how can you tell? How can you be so sure? I mean, you can't be.'

'Oh yes I can. And you'll just have to take my word for it.'

She was incredulous. 'But how on earth - '

'Actually, it's got more to do with Heaven than earth,' he interrupted, smiling.'

If she had felt perplexed and anxious before, that was nothing to the way she was feeling now. She just could not think straight. His face was less than a foot away from hers - and getting closer. There was nothing left for it now; she would have to tell him her reason, and she had better be quick about it. She spoke in a rush. 'Okay, you win. I'll tell you why I decided not to have any more relationships.'

He leant back, giving her space, but still holding her hands.

'If we did get … close ... then I'd end up doing my usual, and running away. That's what always happens, and it would happen again. I'd find some excuse, and I'd be off. I just can't help it. And you, nor anyone else, would be able to stop me. Don't you see? It's far better to stop now, before anything does … develop. I don't want to leave; I like it here. I've been searching for a place to settle down, and now you've come along … just when I thought I was okay. I just can't, *I mustn't* get involved with you - or anyone.'

She tried to pull her hands away, but his grip became firmer. Now it was his turn to sound incredulous. 'You run away?'

'Yes. And I'll do it again if you don't leave me alone. Now please let go of my hands!'

But he persisted, 'Why? What are you scared of?'

'*Alex!* You've got no right to ask me. I've already told you more than I've ever told anybody else. You'll just have to believe me ... this is for the best. Now, will you *please* let go of my hands!'

He released them slowly, his mind racing to grapple with this new, unexpected problem. 'You can't help it? So, are you saying that it's a ... a sort of self-preservation thing?'

Bowing her head, she answered in almost a whisper. 'Yes, but not just for my sake. It's more for the sake of anyone who...who's unfortunate enough to get involved with me.'

He could almost physically feel her discomfort; there was so much sadness there, so much hopelessness. Now he was filled with compassion and guilt, knowing that he had forced her to reveal what she had tried so hard to keep hidden. He reached over to kiss her tenderly on the forehead, and with a voice full of emotion, said softly, 'Oh Yvonne, Yvonne. I'm sorry.'

The touch of his lips on her skin and the tone of his voice were too much. This was unknown territory, and she was scared, and now dangerous tears were beginning to form behind her eyes. How had things backfired like this? All she had wanted to do was to warn him off, but instead, somehow, she had only succeeded in drawing him closer! She almost pleaded, 'Please, I must go.'

He stood and took a few steps back. This needed some serious prayer. 'Alright. And thank you for being so honest with me. I appreciate it. I can see how hard you found it.'

'I'm really sorry, Alex.'

'No need to apologise. You've done nothing wrong, sweetheart. We'll just have to think again.' He smiled at her reassuringly, then glanced at the clock. 'Right, give me a minute, I've got to check on something upstairs, and then let's get you back to the Inn.'

*

He made an effort to lighten the atmosphere on the journey back, but she was only able to reply in monosyllables. She almost leapt out of the car when they arrived and hurried to retrieve her shopping from the back seat, saying, in what she hoped was a matter-of-fact tone, 'Thanks for the outing. I'm sure the Manor will look great when everything's done. Bye for now then.'

But he was not to be dismissed so easily, and called after her, 'Hey, hang on a minute!'

Reluctantly, she turned to face him. *When* was this going to end? 'Yes?'

The car's dim interior light revealed the strain on her face, and again his heart went out to her. 'It's been a good day, despite everything, and thanks once again for your help. Now, listen to me Yvonne, I want you to know that everything's going to be fine; things will work out for you here. So, don't you even think of leaving. Okay?'

Puzzled, she nodded, and managed a not very convincing, 'Alright.'

Firmer now, he said, 'I mean it, Yvonne. No running away!'

'I ... I can't promise.'

'But you'll try?'

She nodded.

'Well then, guess that'll have to do.'

She turned and walked away. As far as she was concerned, the matter was settled, the deed was done. It had to be. If only her heart didn't feel as heavy as her bags.

*

Donald was in the kitchen, stooping and staring at something in one of the ovens. His sinuses were still playing up and his head ached. He turned his head slowly as she entered. Spotting the bulging bags, he said conversationally, 'Ah, you're back! Dinner won't be long. Bought anything nice?'

'Just some books, wool, things like that.'

'Going to make a woolly jumper? You'd better get on with it; more snow's on the way.'

'No, a quilt.'

'Very nice. For your bottom drawer?'

She had reached the door to the staff stairs, and turned to reply, curtly, 'No! Definitely not.'

'Ah!' Now what type of a reaction was that? Georgy would know if she was here. Sometimes he couldn't fathom these youngsters out at all.

Realising that she had sounded a bit too abrupt, she added, 'I'll give it to a friend if it turns out alright, for her bottom drawer. And, if you don't mind, Donald, I'd like to skip dinner tonight; I've had a good lunch.'

'Righty-o! Oh, nearly forgot, the couple in room eleven have booked early morning tea for quarter to six.'

'Okay, well, good night.' She climbed the stairs wearily and thought how pitiless life could be sometimes. Here she was, feeling sorry for herself and needing a proper night's sleep, and now she would have to set her alarm even earlier, just so that she could make that all important cup of tea for some complete strangers. She had left her room nine hours before, determined to discover if her suspicions about Alex Grant were real or imaginary. Then, she had known exactly what she wanted - or rather - did not want. Now she was utterly confused. His frankness and concern had weakened her resolve, and she had ended up revealing private, disturbing things. At least now she knew just how fragile her defences were when it came to him. Somehow, she would have to forget how quietly thrilled she had felt when he said that he liked her, he liked her 'a lot', and how her heart had leapt when he told her that he was 'already in too deep'. She must be careful - extra careful - from now on. This was bad. This was very, very bad. Or was it? Of course it was!

*

Despite the disappointing end to the day, Alex felt a sense of peace and assurance as he drove back to Rosedale. He should have known that it wasn't going to be easy. What was it Charles had said - something about, 'the devil being busy on the inside when God was building a church'? For a split second, he wondered if he had been guilty of manipulating circumstances, and if so, maybe by too much. Then he remembered the few positive sounding remarks she had made, guarded though they had been. That 'maybe' of hers about already being in too deep was encouraging, and she had clearly, even emphatically, stated that she had found what he had told her about his faith 'wonderful'. She had even managed to confess that she found him 'very attractive'. He had seen the way she looked at him when she thought he was looking elsewhere; those were not the looks of someone disinterested - quite the opposite! No, he could truthfully say that he had not forced the issue - maybe encouraged, possibly eased it open a bit - but not forced.

Another of Charles's frequent quotes came to mind: 'Our faith is lived in the present, but oftentimes we only come to understand the whys and wherefores of parts of our walk with Him when we look back.' The living bit could be tricky, especially at times like this, but he knew that the time of understanding would come. What was the point of having a faith if you were never given the opportunity to use it? And somehow, he felt a real peace about the situation. He had no doubt now, that one day, he would be able to tell her how he had known all along that they were meant to be together. And he was already looking forward to that day - very much.

CHAPTER 24

Throughout the coming weeks the weather was to dominate everyday life for those living in that part of the Highlands. The prevailing winds drove heavy clouds before them which opened to spill vast quantities of snow onto the whole area. Animals, that been allowed out to graze, were brought back into the safety and warmth of indoor shelters. There were days when all but the most desperate, or foolhardy, ventured any distance out of doors, and small communities soon found themselves isolated from the outside world.

Much to everyone's relief, all the main utilities remained unaffected at the Inn, although the daily deliveries of milk and mail became sporadic. Overnight temperatures fell to well below freezing, and the morning stillness would often find Yvonne gazing out, spellbound, at the silent beauty around them. Another pair of eyes, although of a more anxious kind, regularly scanned the near and distant slopes for any sign of Rabbie's brown and lumbering form. Donald was earnestly willing the stag to find enough food and shelter to see this current spell of inclement weather through. If only he could shake off this uneasy feeling that something bad had happened to him; what a fuss he would make of the old boy when he did eventually show up.

*

Around twelve noon on the first day of this dangerously beautiful time, a heavily equipped Land Rover belonging to the Hydro-Electric Board, came to a none too graceful stop outside. The two surveyors, who stomped and stamped their snow-clad boots into reception two minutes later, had left Strathlochy earlier that morning, hoping to outrun the storm. However, they had been caught out, and skidded more times than they cared to remember. Greatly relieved at coming across the Inn, common sense prevailed, and they wisely elected to take refuge until the worst was over.

*

Flora had been told to stay away for the duration, and Yvonne sorely missed her company. If she had expected to be given a reduced workload, then she could not have been more mistaken, for Georgina decided that this would be the perfect opportunity, 'to give the place a good going over'. Thus, she found herself being just as busy as ever as she embarked upon giving the Inn a thorough spring clean. Georgina encouraged Donald 'to tidy-up the bar', as she worked methodically through the office and reception area before attacking the flat, much to his dismay.

Although Yvonne would have run a mile from being a full-time cleaner at any other time or place, she found herself actually enjoying the work. The hours she spent alone passed quickly enough with the aid of her radio, whenever she could pick up a signal. She took pains to avoid the station broadcasting an endless stream of love songs; let others wallow in romantic longings and fantasies, or pine away with broken hearts. It was a mug's game, and she, for one, was glad to be out of the whole sorry mess.

Whenever it was calm enough outside, she would wrap up warmly, select her favourite stick from the collection kept for guests' use in reception, and venture outside for a short walk. For the first few minutes she would take long, deep breaths, imagining her lungs emptying of the cloying effects of the bleach she had been inhaling all morning, then filling with the purer, crisper air. The loch was her favoured destination, and she would often stand beside its frozen edge, trying to detect any movement through the thick layer of ice. At times, especially on brighter days, its dark surface would reflect a lighter grey. Grey, like someone's eyes.

The evenings also passed quickly, thanks to her plentiful supply of wool, reading material, and some challenging jigsaws. Her latest letter to Sandra and Tom was gradually turning into a major essay. She wrote how thankful she was that Niall's departure had been so timely; there was no doubt in her own mind that he would have been even more unbearable in these more restricted circumstances. Thank God they had been spared! She gave Alex the usual, cursory mention; better to keep referring to him as being just another local, and no one special, for that is who, and what, he must remain. She would often wonder how the weather was affecting the work at the Manor. He had sounded confident about Conroy's ability to carry on; but even if their wagon was able to get there, could concrete, plaster and paint dry in such conditions? Sometimes the ground was treacherous, especially when it rained over the layers of ice. He must be finding it hard to take even a few steps outside; it was difficult enough for her, and she was able-bodied. Then she would scold herself for spending just a bit too much time thinking about someone who was probably far more capable of looking after himself than most. What an idiot she was!

Curiosity had led her to borrow a *Gideon New Testament* from one of the guest rooms, and she had acquired the habit of reading a few pages each night before turning off her light. Now, instead of reliving and fretting over that last scene with Alex, or wondering if Niall had contacted Maggie, she would find herself drifting off to sleep thinking about what she had just read.

*

The wind changed direction on the tenth night of their enforced isolation, and by noon the thermometer showed that the temperature had gone up by a full ten degrees. She had just finished laying the tables for lunch when she noticed the surveyors talking to someone outside. The man had his back to her, and looked all too familiar, and judging by the look on the surveyors' faces, he was not giving them good news. In fact, Alex was advising the men to stay where they were; the forecast for the next few days was bad, and the roads further north were still impassable. He hinted broadly that the local crofters and tractor-owning farmers would not take too kindly to being called upon to risk their own lives and equipment on rescuing people who had been foolish enough to leave such a safe refuge.

The small group headed for the door. Alex spotted her and waved. She waved back and went to wait in reception, grasping the end of one of the long plaits she had frivolously styled her hair in that morning. Deeply embarrassed, and feeling like a silly schoolgirl, she smiled coyly as he entered, and was rewarded with such a brilliant, almost gleeful smile back that she felt uncertain how to respond. Was he really *that* pleased to see her? He removed his sunglasses, and she noticed how clear and bright his eyes were, even his skin seemed to glow with a slight tan.

Hoping to sound welcoming, she said, 'Hello Alex. You look well. Have you been away?' and immediately felt even more ridiculous. Of course he had not been away; no one had been away!

He laughed. 'Chance would be a fine thing! I've been shovelling snow and must have caught the sun. Actually, I've just been telling your guests here that there's more on the way.'

Donald emerged from the kitchen after hearing voices and was obviously delighted to see a different face. Lunch was just about to be served and he insisted that Alex be their guest. Alex had intended to leave as soon as he had seen Yvonne, but changed his mind when he learned that everyone, including her, would be eating together. The snow chains on his tyres had done a good job at getting him around that morning and should get him back safely. It would be worth the risk if he could spend a bit more time with her; she was looking cute enough to eat.

Donald returned to the kitchen as Georgina appeared. She led the small party into the dining room, instructing Alex to sit next to her as she made the introductions. He was disappointed to see Yvonne take a seat at the opposite end of the table, flanked on either side by the surveyors.

Donald reappeared and began to ladle generous portions of soup into bowls. 'I'm afraid it's nothing fancy, all tinned. You've probably heard that we've lost our chef? Yours truly is back on K.P.'

'Tinned rations are fine by me,' Alex replied, 'and yes, I did hear something. Dot tells me that Maggie's still struggling to come to terms with things. Let's hope you'll be able to get someone who's a bit more reliable next time; more of a teamplayer.' He glanced at Yvonne, and was just in time to see the merest flicker of a frown cross her face.

Georgina spoke up sharply. 'I've instructed the Labour Exchanges in Beaulane and Starold to send us some suitable candidates when the roads are clear.' Then, keen to change the subject, went on to ask, 'Things must have come to a full stop at the Manor?'

'For the time being, and we expected delays like this,' replied Alex. 'Actually, it's been useful in giving me more time to concentrate on a project I've been working on lately.'

The soup served, Donald put down the ladle and began to blow his nose noisily. Peering over his handkerchief, he asked, 'Project, eh?'

'Yes. Mainly to do with researching alternative types of work for our younger guests. It would be good to be able to spark some interest in them, especially those who feel they've come to a dead end. It's turning out to be a big job.'

There was just a hint of sarcasm in Georgina's voice, as she asked, 'Work! Surely you don't plan on becoming some sort of employment agency as well?'

'No, but it would be good to help them realise that there could be other options for them out there.'

Donald finished wiping his nose. 'Well, if you don't mind me saying so, I think you're a fine example. From soldier to, what, convalescent home owner? Pretty imaginative, I'd say.'

Alex raised a tumbler of peat-tinted water in his direction. 'Kind of you to say so, sir. The re-mustering side of things is something I'm particularly keen on.'

The subject changed to the weather conditions, and the meal progressed as the small group continued to chat amiably amongst themselves. They were an eclectic mix of souls: a couple in their late fifties, biding their time managing a Highland inn; two surveyors, temporarily stranded en route to some distant loch, which would be changed forever as a result of their report; an ex-soldier, now dedicated to helping others with the same help he had received; and a young woman, determined to stay where she was and settle down - and especially to remain single.

Alex would have enjoyed the lunch far more if he had been allowed to sit next to Yvonne, but at least from this vantage point he was able to observe the admiring glances the younger surveyor regularly cast in her direction. He was relieved to notice that she did not respond, but then, she wouldn't - The Boss never made mistakes.

The conversation turned to photography when he admired the large framed print of Rabbie, hanging on the opposite wall.

Donald became animated. 'That's one of Robert's. He took it a few years back. Great one of Rabbie isn't it? I don't suppose you've come across him recently, or heard if he's been seen anywhere around?'

'No, can't say I have. But that's an exceptionally good study.'

Donald smiled affectionately at the picture. 'One of my favourites.'

Alex remained silent for a while, deep in thought, before saying speculatively, 'You know, the Manor's going to have a lot of bare walls, and I think something like that,' he gestured towards the photograph, 'would look great; a local character in a local setting. I don't suppose - '

'You'd like a copy?' interjected Donald, hopefully.

'Well, yes. That is if you've got a spare print, or even the negative?'

'Ah! Not sure now. We did have some of his earlier stuff around the place, but I've got a feeling he had a clear-out when he was last here.'

Hoping to be helpful, Yvonne joined in the conversation. 'There's a lot of photos in that tallboy in the staff room.'

'Really?' Georgina exclaimed. 'He must have put them there himself. I do wish he'd have told us; anyone could have got their hands on them.' Patting the frizzy tuft of hair, and looking sternly across at Donald, she added, 'And I think we ought to consult him before we let anything go.'

'Naa! He won't mind, why should he? Especially if the negatives are there. I know he took several portfolios away with him, so he can't be that fussed about the rest. Tell you what, why don't you run up after lunch and take a look

Yvonne? Or, better still, why don't you go as well Alex? See if there's anything that takes your eye?'

Georgina muttered something incomprehensible before sighing with resignation, and saying, 'Have it your way dear, but I'll be telling him anyway.'

A dessert of tinned fruit and evaporated milk followed. Coffee was being served when Yvonne, who had been feeling tense since Donald had suggested that Alex went with her, stood abruptly, and announced that she would go and see what she could find, adding, 'Why don't you stay down here Alex? It'll be cold up there.'

But he was having none of it, and grabbing the small packet he had walked in with, insisted on accompanying her. Which he did.

CHAPTER 25

Both remained silent as they made their way through the kitchen and up the staff stairs. Yvonne found she could hardly breathe; the thought of being alone with Alex again was nerve-racking. He was more confident, and hoping that this was going to be another of those God-given opportunities he had been waiting and praying for.

She showed him into a fairly large room filled with an odd assortment of furniture which had obviously seen better days. One wall was dominated by an impressively high tallboy, another by a table on which a large jigsaw was nearing completion. The rest of the room was taken up by three small armchairs and a two-seater settee facing a radiogram and a television set. The room felt cold and unfriendly, and he tried to imagine her sitting there alone at night, crocheting and watching the television; a solitary figure.

She knelt to light the gas fire. 'Don't expect we'll be in here long, but I'll light it anyway.'

'Okay. So how've you been?'

The flame leapt into life. 'Oh, you know, alright.' She turned the gas down, 'Been kept busy with spring cleaning.' She stood, walked over to the tallboy, and began pulling open the top drawer, obviously struggling.

'That looks heavy, here, let me,' he said, going towards her.

'No, it's okay, I can manage,' she replied, reaching up on tiptoe to peer in.

He sat on the nearby armchair, and asked, 'Those two likely lads aren't being a nuisance, are they?'

The drawer contained piles of old faded linen. 'Who do you mean?' she asked, closing it. 'Not the surveyors?' The next drawer contained more of the same.

'Well, yes. That young one's got his eye on you.'

She turned to look at him with obvious surprise. 'You're joking! He's ... they're both married. Their wives are always phoning up. And anyway, he's a family man; he's got two children.'

'Not always a deterrent.'

Surely he wasn't accusing her of flirting, or even worse - and with a married man! Jamming her hands into her waist, she asked, 'What are you saying? That I've been egging him on - or something?'

'No, not consciously.'

'What then, unconsciously?'

Taking no notice of the alarm bells that were beginning to ring in his head, he replied, 'Hey, let's face it, you've all been cooped up here for days; it's only human nature.'

She was scandalised. '"Human nature!" Well then, let me tell you, *Mr* Grant, that it's not in my *human* nature to egg anyone on, married or not! And you've got a short memory, after...what I told you the other day. How could you even *think* that I'd do such a thing, consciously or unconsciously? He's, they're both, you know ... just being friendly.'

Those bells were ringing loudly now; still he ignored them. 'So you haven't noticed the way he looks at you?'

'No, I certainly have not!'

'Well, you can take it from me, he certainly does! And I can't say that I blame him.'

She chose to ignore that last remark. 'But ... I had no idea! Are you sure?'

'Oh yes!'

'Anyway, even if you're right, there's no way I'd do anything about it. Apart from anything else, it wouldn't be right. It would be ... unprofessional; he's a guest.'

'Maybe so. But I don't think there's any law against it.' Now he did take notice of the bells, and felt annoyed with himself for persisting when it was obvious that she had been offended. Embarrassed, he picked up his stick and started to poke the end into a threadbare patch of carpet. 'At least now you're aware of it. And I certainly wasn't accusing you of behaving improperly.' He looked up. 'Pretty stupid of me. I'm sorry Yvonne. No excuse; I was well out of order. Friends again?'

She sighed and relaxed. There, he was doing it again, challenging and upsetting her, and then sounding really sincere when he apologised and tried to make peace. What was it about this man that had the ability to arouse such strong feelings in her? Why couldn't she just laugh his comments off, or dismiss them as not being worth fretting over? And why did it bother her that he could even *think* things like that about her?

'Well okay, apology accepted,' she said.

The next drawer contained dozens of picture frames that had been carelessly stacked, causing several pieces of glass to shatter. 'Looks like we're getting close,' she remarked. She opened the last drawer, and was relieved to find several boxes of slides and a large pile of loose photographs and negatives. 'Bingo!' she exclaimed, kneeling down to take a closer look.

She was very close to him now, her face level with his, and it wasn't long before he found his whole attention shifting from the drawer's contents and onto her. How could he ever have dismissed her as not being worth a second look? He must have been blind! Magnanimously, he even felt a twinge of sympathy for the young surveyor who was obviously attracted to her. Her hair was doing that wispy thing around her face again; he would give a hundred pounds to be able to touch one of those curls, especially the one touching the corner of her mouth.

Yvonne was only too aware of his closeness and was doing her best to concentrate on her task. She began to feel warm all over, and not just because of the growing heat from the fire. Her skin seemed to have taken on a life of its own, she could sense every nerve ending, vibrant and expectant; somehow she knew that he was going to kiss her. And she also knew that she wanted him to. But she must stop this, it was madness! If she didn't do something about it this very instant, then she would have no one to blame but herself.

On automatic now, she uncovered a large photograph and recognised Rabbie's erect figure, standing proud, with the evening sun casting a pink glow on the slopes of Ben An-t-

Earrach in the background. She held the photograph up and turned to face him. 'This looks like the one downstairs. What do you think? Do you want it?' He was staring intently at her. She held her breath as he reached out and slowly stroked her cheek with the back of his hand, before taking a piece of her hair and coiling it between his fingers.

'Yes, I want it. It's just the one I want,' he said slowly. There was no mistaking his meaning, but in case she had, he leaned the last few inches towards her and began to kiss her gently, but firmly, on the mouth. And she let him.

The kiss was shattering. The photograph fell from her hand as his mouth pressed down harder on hers. She liked the feeling, very much. She closed her eyes and turned her body towards him, allowing him to draw her closer. She knew she should be pushing him away, but instead she found her arms going up and grasping the back of his jacket. One of his arms was around her waist and he began to caress the back of her head with the other, making it impossible for her to stop herself from responding. He felt her melt against him, and was almost overcome with his want of her - his need of her. Now he knew that he was a lost man; no matter what she said or did from this moment on, for him, there would be no turning back, no retreat. He had kissed many women - too many - but never had he wanted to kiss one the way he wanted to kiss her now.

At last, their lips parted, and he gently pushed her head onto his shoulder as he continued to stroke her back as gently as if she was a new born baby. His voice was full of desire as he spoke, 'Yvonne, Yvonne, I've been wanting to do that so badly.'

When she did not reply, he tilted her head towards him and kissed her again, thoroughly. She swayed slightly, and he had to use both arms to steady her. Time passed. Eventually, he nuzzled against her smooth, hot face, and spoke softly in her ear, 'Oh my Good Lord, Oh My Lord! You feel it too, I can tell. We must be together. You know that don't you?'

At last, she found her breath and her voice. 'Yes, but ... I wish I didn't.'

'Why?'

'You know why! I told you ... my decision.'

He gave a small, dismissive laugh. 'Oh that! Now don't worry sweetheart. In a way, I'm glad you made it, especially if it helped to keep you away from other men.' He kissed her cheek, her forehead, and was about to kiss her again, and would have, if she had not found the strength to pull away.

'No! We can't do this. It won't change things.'

Even as she objected, part of her was willing him to say something, to *do* something - *anything* - to show her that she was wrong, that this time it really would be different. But then, didn't she already know that it was different? No man had ever kissed her like that - and how she had wanted him to.

He held her at arm's length, studying her troubled face. He knew that there was real happiness waiting for them, but now it was beginning to sound as though that decision of hers could become more than just a passing nuisance. 'Alright, then maybe we should talk about it. You don't have to go back to work right now, do you?'

'Soon, but I've already told you enough - why I had to make it.' She hesitated, then risked looking up into his searching eyes. 'And when I came here, I was determined that it wasn't going to happen again, but ... then ...'

'Then I came along?'

She nodded. How could she tell him what affect he had upon her? She had never spoken intimate, private words to any man; she had never wanted to; and anyway, they just didn't seem to be in her vocabulary. Nor could she tell him how frightened she felt, and not only for her own sake, but for his too. There would be nothing but pain ahead for them both if she did not put a stop to this - and right now.

He repeated, 'Then I came along ... and did this.' He took her face in his hands and kissed her again, wanting his lips to convey to her something of what was in his heart. His first two kisses had taken her breath away, but the one he gave her now was full of such tenderness that every part of her felt awed with the wonder of it.

When they parted, he raked his hands roughly through his hair, and said, 'Oh Lord! We've got to stop.' He stood slowly and moved over to the settee. 'But we need to get this sorted out. Tell me a bit more about this decision, and how long have you've had the ... problem?'

The kisses had left her feeling woolly headed, and she felt like going away somewhere private to curl up and bath in the unfamiliar glow that had worked its way through her body. She sat back on her heels and looked at him, knowing instinctively that he would take whatever she said, and handle it - handle her - with care. Now how on earth did she know that? Resuming her search through the prints, she replied, half-heartedly, 'I don't really know. I think ... a long time.'

'You can't remember when you first became aware that there was something ... not quite right?'

'Well, maybe sometime after my mother died. I couldn't seem to settle anywhere, and just kept moving. I suppose it just became a habit.' Willing him to understand, she looked up at him again, and said with a voice full of anguish, 'I know I'm repeating myself, but can't you see? If I do get involved with you, it would only happen all over again. Then I'll have to pack my bags and leave; I won't be able to stop myself. And I'm so tired of being the one who's always doing the leaving.'

He hesitated, then reached over to take her hands in his. 'How old were you when your mother died?'

'Sixteen.'

'So young. And what about your father?'

'What about him?'

'Well, you said the other day that he went back to Wales. When did he go?'

'Six weeks after my mother died.'

'Six weeks! And you didn't go with him?'

'No.'

'Why not?'

She hesitated, beginning to grow anxious about where this line of questioning could be leading, then answered, 'We didn't really get on. And look, I really don't want to discuss this now. But I will tell you that my father ... that he wasn't ... I mean, he wasn't much of a family man.'

'No happy childhood then?'

She laughed mirthlessly. 'Er, no.'

'So, you left King's Lynn and hit the road. Where did you go?'

'Oh, you know, the coast, seasonal work. Mainly in hotels and holiday camps. Anything that gave me a roof over my head. And I did stay longer in some until … until …'

'Until you got involved with someone?'

She shrugged. 'Maybe.'

'And as soon as things got serious, you moved on?'

Now she'd had enough, he had hit her boundary. She pulled her hands away, and said firmly, 'Okay, Einstein! I don't need you to tell me that I've got a problem with commitment, and that it all stems from my childhood. And what's wrong with me wanting to do something about it? I think I was acting responsibly to make that decision.' She started to gather up the prints, and then said in a more conciliatory tone, 'Anyway, seemed like the right thing to do at the time.'

He gave a half smile. 'And now?'

Seconds passed before she was able to reply, 'Probably, and I know you'll thank me for it … one day.'

He looked askance. 'Is that right? Well then, believe me, no. No, I won't. Look sweetheart, I'm no expert on this kind of thing, but it sounds to me as though you made a type of vow, and you're not giving yourself permission to be free of it. I reckon that all we have to do is to find a way for you to do that, and be … released.'

She was silent for a while, then said thoughtfully, 'But what if I don't want to be released?'

'Oh, I think you do,' he replied softly, his body still feeling the after-effects of their obviously mutually enjoyable embrace.

'But how do you know that I'm not doing the right thing, for myself and for…others?'

'Believe me, I know. And remember, this involves me now, and I can't accept that. I *won't* accept that.'

Something in her was glad that he was not prepared to let go, and for a few moments she allowed herself to think about reversing her decision, to, how had he put it…to be 'released'? After all, she'd had no notion that such a man even existed when she had made it. Maybe she could take the risk, this one, last time? Maybe, by some miracle, it might work out, and she could settle down and be normal at last. Why shouldn't she allow herself to free fall into his open arms? She wanted to. She really wanted.

But she was not allowed to bask in the warm glow of such feelings for long, for like some awful, persistent echo, the poisonous mantra began to pour once again into her mind:-

Doley, Doley. Remember, you're nothing but a nuisance. You'll never amount to anything. Good for nothing; never were, never will be. Sneaking in through a hole like that. Taking up someone else's space. You're a waste of time. Just you remember … remember …

Unable to block out the venomous words, she turned away, knowing it was useless - she was useless. With a voice full of dismay, she asked, 'But what if I can't be released? What if I'm stuck?'

He had watched the bleak, hopeless expression come into her eyes, and asked, 'Is that how you feel?'

She nodded.

'Then we'll have to find a way of getting to the root cause of those feelings - and get them dealt with.'

The *we* was not lost on her. So he was not letting go, not yet.

He was determined to find out more. It was in his nature to do battle with anything he believed to be unjust or downright wrong, but now he felt a growing awareness that he would have to tread carefully. He might do more harm than good if he persisted in wading in and stirring up some obviously very troubled waters. The problem might need far more sensitive handling than he was capable of. If he had any sense, he would stop probing and step back right now, or there might be a real risk that he could push her too far and she would carry out her threat and take flight.

'Right. Look, this is a bit out of my depth, but if there was someone who could help, would you be willing to have a chat with them?'

'What, like a psychiatrist or something?'

'Not exactly.'

'Who then?'

'Do you remember me telling you what a mess I was in before I met Charles?'

'Yes.'

'And how he helped me by listening, and letting me talk things through?'

'I remember. Oh, I see! You think I should talk to him?'

'Well, why not? Worth a try isn't it?'

She looked up and into his hopeful expression. It had been difficult enough to talk about such deep, personal things to him, but the thought of confiding in a complete stranger, especially one who just happened to be such a good friend of his, was unthinkable. 'But won't he have enough to do when he gets here? I'm sure I'd just be wasting his time.'

Alex had expected this evasive type of reaction, and had learned, through his own experience, that just being willing was half the battle - and a battle that he was trying so carefully now to show her that she might have to fight. He persevered, 'I think there'd be no harm in getting it checked out. And if you don't fancy talking to Charles, then how about his wife? She's a trained counsellor too, and I'm sure she'd be just as willing to have a chat with you.'

Yvonne dug her heels in. 'I know you're only trying to help Alex, and I appreciate it, but I'd rather not, if you don't mind.'

'You know Yvonne, you'd have no problem accepting help if you'd broken an arm, or a leg, would you? It's like that with emotional problems, sometimes we all need a bit of help to get them ... straightened out ... untangled.'

She knew he was talking sense, but still something in her would not allow her to even contemplate taking such a risk.

'Thanks for trying, but I'd rather leave things as they are. I know it's for the best, honestly.' She stood and walked towards the door. 'Anyway, I think we'd better get back; we've found what we came for. I'll come and tidy up later.'

'Yvonne.'

'Yes.'

'I get the message. But will you at least think about it?'

She did not need persuading. Of course she would think about it. How could she not? She replied half-heartedly, 'Alright, but I'm not promising anything.'

'Then that's all I need to hear. And you know sweetheart, everything will sort itself out in time, one way or another. I know it will.'

'There you go again!' she said, sounding exasperated. 'Why do you keep saying things like that?'

He went to stand beside her and began to twist a tendril of her hair around his finger. 'I'll tell you all about it one day, but not today. And you do agree, don't you, that it would be daft for us to ignore each other - and pretend that we don't want any more of these?' He kissed her again, lightly this time, and so tenderly. 'And God knows all about it. We can trust Him to help us. Ah now, that reminds me.' He bent to pick up the packet he had brought up with him from the chair. 'I meant to give this to you after we'd been to Strathlochy.'

She took the small package from his hand and opened it. It was a book. Embossed in gold letters on its brown cover were the words:-

Good News for Modern Man
The New Testament in Today's English Version

'A Bible! Thank you.'

'My pleasure, and it's just the New Testament.'

Her apprehensive look had melted away by now and had been replaced by a more relaxed expression. 'Thank you Alex. I promise I'll read it.' It was on the tip of her tongue to tell him about the small *Gideon* beside her bed, but she felt strangely shy about doing so.

'Atta girl!'

'Are you two alright up there? Have you found anything?' Like an unwanted visitor, Georgina's shrill voice broke into the room.

Yvonne called back, 'Just coming.'

But Alex was still not ready to let her go, and asked, 'Can I telephone you?'

'Er, I don't know.'

'Yes you do. No games, remember?'

She sighed. 'It's not that easy.'

'Why?'

'The office is locked at night. I have to use the one outside.'

'Can't you use one in reception?'

'Well - '

'We can arrange a time.'

She tried to think, which was hard because she liked the way he was stroking her back. Evenings were difficult, but the reception area was usually deserted by the time she went out for her afternoon walk. Donald had finished in the kitchen by then and had joined Georgina in the flat. The surveyors usually retired to their own rooms after lunch, and would not reappear until well into the afternoon.

'I suppose you could try at two, at least while the weather's like this.'

'That'll do. Alright, we'll give it a go.' He released her reluctantly. She bent to pick up the photograph of Rabbie. 'What about this?'

He took it from her and studied it. 'I'll leave it, it's too badly creased. Let's hope the negative's here. You know, I've got fond memories of this old fella.'

'Why's that?'

'He's part of the team too. Remember, that day we met? And he's the reason we're up here now.'

'Don't you bring that up again, or I really will make you tell me what all that shouting in the heather was all about!'

He laughed as he stooped to kiss the top of her head. 'And as for the answer to that mystery, my love, you will also have to wait.'

'Oh no! Not another mysterious thing you just *happen* to know.' Now he had called her his 'love', there was so much for her to think about - so much.

*

They found Georgina loitering near the desk when they walked into reception.

'Any joy?' she asked, rather too sharply.

'Yvonne found the photo, but it was damaged,' replied Alex. 'She's kindly volunteered to go through the negatives.'

Georgina was determined to have the last say in this matter. 'I see. Well, I'll have to talk to Robert about it, but I wouldn't be surprised if he's got plans for them all when he comes back.'

'Fair enough,' Alex said, not feeling inclined to make an issue out of something which he considered to be a trivial matter. 'Now, how much do I owe you for lunch?'

Satisfied that she had reclaimed some territory, Georgina decided to be gracious. Patting her frizz, and pretending mock horror, she exclaimed, 'Goodness me, I wouldn't hear of it! You were our guest after all.'

'That's very kind of you, Georgina. Right, I'd better be making a move; it's not looking too good out there. Tell Donald that I'll listen out for any news of Rabbie.' Turning to Yvonne, he said, 'Two o'clock tomorrow, don't forget.'

She smiled and nodded.

He turned and left.

She watched the car pull away; the snow chains crunching noisily as they broke through the hard layer of ice.

CHAPTER 26

That evening, Yvonne found several photographs that Alex might like. The matching negatives were difficult to find, but she made a good effort. Satisfied, she prepared for bed early. She opened her New Testament, and because it was quite a short book, read the whole of *The Gospel of John* before turning off her light. She fell asleep almost immediately, but awoke in the early hours, and was unable to stop her mind from roaming undisciplined over the events of the previous day. She could almost feel again the thrill that had coursed through her when Alex had kissed her so passionately. How unexpectedly safe she had felt in his arms; and those fine, strong hands of his, tenderly touching and stroking her head and back. At last, common sense prevailed, and she told herself to stop being so pathetically romantic and stupid. Why, oh why hadn't she had the good judgment to move away from him before that first kiss? How could she ever look at him again, or even be anywhere near him, and remain detached when her own emotions and body refused to co-operate? If she carried on like this, then she would soon find herself having to say another 'goodbye'. Maybe it would have been better if she had left after all, but circumstances seemed to have conspired to keep her here. If only Niall hadn't lied; if only the snow hadn't arrived; if only replacement staff were easier to find; if only the season was not about to start; if only the MacMan's hadn't already begun to rely upon her … if only … if only … if only …

She turned over and tried to force all thoughts of Alex out of her mind, but had to give up after another long spell of concentrated effort. Something would have to be done if she was to get any more sleep. She switched on her light and began to read through *The Gospel of John* again, having felt that there had been something almost calming about it. But even now Alex invaded her mind: he was real, he was flesh and blood, sight and sound, taste and touch. Jesus was too vague: He was only to be found in the pages of a book; there was nothing real or solid about Him. Another hour passed, and still sleep evaded her. Maybe she should try to pray. Why not? It couldn't do any harm. She closed her eyes and clasped her hands together.

'Dear God, I mean, Jesus, Who art in Heaven. I'm so confused, but then, You already know that, because You're supposed to know everything.' She paused, wanting to add, 'If You do exist,' but felt that might sound a bit rude, so went on to ask, 'Please show me what to do about Alexander Grant. You know I really don't want to be the cause of any upset, especially as he's involved in such a worthwhile cause. And I'll only end up doing my usual and leaving if things do ... develop between us. And then the MacMan's wouldn't be too pleased at having to find someone else again so soon. I just want to do what's right for everybody's sake. So, if You could somehow sort things out, I'd be very grateful. Er, thank You very much. Amen.'

She felt more relaxed and even peaceful now; maybe she should try to pray more often. Sleep came soon after.

*

More snow fell during the night, and she awoke once again to a quiet, white world. She went down for breakfast and found Georgina in a state of agitation over a problem with the telephone. Donald was trying to pacify her, but obviously failing. 'The line must be down. We're lucky it didn't happen before now. Come on, Georgy, they'll sort it out before long, and there's nothing spoiling.'

Georgina replied irritably, 'Why don't they use stronger wires and put those poles in deeper? There must be something they could do to stop this from happening every time we get a bit of wind and snow. It really is too bad of them, leaving us to cope like this. And I *really* needed to call Robert today.'

'How long do you think it'll be before we're reconnected?' asked Yvonne.

'Days!' Georgina replied testily. 'And we've got to put up with this in the meantime.' She shook the instrument furiously, as though the action could somehow bring it back to life. 'I'm in two minds about paying the bill. They'd soon chivy themselves up if people turned awkward on them.'

*

Yvonne entered reception just before two o'clock that afternoon and was relieved to find the area deserted. Picking up the telephone receiver, she tried to convince herself that it would make no difference to her if the line was alive or dead. She heard only silence. Well, that was good, wasn't it? Now she would have more time to think about what to do about things. Yes, of course it was good.

*

The days passed, and Yvonne was kept busy in the usual manner, the only exception being that now she kept a wary eye on the young surveyor. Every so often she caught him looking at her with an odd expression on his face, which made her wonder if Alex had been right after all.

During the past few days she had begun to see some things a bit more clearly, and was becoming increasingly alarmed at the realisation that that decision of hers had gone so deep that she might actually need some sort of counselling to be free of it. And how strange that this ... thing with Alex had happened here and now, and that he just happened to know people who did that kind of counselling - the very people who would be here in just a few weeks' time. He had made it all sound so logical and matter-of-fact. But maybe it was. Maybe she should try a session or two; it might actually work. Wasn't she worth a try? No, probably not. But Alex, wasn't *he* worth a try?

However, whenever she reached this semi-positive state of mind, the poisonous mantra would rear its ugly head and insist on shouting such thoughts down. Recently she had been thinking more about it, and was beginning to recognise and analyse it for what it was: the toxic arrow of self-worthlessness her father had continuously shot into her throughout the first sixteen years of her life. Now she found herself becoming even more angry with the thing, as well as her father - but more especially with herself. Why had she allowed the destructive thing to dominate and spoil her life for so long? If only she

237

could control the fear that rushed in with it, the fear that it - he - might be right, and that, just by being here, she would almost certainly end up unnecessarily complicating and upsetting Alex's life too.

She stood back to cast a critical eye over the large family room she had been working on for most of the morning. Yes, it would pass muster. It was nearly lunchtime and there was no point in starting anything else. She sat on the stool and rested her elbows on the dressing table's polished surface. Propping her chin up in her hands, she closed her eyes and thought how exhausting all this self-analysis and mental toing and froing was; she was feeling quite worn out with it all. And then, without any conscious effort on her part, some words came into her mind:-

I am the way the truth and the life. (John 14:6).

Startled, she opened her eyes and stared at her reflection in the mirror. The words were somehow familiar. Overcome with curiosity, she went over to the bedside drawer and took out the *Gideon's Bible*. She returned to the stool and began skimming through the pages of *John's Gospel*. There they were: *Jesus answered, 'I am the way the truth and the life ...'* Good, strong words, sounding almost like a promise. Now she thought about it, wasn't that exactly what she had been searching for all this time - another way of life: a good, honest and truthful way? And not just to get by, or make do, or survive, but a really worthwhile, meaningful way of life? And now here was Jesus claiming that *He* was somehow that way - *the way*. But what about the other ways that people chose to live? What about all the decent, kind and hardworking people who never talked about God, or professed to have any kind of faith? And what about all those followers of other religions? Didn't 'All roads lead to Rome' anyway? Did it really matter what route, what way, a person came by - as long as they reached the same destination? She read on:-

No-one comes to the Father except through me.
(John 14:6).

So, Jesus was claiming to be *the* way to *the Father*.

And His father was God. Well, she supposed, with a Father like that, anyone would be satisfied!

She looked at her watch, still another five minutes to go before lunch. There had been something about a shepherd in the reading, and she had liked that. Now, where was it? She flicked quickly back through the pages, then her eye fell on a heading and the passage beneath:-

The Shepherd and His Flock

...I tell you the truth, I am the gate for the sheep. All who ever came before Me were thieves and robbers, but the sheep did not listen to them. I am the gate; whoever enters through me will be saved. He will come in and go out and find pasture. The thief comes only to steal and kill and destroy; I have come that they may have life, and have it to the full.

...I am the good shepherd. The good shepherd lays down his life for the sheep. I am the good shepherd; I know my sheep and my sheep know me - just as the Father knows me and I know the Father - and I lay down my life for the sheep. I have other sheep that are not of this sheep pen. I must bring them also. They too will listen to my voice, and there shall be one flock and one shepherd.

(John 10:7-11; 14-16).

She liked the imagery: Jesus was the gate, and everyone who went in through Him would be saved from the thief - that must mean the Devil. He promised to give life to those who entered through Him, but not just any old life, but life *to the full*. And He must have been referring to His death on the Cross when He said He was prepared to lay down His own life for his sheep - His followers. She wondered if Buddha, Confucius, or any other founder of any other religion had laid down their lives for their followers? Probably not. And even if they had, had they been resurrected? Not that she was aware of.

But why had He called Himself *the Truth?* That was a strange thing to call oneself. Was He saying that he was like some sort of Magna Carta, or Declaration of Independence? Nations had taken such noble, aspirational words, and used them as a foundation upon which to build their own societies. But wasn't that exactly what she needed - her own personal Magna Carta - some sort of firm foundation, something worthwhile and secure that she could build her own life upon? She was only too aware that she had not done a good job so far. In fact, it would be fair to say that her foundations were anything but firm, especially with regard to her working life, and most especially her relationships, which, apart from those with her mother and Sandra, had not been particularly healthy. Nor had she been able to carve out a decent career for herself. But then, even if she had, and if she had managed to have a few more meaningful relationships, could such things always be relied upon? Weren't they like everything in life - transient? Everybody and everything always came to an end. So what foundations had she been using to build her own life upon? Her own common-sense, intuition and wisdom; limited though they were? But she regularly made wrong choices, and even wisdom was subject to change: what was considered right and wise today, was often thought as wrong and foolish tomorrow. Now she thought about it, *really* thought about it, wouldn't it be more sensible, logical even, to change her focus - and put her trust in something, Someone - Someone steady? Someone who never changed? Someone eternal?

She had to admit that Jesus's claims at being *the way* and *the truth* were beginning to sound very appealing.

That just left His *life* claim. Then she recalled Alex describing how helpless and hopeless he had felt in hospital before becoming a committed Christian. He had said something about his new life having a real sense of purpose and fulfilment, even more than his old one, good though that had been. He was certainly a good advertisement for another way of life - this other *way*. By following Jesus's way and living by His truth, he seemed to be living a full life - a fulfilling life. What a difference there was between them both:

she, searching for a decent, settled life, and he, claiming to have found one.

And somehow, amazingly, and now she could hardly breathe as the incredible pieces began to slot into place, maybe it had been no coincidence that the two of them had met! Maybe they had been guided towards each other. If that was the case, and she had to admit that it did seem to make some sort of sense - did that mean that God was *interested in her too?* No, it couldn't be! But really, without luck or fate having a hand in it, what other way of looking at it was there?

She closed the book. This needed more thought, but she was already late for lunch. Time to stop thinking such unworldly thoughts and step back into the real world - or was it the real world? What if God was trying to get the message across to her that there really was another one: a better, happier and more fulfilling one - and that Jesus really was *the way* there?

She spent the rest of the day in a haze as she read and re-read the passages, searching for any other possible explanation. But no matter how hard she tried, she could find none.

*

The telephone became live again later that night, but no one was aware of it until it rang at nine o'clock sharp the next morning. Georgina sprang into life and returned soon after to announce, 'Looks like we'll be losing the surveyors tomorrow. Their head office reckons there's some clear places around. Shame really, they've been good company. Oh well, I'd better go and start totting-up their bill.'

*

At two o'clock Yvonne went into reception to wait for a call that might, or might not, come. She felt a bit edgy and jumped when it rang seconds later. 'Good afternoon. The Tananeach Inn. Can I help you?'

'You certainly can! Got you at last,' replied Alex.

Her heart leapt at the sound of his voice, and she tried to sound casual as she replied, 'Hello there Alex. How are you?'

'Much better now for hearing you. How is everyone?'

'Fine thanks, although Mrs Mac's been a bit fed up and starting to make sounds about cancelling the next ceilidh, but Donald reckons the worst is over.'

'He's right, the roads are almost clear this end. Right, listen-up, I can't be long, Dot's expecting a call. She's invited you over for tea tomorrow, and some bright spark's going ahead with showing a film in the church hall in the evening. Don't expect there'll be much of a turnout, but we could boost the numbers. How about it? You must be desperate to escape.' Then, in a softer timbre, added, 'And I *really* want to see you again.'

Part of her knew what she should be saying, but the other part seemed to win, when she heard her voice asking, 'What's the film?'

'*The Planet of the Apes* with Charlton Heston. Strange combination, but had some good reviews. Anyway, do you fancy it?'

'Go on then, you've talked me into it.'

He laughed. 'Don't tell me you're a Heston fan?'

'He's not bad, but I haven't seen a monkey for years.'

'Oh yes you have. How's he been? Behaving himself?'

It took her a few seconds to realise that he was talking about the surveyor. 'He's been no problem. Anyway, they're leaving tomorrow; apparently they're going to be flown to that place they were heading for before they got stranded here.'

'Excellent! By the way, how did you get on with the photos?'

'Okay, I've found some you might like along with what could be their negatives. Mrs Mac's spoken to Robert, and he's fine about it, but he says he'd like to sign any prints you do get developed.'

'Good idea. I'm looking forward to seeing them. But how about you? Have you managed to get out at all?'

'Only for short walks, usually around this time of day. It's so still out there. I keep looking around for any deer tracks, you know, Rabbie's. Don't suppose you've heard anything about him, have you?'

'Unfortunately not. There've been a few sightings of other stags, mainly in the forest areas, but no one seems to have spotted him.'

'How can they tell the difference?'

'Apparently he damaged his head during the rut some years ago, and ever since the antlers on that side grow at an odd angle. It's quite distinctive.'

'Donald says he's never known him to keep away this long before.'

'Hmm, I wouldn't be surprised if something has happened, but I hope I'm wrong. Now, getting back to tomorrow, okay to come and fetch you at half-past-four?'

'That should be fine. I'll meet you in reception.'

'Great. Right, I'd better ring off. Until tomorrow then.'

'Okay. See you then. And thanks for calling.'

'And thank you for answering! Now just you take care of your lovely self out there; I don't want anything to happen to you. Well, God bless you for now.'

She replaced the receiver thoughtfully. He really did have the knack of making her feel as though she was someone worth bothering about - as though she was someone precious.

Her progress along the loch shore was slower than usual that day. She paid little attention to her surroundings, so preoccupied was she with the realisation that, no matter how many times she promised herself that she would say 'No' to him, she was becoming aware that another part of her, and an increasingly dominant part of her, was wanting her to stay calm - and say 'Yes.'

CHAPTER 27

By half-past-four she was ready and waiting in reception, under her coat she was comfortably dressed in the cream Aran jumper and fitted dark green slacks she kept for best. Her hair was loose and provided extra warmth as it fell over her shoulders.

Georgina came through from the office. 'Hello Yvonne, going anywhere nice?' she asked.

'Just tea with the Tweedie's and then onto the film in the church hall.'

'It's still on then? Is Alex taking you?'

'Yes,' she replied, realising that from now on it would be common knowledge that she and Alex were seeing each other, and not just spending time on Manor business.

'Does Donald know you won't be in for dinner?'

'I told him earlier.'

'Are there any early morning teas booked?'

'Only one, at half-past-seven.' She spotted Alex's car approaching and headed for the door, eager to escape before being asked any more questions.

'Well, have a good evening. And say hello to Dot and Angus for me, would you. Oh, and by the way, tell them that we've decided to go ahead with the ceilidh.'

'Okay,' she called behind her.

Georgina watched them drive off before hurrying to discuss this new development with Donald, who was then obliged to spend a good part of the evening trying to reassure her that a date did not mean a marriage. However, from that time on, she decided to watch points very carefully; something in her bones told her that she had been right about those two all along. She felt more than a little peeved; the last thing she needed now was to start thinking about finding another general assistant as well as another chef. That was the trouble with employing young, single women, as soon as a man came on the scene, they were off. Give her an older woman any day, so much more reliable. Pity though, Yvonne had not struck her as being the type.

*

Yvonne remembered the Tweedie's from the ceilidh. Angus reminded her very much of Hamish, and it was no surprise to learn that they were first cousins. Dot was a cheerful, friendly soul, and the proud owner of a recent home perm that was destined to turn Georgina green with envy.

She was invited to sit at the table whilst Alex took charge of the teapot. Dot disappeared into the kitchen, reappearing a few minutes later with plates of scrambled eggs and the square, flat sausages that Yvonne had grown accustomed to. A selection of homemade cakes followed, including the obligatory shortbread, warmed to bring out its buttery taste. The couple were easy to get along with, and she soon found herself relaxing in their company. At regular intervals she looked around appreciatively at the quaint, old-fashioned surroundings, wondering if this was what a really settled home looked like.

*

They arrived at the church hall in good time and chose seats in the middle of the large room. Plenty of curious glances were cast in their direction. Alex appeared to know several people, some of whom came over to be introduced. Eventually, the projectionist left his last-minute ministrations on the powerful looking machine and went to stand in front. Clapping his hands noisily to attract attention, and much to some people's growing frustration, he began to make an overlong introduction to the film. Satisfied at last, he resumed his post as the lights were dimmed. A young woman giggled from somewhere near the back, resulting in much censorial tut-tutting and shushing. A bright beam of light streamed from the projector onto the screen, revealing myriads of odd shaped particles of dust scattered amongst a miscellany of mysterious symbols.

The film was as fascinating as it was disturbing. Afterwards, there was a marked silence as people made their way out into the cold, black night, treading carefully along the narrow path that had been cleared through the slush.

Alex kept his eyes on the road as they chatted about the film on the journey back. When they arrived, he insisted on escorting her inside, which was something she knew she had to prevent. With the exception of the public bar, one of the many unwritten rules that she was expected to comply with as live-in staff was the ban on using any of the Inn's facilities to entertain friends, especially those of the opposite sex.

She turned to face him at the main door. 'Thanks for tonight Alex. It's been good to get away. I'd ask you in for coffee, but I'm not supposed to ... you know. And I'll send Dot and Angus a thank you note.'

'Not so fast, young lady,' he said, reaching behind her to open the door. Then, taking her hand, he led her into the lounge. 'Someone should tell them you're an adult now and that you actually *live* here.' The room was dark and felt comfortable with residual heat. 'And I'm not leaving until I've done what I've been wanting to do all night.' He pulled her to him, wrapped his arms around her, and gave her the first of several long and mutually enjoyable kisses.

They heard a light being turned on in the kitchen a few minutes later, followed by a succession of noisy throat-clearings. Alex laughed and called-out, 'Hello there!' He kissed her again, his lips resting lightly on hers, playing havoc with her equilibrium, and said, 'Well, suppose I'd better hit the road. I'll call you tomorrow, same time.'

Donald emerged, looking slightly sheepish. 'Sorry about this, folks. Just doing the rounds.'

'No problem, I was just on my way anyway,' said Alex, squeezing Yvonne's hand before heading for the door. 'Well, goodnight, and may God bless and keep you both in His care.'

*

During the following weeks stubborn, upland patches of snow were gradually washed away by a mixture of late spring rain and bright sunshine. It was on one such showery day, just as another rainbow formed in a busy sky, that Frazer Brown, the new chef, arrived. He had been offered the position on a month's trial basis, having already had his references meticulously checked, and been subjected to no less than two rigorous interviews. Apparently the Inn would suit him very well, for he had let it be known that, 'This is just the quiet sort of backwater I've been looking for to help me make a start on the book I've been pregnant with these many years.' The proposed title was impressive: 'The Definitive Work on The Influence of Scottish Cookery on World Cuisine'. Georgina had speculated that, should this masterpiece ever actually make it to print, she could see no reason why the Inn should not share in some of its reflected glory. Even Robert had sounded keen when she had put the idea to him.

*

Yvonne and Alex continued to meet as often as they could. She began to recognise some subtle changes in her behaviour as they grew closer, and marvelled at the fact that she was still there, knowing that, in the not too distant past, she would almost certainly have extricated herself from the relationship and place long before now. It was a mystery. However, at times the old panic would return, fuelled by the malevolent voice that persisted in tormenting her, especially at night. Sometimes she would ask Alex about that other mystery, namely about the timing and significance of their meeting. But he would only smile and kiss her questions away.

Her reading of the Bible was progressing, and she was just about to make a start on *Hebrews* when Alex suggested that she would probably benefit more by reading the four Gospels again. Her curiosity about Jesus had continued to grow. Now she felt awed that such a Person could ever have lived on Earth, and that He was an actual, historically proven figure. Whenever she read the passages about His crucifixion, she would imagine herself standing at the foot of the Cross, looking up into His tortured, bleeding face, and wondering if He really was allowing Himself to hang there for the likes of her. She could even picture herself in the Garden, three days later, observing the angels roll the stone away, and watch Him step out of the tomb, miraculously resurrected.

Now she had no difficulty in believing that He was still alive, albeit in that other dimension, Heaven. And she began to seriously envy those who were able to accept Him as their *Way,* their *Truth,* and their *Life.* She wished she could too, but there was a problem: it was clear that if a person could not forgive, then they would not be able to make a genuine, heartfelt repentance - which meant that they were not free to accept God's forgiveness - and His gift of a new life. And that was her dilemma, for now she knew how spiritually impoverished she was, and how very much in need she was of *The Good Shepherd.* But how could she even begin to repent when she was so unwilling to forgive? And she had no idea what she could do about it.

CHAPTER 28

Charles and Izzy Harmer's arrival was imminent. Despite his assurances that they would love her, Yvonne still felt concerned about meeting these very special friends of Alex's. She was a firm believer in the importance of first impressions and really wanted to make a good one. However, before then, there was a busy day ahead. Two coaches were due in for morning coffee, and it had been a rush to get the bedrooms done. Just before half past ten, she left Flora to sort out the laundry and went to join Georgina in reception.

Within minutes a swarm of noisy passengers had invaded every inch of the public areas, and a considerable queue had formed by the toilets. Georgina's face ached with the effort of maintaining a fixed smile as she pointed at a large sign indicating that there were more facilities along the guest corridor. Donald and Yvonne were in the lounge, pouring drinks from two large aluminium kettle-shaped tea and coffee pots. As soon as everyone had been served, Donald slipped outside; he was finding all the noise and activity just a bit too much. He was also extremely concerned about Rabbie, and had convinced himself that having such great, noisy vehicles like this parked outside the place nearly every day was frightening the old boy away. Yvonne was busy doing the re-fills, and did not see him re-enter a few minutes later with a middle-aged couple.

From their vantage point in reception, Charles and Izzy Harmer were strategically placed, and possibly the only two witnesses to the scene that followed in the crowded lounge. They watched with fascination as a burly, red-faced fellow reached over and pinched the bottom of a young woman carrying what looked like a very heavy teakettle. They looked at each other, curious to see what would happen next, and did not have long to wait when the young woman stopped what she was doing and turned to give the culprit a fierce glare. It appeared that the man must have uttered something deeply offensive, for she marched over to the nearby sideboard and put down her burden before returning to stand directly in front of him. She bent to say something close to his ear; the man shrugged his fleshy shoulders and dismissed her with a wave of a hand. The young woman bent to say something else, and this time the affect was immediate. The man's head jerked up; his previous self-assured expression now replaced with one of concern. Satisfied, the young woman went to retrieve the teakettle and resumed her pouring, making sure to give the man a wide berth whenever she was obliged to go near him.

*

The registration process complete, Donald showed Charles and Izzy to their room. The couple looked around approvingly, pleased to see how large and comfortable it was.

Izzy sat on the bed, and remarked, 'Good, nice and firm. And what about that scene back there! I think I might have been tempted to step accidentally and very heavily on that awful man's foot if he'd done such a vulgar thing to me.'

'Oh, I don't know, I thought that young woman handled it well enough,' replied Charles, laying the cases down next to her. 'She's probably used to things like that happening anyway, and it might have caused embarrassment all round if she'd have made a scene. You have to consider, my dear, that that lot were probably from the coach, and will be cooped-up with him for days yet, and learning that they've got a lecher amongst their number wouldn't be very pleasant. But I'd like to have been a fly on the wall and heard what she said. Certainly seemed to shake him up a bit, anyway.'

'Charles!'

'Yes dear?'

'Don't you realise who she was? Remember Alex told us that there's only three other staff here: the cook, an elderly woman, and her'

'W-e-ll, I did wonder.'

'I'd bet my bottom dollar on it. He said she was no pushover; looks like he was right.'

'Interesting, very interesting. Looks like our Alex has got himself a bit of a fire cracker!'

Izzy shivered and went to study the gas fire. It had been lit earlier that day and was still on a low setting. Charles was more concerned about what type of view they had, and went over to look out of the large picture window. He pushed aside the net curtain and let out a long, low whistle. 'Glory to God! Just come and look at this.'

Having turned the gas up, she went to stand beside him. 'Looks warmer out there than in here.' Being a keen walker, her eyes automatically scanned for any potential tracks, thankful now that she'd had the foresight to put Ordnance Survey maps of this part of Scotland on the wedding present list. 'Maybe I'll be able to get some walking in before we get too busy.' She put her hand in his, and trying to sound appealing, asked, 'Are you sure you won't join me for the odd stretch?'

But Charles was not to be persuaded; his days of long, tortuous route marches were well and truly behind him. Now he preferred to exercise his appreciation of all things rural from the comfort of a moving vehicle or a fixed television screen. 'Sorry petal. You'll have to hunt out the local hiking club, but I will stick to my promise and take regular half-hour jaunts with you. And anyway, you're not up to long treks yet; give it a week or two.'

'Yes sir!' she replied, giving him a mock salute, and still trying to come to terms with the fact that this was going to be one area of married life that she would never be able to share with him.

He could hear the disappointment in her voice and turned to give her a hug. 'And you know you'll have the Lord with you up them there hills. Just think, you'll be able to chatter on to Him to your heart's content, and ask Him why He let you fall into the clutches of such a monster of a man!'

'Oh, I've already done that. And don't mind me dear, I'm still adjusting my expectation and reality dials.'

He kissed her lightly on the cheek. 'Well Mrs Harmer, you've blown my dials right out of the water!'

She put her arms around his waist and pressed him even closer to her. 'Mmm, is that so? You know, I think mine could do with a bit more adjusting - '

Just then, their pleasant, romantic interlude was rudely interrupted when someone knocked on their door. Izzy cooed, 'To be continued,' seductively in his ear, and reluctantly extricated herself from his arms.

'I'll hold you to that,' he said, crossing the room, and opening the door to reveal the figure of the young woman involved in the bottom-pinching incident.

'Mr and Mrs Harmer? You wanted coffee in your room?' asked Yvonne.

'Ah yes! And you must be Yvonne?' He replied, relieving her of the tray she was holding and handing it to Izzy.

'Yes, that's right.'

He held out his hand. 'I'm Charles Harmer, and this lovely lady's my wife, Izzy. It's good to finally meet you Yvonne.'

Yvonne's mind raced as they shook hands. 'And I'm pleased to meet you too.' So, here they were at last, the people Alex was planning to live and work with - and the man she was going to have to reveal her innermost thoughts to. She looked into a pair of kindly, deep-set hazel eyes. With his sandy brown hair and Van Dyke-style beard - complete with reddish tips - he looked nothing like the archetypal elderly minister she had been expecting, especially because he wore no dog collar and was casually dressed in slacks and a well-worn, hand-knitted jumper.

Free of the tray, Izzy approached and held out her own hand. Her fair hair was short and straight, and set off a pair of shrewd looking brown eyes. Despite all the travelling they had done, her navy blue, sharp-pleated trouser suit and cream blouse looked immaculate. There was no sign of make-up on her tanned face, now fading, and there was nothing of the middle-aged spread about her very neat, trim figure. In fact, everything about her appeared to be very much in place and under strict control.

'Hello Yvonne, I'm sure I don't have to tell you that Alex has told us a lot about you.' She was a quick judge of character and liked the look of this young woman who looked at a person straight in the eye, and who, judging by the slightly rough feel of her hand, was obviously used to hard work.

'Yes, and he's told me a lot about you too. I hope you're feeling better?'

'Well on the mend now, thank you,' replied Izzy.

Definitely no push-over, thought Charles. 'And now you're going to find out if it's all true. Actually, I think I'll go and give him a ring and let him know we're here.'

'There's a phone box outside, or you can use the one in reception if you prefer. There's an honesty box just by it.' Even before she had finished uttering the words, Yvonne began to feel embarrassed; what was she thinking of, reminding this man of the cloth to be honest!

He laughed, then surprised her by quipping, 'You'd probably do better to have a swear box. Come on then, lead on MacDuff!' Turning to Izzy, he said, 'Back in a minute petal. Now no going A.W.O.L. up them there hills!'

As they made their way through to reception, Yvonne wondered at the fact that here was yet another bearded man: Donald's bushy mixture of grey and brown was the grandest of the three; Alex had the neatest, fair and always closely trimmed, and now here was one of those artistic, pointed, reddy-brown ones. Three men; all bearded, and all significant in her life. So much for trying to steer clear of them!

*

Alex arrived just before two o'clock. He heard noises coming from the kitchen, and rather than ring the bell, decided that the time had come for him to behave less formally. He knocked on the door, peered in, and found Donald unpacking the contents of a large box of exotic looking ingredients that Frazer had ordered from a store in Glasgow.

'Hi Donald. Is Yvonne about? She's expecting me.'

'In her room I expect.' He hesitated, then said, 'Go on up.'

'Are you sure? I don't want to upset the applecart.'

Donald winked. 'I won't tell if you won't.'

Yvonne heard footsteps on the stairs and was startled when someone knocked on her door, and even more startled when she opened it to find Alex standing there, grinning.

'Alex! What ... who let you up?'

He kissed her lightly on the cheek. 'Donald, he's on our team. Are you ready?'

'Just. Actually, I've already met your friends. They seem ... really nice.' She knew how weak this sounded, but it was all she could think of right now. It would have to do.

*

'That'll be him' exclaimed Charles, sitting up quickly. 'Enter if you're tall and fair, otherwise go away.'

Alex laughed as he opened the door and ushered Yvonne in ahead of him. Isabelle sat up and began rubbing her eyes, attempting to hide a discreet yawn as she slid gracefully off the bed.

The three friends greeted and hugged each other affectionately, then Alex went to put his arm around Yvonne and drew her further into the room. 'Come on, sweetheart. I know you've already met, but let's do the job properly. Yvonne, I'd like to introduce you to my very, very dear friends, Charles and Isabelle Harmer. And Charles and Izzy, this is Yvonne Williams, who, as you know, is very, *very* dear to me too.' He planted a firm kiss on her forehead, and added, 'And The Boss's gift to me.'

There was no time for Yvonne to wonder at this, as, just to please Alex, she found herself having to shake the couple's hands again.

Charles spoke first. 'Hello again, Yvonne. I know we'll soon become firm friends. Anyone who can make Alex grin so idiotically is A.1. with me.'

Izzy had felt moved at the sight of Alex's obvious happiness and pride in the young woman, and began to hope that she really would turn out to be a gift - and not a stumbling block. 'Don't take any notice of him, dear. I think he's had too much Mediterranean sun. And Alex, for goodness sake, put him out of his misery and take us to the Manor; he's all of a fidget. I had the dickens of a job trying to stop him from taking

254

a sneaky look on the way here. How about you, Yvonne? Can you join us?'

Alex beamed, he was going to suggest that Yvonne be included, but the fact that Izzy had invited her was doubly encouraging.

'I'd love to, but I'm back on duty in half-an-hour,' explained Yvonne.

'That's a shame,' said Izzy, 'and after all the help you've been too.'

'Indeed,' agreed Charles. 'Alex has kept us fully briefed, a woman's touch and all that. Izzy was relieved when you stepped into the breach after he'd given the interior designers their marching orders. The place was like a Hammer House of Horrors when we last saw it, and we're pretty keen to see what's been going on.'

Izzy looked askance at him. 'Yes, I was relieved, but not as much as you, kind sir! I kept telling you not to fret.' She turned to Yvonne. 'I knew the Lord would have another plan up His sleeve.'

Yvonne looked bemused, surely she didn't mean her? She spoke up quickly. 'Well, in that case I hope you won't have even more nasty shocks when you see the staff rooms.'

Charles was quick to reassure her. 'I'm sure we won't, in fact, I *know* we won't. They'd have ended up looking like barracks if it'd been left to us old fuddy-duddies.'

Alex squeezed Yvonne's shoulders again. 'There, what did I tell you? Part of the team.'

She blushed and decided to study the carpet. 'Well I ... it made a nice change.'

Alex laughed. 'You can say that again! And if those walls could talk, they'd be hugging you too.' He released her and began rubbing his hands together, eager to get on. 'Okay you two, if you're ready, I'm doing the driving, you've done enough these past two days. And don't worry Izzy, I've had the heater fixed.'

*

They arrived at the Manor and had to pick their way carefully around an assortment of tools and tins that lay scattered around. Sheets covered the cleaned and re-polished oak floorboards and electric sockets hung, half-wired, from freshly plastered walls. At times, it was difficult for them to make themselves heard, such was the collective din coming from transistor radios, men shouting, and a variety of mechanical whirring and screeching noises.

Alex was relieved when the couple expressed themselves to be delighted with the progress and enthusiastic at the sight of the few rooms that were nearing completion. The inspection complete, they retreated to the comfort and peace of the Tweedie's sitting room to plan, talk and pray.

*

He drove them back to the Inn just before six o'clock. They were looking tired, so he declined their offer to join them for dinner. He looked around for Yvonne, knowing that she would be keen to hear how the visit had gone. Spotting her in the dining room, he felt the usual rush of desire as he watched her lithe, young body move effortlessly between the tables. As though sensing his presence, she turned and saw him. She waved and smiled as he mimed putting a telephone to his ear and held up nine fingers. Someone touched her arm and distracted her attention, making her miss the kiss he blew towards her.

He turned and left, resigned to spending yet another evening without her. It had been a good day; a day he had been looking forward to for some time, but now his feeling of anticlimax was almost palpable. Try as he might, he was finding it increasingly hard to have just himself to please and organise during the long nights. It had been relatively easy to fit her time off into his flexible schedule, but that was about to change now that Charles and Izzy had arrived. Apart from the car, finding a warm place to be alone with her was always a problem; at least Donald understood, but Georgina was another matter. Even Dot and Angus seemed to have taken on the role of unofficial chaperones.

He drove off, feeling that the sooner he could get his own private space sorted out, the better, and reminding himself, yet again, of the need to continue exercising self-restraint. But there was hope; recently he thought he had detected signs that The Boss was at work in her spirit, awakening a curiosity and recognition of her own need of Him. He knew that his part was to stand back, and let Him reveal Himself to her in His own good time. Charles had frequently found it necessary to remind him that God's timing was perfect, and if Yvonne needed more time than he could cope with, then that would be his problem, not hers. Far better for her to reach a rational, well thought out and genuinely heartfelt decision than be persuaded to give in to a quick impulse, and one created and manipulated by his own impatience. He must bide his time, and trust that it would not be too long before she would choose to walk with The Boss for the rest of her life - and that he would be the human companion she would choose to walk along that same path with.

CHAPTER 29

Alex had an appointment at Invermaden Infirmary a few days later. He had asked Yvonne to go with him, seeing it as an opportunity to discuss his physical condition in more detail than the vague generalisations he usually gave her; however, she only had the afternoon off and was unable to accompany him.

Charles was keen to spend some time in the almost completed office at the Manor, and, not needed for anything in particular, Izzy decided that she would go for her first hike. She had been praying for a way to spend some time alone with Yvonne, and lost no time in inviting her to go along. But Yvonne was reluctant, knowing that Georgina would not approve of her fraternising with a guest, even for something as innocuous as a country walk. There was also the problem of suitable footwear, and she felt sure she would only be a hindrance. When Georgina did object, Izzy dealt with her efficiently and diplomatically by hinting how useful it would be to have a member of staff, besides her son, who could talk knowledgeably to the guests about the local walks. Donald produced an old pair of wellington boots that had been left behind by a former guest, and a comfortable fit was achieved with the help of two pairs of thick socks. Then, reassured that she would be no hindrance at all, the two women left the Inn soon after two o'clock that same afternoon.

Izzy was a considerate and interesting companion, and Yvonne soon found herself able to relax. The former confident, authoritarian nursing sister was mellowing now that there were no malingering pupil nurses and raw junior doctors to keep tabs on.

They entered a dense, tree-lined part of the route, where the air was still and silent with no bird song. Yvonne often found that her imagination could run away with her in here, and had described it as being, 'Eerie, foreboding and somehow threatening,' in her last letter to Sandra. But today it was different. With Izzy's sure stride and confident presence beside her, she was able to appreciate the colourful variety of wild plants and grasses growing alongside the rivulets that trickled down from the sodden earth above.

'I usually rush through this bit,' she confessed, pointing into the gloomy darkness between the trees. 'I know it's silly, but I can't help imagining that there could be something sinister lurking in there.'

'Not silly at all. The best of us can get spooked. But I'm used to walking alone, and it looks like that won't be changing any time soon.' She sighed. 'I can't get Charles to come with me for love nor money. He's getting into some bad habits now he doesn't have to keep his fitness level up. Even Alex sounds as though he's more active.'

'Really?'

'Well, that's what it sounds like. Always out and about, isn't he? Tells me that he tries to walk at least a couple of miles every day.'

'Yes, but he suffers for it, you know, his leg. Although he never moans, but I can tell.' She paused, and considered whether or not she should ask one of her important questions, the ones that she wanted to ask Alex when, and if, the time would ever be right. Deciding that there was nothing to lose, she continued, 'Do you think he'll ever get any better, I mean, move around more freely? I have asked him, but all he'll ever say is that, "that's the plan". It's obvious that he doesn't want to talk about what happened. All I know is that he was working in bomb disposal in Northern Ireland, and there was some kind of explosion. I can only imagine how serious his injuries were.'

Izzy smiled inwardly. The Lord was good. Here she was, puzzling how to broach this very subject, and Yvonne herself had just given her the perfect opening. Businesslike, she replied, 'Normal reaction for someone who's been through that kind of trauma. But don't take it personally, Yvonne. The Lord has used Charles to help him with the spiritual and emotional side of things, but as for his physical state, well, that's just a matter of time. He'll get there in the end, especially with his determination.'

'Do you really think so?' asked Yvonne, a note of real optimism in her voice.

'I'm sure of it. He's made excellent progress so far, and I'm fully expecting him to come back with a favourable report tonight.'

Yvonne digested this encouraging piece of information as Izzy paused to consult her map. Satisfied, they walked on, the only sound the crunch of their soles on the undulating, gritty track. Several seconds passed before Izzy broke the silence to ask, 'Is it important to you - to know that he'll improve?'

'No, I mean, yes! But not for my own sake … for his. It's awful knowing he gets so much pain, and I know he gets frustrated at times.'

'He handles it well though, doesn't he? But, for argument's sake, let's say that he doesn't improve, that what you see now is what you get - forever. How would you feel about him then?'

They emerged from the semigloom into an expanse of young spruces. Looking up, they saw the mountainside decorated with gorse bushes, vivid gold amongst a hazy cloud of bluebells. Izzy was well aware that she was a plain speaker, and expected as much back, although she was invariably disappointed. She had asked this young woman a deeply personal question, and one that could prove awkward to answer, but she was keen to learn just how much Alex had revealed to her about his injuries. For all their sakes, the sooner they found out about her true feelings for him the better; there was a lot at stake.

Yvonne replied thoughtfully, 'It wouldn't make any difference to me. I know he's got … limitations, but somehow they don't seem to matter, or get in the way. He's such a strong kind of person, so positive and focused.'

'And those "limitations", has he told you the nature of them?'

'No, not really. Although I know he gets cramp if he's in the same position for too long, and he won't touch alcohol, and gets stomach ache every so often, but I've always assumed that's because of the tablets he's on.'

'Ah!' Izzy's pace slowed. So that was the lie of the land. Obviously Alex had his own reasons for not telling her the full extent and consequences of that blast. Could it be that he was scared of frightening her off? Or maybe he was waiting for the right time? The trouble with that was, the longer he waited, the more difficult the task might prove to be when he did get around to it. In her opinion, if he really did believe that the Lord had brought them together, then he should be stepping out in faith with this, as he was doing so confidently with everything else. It was no good burying his head in the sand and hoping that things would work themselves out. Any new wife of his would have enough to cope with, never mind the shock of realising that she would have to sleep with someone so disfigured for the rest of her life. She might feel that she had been tricked, and could even lose some trust - and that would never do. Certainly, she would not have liked to have been confronted with a new husband with such ugly scars and half his groin missing on her honeymoon night! And she was used to such sights. But this young woman had no medical background. Somehow it didn't seem fair. Could it be that the Lord had given her this opportunity to forewarn her? Surely it would be an act of kindness to give her some idea? Hadn't she felt almost compelled to invite her along today? She had prayed, and all the circumstances had fitted together nicely. Yes, she would do it.

Yvonne glanced at Izzy's serious expression, and hoped that this was her chance to find out exactly how badly affected Alex really was. She knew that whatever dreadful thing she might be about to hear would make no difference to the way she felt about him. In a way, she was damaged goods as well, and look how he was standing by her. If things did work out between them, then she would stand by him too, no matter what. Resolved, she decided to take the initiative.

'I wish you'd tell me, Izzy. I do care for him you know, very much. And please don't worry, I won't let it affect me. I promise. In a way, I'm already expecting to hear that he's ...'

She paused, then forced herself to continue, she had come this far - just a bit further, 'You know, impotent ... or something. I can understand that he'd be embarrassed to tell me, but it really wouldn't make a scrap of difference to me. So, if there is something that I should know, I'd rather be told now, and have time to get used to the idea, if you see what I mean.'

That was all the persuasion Izzy needed. She began to wonder if she and Charles had been so concerned about Alex's welfare, that they had been a touch guilty of neglecting this young woman's. If so, that would never do. 'That's fair enough,' she said. 'And I'd like to put you in the picture. But, before I say anything else, I need to know how you *really* feel about him Yvonne. You said that you cared for him; he's not just some passing fancy then, just another boyfriend? Tell me truthfully, are you serious about him, and maybe hoping that you might have a future together? Be honest now. There's an awful lot at stake here.'

Yvonne reminded herself that here was one of Alex's dearest friends; it was only natural that she would be concerned about him, and she liked her for that. 'I'm *very* serious about him; I couldn't be more serious, and I think ... I know ... he is about me too. But it's not easy, what with one thing and another.'

'Oh, no doubt! There's always some sort of fly in the ointment,' remarked Izzy, making her mind up fully now. 'Well, okay.' She sent up the swiftest of arrow prayers, then began, 'Unfortunately, he sustained very serious injuries, and not only to his legs, but to his abdomen as well, especially around the groin area.' She stopped to peer down into the black-brown, peat stained water of a small pool beside the path. 'His spleen, left kidney, and part of his small bowel were removed, and there was some damage to his liver. He's got quite a bit of metalwork in his left hip and leg.' She looked up, watching Yvonne's face closely as she continued, 'The damage to his private parts was also quite extensive.' Seeing no obvious sign of horror or disgust on the younger woman's face, she went on to say, 'He'll never be ... complete in that area. Do you understand what I mean?'

262

'Oh, I see. Er, well …' Yvonne paused, needing time to think. So that was it! She had spent many a night, and day, thinking about the physical side of their relationship, or lack of it. There was an undeniably powerful attraction between them; she had felt his desire, his need, as much as her own, but had assumed that his faith was the only reason for his tremendous self-control. Tears began to prickle at the back of her eyes. Oh, but Alex, what he must have been through! How brave he had been to fight back, to be willing to live life again, even to enter into a relationship. But why had he chosen *her* when there was any amount of decent and uncomplicated women out there that he could have set his cap on? What a situation: both of them damaged, him physically, her emotionally. In a way, they were only half the people they should have been. But maybe that was it, maybe with his strength of character, and her strong body, the two of them together could make a whole!

At last, her voice trembling slightly, she replied, 'Yes, I think I do. If what you're trying to tell me is that he doesn't have the … necessary equipment, and could I live without sex, then the answer is yes. I know I could. And, anyway, there are other ways for a couple to … you know, satisfy each other. But I'm not interested in him in just that way, even though I can't deny that I am very attracted to him. But sex isn't the be-all and end-all to a successful relationship, is it?'

Izzy smiled and reached over to squeeze Yvonne's arm. 'Well, it helps. But I'm very glad to know that you feel like that.'

They walked on in silence, both deep in thought. Yvonne was trying to come to terms with the news that Alex was impotent. So what? It wasn't his groin that she had been drawn to, but the man himself. She had come to know him as a thoroughly decent person; he had a strength of character that was out of the ordinary, and he stood head and shoulders above every other man she had ever met. It was the essence, or, as he might put it, the soul of him that she had grown to love. So what if there could never be any sex? It was overrated anyway. Then again, she had often wondered…with the right man … with Alex … but no! She must stop thinking like that. It didn't matter, it really didn't matter. If she could be freed from her demons, and they did end up together, then there were other ways they could achieve mutual satisfaction. And as far as children went, well, for her part, she would certainly not be averse to adopting a child or two.

Izzy was also doing some hurried thinking of her own. From Yvonne's reaction she could only assume that the couple had not yet been intimate. Good for Alex! His faith was standing him in good stead. But somehow she began to feel uneasy. Maybe she had been a bit too negative about his capabilities, and inadvertently given Yvonne the wrong impression. If that was the case, then she would have to put it right. Biting her lip, she realised that she would have to disclose even more intimate details about Alex. But she really couldn't let the poor girl go on believing the worst.

Tentatively, she went on to say, 'He does have some rather unsightly scarring across his abdomen, but they may be able to do something about that. And while it's the case that his private parts have been considerably … altered, the only real problem he has in that area is that one of his testicles was so badly damaged that it had to be removed. But, I can tell you that there's no physical reason why he shouldn't be able to enjoy a full sex life; when he gets married, of course. And he's still quite capable of fathering a child.'

Yvonne could not decide if she was more relieved than embarrassed. The yo-yo of emotions she was being bombarded with was almost unbearable, and she wondered at the unexpected surge of relief she felt.

Izzy continued, 'But you know, Yvonne, I've told you more than I should have. And I do think that it's only fair that Alex knows that I have.'

'Yes, I agree, but I'm so glad you have. And I think it should be me who tells him; I don't want there to be any secrets between us. I'll just say that I persuaded you to tell me more about his … condition. Well, I did, didn't I? It's only the truth.'

'That's good of you. But be prepared, I don't think he's going to be too happy about it. We might be in for a rocky ride for a day or two.'

'Maybe. But I think it'll be worth it. I hope so anyway. And thank you Isabelle, I'm glad I know now.'

'That's alright, my dear. Now, let me just check the map to see if there's a good place for us to stop nearby; I'm starting to feel peckish already.'

CHAPTER 30

The two women walked on, joining the main road before entering another area of woodland, only this time the trees were native and deciduous. A breeze began to stir the leaves. As though in greeting, sprays of golden, late flowering daffodils waved their trumpets gently as they walked past. Izzy proved to be a knowledgeable guide, identifying various animal tracks and many of the birds that fluttered through the branches and flew above them, singing to attract mates, and proclaiming loudly over their territory. Every so often they met other hikers, some still lively and fresh faced, others quiet and trudging wearily. One young couple, dressed in the very latest of hiking attire, asked them the time.

'Twenty past three' replied Izzy, 'and a good time to seek the Lord!'

The couple hurried past; the girl could be heard laughing loudly a few seconds later. Yvonne made no comment as Izzy shrugged and said, matter-of-factly, 'Pay no mind to them dear. They think they've got all in the time in the world before they meet Him. Anyway, how are those wellies feeling?'

'Okay so far, thank you,' she replied, realising that she would have to get used to this woman's no-nonsense, straight talking ways.

Several minutes later, they came across a small wooden bridge crossing a stream and decided to stop and rest. The heady mixture of vanilla and coconut from some nearby gorse blossom wafted their way, and welcome shade from the persistent sunshine was provided by a Scots pine that had seeded itself by the water's edge years before. This time, Izzy felt no qualm about broaching the other delicate subject that had also been exercising her mind recently.

'Actually, Yvonne, I hope you won't mind if I ask you another personal question.'

Yvonne had been struggling to open a flask of coffee. Succeeding, she began to pour the steaming liquid into the vacuum cups. 'What's that then? Sugar?'

'No thanks.' Izzy reached into one of the side pockets of her rucksack and drew out a miniature pill box containing saccharine tablets. 'Alex told us about that decision you made, and I know you're going to talk to Charles about it. But I was wondering if you couldn't bring yourself to tell me a little something about it now?' She dropped two of the small pills into her coffee and began to stir, looking over expectantly at Yvonne.

Yvonne unscrewed the top off a small jar of sugar, and began to absentmindedly stir two spoonfuls into her coffee as she silently debated with herself how much to reveal. She grimaced at the too-sweet taste after taking a tactical, time-delaying sip, trying to decide if she should avoid the subject by saying that she would prefer to wait until she saw Charles, or use this as a sort of rehearsal. She chose the latter, and replied, 'Okay. But, you know, I had no idea that it would cause all these problems when I made it. It just seemed to be the most logical thing to do at the time, and the only way I could think of to … to …'

Izzy had been delving into her rucksack. She drew out a greaseproof bag, and offered Yvonne one of the substantial slabs of Dundee cake that Donald had contributed. 'To what?' she prompted.

'Well, you know, protect myself.'

'Really? From what'

'Relationships, and the complications that go with them. It's hard to explain, and to be honest with you, I don't really understand it all myself. Although, I thought I did at the time.'

'But you obviously found a way. You're having one with Alex now, aren't you?'

'Well, yes, but I can't seem to…move forward.'

'Ah, I see,' said Izzy, taking a mouthful of the cake.

'It's like I can't give myself permission to go deeper, to commit.'

'Hmm. Well, from my experience, things like that are usually caused by some deep-seated and unresolved problems from someone's past. You know, there's a root cause that holds them back. And some of those problems can be so damaging that they can have the effect of emotionally crippling people in some way, although they really ought to be shouting "help" before things get to that stage. And it sounds very much like this is your time you to do so, my dear.'

Despite experiencing a vague sense of unease, Yvonne felt that she should allow the conversation to continue, no matter how embarrassing or uncomfortable it might become. 'Yes, I think you're right.' Then, haltingly, she began to explain why she had found it necessary to make the fateful decision. Somehow she managed to describe all the lonely, hopeless years of trying to fit in, of being befriended, even wanted, and then how the inevitable feelings of worthlessness, even fear, would overtake her, and how she would always end up running away.

Izzy listened intently. It was clear to her now that Alex had not been exaggerating; the poor girl really did have a bit of problem. She searched her rucksack again and retrieved a plastic bag containing some damp tissues. Offering one to Yvonne, she said, 'You know, it sounds to me that your problems could well stem from your childhood, especially after what you said about your home life. But it wasn't until you were out in the world that they showed themselves, especially when you embarked upon your first real relationship outside the family unit.'

By now Yvonne had curled-up into a ball, her arms wrapped tightly around her knees. Izzy read the defensive body language, and said, reassuringly, 'Now, don't you worry my dear. The Lord can sort it out, especially with Charles on the case. He's good at handling these sort of issues, and has a great track record. You'll be fine, I'd bet my bottom dollar on it. Anyway, come on, chin up and eat up! We've still got a way to go.'

Yvonne lifted her head and looked up at her hopefully. 'You don't think I'll be wasting his time then? You don't think he'll have enough on his plate without listening to my sob story?'

'My dear girl! Let me assure you, Charles will take all the time he needs to help you, and I certainly wouldn't call it a mere "sob story". You've got a genuine problem, but, like I said, nothing that can't be sorted out. And I know you're reading your Bible, and that should help. I often feel like I've had a good dose of emotional medicine after a bit of Bible study. How far have you got, by the way?'

'I'm up to The *Hebrews*. I'd have got further, but Alex suggested that I read the Gospels again.'

'Good idea. But it's *Hebrews*, just *Hebrews,* like *Romans.* And what about the Lord, how are feeling about Him?'

'Er, in what way?'

'Well, for a start, do you believe that He's still alive?'

'Of course!'

'Oh yes, and why's that?'

Yvonne had to consider. What she had so boldly stated just now had been the truth. She really did believe that Jesus was still very much alive and active, and not just in Heaven, but here on Earth too, after all, she had been witnessing firsthand how very involved He was in Alex's life all summer. Now her careful reading of the Gospels provided her with the answer. 'Because He was resurrected, wasn't He? And, so far, there's no mention of Him having died again, and it says that He's in Heaven now, with God, and there's no one dead, I mean, no corpses, in Heaven, is there?'

Izzy laughed as she slowly raised herself to her feet and brushed herself down. 'No! There certainly isn't. You'll have seen that bit in *Corinthians,* where Paul talks about Him appearing to over five hundred people at the same time *after* His resurrection?'

'Yes, that was a real eye-opener. I'd like to have been part of *that* crowd.'

'Me too! So, does that mean that you're thinking seriously about asking Him into your life?'

Yvonne pulled the cord on her duffle bag and rose effortlessly to her feet, reminding herself that this woman was a plain speaker, and hoping that she would not mind being spoken to just as plainly. Izzy sighed at the sight of the young, supple body, knowing that, for her, those days had gone forever; years of lifting and heaving patients around had taken their toll on her poor vertebrae.

'I ... want to, but I can't,' confessed Yvonne.

'You can't?' exclaimed Izzy, with obvious surprise.

'No. I can't.'

'But why on earth not? You sound as though you want to.' There had been many times in Izzy's life when she knew that she had been just a bit too forward, and now she began to wonder if this could be another. Nevertheless, she persevered, 'Or are there some things you don't understand? Parts of the Bible can be difficult to grasp. Let's face it, it is a *super*-natural book, and I don't mean supernatural in the sense of the occult. I mean that it's above and beyond the natural. Greater than. Is there one particular bit you're having trouble with? If you tell me, maybe I can shed some light on it for you.' She looked at Yvonne's serious expression, then added, 'Or, are you going to tell me to mind my own business?'

Yvonne suspected that Izzy was not the type to be told any such thing, and also suspected that, one way or another, she would eventually succeed in wheedling the truth out of her anyway. Maybe it would be best to get it over with.

'Because, from what I've read, if someone can't forgive ... someone ... then they can't repent ... and ask Jesus into their hearts. You *have* to forgive, don't you? To become a Christian? Now I know that's what Jesus was doing on the Cross - taking our place, taking all our sins upon Him - so that God can forgive us. And if we can't forgive others, then we've got no right to accept His forgiveness and sacrifice on our behalf. I've got that right, haven't I?'

Izzy watched Yvonne lift her bag until it rested on her back, the symbolism was not lost on her. It had been many years since she had repented, and laid her own burden of confusion and guilt down at the foot of the Cross. 'Well, yes, you're almost right. God looks at Jesus - and pardons us. But, you know, it was love that kept Our Lord on the Cross; His love for His Father, and for us. That's the *real* message of the Cross. When we come to recognise how much we need His love, we really shouldn't let our ... hindrances ... prevent us from coming to Him. And we all have some; some more than others. We just have to be sincere, and willing to let them go, and surrender everything to Him.'

They set off to join the path again. Sounding as dejected as she looked, Yvonne went on to ask, 'But what if a person isn't willing to let go of one of those ... hindrances? Or maybe they want to, but just can't?'

'Well then, I'd say they definitely need some help,' replied Izzy, realising that this young woman's problems might be even more serious than she had suspected, and that Charles might have his work cut out. If she could not make a genuine, heartfelt decision to become a Christian, then it would be better for Alex to put an end to the relationship sooner, rather than later. Any woman who became his wife would have to be supportive in every way: physically, mentally, emotionally, and most definitely spiritually. An unequal yoking with an unbeliever could cause him a great amount of grief, not to mention have a detrimental effect on the ministry of the Manor. Intentionally, or unintentionally, a non-Christian wife could put all sorts of spokes in the wheel.

'Have you spoken to Alex about all this?' she asked.

'Not really, the subject hasn't come up. I only came to understand this forgiveness issue myself just recently. And I know he'd like me to become a Christian, but I won't pretend. I don't think a person can pretend something like that, can they? I couldn't live a lie like that. He should marry a Christian shouldn't he ... if he does ever get married ... someone who shares his beliefs?'

Izzy nodded.

'And he'd be bound to find out sooner or later, I mean, if I did make all the right sounds about becoming a Christian, but wasn't being genuine. And God would know all the time anyway. The relationship would be built on a lie.'

Again, Izzy nodded, struggling to find something positive to say. 'You know, Yvonne, I suspect it's all tied up with that decision you made. I wouldn't be at all surprised if you'll find yourself being able to forgive that person once that issue's been dealt with. We often find that when one problem gets resolved, others get sorted out at the same time, or at least they can be easier to deal with.'

'Really? Do you think so?'

Izzy looked at Yvonne's hopeful expression, and exclaimed emphatically, 'I do. I most certainly do!'

For the first time, Yvonne found herself beginning to look forward to the counselling sessions. If she had just experienced a short taste of what they might be like, then she might have reason to believe - even to hope - that one day she really could be free.

They strode on, chatting about life at the Inn, when Izzy remembered the groping coach passenger, and laughingly revealed that she and Charles had witnessed the whole scene from reception. Yvonne was mortified, and revealed that that was not the first impression she had wanted to make on the couple. However, Izzy was quick to reassure her that they had been greatly impressed by the way she appeared to have handled the situation, and went on to ask, 'So what was it you said to him?'

'I threatened to tell the driver about him, but I don't think he believed me. So I told him I'd stick his hand up in the air, and ask if anyone knew who it belonged to, because I'd found it somewhere where it shouldn't have been.'

Izzy laughed out loud. 'Wonderful! Good for you. And what did he say to that?'

'Oh, just spluttered some sort of apology. But I told the driver anyway.'

They were passing by a deserted croft that was almost completely surrounded by a wilderness of rhododendron bushes and thick bracken. Izzy was at that age when many women find that any sudden cough, sneeze, or outburst of any sort, could prove embarrassing, and exclaimed, 'Oops! Now I need to find a friendly bush. Back in a minute,' and was obliged to make a quick dash behind the tumbling stone walls.

Looking around, she spotted a large, brown shape, resting against a pile of smaller stones. There was something different and out of place about it, and having finished, she tentatively made her way across the tangle of bracken and nettles. It appeared to be the decomposing body a large animal.

Emerging a few seconds later, her expression grim, she announced, 'Well, that wasn't very pleasant. There's a dead stag behind there. I wonder if it's that one that Donald keeps on about? Poor thing, it must have gone there to breathe its last.'

'What? Oh no!' Yvonne did not wait to hear any more as she rushed behind the croft to see for herself. *'Oh God, oh God, please, please don't let it be Rabbie!'*

He was easy to spot. The deformed antler was conspicuous as he lay with that side of his head uppermost. She stood, transfixed and horrified at the sight of the once powerful body, now lying lifeless and rotting. And alone. So alone.

'Oh no! Rabbie! Rabbie!' she cried. She had not known him long, only encountering him on maybe half a dozen other occasions after the telephone box incident, but she had come to know him for what he was: a splendidly handsome animal, although she had often wondered if he was a bit too curious and friendly for his own good. Now he was dead. Donald would have to be told. And she would be the one who would have to tell him.

Izzy had followed. She bent to examine the body, and noticed what appeared to be a long, straight cut running from the back of its neck and along its spine. Maybe he had been fatally wounded during the rut, but she knew enough about that event to know that it only occurred around October - and it was only July. Then again, the cut was too straight and regular to have been made by another animal, too neat to have been made by nature. It was like an incision - like a long stab wound.

At last she stood. Taking Yvonne's arm, she led her away from the heartbreaking scene. 'Come on dear, let's get back. We can't do anything for the poor thing now. His suffering is over.'

CHAPTER 31

Yvonne was frustrated. She began to wonder if circumstances were conspiring to keep her and Alex apart. Four days had passed, and still there had been no opportunity for them to spend any time together. He had moved into his small flat at the Manor two days earlier, and now found himself being called upon by an endless stream of tradesmen, needing to know about the finer details of the work.

But, at last, they were alone. She was feeling apprehensive about what the next few hours might bring. The only thing she knew for sure was that, above all else, she wanted to be absolutely honest with him. She kicked off her shoes and curled up into the corner of the sofa. This was the first time she had seen the room furnished, and she began to imagine what changes a woman could make. Textured wallpaper on one of the walls would create a contrast to the plain, blue silk paint, a thick sheepskin rug on the plain, blue carpet, and an assortment of carefully selected prints and indoor plants would give it a more homely feel. At least there were framed photographs of family and military groups on the unit's shelves; all neatly lined up, as though on parade.

Alex was busy in the small, adjoining kitchen. He raised his voice above the noise of the kettle. 'Haven't seen much of the MacMan's lately. Every time I call in, you and Frazer seem to be the only ones around.'

'Georgina's not well and only comes out of the flat when she has to,' she called back, 'and Donald's not up to much; he's taken Rabbie's death really badly. Actually, I'm upset about it too; to think that Niall could be so vengeful - if it was him. Poor Rabbie, what a horrible way to die; it feels all wrong to think that we'll never see him again.'

He reappeared with the drinks and came to sit beside her. 'Must have been bad, finding him like that, but the finger definitely points Niall's way. Apparently, there's been no history of anything like that happening around here before.'

'It was awful, and I can't help feeling that I'm somehow to blame. Maybe it wouldn't have happened if we hadn't have clashed like that.'

He looked surprised. 'Sounds to me like he clashed with everyone! And why should you feel bad about it? It wasn't you who took the knife to him.'

She flinched, and he immediately regretted his choice of words. 'Sorry, sweetheart, I could have put it better than that.'

'It's alright, but I keep thinking that if only I'd have spoken up sooner ...' And, at last, she was able to talk about the guilt she felt, even shame, at what she considered to be her part in the tragedy, especially the thought that, if she had not come, then the whole dreadful chain of events might not have happened. She had tried confiding in Flora, but she had only dismissed her feelings as being 'unwise' and 'mere folly.'

Alex was shocked to learn of her feelings, and set about trying to sooth her with repeated assurances that she was not responsible for Niall's actions. 'In fact,' he stressed, 'if anyone should be feeling any blame, it should be the MacMan's. Instead of taking steps to protect their guests and staff from such a loose cannon, they had been in dereliction of their duty by choosing to ignore his antisocial and volatile nature, and keep on employing him.'

Yvonne wanted to be persuaded, but the image of Rabbie's slaughtered body was hard to shake off. She told how her initial fear of him had been replaced by one of a growing fondness, and how she was beginning to get quite used to seeing him around the place. There was something almost regal about the way he ambled along with his head held high, as though he was the natural owner of the land: the real *Monarch of the Glen*. Her tears fell unchecked as she described how Donald and Frazer had wrapped his poor body in a tarpaulin, and lowered him into a deep, black hole at the back of the Inn. All she could do for him now was to put bunches of wild flowers on his grave, and tell him, over and over again, how very sorry she was.

Alex tried hard, but was still unable to convince her that she had got her wires crossed about the whole sad affair. He knew that she was only trying to appease him when she agreed that he was, 'probably right,' and went quiet.

'By the way,' he said, attempting to lighten the mood, 'I'll be disappearing for a few days next week. I'm going into hospital for a minor procedure. Timing could have been better, but Charles and Izzy insist I grab the chance, and go for it.'

'What kind of minor procedure?' she asked, all thoughts of Rabbie suddenly pushed to the back of her mind.

'Just some tidying up of the scaring; it's all healed up, but, let's just say, there's still room for improvement.' He put an arm around her, 'So, will you miss me?'

'Oh, expect I'll survive,' she replied, realising that he had just given her the opening she needed. Now that he had brought the subject up himself, maybe she could somehow tease the more intimate details of his medical condition out of him. She could even pretend that this was the first time she had heard about them, and then, just as quickly, dismissed the idea, recognising that that would be a sort of deceit - and she could not, would not, allow herself to contaminate their relationship.

She uncurled her legs and sat up. 'You know, you've never really told me about what happened to you in Ireland. And you don't have to, I mean, why should you? But, I've got to tell you ...' She hesitated, then braced herself, and continued. 'The truth is ... I know...that you had some parts of you literally blown away, and that you had to have extensive surgery, but that they couldn't repair ... everything.' She paused, beginning to feel daunted as she recognised that same unwavering, questioning look that had so unnerved her when they had first met.

'I see. Who told you? It couldn't have been Charles,' he asked, his voice low, his words measured. 'That leaves Izzy. Was it her? It must have been. And exactly *what* do you know?'

What remained of her courage was fading fast, but she was determined to see this thing through, no matter how hard his eyes bored into her. Her nervousness was obvious, and he watched as she began to twine her hair through her fingers, part of his mind thinking how lovely it was, the other, keen to know the extent of her knowledge. She began to relate the conversation that she'd had with Izzy days before. When she finished, she stressed, yet again, as she had done so throughout, that Izzy should bear no blame.

'I'm sorry but it … it just sort of happened. I know she hadn't planned on telling me, but it just seemed to crop up naturally, in conversation. She wanted to tell you straight away that she'd told me, but I asked her not to. I felt it only right that I should tell you myself. But I want you to know that I'm glad she told me. I … I've wanted to know.'

He had remained ominously silent throughout her speech, and now, hardly able to breathe, she waited for some reaction from him. Would there be a controlled, but barely concealed, flash of anger, or a continuation of this excruciating silence? From her knowledge of him so far, she knew that he was not the moody type, nor given to sulking, but he could be a bit of a cool character at times. As alarming as it would be, she felt she would cope better with the former reaction.

At last he spoke, 'I can't deny that I'm not very happy about it, and it sounds like she didn't spare you any of the finer details.'

Yvonne reached for his hand, covering it with her own. 'It makes no difference to the way I feel about you, Alex. Absolutely no difference at all.'

His eyes softened. 'Is that right? And just how do you feel about me?' He turned his hand over in hers and squeezed it. It was the smallest of gestures, but its impact was great enough to make her want to cry with relief. With the other hand he began teasing the fine wisps of hair by her cheek. 'Or maybe I already know, but it would be kind of nice to hear you say it.' His brow furrowed again as an unwelcome thought struck him. 'Hey, you don't feel sorry for me, do you? That's the last thing I need, you treating me with kid gloves.'

She recalled the momentary pity she had felt when learning about his injuries, and how she had dismissed the emotion almost immediately. 'What? *No, no!* Nothing like that. If you must know I …' ***Stop!*** She faltered, aware that the hated, malevolent inner voice was beginning to pour its unwelcome words into her mind again:-

What do you think you're doing? You're on dangerous ground now. Don't let yourself get carried away and let your secret slip out - then what kind of a fool would you be? You're so stupid, believing that such a man could ever want you or take you seriously. You know you'd be nothing but a millstone around his neck. You're getting too big for your boots my girl. Remember, you're nobody, nothing but a waste of space. Remember now ... remember ...

'Well? Yes, I must,' broke in Alex.

The battle raged within her, desperate now to find a way of telling him something, *anything* of how she felt about him without speaking those most dangerous of words. Guardedly she managed to say, 'I ... quite the opposite. I admire you ... all that you've been through, and how you've come through it all. You've got on with your life, in fact, you've turned it around and are going to do something wonderful, wanting to help others. You're not sorry for yourself, so why should I be?'

A smile played at the corners of his mouth. 'Very noble sentiments, I'm sure. But is that all? Just admiration? And there's really nothing else you feel about me?'

She had a sudden flash of inspiration, and smiling up at him, said coquettishly, 'Well now, as to that, my dear Alex, you'll have to wait. Maybe I'll tell you all about it one day. But not today.'

He laughed. 'Looks like we've both got things to reveal to each other - but at the right time. And maybe if that was the way The Boss chose to let you know, then who am I to complain? And, I'll be honest with you sweetheart, I can't deny that I'm kind of relieved. You know, I actually had intended to tell you last week; that's why I asked you to come with me to that outpatient's appointment. Still, taking everything into account, I guess Izzy's done me - us - a big favour, and I suppose I should be grateful to her for that.'

The danger time was over, and overcome with relief, she grabbed his hand and pulled it close to her chest. 'Oh, thank God! I've been so worried. But I should have known you'd take it so well. What a wonderful, *wonderful* man you are! I do love you so much!' She gasped, 'Oh, I …' her eyes becoming huge as she realised, with horror, that she had allowed the dangerous words to escape. How hard she had fought to keep them locked up and buried deep inside her, unwilling to allow them to roam free in her own mind and heart. And now she had let them escape. Now he knew. Now the awful, inevitable chain of events would follow. Now she had ruined everything.

He watched her face cloud over, her smile fading the instant she had spoken those words; words he wanted to hear her say again. 'You love me?'

Without realising what she was doing, she cast aside his hand and stood up. All she wanted to do now was to run. Run away, as far and as fast as she could:-

Get away, go! Leave this place. Leave him before he finds out what you're really like, before he rejects you, before he despises you, before he discovers just what a piece of rubbish you really are.

She cried, 'Oh Alex, I don't want to! I mustn't. I'll only end up hurting you. I'm no good for you. Please, *please* try to understand. *I can't!*'

He recognised what was happening. And now the anger came - although not with her, but at the devilish thing that was inside her, tormenting her. He felt desperate to comfort and protect her, to somehow pour his love into her. He stood and put his arms around her tense body, holding her close and stroking her back in an effort to sooth and calm her.

'Hey, hey! Come on, sweetheart. What's all this? It's alright, it's alright. I understand. Now listen to me, everything's going to work out, everything. I know it will, *I know*. Do you hear? I love you too. I love you Miss Yvonne Williams. I love you, and I'm not going to hurt you, and you're not going to hurt me. You don't have to be afraid. Remember,

The Boss is in this with us. I know He brought us together. I *know* things will work out for us.' He stopped abruptly. How close he had come to revealing his own secret. But no, he must not. Not yet. But how he wanted to!

She pressed her face against his shoulder. What words were these? What wonderful, wonderful words? Her heart leapt within her, just as somewhere, deep inside, a door felt like it was shutting. For a fleeting second, she had glimpsed real happiness. But just for a second.

'Oh, please don't! You mustn't. You *don't* understand! It wouldn't work. I'll only end up dragging you down too and making you miserable, and then you'll start resenting me. You *must* understand!' She managed to extricate herself, and pulling a tissue out of her sleeve, began to rub her eyes hard. 'And, anyway, I'm not a Christian.'

'But, last week you said … what was it … that you were feeling drawn - '

'I am. But I mustn't. It would be wrong.'

'You mustn't? Why? How could it be wrong? Especially if you feel drawn - '

'Please stop Alex! Don't ask me. I can't. Can't you just accept that? Can't you see now why we mustn't - '

Firmer now, and becoming more than a little anxious, he interrupted, 'No, you're really going to have to explain it to me. You've come this far; you might as well get it all off your chest. I think I've got a right to know.'

She stood perfectly still, struggling to compose herself and find a way of putting the awful truth into plain words. Yes, he had every right to know: this innocent, lovely man who loved her; this man who she was already starting to hurt.

'There's someone I…I can't forgive. I just can't. And you have to, don't you? That's a big thing in the Christian Faith, isn't it, forgiveness?'

'Well, yes. We forgive, just as we've been forgiven.'

She looked down, her whole demeanor one of utter dejection. 'Thought so.'

'So, who is it?' he asked. 'Your father? Niall? Or is there someone else?'

'My father … things he used to … but I'm having trouble over Niall too …' and then, unable to say any more, and despite promising herself that she wouldn't, she began to cry.

So, that was it. He felt a flash of anger towards that damn chef and this unknown, so-called parent. Forcing the strong feelings to one side, for he was more concerned about her now, he firmly, but gently, drew her back into his arms. 'It's okay sweetheart. You don't have to say any more. You'll be starting your counselling soon, and you'll be free, I promise you. The Boss will help you. He's brought you this far, He'll see you through.'

He continued to speak words of comfort and reassurance to her. He loved her and she loved him; wasn't that all that really mattered? All they had to do was to trust in The Boss. But she wasn't to worry, because, for now, he had enough trust for them both. At last she became calm. The storm was over, at least for now.

*

Later, he kissed her goodnight and watched her walk away. With his own heart sinking, he noted that her step was not as light as a young woman's should be, nor did she give him her usual bright smile when she turned to wave as he drove off. Despite his best efforts he knew that she was still consumed with feelings of sadness and guilt. He had done his best to calm and comfort her, but counselling was not one of his fortes. This was one battle he would have to watch from the sidelines, as others, gifted in the area, waded steadily and carefully in, to wield their own spiritual weapons.

'So much heartache, Boss, so much pain and false guilt over Rabbie. It's like part of her personality is being tortured. Hurry up and work a miracle through Charles and Izzy; let the counselling start soon. Let me have the girl you died for me to have. Soon, Boss, soon.' His innate obedience preventing him from putting into words his next thought, which he knew The Boss was fully aware of anyway, and a thought that he was finding increasingly hard to ignore: he would have her - whether she became a Christian or not. They belonged together. She *would* be his.

CHAPTER 32

The last hint of the pungent aroma of gloss faded just a week before the first guests were due to arrive at the Manor, but before then it was felt that the venture should be marked with some sort of celebration. After much deliberation, it was decided that a housewarming-come-ceilidh would be a suitable type of event, and Izzy set to work, ably assisted by the two new members of staff who had recently arrived. Retired, but still fit in mind and body, Sergeants George Andsover and Fred Owens, both of whom Charles had known for years, had been recruited after expressing themselves keen to support the project. Although regular church goers, neither were committed Christians, however, this was not considered to be a major obstacle. The truth of it was that, having no strong family or other civilian ties, both were grateful for the chance to belong somewhere even vaguely military again.

*

Things were not going so well at the Inn, especially for Georgina, who felt that the past three weeks had been truly dreadful. Not only was she still suffering from some sort of virus and had just been told that she was anaemic, now she was at her wits' end trying to cope with a seriously depressed Donald. He hadn't had an episode like this for over twenty years, in fact, not since the time when they thought they could lose Robert to meningitis. Now he only picked at Frazer's tasty concoctions, and had developed the unfortunate habit of raking his hands through is already tousled hair, giving him the appearance of an aged and scruffy beatnik. As if all this wasn't bad enough to cope with, he was tossing and turning so much in bed at night that she had found it necessary to banish him to Robert's old room. She just knew she would scream the next time he uttered his tormented cry, 'It's my fault, all my fault! He'd still be alive today if I hadn't encouraged the dear old boy. He was too trusting of humans. That damn Niall! I was too soft on him. We should have got rid of him much sooner. Oh God, Oh God!'

The one good thing about the whole dreadful affair was that all the official parties concerned had agreed to handle everything with the utmost discretion. Both the police and the vet had reached the same conclusion as Mrs Harmer, that death had been caused by a fatal knife wound. There was no doubt in her own mind now that Niall had been the culprit, and her anger and resentment towards him simmered deep in her heart. They knew he had been carrying knives; Donald said how he had watched him pack the block that day they had fired him. Full of rage and spite, he must have come across the stag soon after. Poor Rabbie, in her own way, she had been really quite fond of him. It was just his bad luck to have been in the wrong place at the wrong time.

Hoping that it would help Donald to come to terms with things, she had foolishly given in to his pleas to have the body laid to rest in a secluded spot behind the Inn. However, she was to be disappointed, for now he had taken to spending long hours by the graveside, 'Keeping the dear old boy company'. At least the guests were spared the sight of the forlorn, dejected figure, standing vigil, hour after hour out there, come rain or shine. As yet, none had commented upon the pathetic sight loping through the Inn; so much obvious misery seeping from every pore. Niall had certainly found an effective way to take his revenge and hurt them all, for now she was left with an almost useless husband - and just as the Inn was at its busiest.

*

Charles and Izzy were enjoying a quiet night in front of the television when their telephone extension emitted one long, uninterrupted ring, denoting an internal call. It was Alex.

'Sorry to bother you chaps, but I've got Georgina here. Say's she'd like a word with you Charles.'

Charles relayed the news to Izzy, who sighed heavily and began to think fast. The work they would soon be engaged in would be demanding in every way, and definitely not of the nine to five variety. As a consequence, they had decided that their private accommodation was sacrosanct, and that only family members and close friends were to be admitted. More than a little peeved, she whispered, rather too loudly, 'What can she want? Can't be about the house-warming, I only spoke to her about it this morning.' She sighed heavily again, 'Oh well, suppose I'd better come too. Tell Alex to put her in the lounge.'

They descended the stairs and met Alex coming out of the kitchen carrying a mug. He spoke quietly. 'This is for her, looks like she could do with it. Reckon she's a bit out of sorts. I've put the fire on.'

Izzy took the mug from him. 'Thanks, we didn't hear the bell.'

'Disconnected; got a fault. The electrician's coming to reroute it tomorrow, and I was down here anyway.' He pointed towards a small stack of picture frames leaning against a wall. 'Just finding homes for these. This is where I could do with Yvonne again.'

They found Georgina perched on the edge of one of the armchairs, her hands folded tightly in her lap, her mouth set in a grim line. She nodded, but did not stand when they entered.

'Hello Georgina! Welcome to Braegarroch Manor,' said Charles, crossing the room and going to sit opposite her. 'I believe this is your first visit for a while?'

Izzy took in the stiff, anxious bearing of the woman as she placed the mug on the table beside her, before joining Charles on the settee.

Charles was right; Georgina had not set foot inside the Manor since falling out with the wife of the previous owner, who, in her opinion, was a bit too fond of the bottle and prone to making an exhibition of herself at the ceilidhs. She had made a cursory inspection of the place whilst waiting for them, and from what she had been able to see so far, felt that it was a touch too modern for her taste. And the carpet was a bit too plain - so impractical. The whole thing must have cost a pretty penny, but then, it was alright for some; not everyone was able to access all types of grants.

Trying to sound only mildly interested, she replied, 'Quite a while. I must say, it's all very … modern. Of course, you'll need to keep on top of it. You'll soon discover that it's a lot of hard work keeping an establishment up to the mark. Have you got some girls coming in from Braegarroch to do the cleaning? There's no one I can think of in Ardgeal.'

Izzy was not in the mood for shop talk, and hastened to explain, as graciously as she could, that both she and Charles had vast experience in organising people and places, and that they already had sufficient staffing levels. 'But now,' she asked, 'why have you paid us the compliment of this visit, and where's Donald?'

Georgina sat back and began to smooth imaginary creases off the chair's armrest. 'Actually, he's the reason I'm here. But, before ... that is ... you know, of course, at least, I *assume* you know, that we're Church of Scotland? I'm not quite sure that we shan't be expected to join in ... things here ... if we find that we might need to accept any kind of ... er, assistance in any way?'

Charles understood her discomfort, and quickly stepped in to explain, 'By no means! There's no strings attached to any of the ways we'll be helping here, and we're not going to be a closed shop,' then added, smiling, 'even neighbours are welcome.'

Feeling that enough time had been spent on pleasantries, Izzy ventured, 'Well now, Georgina, it sounds as though things have been rather difficult for you all at the Inn recently?'

Charles smiled inwardly as Georgina's hand shot up to pat a frizzy portion of her hair. This new wife of his was impetuous, impatient and impossible - but quite a marvel! She had proved right on more occasions than he cared to remember, and was probably doing it again. And he was glad of it.

Recovering, Georgina picked up her mug, which she considered to be very uncouth, and replied tersely, 'Well, I wouldn't have put it *quite* like that myself, Mrs Harmer.'

'Isabelle, remember?' reminded Izzy.

'Oh, er, yes. But now you mention it, poor Donald's been in a terrible state since that ... thing ... happened to Rabbie, and he just can't seem to snap out of it, and we're so busy now.

He's usually so conscientious, but all this moping around that grave, and he's looking so peaky ...' Her voice cracked, she sipped her drink and grimaced. Instant coffee, typical! She went on, 'And between you and me, I'm finding the whole thing very tiring. He's always been too fond of that stag. But one doesn't expect one's husband to go around moping like this. For goodness sake, you'd think he'd lost a child or something!' She paused, even she could hear the wretchedness in her voice.

Charles studied her pale, strained face, and felt that Donald was not the only one going around looking peaky. He had not known Georgina long, but from what he had experienced of her so far, judged that she was the confident, self-contained and stiff upper lipped type. Things must be very bad indeed for her to admit to any kind of weakness in her world. 'A painful time for him, and hard on you too, I imagine?' he asked.

Isabelle suddenly remembered that there was a son somewhere, and added, 'You have a son, I believe? In the hotel trade too, isn't he? Can't he come and help out for a while?'

Georgina let out an exasperated gasp as she replaced her mug and slapped her hands down hard on her knees in a gesture of impatience. 'Robert? Oh no! We couldn't possibly involve him. Their conferences are well under way, and it wouldn't look good if he suddenly up and disappeared. No, I'm afraid Donald's got to snap out of it. I've tried reasoning with him, but he just looks at me blank, and all Doctor Anderson could do was to offer him sleeping pills, and tell me to be patient. *Patient!* Reverend Gunn was next to useless too. Er, I happened to bump into him the other day. "Give him time," he said, "be gentle with him". As if I needed telling! If that's the only help he can give ...well!' She gave a ladylike snort of derision. "Be gentle," indeed! For goodness sake, Rabbie was just an animal! No, Donald's just needs to come to terms with things, and pull himself together.'

The outburst over, she glared at the faces opposite, her irritation towards Donald reaching new heights. How could he do this to her, and put her in such an embarrassing position? Regaining some control, she looked directly at Charles, then said in a much lighter tone, 'Then it occurred to me that you're supposed to be used to dealing with certain problems of ... an emotional nature, and maybe there was something you could do, you know, like have a quiet word with him?'

'Well now, that depends,' said Charles, 'has he mentioned anything about wanting to talk to someone, apart from Doctor Anderson?'

'Er, no. I don't think it's occurred to him,' she replied. 'But surely ... there's some way, something you can do? I'm really at my wits' end. Do you know, I even had to tell him a little white lie just now, just so I could slip out? All this skulking and moping around is so tiresome. We simply can't go on like this. Where will it all end?'

Charles studied her strained face and considered. The poor woman certainly looked desperate, but Donald sounded even more so. Making his mind up, he said, 'Okay, I'll see what I can do.'

'You will? Oh, that is good of you!' She exclaimed, allowing a flicker of a smile to cross her face.

'So, how do you want to play this?' asked Charles. 'Shall I phone first, and try to arrange an appointment? Or would it better to invite him to come here?'

'Er, I don't think that would be quite the thing. Can't you, you know, just drop in ... casually, one day?'

'Well, I suppose ... but that's not our usual way of doing things.'

Izzy felt she should intervene here. 'You know Georgina, it would be better if he came to us in his own time. One should never try to manipulate ...' she paused, noticing that their visitor was becoming visibly distressed again.

Charles quickly intervened. 'Although, I think we can make an exception in this case. I could call in tomorrow; see if I can catch him, and maybe have a chat?'

Recovering, Georgina made a great show of considering the matter, although all three knew this was exactly what she had been hoping for. 'Oh, I see. Well, I think ... I expect that would be alright.'

'Fair enough,' said Charles, 'and gently does it. Let's see if he's ready and willing; we aren't in the business of forcing ourselves on anyone.'

'Well of course not!' Georgina replied indignantly, obviously feeling more like her old self again. 'But honestly, all this fuss and bother over an animal! Although, don't get me wrong, I was actually quite fond of the stag myself. And even I was quite upset about the way it was killed. What on earth possessed the man to do such a dreadful thing?'

'Huh! More like *who* possessed the man,' remarked Izzy.

'Pardon?'

Charles interjected quickly, feeling that this was not the most suitable of times to embark upon an explanation on the sources of evil. 'From what I hear of it, Georgina, Rabbie was quite an exceptional character, and he and Donald had a special type of bond. It sounds to me as though he's going through just as painful a grieving process as if he'd have lost someone dear to him.'

Georgina stared at him. 'Well, even so - '

Now it was Izzy's turn to interject; she had heard quite enough, and was suddenly feeling very tired. 'Okay, so, shall we say sometime tomorrow morning? We're not booked until later. Say around the ten o'clock mark?'

'No, that won't do. The afternoon would suit us better.'

Izzy felt piqued. Not only had the woman infringed upon their precious private time and extracted a promise of help, now she was actually trying to dictate when that help should be given! 'Can't do, I'm afraid. Morning only. We've several appointments in the afternoon, and it's a bit late to for us to start re-arranging the whole day.'

The two women stared at each other, both understanding the unspoken challenge. Charles remained silent, inwardly asking the Lord to bring His peace to bear. How alike these two women were; both possessed strong, assertive characters; it was inevitable that they would clash sooner or later.

Finally, Georgina conceded, albeit grudgingly. 'Very well. Only I can't promise that we won't be busy, there's a coach in at eleven.' She sighed, heavily and gave them a pained look of resignation. 'But I suppose we'll have to cope.'

'Ten o'clock it is then,' announced Charles cheerfully, and rising to his feet. 'Now, how about a quick tour? I'm afraid Izzy won't be able to join us, but I'd be interested to hear your opinion on what we've done to the place.'

And, feeling relieved, Georgina felt that she would be more than happy to give it, although it would have to be a somewhat tempered version - the man had agreed to try and help after all.

CHAPTER 33

Having checked, and re-checked the stock, then spent the next ten minutes wiping the already spotless bar, Donald gave in to the struggle going on inside him, and went outside. It was cold, he shivered, but that didn't signify, for the dear old boy's body was somewhere far, far colder. All that black earth, great mounds of it, and piled so heavily on top of him. At least the tarpaulin would keep the worms off for a while. But those maggots! N*o! Don't think of it!* Think of the warm, the dry, anything. If only he wasn't feeling so alone now. So very alone.

He stared at the vase containing a fresh bunch of wild flowers, and wondered when Yvonne had been there; he knew it was her, he had spotted her out here several times arranging similar bunches. Her thoughtfulness touched him, just as he'd felt touched by the genuine upset of the small crowd that had gathered to watch and help with the burial. Burial. Death. Gone forever. Words that had come to define and dominate his life now. Yes, the dear old boy was dead, but oh, still alive, so *very* alive in his heart. Maybe later, when the ground has settled, he would arrange to have a small stone erected with some meaningful words carved on it. Yes, that would be fine thing to do, despite what Georgy might say.

It began to rain, he'd forgotten his coat, but that didn't signify either; at least he'd be put out of his misery if he caught pneumonia and died. Then, if Georgy allowed it, he'd like his ashes interred with the dear old boy, and then maybe someone would say some kind, graveside type words over them both; that would be good. Thinking about it, maybe he'd been a bit too hasty refusing to allow Charles to say a few words that day. After all, what harm could a few prayers have done? It might even have been a sort of compliment, an acknowledgement to the rest of the world about what he'd always known: that Rabbie was far more than just a mere, dumb animal.

*

Charles stood in the open doorway, watching the solitary figure. Quietly, not wanting to startle him, he cleared his throat and went to stand beside him. 'Hello Donald.'

Donald gave a small start, and turned his downward gaze up to meet Charles' kindly and concerned expression. 'Oh! It's you!'

Charles noticed that Donald had been crying and made a sweep of his arm, taking in the mountainous background. 'You chose a good spot for him. I'm sure he'd approve.'

Donald's chin twitched uncontrollably under his beard. Charles recognised that the man was on the verge of spilling more tears.

'He used to ...' he turned his head towards the side gate, 'wait for me there sometimes ... I'd find him ... you know, his spot. He was a canny one.'

'Clever as well then? A real character?'

Donald nodded. 'Strange you should turn up. I was just thinking ... you offered to say a few words, you know, that day?'

'Yes, I remember.'

'Well, I was wondering, are there time-limits to that kind of thing? Because, I think, I wouldn't mind - '

'Of course. And it's never too late.' Charles gave an involuntary shiver; the light drizzle was beginning to turn heavy. 'But why don't we go inside and warm up? Maybe we could talk about it in there?'

Donald looked uncertain. What did the wet and cold matter? All he wanted was for the man to say a few words. Why couldn't he do it now? He didn't need to *talk* about it. He just wanted to get the thing done ... for Rabbie.

Charles put his hand on one of the stooping shoulders, and said comfortingly, 'Come on Donald, let's go inside and find somewhere warm and quiet. You know, I think I'd like to hear a bit more about him; maybe you can tell me about some of his little ways?'

Donald peered at him through bloodshot eyes. A chance to talk about the dear old boy. Yes, he'd like that.

Georgina had been watching events from the kitchen window, and appeared as the two men entered.

Charles quickly took the initiative. 'Ah, Georgina! Good day to you. I wonder if there's somewhere quiet Donald and I could go for a few minutes?'

'Well, I suppose, the flat. And for goodness sake, Donald, take those wet shoes off! Look at the trail you're leaving behind you.'

*

Donald led Charles up into their private sitting room, which turned out to be an overwhelmingly plumped up chintz affair. He made coffee, and with a slightly shaking hand, held the dainty bone china cup and saucer out to Charles, explaining, 'Mugs were banished up here when our son left home.'

Not one for social chitchat, and knowing that time was short, Charles took the rattling crockery, and launched straight in. 'Makes a nice change. Now, about Rabbie, you're missing him a great deal, aren't you?'

Donald bent and seemed to crumple into his chair. 'More than I can say. But that must sound odd to you?'

'Not at all, sounds very reasonable. You two had a special bond. I can quite understand that.'

Donald looked up in surprise. 'You can? And you don't think I'm being, you know, that I've gone soft in the head or something?'

'Certainly not! A character like that can leave a huge gap in the life of someone who's fond of them.'

'You can say that again! I just don't know how ... I just can't get used to not having him around. Georgy thinks I'm crazy, but she never ... you know.'

Charles nodded. 'Some people have a special affinity with animals, and I personally believe that part of our soul remains asleep until we have experienced the love of one. It's a very special type of love, and one which many find hard to understand. But it's certainly nothing to be ashamed of, or hide under a bushel. I believe it's God-given.'

'You do?'

'Most definitely!' He paused to give Donald a thoughtful, kindly look, before adding, 'And I also believe that you feel that your poor heart has been broken, and you don't think it will ever heal. You can't imagine how to live your life without him being part of it.'

Donald leaned forward, relieved that here, at last, was someone who actually seemed to understand. But hearing the kind sentiments spoken out loud was more than a little harrowing. He cradled his head in his hands and wrung out his reply. 'I can't seem to ... to get on ... and ... yes, it's like my heart ... you know. It was awful, *awful!* If only he'd have died naturally ... but to be killed ... murdered ... butchered ...'

Charles leaned towards him and patted the bony knee. 'Don't torture yourself like this Donald. You know, your heart will heal, especially if you let God into the picture. He loves Rabbie far more than you do; bound to, He created him. Here, if you'd allow me.' He drew out a small Bible from his pocket, its black leather cover softened by years of regular handling. Patting it, he said, 'They're all in here you know, the answers.'

Even in his distressed state, Donald reasoned that this was fair enough; he had asked the man to speak a few words over the grave, and being a man of the cloth, it was natural that he'd want to dip into the Bible. He was sinking here, and a drowning man couldn't be too fussy about what type of lifeline he was thrown. And anyway, he was curious. Resigning himself to the inevitable, he sat back, and asked, 'Answers, what answers?'

'To questions. Questions many people ask at times like this,' replied Charles, opening the small book. 'Such as: "Has my cat, or dog...my beloved pet...gone to Heaven?" He quickly found what he was looking for. 'Here, listen to this:-

Are not five sparrows sold for two pennies?
Yet not one of them is forgotten by God.
(Luke 12:6).

And I'd have to include our budgies, cats, dogs, guinea pigs, hamsters, donkeys and horses, even stags. All of which, just like the sparrows, will not be *forgotten by God.* Sounds to me like they're all stored away, safe, in God's memory. Not a bad place to be, wouldn't you say?'

Donald felt his heart quicken. If this was true, then could it be that Rabbie wasn't out there after all, alone and rotting in his grave? To be sure, his poor body was, but was it really possible that the *real* Rabbie, the part that he had befriended and loved, his own special character, might actually be ... somewhere else? Somewhere safe? The notion that God could somehow reach down to take him, and store him safely away in His very own memory - was plain crazy! But somehow ... He was so taken with the idea that he decided he would like to hear more things like this, even if they were too good to be true.

As a result, Charles found himself conducting a spontaneous Bible study. 'God gave *every* living thing a soul, you know. Here, listen to what He said to Job:-

> *In his hand is the life of every creature*
> *and the breath of all mankind.*
> *(Job 12:10).*

Some of the older versions use the word *soul* instead of *breath.'*

Donald looked puzzled. 'So, you're saying that animals have souls - as well as humans?'

Charles nodded and tapped the open pages. 'That's how I read it. They're certainly more than mere flesh and blood, no matter what some people think. And John's vision in the book of *Revelation* includes all manner of creatures, not just us humans. Let me see now ...' He turned to the back of the Bible, and quickly found what he was looking for:-

> *'Then I heard every creature in heaven and on*
> *earth and under the earth and on the sea, and all*
> *that is in them, singing: 'To him who sits on the*
> *throne and to the Lamb ...' (Revelation 5:13).*

There you go: *every creature* again.'

'Well, Rabbie was definitely more than just a big lump of flesh! And he did have something kind of...soulful about him. If you'd have known him, how he used to look at me sometimes ...' And so he went on to describe many of Rabbie's little ways, including how he would rub his muzzle against his hand and give him long, slow licks, whilst giving him gentle, ponderous looks with his big brown eyes; so docile, so trusting, so gentle. So soulful. He was forced to stop when his throat began to ache unbearably with the strain of keeping the sobs at bay.

Charles listened attentively, occasionally making sympathetic and encouraging comments. Now he said, 'He was obviously extremely fond of you Donald. But your experience is not uncommon. Many of us know what it's like to have the companionship, friendship, loyalty and love of an animal. And I often think that, in many ways, they put us humans to shame. Look at the joyful greetings and unashamed affection they give their owners when they come home. And what about the many reports there are of those that have put themselves in harm's way to save a member of their pack? Even their human 'pack'! I don't know what you call behaviour like that, but I'd call it sacrificial. Certainly not the actions of a *soulless* being.'

Donald was aware that something in him was beginning to warm up, and now he *really* wanted to hear more.

Charles flicked the delicate pages over quickly. 'God knew Rabbie, and still knows him.' He held the book open and turned it towards Donald. Pointing at the verses, he said, 'Here, look at this.'

Donald lent forward and read:-

'...for every animal of the forest is mine, and the cattle on a thousand hills. I know every bird in the mountains, and the creatures of the field are mine.'
(Psalm 50:10,11).

He gave a short whistle. 'That's good! I like that. And Rabbie was an *animal of the forest*. So they all belong to God?

And is that why they all go to Heaven when ... you know ... afterwards?'

'When they die? Remember what we read, about how God doesn't forget even the sparrows? And about *all* creatures worshipping God in Heaven? John's vision in *Revelation* mentions horses. And Peter saw all manner of birds and animals coming down from Heaven - and then going back up again in his vision in *Acts.*'

'Really? But ... but what if someone doesn't go along with, er, everything, you know, in the Bible? I do of course, but there's plenty that don't.'

'You know Donald, we're all free to make our own choices, but would they really want to throw the whole lot in the bin? I've witnessed many who find themselves thinking again when their own end comes. And I always find it strange when people continually use God's name in their everyday speech - and then claim He doesn't exist! Why not use Santa's name, or the Tooth Fairy's? Why is it always God's name? Worth thinking about, don't you think?'

Donald shifted in his seat, knowing that his everyday speech was littered with all manner of references to the Almighty. Maybe he should think about all this, but at some other time, when he felt up to it.

'Have you had enough, or do you want to hear more?' asked Charles.

'Yes, go on, if you've got something...about animals,' replied Donald.

'Alright. Then maybe this will sound familiar,' he turned back to *Genesis.* 'It's before Eve came on the scene:-

The LORD God said, 'It is not good for the man to be alone. I will make a helper suitable for him.'
Now the LORD God had formed out of the ground all the beasts of the field and all the birds of the air.
He brought them to the man to see what would name them; and whatever the man called each living creature, that was its name.
(Genesis 2:18,19).

So, it appears that God's original plan was for humans and animals to co-exist. And I especially like this bit.' He leafed forward a few pages. 'It's the very first covenant God made with mankind, to Noah and his family, after the flood:-

Then God said to Noah and his sons with him: 'I now establish my covenant with you and with your descendants after you and with every living creature that was with you - the birds, the livestock and all the wild animals, all those that came out of the ark with you – every living creature on earth.
(Genesis 9:8-10).

Seems to me that God was keen to get His message across: *every living creature.* and again, *every living creature on earth.* Let's face it, it would have been far quicker and easier for Noah to build the Ark if it was just to save him and his family - by the way, that was only eight humans. But God obviously wanted to include representatives from all parts of His creation. And as to why He felt He had to wipe out all other life on earth, we need to take into account that the people of that day were into all sorts of unsavoury practices, especially bestiality - that was very common. As a result, demon possession must have been extremely widespread, unfortunately in the animal kingdom too; they became contaminated, infected, as a result of mankind's sinful and rebellious activities.'

Donald was fully alert now. Gone were the rounded shoulders, he was sitting upright, his face alive with interest, as he exclaimed, 'You're joking! Any more things like that in there?'

'Well now, seeing as you asked, but let's get back to the present, and your situation. In a way, you could say that Rabbie's gone ahead of you.'

Donald frowned. 'What do you mean, "Gone ahead". In what way?'

'We believe that God doesn't wash His hands of us when our earthly life comes to an end. Our spirit, the part of us that is our connection with Him, returns to Him at our physical death. But only for those who've made that choice.'

'Choice? What choice?'

'To take Him seriously, before it's too late, and by responding to His love in Jesus.'

Donald wondered where he was going with this. 'Er, you're losing me now.'

'We each have to make our own personal decision to want to be right with God. You know, you can't just slip into Heaven, or trick yourself in, nor can you get in by hanging on to someone else's coat-tails. Good works, or leading a good life, won't get you in either. We've all been given freewill; we can choose to accept God's love, or reject it, and Him. And the choice is free, there's no charge. His Son, Jesus, paid the price in full by dying on the Cross for each one of us. The choice is ours to make: accept Him, or reject Him - and suffer the consequences when our time comes to face Him.'

'But I ... er, hadn't heard. At least, I can't remember ...'

'Worth doing some serious thinking about though, wouldn't you agree?'

Donald considered, and tried hard to remember when, apart from this man, Alex, and Reverend Gunn, he had ever known anyone who had thought seriously about God. Had he? No, probably not. Then Niall's unwelcome image crossed his mind; now there was someone who needed to be serious about these sort of things. He let out a long, low whistle. 'Hell's bells! I wouldn't want to be in Niall's shoes on Judgement Day. I'm damn sure it was him who did for my Rabbie.'

'You know Donald, even he can be forgiven if he's sincerely sorry and wants to make his peace with God.'

'Huh! That doesn't seem very fair to me! I wouldn't let him off. I'd make him pay for what he's done; I'd make him suffer.'

'Well now, when it comes to justice, best to leave that sort of thing to the law, don't you think? Appropriate human justice is to be desired. But *eternal* justice, now that's another matter, and best left to God: the Judge of all souls. But what about you?'

'What about me?

'Are your hands clean? Haven't you ever done anything you're sorry about, or ashamed of? Haven't you ever caused some misery or pain to someone else? Or have you led a totally blameless life? If so, I'd like to shake your hand. You'd be the first perfect person I'd ever met!'

'Well, I ... er, can't say that I've not done the odd thing here or there which might be considered ... you know. But nothing like what *he* did. Nothing like that - *that* bad.'

'Hmm. Just little sins, then. Sorry, but still enough to keep you out of Heaven. No sins allowed in there - or it wouldn't be Heaven anymore!'

Donald shifted position. The focus of the conversation had somehow moved onto him, and he was beginning to feel a touch uncomfortable about it. 'Er, but what about Niall? I still say that it can't be right that he'd be allowed to get off scot-free.'

'And he won't! You can be sure of that. Unless he genuinely repents, one day he'll have to stand before God, and account for all his actions - and face the consequences.'

'Huh! I can just imagine him trying to wriggle his way out of it. All he ever did was mumble and curse. And what are these consequences anyway - that he'll have to face?'

'In a nutshell, to spend eternity away from God's presence, and all that that means.'

Some of this was going over Donald's head, but something in him felt satisfied. He liked the idea, that, although Niall might have escaped justice on this side of death, it sounded as though he would not escape it on the other. He uncrossed his legs and scratched a recent midge bite. So much for Niall, but what did fate have in store for these blasted pests?

'And what about midges, and things like snakes and man-eating tigers, and so on? What good are they to anybody? Why the heck did God create them?'

'Ah, we're getting in deep now. Briefly, and I mean *very* briefly because we're into sermon-land, *Genesis* tells us that the *whole* of creation fell in The Garden of Eden. Adam and Eve didn't appear to have had any fear of the animals, or have any thorns or thistles to deal with - that is, before they disobeyed and rebelled against God. Everything in the Garden was perfect; humans living in perfect harmony with nature and animals; all bound-up and integrated. The sad truth is that when sin entered the human heart and we fell from grace, nature was dragged down with it. Mankind, who God had made perfect and in His own image, became infected with sin. The result was that humanity and nature, including the animal kingdom, began to produce ungodly things and suffer from ungodly traits - like suspicion, fear, aggression, hate - and poison. In other words, humanity became distorted and warped, as did nature, and the once good ground began to yield thorns and other problematic vegetation. But, and I'm sure you'll be pleased to know this Donald, God has a rescue plan. Paul indicates in *Romans* that there will be a glorious time when God will free *every* part of His creation from the effects of the Fall. *Every* part will be rescued - and freed! And that includes Rabbie.

'Rabbie, rescued!' exclaimed Donald. Sitting bolt upright now. 'How…what do you mean? How will he be rescued? How can he be freed?'

'At the risk of repeating myself, remember what I said about nature and humans, all being bound up with each other? They were then, they are now, and they always will be; interdependent, integrated. God has promised in His Word that there's going to be time - a *glorious* time - when harmony will be restored. He's going to create a new Heaven and a new Earth. Animals won't fear us any more, nor we them. And incidentally, the account of Creation in *Genesis* makes it clear that God's original plan was for us, and them, to be herbivores - vegetarians! There were reasons why that changed after the Flood, but I shan't go into them now. But when God's plan is fulfilled, we won't have the desire to eat them, nor will they want to eat each other. Here, listen to this. This is something I'm really looking forward to:-

The wolf will live with the lamb, the leopard will lie down with the goat, the calf and the lion and the

*yearling together; and a child will lead them. The cow
will feed with the bear, their young will lie down
together, and the lion will eat straw like the ox.'
(Isaiah 11:6,7).*

He closed the Bible slowly and slipped it reverentially back
into his pocket. 'All I can say is, and please be assured that this
is what I truly believe Donald, that Rabbie is resting peacefully
- maybe even running free - in God's very Presence.
Remember the sparrows? So please try and rest easy, knowing
that Rabbie's in a safe and loving place. And remember, it's up
to you if you make that choice to go and join him one day. And
just on the off chance that you start doubting God's
commitment towards animals, remember the circumstances of
His own Son's birth?'

'What, you mean in a manger?'

'Exactly so. Animals involved again. And consider one of
Jesus's titles: *The Lamb of God.*'

The silence in the room was almost palpable. At last,
Donald spoke, 'I'd like you to say things like that over him,
over his grave, about the sparrows, and Heaven ... and him
being one of God's creatures ... and safe and all.'

'I think I'd like that very much.'

*

And so it was decided that Charles would conduct a short
service after breakfast the next morning. In the meantime,
Donald would invite any who wanted to come. The discussion
over, the two men shook hands warmly. Something in Donald
recognised that he had heard the truth, and the truth was that
this wasn't the end of Rabbie's story. He had simply moved
on. He was safe with God Almighty. Almighty! He liked the
sound of that. Such a powerful word. As for the rest of it, that
choice, well, he'd have to think about that another day. But
think about it he would: Rabbie was waiting for him.

He watched Charles drive off, glad there were such people
in the world. He took his comb out of his pocket and attempted
to tidy himself up. The coach was in. Georgy would be needing
him.

CHAPTER 34

Chauffer-like, Donald opened Georgina's door and helped her emerge. Resplendent in her mink stole and finest evening gown - a shiny brown affair, he quietly thought she looked every inch the lady as he steered her towards the Manor's main entrance. Held tightly under his other arm was a pair of large framed photographs of Ben An-t-Earrach and Loch Laith. It had been useful to rediscover Robert's old prints, and he had every confidence that these would prove to be acceptable house-warming gifts for any blank spaces there may still be on the Manor's walls.

It was a mild evening. The tinkling of ice cubes could be heard mixing with the noisy chatter coming from the lounge's open windows. Georgina peered in and recognised many of the faces.

'What a crowd!' she exclaimed. 'Everyone and his neighbour must be here. The place is lit up like a Belisha beacon. Goodness knows what their electricity bill will be!'

Donald, who had been thinking how tidy and attractive the outside was looking, replied, 'Can't miss it, that's for sure. Hey, isn't that old man Morrison over there, and Kathleen too? Haven't seen them for a while. Come to think of it, didn't Alex say something about him doing a stint or two in the garden?'

'Humph! Gardeners indeed. What next, a swimming pool?' she replied, tartly.

His own anticipation at attending the Manor's official house-warming suddenly experienced a slight chill. 'Come on, Georgy, you know he's been lost without Lassie. Probably glad of something to do, being an old soldier and all.' He was a bit fed up of her continuing negative attitude towards the place, and could only assume that she was suffering from a dose of good old-fashioned jealousy. Speaking for himself, he wished the venture every success, and the more so since he had personally experienced a taste of what they would be offering to others. Although he was still grieving over the dear old boy, the awful black cloud of depression had been lifting a bit more each day since he'd had that chat with Charles. It would be good to support the man now.

They approached the porch steps and took their position behind several other couples waiting to be greeted by Charles, Izzy and Alex. An assortment of cards, packages and bottles were being offered to the small welcoming party. Immediately behind them stood a man, new to the area, whose task appeared to be to discreetly relieve them of the gifts and stack them onto a nearby table.

'I thought this was supposed to be a housewarming, not a wedding reception,' whispered Georgina, sarcastically.

'Buck up, Georgy!' Donald replied, a firmer tone than usual to his voice, and hoping that no one had heard her. 'Only chance we'll have for a night out for a while, anyway.'

She fixed one of her tight smiles on her lips as they reached the head of the queue. Donald held out the pictures. 'Hope you like them. Home grown, you might say, and personally signed.'

'How very kind! Thank you,' said Charles, accepting the packages. 'Do you mind if we open them later? And may I say how splendid you're looking Georgina?'

'Yes, indeed,' exclaimed Izzy. 'How good of you to spare the time to come to our little gathering. I hope you'll be able to relax and enjoy watching someone else do all the work for a change. And I know you're keen to hear the band.'

The main entertainment of the evening was the well known Starold Star Ceilidh Band, who, along with some of the other guests, would be staying overnight at the Inn; a fact that Georgina would have the need to drop into several conversations throughout the evening. Feeling suitably welcomed, she patted her carefully shampooed and set hair, every part of which was now satisfactorily waved and lacquered, and replied dismissively, 'Well, that all depends. If they're any good then we might consider them for a ceilidh, as long as they're not too coarse or amateurish.'

Polite smiles followed as Donald shook Alex's hand and gestured towards the blue-pink sky. 'You've got a good night for it anyway. Looks like it'll stay clear; fortunate that.'

Alex nodded. 'Another blessing. But please go on in and make yourself comfortable. There's refreshment in the lounge.'

Donald guided Georgina through the crowd, hoping that there would be at least some sherry on offer; that should loosen her up. If not, he would make it his business to add a few discreet nips to her glass from the contents of his trusty hip flask.

*

Yvonne had just enough time to change before Alex came to collect her. Desperate not to let him down, she studied herself critically in the mirror. The Spastics Shop had done her proud; the cream, embroidery anglaise blouse looked good against the black, full-length evening skirt. Thank goodness her hair had co-operated for once; the French plait looked tidy enough, and it was kind of Flora to lend her the delicate mother-of-pearl combs.

He was talking to some of the guests and had his back to her when she approached the lounge. She felt maddeningly shy as she walked towards the group. Unlike Niall, Frazer had no qualms about taking a turn behind the cocktail bar, and nodded in her direction as she entered. 'Here she is,' he announced, 'and looking aye bonnie if I might say so.'

All eyes turned towards her, and despite her best efforts, she found herself blushing furiously, thereby immediately sabotaging her hope to appear as graceful and stylish as she possibly could from the very start of this most important of nights. The handsome, elegant man waiting for her, deserved, and needed a mature, graceful companion; not some gawky Eliza Doolittle lookalike.

Alex turned and gave a slow, soft whistle, his eyes lighting up as he held out his free hand towards her, the other clasping the handle of his stick. He bowed and pressed a firm kiss onto the back of her hand. 'Well, hello beautiful! You'll have to keep reminding me to keep breathing tonight.'

She would have liked to have told him how he took her breath away too, instead, she could only manage an uninspired, 'Thank you. You're looking very smart.' She glanced the full length of him, taking in his freshly cut hair, the razor-like pleat of his trousers, and the mirror-like shine of his shoes. He was in civilian clothes, but she felt sure he was up to military inspection standard.

'Well, do I pass muster?' he asked, smiling, his eyes warm, and still full of her.

'Oh yes! You certainly do!' she replied, managing to regain some composure, despite the ongoing blush.

He laughed. 'Thought I'd better make a bit of an effort. Anyway, there's quite a crowd there already; we'd better be making tracks.'

They said their goodbyes. Once outside, he looked back to make sure that no one was watching, then took her hand and led her around the front of the car. 'Come here,' he said, gently pushing her against the bonnet, 'there won't be much chance to do this for a while.' He began kissing her softly on her face and neck, before settling on her mouth. The kisses became more urgent as he pressed himself hard against her. Eventually, he was able to make himself stop, and said close to her ear, 'Don't you leave my sight tonight, you hear! Every man in the place will be after you, and they've got to know - '

But she did not allow him to finish. Lost in the longing to be part of him, she reached up, and wove her fingers around the back of his head, pulling his face back towards hers. She kissed him as ardently as she knew how, desperate for him to know how much she wanted, desired, and needed him too. She was his, totally and completely.

A door opened somewhere and voices broke into their world. Slowly, reluctantly, they released each other.

He had a monumental battle to control himself on the journey back to the Manor. He wanted her so badly now that he seriously doubted if he could hold back much longer. And tonight, for the first time, she had revealed how much she wanted him too. And now he knew he was in real trouble. Thank goodness they would be chaperoned by the crowd tonight. But what about tomorrow, and the day after? Christian or not, it was all he could do to stop himself from turning the car right around there and then - and heading for Gretna Green.

*

Three days had passed. He was sitting at his desk in the office, holding the small stone, recently brought into service as a paper weight, and studying the framed picture facing him. Such simple gifts, yet already he was beginning to treasure them.

Yvonne had given them to him on the evening of the house-warming. She explained how the stone had caught her eye as it lay glistening on the pristine, white sand of a beach they had visited one gloriously sunny day. Without knowing why, she had picked it up and slipped it into her pocket. She had liked the feel of it in her hand where it seemed to almost nestle. Grey, and speckled with black, pink and silver dots, it was certainly eye-catching. She explained how she felt it represented their lives, the main part of which was made up of a humdrum existence, but made special by the welcome interruption of many smaller, happier, even sparkling experiences and events; like that very night.

The picture was of a tree she often passed on her walks. Many years before it had died, leaving an empty husk, inside which a regenerated version of itself had grown. Everything about it spoke to her of hope and new life. She had taken several photographs of its changing state over the spring and summer months, and, feeling in an artistic frame of mind one evening, had sat to create the small painting, using the basic set of water colours she had come across in the staff room.

'You've often told me that you're a new creation now,' she had explained. 'So this is like you: something new and whole, like your new life, growing out of something old and broken; your life before you became a Christian.'

It had been a good night. Everyone seemed to have enjoyed themselves, even the MacMan's, and the band had gone down well. But that woman, Sky McLoud, the only female member of the foursome, had been a shameful flirt, and had made a great show of singing nearly every song in his direction. But it had been easy to ignore her blatant overtures towards him; how could he not, when the only woman he had eyes for was sitting close beside him.

He half-smiled as he remembered the bittersweet relief he'd felt when Donald had offered to take Yvonne back to the Inn afterwards; The Boss must have had a hand in that. Yes, it had been a good night, but he was still single, still trusting - and still impatient. Tomorrow would be a quieter day, maybe he should fast and pray; he definitely needed more help and strength when it came to this temptation issue.

His reverie was disturbed when Izzy popped her head around the door, and asked, 'Coffee? Wonder if Stephen will join us today?'

'Right, let's go and see,' he replied, standing and following her through into the lounge. They had eleven guests in, with one more expected to arrive later that day. All but one appeared to be settling in well; Lieutenant Stephen Duncan, (Retired), was obviously finding it difficult to integrate, and had barely left his room since his arrival. Thankfully, Charles did not appear to be overly concerned, exuding an air of quiet confidence as he went about the day's business. Good old Charles, Izzy too; both as steady as a pair of rocks. How blessed he was to have been given the gift of such people in his life. By the world's standards, he had not known them that long, but then again, The Boss's standards were entirely different - and for that he was truly thankful.

CHAPTER 35

Yvonne dismounted and put the bike she had recently acquired into the rack; it was old but solid, and she was grateful for the measure of independence it was giving her. She knew Alex would not be around; he had telephoned a few days earlier to say that he was going into Invermaden to look at a minivan that was for sale. The excursions he regularly offered to the guests were proving popular, and the decision had been taken to invest in something larger than his estate car. Izzy had offered to come and fetch her if the weather was bad, but it had turned out fair, and she had enjoyed the thirty-five minute ride.

Her counselling had started three weeks earlier. Today was to be her fourth session. The first had been exactly what she had expected; a fairly long discussion about her early years, with special emphasis on her relationship with her parents - especially with her father. She learned that her image of herself had been adversely affected as a result of that relationship. It was clear that he had rejected her, even before her birth, and her childhood had been marred and scarred as a result. Self-rejection inevitably followed, and later, as a young woman, she had developed the survival technique of catapulting herself out of any relationship that threatened to became serious. In effect, she would unconsciously protect herself by rejecting others before they rejected her.

During the session, Charles had drawn a perfectly formed circle with a cross in its centre. Beside it, he drew a badly misshapen one, empty of a cross. He went on to explain that the former was a representation of what God had intended for her life: flawlessly rounded and full of good things. Then, tapping the misshapen one with the tip of his biro, he went on to say, 'Now this one's more like you. This big dent here, let's say that that's the result of your damaged relationship with your father. And this one,' pointing at another, 'the pain and loss you felt as a result of your mother's death.' And so he went on, pointing at other dents, and detailing other negative experiences she had found herself telling them about, including more recent ones, namely her problems with Niall, and guilt over Rabbie. Summing-up, he said, 'Some were inflicted upon you, but others were self-inflicted, like that decision you made before coming here.' He noticed her concerned expression and quickly added, 'But don't get too worried. We're all misshapen in one way or another, some of us more so than others. We can try as hard as we like to reshape ourselves, and, to a point, we may even succeed. But only God can truly heal and restore us to our proper shape.'

He drew a cross in the middle of the misshapen circle and a series of arrows radiating out from its centre, the points ending in the gaps formed by the missing boundary. He began to shade and fill in each gap, until the circle became whole again, like the perfectly formed one next to it. As he did so, he explained, 'He's the only One who can realistically fill in those damaged areas; the only One who can genuinely re-create a broken life and spirit.' Finally, he pointed back to the cross. '*If* we let Him in.' He tore the page out of his notepad and handed it to her. 'Here, you might want to take a look at it again, when you feel up to it.'

The idea of the reformed circle strongly appealed to her, and she had often spent time studying the two diagrams. Now she understood, and could even believe, that God wanted to re-create - or re-shape her - as Charles had so effectively put it. And she wanted, *really* wanted to become a whole circle. If only He would wave a magic wand and show her how she could forgive. How she would like that.

*

Her unresolved feelings of grief and guilt over Rabbie's death took up most of the second session, and Charles had found himself repeating the short Bible study he had shared with Donald.

'But, what I don't understand is, if God loved Rabbie so much, why didn't He stop it from happening in the first place?' she had asked.

'Ah now, what you're really asking is, why do bad things happen to good people? Or, in this case, to an innocent animal? replied Charles. 'Remember what I just said about mankind being given freewill? And how we use that freedom to rebel against God, and go our own way? The result is that we've all been born with self on the throne of our lives, the place where God should be. To put it another way, we've got an innate propensity towards selfishness in all its forms: self-interest, self-absorption, self-indulgence, self-gratification, self-promotion, self-glorification, and so on - right at the core of our being. Is there any wonder there's so much misery in the world? And it starts from an early age; children don't need to be taught how to be naughty, but they certainly *do* need to be taught how to be good! Be honest now, don't you have to remind yourself, and sometimes find it's a real effort, to be good and to do the right thing, even though something in you really wants to do the opposite?'

Yvonne thought hard, and had to admit that this was often the case. 'Well, yes, I suppose so.'

'And God isn't a dictator. He doesn't want slavish, unthinking obedience. He's graciously given us all the freedom to choose Him, or reject Him. We have the freedom to be good or bad. Jesus tells us that He is *the Light of the World,* and if He doesn't live in us, then we can be filled with darkness, either of our own making, or as a result of the sinfulness of others. And I believe that Rabbie's killer was influenced by that darkness.'

'And that darkness ... does it come from the Devil? she asked cautiously, remembering what she had read about him in her Bible.

Charles nodded. 'I'm afraid so. You know Yvonne, he's very much alive and kicking, and like God, he also works through people. In our modern, scientific, and so-called enlightened age, his presence and activities are often dismissed as mere superstition. Sometimes his influence is very obvious, but many times it's not. He can be very subtle. Anyone who thinks that there's no such being, or that he's just a character made-up by Hollywood - with horns and a tail, and not to be

310

taken seriously - has already fallen for one of his most effective lies. Let's not forget that Our Lord called him "the father of lies" in *John 8*.'

'And you're saying that Niall was influenced by the Devil when he behaved the way he did, and when he…did that to Rabbie?' she asked, obviously disturbed by the idea.

'Assuming it was actually him, then unfortunately, yes. Although, it would be more accurate to say that his behaviour was probably the result of a combination of things. Like you and me, he was born a sinner, and possibly not helped by being damaged by life's circumstances: childhood, and so on. Remember those circles? Then, as he got older, either because of ignorance, or through his own deliberate choices, he kept going his own way, and unknowingly opening himself up to some unhelpful influences, instead of coming to his right mind and realising his need of a Saviour.'

'Golly!' she exclaimed. 'I thought I was just doing battle with him. If I'd have known that the Devil was behind it! What an evil monster he was - '

'Careful now!' he warned. 'You need wisdom, and to be able to discern objectively, otherwise you're actually pointing three fingers back at yourself when you're pointing at someone else. And, if it was him, don't you think it best to let human justice prevail?'

Once again, she became uncomfortably aware that she was not as white as snow. Nevertheless, she persisted, 'But I still can't come to terms with the way that some people suffer, especially if they haven't done anything to deserve it. Why does God allow it?'

'Alright. Let's think of more examples of how people point the finger at God, and then go on to blame Him when things go wrong. For argument's sake, let's say the planning department of your local council accepts a bribe from a local developer to build homes too near a known flood area, and then your home gets flooded. Who are you going to blame? God? Or the corrupt councillors who accepted the bribe in the first place? Wouldn't that be a case of people exercising their freewill in the wrong way, and resulting in innocent lives being affected?

And what if I use my freewill, my freedom, to ignore the speed limit, and then crash, or kill someone? God's fault? After all, He should have arranged it so that the road ahead of me was clear, or prevent that person from being there at the same time. Can't you see, that in both instances, the wrong use of freewill - or, to put it another way, human rebellion and Godlessness - was actually the root cause of both problems?'

And now, for some reason, the image of her father returning home after a heavy night's drinking at the Ex-Servicemen's club came into Yvonne's mind. She recalled how he would curse everybody and everything for his self-inflicted nausea as he staggered up to bed in the early hours. 'And my father, you think that he was … somehow … that that same darkness … was in him?'

'Quite possibly. No doubt something happened to cause him to be the way he was. Some childhood trauma, or unhappiness, or maybe some disappointment later on in life. Instead of dealing with it in a proper way, and going to the One who has the *real* medicine, he chose to nurse it along, allowing it to grow and fester, like a silent cancer, eating into and damaging…warping his soul. If that was the case, then unfortunately, you and your mother were in the firing line.'

Yvonne sighed. 'Well, I wish God would have done something about it, and helped us in some way.'

'He did! Jesus has been around all the time. He tells us to … *seek and you will find; knock and the door will be opened to you.* But from what you've told us, I'd say that your father didn't look His way, and probably neither did you, nor your mother.'

'But Mum and I did go to church sometimes.'

'Sometimes?'

'Yes, usually around Christmas, or Easter.'

'Aha, just the odd visit here there then? Well, that doesn't do much for any relationship, especially if you ignore the person in between and treat them as though they don't exist. We have to be serious about our need of Him, about wanting a relationship with Him, not half-hearted. We have to be single-minded about wanting Him; we need to seek Him with our *whole* heart.'

She could see his point, and conceded, 'I suppose that's fair enough.'

'And you know, Jesus was there all the time, waiting for you to look for Him and take Him seriously. He died to reconcile us to God, so that we can come to know His Father as *our* Father: our loving Heavenly Father. I know you may find that hard to come to terms with. People who've never had a father, or have a difficult relationship with theirs, often struggle to accept the fatherhood of God. Another father is the last thing they want. In such cases, many find that the only way they can relate to Him is in Jesus.'

'That's how I've been thinking...you know, just Jesus.'

He nodded. 'That's fine. God understands. Jesus said that He was in the Father, and the Father was in him: *I and the Father are one.* When we talk to Jesus, we're talking to God at the same time. And, Yvonne, please don't make the mistake of judging Him by your father's standard; God is the *Perfect* Parent.

The session had been enlightening. Charles had been right, as far as she knew, God had never figured in her parents' lives at all, nor in hers. Maybe things would have been very different if He had.

*

The third session was all about forgiveness, and had the effect of gently, but firmly, addressing the unfortunate decision she had made regarding her future associations with men.

Charles explained, 'The New Testament was written in Greek, and the Greek word to forgive is *aphesis*, which means *to loose*. It's the same word Jesus used when he told Lazarus's friends to undo his grave-clothes - *to loose* him. In other words, to let him go. He used it again when He was dying on the Cross: *Father, forgive them, for they know not what they do.* Some scholars believe that He didn't say it just the once, but several times; so it could be read as: *Jesus kept on saying - or - said many times - Father, forgive them ...*

'You've read the accounts by now; think how many people needed His forgiveness: the leading teachers and priests of the day, the crowds who turned on Him and cried out for His death, His disciples for deserting Him, the soldiers who mocked, humiliated and tortured Him, and then went on to drive nails into His hands and feet. And don't forget the passers-by who shouted abuse at Him as He hung in agony on the Cross. And all the time He chose to stay up there - dying for them all - asking His Father to forgive them; to loose them; to let them go - to let them be free. The whole of humanity was included in that desperate prayer, and His resurrection proves that His Father said, 'Yes.' Freely we have all received His forgiveness; freely we should all forgive.'

He handed her a cushion. 'Here, hold this. Think of it as representing that decision you made. Use both hands, and don't let go until I tell you.'

Puzzled, she took the cushion and held it to her.

He picked up her drink and offered it to her. 'Drink this while it's still hot.'

'I can't!' she exclaimed.

'Why not?'

'No hands.'

'Alright, well let's try this,' he opened his wallet and offered her a five pound note.

'Go on, take it; I'm guessing it'll come in useful.'

Shocked, she laughed and looked from one to the other. Izzy did not seem at all perturbed that he was offering her the equivalent of a whole week's wages!

'Come on, Yvonne. It's bona fide.' He reached over and took a pencil from the nearby bureau and wrote her name on the note. 'All right. Let's say it's a late birthday present. We'd like you to have it, it's yours now.' He waved it enticingly in front of her. 'Look, it's even got your name on it.'

Faintly alarmed now, she said, 'Tell me you're joking! You didn't even know me then. And I wouldn't accept it anyway, hands or no hands.'

'Why, what's the matter? Don't you want our gift? It's free. All you have to do is to let go of that cushion and accept it.'

'But I can't!'

'Why not?'

'You haven't told me to let go of it yet.'

'So, you don't want to accept our gift? You know, we've grown very fond of you, and we want you to have it. I can assure you there's no strings attached, it's a totally free gift. Please take it Yvonne.'

Exasperated, she shrugged and sighed heavily.

'Okay. Think of me as God. And He says to you: "Yvonne, let go of that cushion - of your burden. Give it to Me. I died to pay the price for it. I love you, and I want you to accept my love, and along with it, my gifts of forgiveness, freedom, peace, and eternal life."'

There was a heavy silence in the room as Charles allowed the implication of the simple lesson to sink into her heart.

He went on, 'Can't you see now, that by holding onto the things you *don't* need, like that decision you made, and your negative feelings towards your father, you're stopping yourself from receiving the things you *do*? Not only are you doing him no good, whether he's aware of it or not, you're doing yourself no good as well. These things are tarring the rest of your life. You've been struggling for too long now, don't you think? Unforgiveness is like that; you have to be *willing* to let it go, so that you can be free to receive. For you, it would be an act of faith, like lying on an operating table and allowing something awful to be cut out of you. You can't do the job yourself, so you have to trust someone else to do it for you. Jesus is like a Heavenly surgeon. You just have to be willing to want to forgive; willing to want to put yourself in His Hands and trust Him to help you. Only then can He remove those old, rotten grave-clothes of unforgiveness from you - and set you free.'

'I ... I wish I could,' she said, obviously struggling to control herself. 'I really want to ...'

'Then let me help you,' he leant forward. 'Just loosen your grip, relax, and let me take that cushion - that decision - from you.'

She stared down at her hands, and saw for the first time how hard they were gripping the cushion. At last, and with some effort, she managed to release her hold. Charles eased it away from her. She gave a small gasp of exasperation, 'You see! You had to do it for me!'

'Yes, but only because you loosened your grip first; you *willed* yourself to let it go. Even though you found it difficult, you gave yourself permission to do so.'

'But I've tried to do that about my father, especially since reading what Jesus said, but it doesn't seem to work. I just know we'd only end up rowing if we ever met again. He wouldn't have changed. He'd do his usual, and chew me up and spit me out.'

'Then he would be like many people; unable to recognise, or even acknowledge their own need of forgiveness. They have no concept of how much God loves them, and longs for them to be free to be the people He created them to be - and the people He died for. All we can do is try to tell them about Him, about His love for them, and point the way. It's up to them how they respond.'

She knew he was right, but it had been hard to hear. But then again, she had let go of the cushion.

CHAPTER 36

Once more, she climbed the stairs to the Harmer's flat and received the usual warm greeting. The room felt as though it was blushing with a mellow light as the afternoon sun filtered through the peach coloured curtains. Now, a few minutes into the fourth session, she found herself having to make a determined effort to stop fidgeting with her handbag strap as she confessed that she was still hesitant to invite Jesus into her heart.

'I'm so, *so* sorry, but I'm afraid I still feel the same, even though everything I've read and that you've told me sounds reasonable, and just plain right! It's still this unforgiveness thing; I just can't seem to do it.'

Izzy crossed her legs and propped one elbow on the arm of the sofa, a mug in her other hand. Charles spread himself comfortably next to her, his Bible on the coffee table in-between them.

Yvonne continued, 'Alex is being really good about it, patient; I know he's keen for me to become a Christian, but it's the sort of thing you have to be genuine about. You can't do it just to please someone else, can you?'

Frowning slightly, Charles nodded his agreement. He remained silent for a while, then, appearing to make his mind up about something, said, 'Fair enough. Let's see what the Lord has to say.'

Yvonne had grown accustomed to the spontaneous way the couple would often stop, at any time or place, and say a prayer. At first, she had kept her eyes open, but now she found that she was more relaxed, and was able to close them and concentrate on the words.

Charles began, 'Lord Jesus, we thank You that You're here and want only to help and bless us in every way. Thank You for Your love. Thank You that You *are* love. Thank You that Your love is beyond anything we could ever imagine. And thank You that we can experience Your love, right here and now.

You know the trouble Yvonne's having trying to forgive her human father, and how it's having an ongoing negative effect upon her life. We feel that he must have been a very unhappy and damaged man to want to hurt her and her mother the way he did. We know that she won't forget, but we pray that the pain and influence of those memories will grow dim and lose their power. The scars will always be there, but we ask that You help her to allow You to work in her heart, so that she will come to know how very much You love her. Please help her to be willing to forgive him, to be free of this burden, and to lay it down at the foot of Your Cross - and leave it there.

May Your Holy Spirit guide Izzy and me so that we can minister Your words of healing and comfort to her. For we ask this in Your precious name. Amen.'

Izzy and Yvonne quietly echoed, 'Amen.'

Several seconds passed, then, with her eyes still closed and her forehead creased in concentration, Izzy began to speak. 'I can see you, Yvonne. You're walking along a path with someone … it's narrow and winding. You're going into a wooded area; it's dark and looks somehow familiar. Ah, yes, it's the Lord. He's very near you, but you're holding back and looking scared - as though you're ready to bolt. But He's standing there, holding out His hand. He wants to walk with you. Hold on! You're reaching out. You're going to take His hand, but … you're … you're pulling back. But you're trying again …' She fell silent, concentrating as she continued watching the scene still unfolding behind her closed eyes.

Yvonne could hardly breathe, and longed to ask what was happening. Did she take His Hand or not? Did she go with Him? Or did she run away?

Just before she felt she was going to burst with curiosity, Izzy continued, 'Oh, what a shame! You just can't seem to do it. You're turning and walking away. Oh dear! But … He's still there … holding His arms out, looking after you … waiting.'

She fell silent, then opened her eyes. She looked so sad that Yvonne found herself wanting to apologise for the actions of this other, unknown self. She knew that this was all imagery; they had already explained that God had given Izzy this gift:

she would be given a picture, and Charles would follow with an interpretation. The amount of time and emotional anguish it inevitably spared the counselee was invaluable. And she had no doubt that Izzy had actually seen what she had described. Why should she lie? Fascinating though it was, and knowing that none of it was real, she found herself bitterly disappointed that even her imaginary self was not able to do what her real self so desperately wished she could.

'Thanks Izzy,' said Charles. 'Do you know such a place, Yvonne?'

'It sounds like that forest bit at the other end of the loch. Remember Izzy? That day we found Rabbie? I told you I used to feel uneasy in there?'

'Ah, thought I recognised it,' agreed Izzy.

'Well, what I believe the Lord is saying, Yvonne, is that He wants and accepts you, just as you are - warts and all,' Charles explained. 'You don't have to wait to get yourself sorted out before accepting His invitation. In fact, He'll minister whatever healing you need if you take His hand. You can trust Him to guide you as you walk together through those dark places. All he wants is that you be willing to trust Him.'

All this sounded logical enough to Yvonne, even though every nerve in her body felt taught. Incredulous, she asked, 'You mean, that even though I can't bring myself to forgive, He'll still … accept me? He still *wants* me?'

'Exactly so. You've just told us again how genuinely sorry you are about your inability to forgive your father. And now you know that you're not only hurting yourself, but others too. I believe that if you can bring yourself to say "Yes" to Him, and invite Him to come into your heart, then I have no doubt that you'll find yourself being able to forgive. It might not happen instantly, although it could, that can happen. You won't have to try to conjure it up yourself, or force it. Come to Him with a sincere desire for Him. Tell Him you know that you're a sinner, and that you believe that He sacrificed Himself for you. Tell Him that you want, and need, to accept His love, and you're ready to turn around and go His way. You're willing for Him to help you to forgive - and let Him do the rest.'

And so for the next fifteen minutes the three embarked upon a short discussion on how several people in the Bible had been helped by simply *wanting* God's healing. Yvonne had already read the passages several times, but Charles had such a clear way of explaining things that she gained a much deeper understanding of each account. Now she came to realise that, like her, not one of those sick people had been able to help themselves, but, unlike her, all of them had been willing to receive help from the Stranger - Jesus.

Reaching over to take a book from one of the bookshelves, Charles said, 'There's a hymn that sums it up nicely in here. Let me see now.' He turned the pages and found what he was looking for. He began to read:-

Just as I am - without one plea,
But that Thy blood was shed for me,
And that Thou bidd'st me come to Thee,
O Lamb of God, I come.

Just as I am - and waiting not
To rid my soul of one dark blot,
To Thee, whose blood can cleanse each spot,
O Lamb of God, I come.

Just as I am - though tossed about
With many a conflict, many a doubt,
Fightings and fears within, without,
O Lamb of God, I come.

Just as I am - poor, wretched, blind;
Sight, riches, healing of the mind,
Yea, all I need, in Thee to find,
O Lamb of God, I come.

Just as I am - Though wilt receive,
Wilt welcome, pardon, cleanse, relieve;
Because Thy promise I believe,
O Lamb of God, I come.

Just as I am - Thy love unknown
Has broken every barrier down;
Now to be Thine, yea, Thine alone,
O Lamb of God, I come.

Just as I am - of that free love
The breadth, length, depth, and height to prove,
Here for a season, then above,
O Lamb of God, I come.'

Yvonne had never heard the hymn before, but she understood. Whoever had written it had also felt tossed about by life, and, like her, he, or she, had "many a conflict, many a doubt" They knew what it was like to be tormented with inner fightings and fears. And they also had come to recognise that God was the only One Who could give them the healing they so desperately needed. She couldn't have put it better herself.

Obviously moved, she said, 'I ... that was lovely,'

'Well?' Asked Izzy, 'Remember I told you that I always feel as though I've had some sort of medicine after I've spent some time reading God's word? Some hymns can be like that too.' She reached across and eased the book out of Charles' hand, then offered it to Yvonne. 'Here, why don't you take it, there's no rush for it back. We've plenty downstairs, and you'll be surprised how relevant many those old hymns still are.'

Yvonne accepted the book. 'Yes, yes, I ... thank you.'

'You know Yvonne,' said Charles, 'He loves you. He always has, and He always will. If we all waited until we get everything right before we asked Him into our hearts, none of us would ever get there! We're all sinners. Not one of us are good enough to deserve His love, nor ever will be. It's a free gift. Pure grace. The Bible says:-

God demonstrates his own love for us in this:
While we were still sinners, Christ died for us.
(Romans 5:8).

And Jesus said:-

It is not the healthy who need a doctor, but the sick.
(Mark 2:17).

You're blessed to have reached this point; now you're aware that you need help. So many aren't. And even when they do hear about God's love for them, they continue to stubbornly trust in their own abilities and resources to get by. That's pride, and it's deadly. A person without God can never be completely healthy in every area of their life, no matter how well and secure they may feel.'

Yvonne was staring at the words of the hymn. Charles saw the strained expression on her face, and knew that it would only take a bit more pressure for her to give in. But that was not his style. He would rather a person go away to some quiet, private place, and thoughtfully and prayerfully open their hearts to the Lord.

Yvonne nodded as she cradled the book in her hands. Could it be true? Really true? Did God really want her? *Her! And just as she was?*

Doley! Don't be so stupid! How can anyone want you? You know you're nothing but a waste of time and space. An accident that should never have been born. You'll be a millstone around His neck, like you've always been around mine. He'll end up hating you. Remember ... remember ... now ...

'Yvonne!' Izzy's voice broke in sharply; she had seen the desolate look come across the poor girl's face. 'Are you thinking of what your father used to say to you again?'

Yvonne could only nod.

Izzy sighed. 'The liar! Just like a thorn, it'll fester till it's out. In the name of Jesus, I ask that The Holy Spirit takes control, and binds that lying spirit; that it won't be allowed to torture you anymore!'

Charles glanced at his impetuous wife, who had gone into spiritual warfare mode without any warning. But he knew that Yvonne needed the more gentle healing of her memories. 'Er, maybe now's a good time to recap, and I'd better explain what Izzy just prayed. All you need to do, Yvonne, is to keep on doing what you have been, that's reading your Bible and talking to Him.'

He paused to give Izzy a conciliatory smile, then continued, 'And, I think it would be sensible that you ask Him to protect you from that voice - which speaks nothing but lies anyway. Every time you hear it, or feel it's influence, just call upon the name of Jesus until it stops. Ask Him to take control of it. Don't be frightened or alarmed in any way. It's very simple, just ask Jesus to help you. Am I making any sense?'

The voice had actually been silenced the second that Izzy had issued the command. Amazed, Yvonne replied, 'Okay, I'll try. But it did stop … when you told it to, Izzy. I can't believe it!'

'Oh, believe it! And of course it did!' exclaimed Izzy. 'You probably started to think of Jesus as soon as I mentioned His name. We know that the light of Christ overcomes the darkness. And that's the thing to do, Yvonne. Every time it tries to drag you down, take yourself firmly in hand, and talk to Jesus. Tell the thing that Jesus is above every name and power in Heaven and on Earth - and under it - and that it has to submit to His authority. I'm afraid it is a battle - '

'Yes, but one that's already been fought and won on the Cross,' interjected Charles, picking up his Bible. 'And now I think it might be an idea to take another look at a few more examples of how Jesus changed the lives of those that were willing to take Him seriously.'

*

It was to be another hour before Yvonne collected her bike and ride slowly back to the Inn. Deep in thought, she was unaware of the summer land around her. She was still trying to come to terms with the fact that God really did love her, and that He had loved her all the time - and that He would accept her just as she was.

CHAPTER 37

Word spread quickly about the benefits of spending time at the Manor, and the waiting list of people wanting to experience its special blend of practical and spiritual help was growing.

One of the first routine activities that Charles introduced was the Sunday morning service. These were held in the lounge, and open to all. They had been a real eye-opener for Yvonne, who always felt a keen sense of disappointment when she was unable to attend. She enjoyed their less formal style, finding the extemporary method of praying and carefully balanced mix of traditional hymns and modern choruses refreshing. Musical accompaniment was provided by Charles and Izzy: he had a fine baritone voice and was able to strum basic chords on the acoustic guitar; she was a reasonable soprano and played a small electric keyboard with some flair. Charles usually spoke for about fifteen minutes, always taking pains to make his message relevant to his listeners. As a result, it was not uncommon for each person to come away with a greater understanding of their spiritual state than when they had entered; some felt themselves to have been comforted and encouraged, others, like retired Sergeants George Andsover and Fred Owens, as well as Yvonne, found they were becoming increasingly curious, as well as challenged.

*

Towards the end of the summer, Yvonne decided to call a halt to her counselling sessions, arguing that others needed the couple's time and help far more than she did. Izzy had given her a small booklet containing daily Bible reading notes, and these, along with Charles' talks, only confirmed to her that the wisest thing anybody could ever do was to take Jesus seriously. *Extremely* seriously. However, despite the fact that her mind had no trouble in understanding that Jesus would accept her just as she was, there was still a small, stubborn part of her that refused to agree, and co-operate. When she did give her life to

Him, as she knew she must do eventually - although how and when she had no idea - she wanted the decision to be unhindered and unpolluted by any nagging remnant of resentment or unforgiveness.

Recently, a new and uncomfortable train of thought had begun to assail her: what if she could see her father again? Counselling had revealed that his unreasonable and intolerant behaviour probably had a root cause; if he was able to enlighten her as to what that was, then maybe she would find it easier to forgive him. Alex seemed to like the idea when she had mentioned it to him, and had promised to do some serious praying about it.

*

But it was not all work and no play for the couple. There were the regular film shows in the church hall and the monthly ceilidhs, even though Yvonne would have to spend a good proportion of the evening on duty. Flora and Dot took it in turns to invite them for Sunday tea. Neither husbands minded too much, as long as Hamish had enough 'baccy' for his pipe, and Angus was left alone to doze by the fireside.

*

Lochlyn and Heather Buchanan, a couple in their early thirties, had recently moved into the area. They had inherited a croft just outside Ardgealish, and began to attend the Sunday morning services at the Manor soon after. For them, there was no great spiritual struggle, and both responded to the invitation to ask Jesus into their hearts after hearing the Gospel Call just twice, and were baptized just eight weeks later. When Yvonne quizzed Alex about the speed they were baptized, he told her that they were only following Jesus's example. 'It's what He did, and He told us to follow him. Some people think of it as an outward sign, or statement, of what's happened to them on the inside. Every new child of God should do if they want the world and the Devil to know that they mean business.'

Although serious about his newly found faith, Lochlyn had a mischievous sense of humour about everything else, and liked nothing better than to play practical jokes. And so it wasn't long before a friendship developed between the two pairs, and a bit more fun and laughter, although of a younger kind, entered Yvonne and Alex's lives.

*

Robert arrived as the summer finally drew to a close. He was a younger version of his father: tall and gangly, although clean shaven, and crowned with a mop of thick, brown hair. However, there the resemblance ended, for he had much of his mother's no-nonsense, black and white approach to life.

It soon became obvious that he was also very ambitious, when, just four days after his arrival, he called a staff meeting to announce his plans for the future of the Inn. But first, Georgina had to have her say, as she embarked upon a small discourse about 'the uncertainty of things, and how adaptable we must be in these modern times'. She was speaking from recent experience, for both she and Donald had needed those four days to recover from the initial shock at learning of their son and heir's determination to implement his new and improved plans. But, more especially, how much it would be costing them.

Strumming his fingers impatiently on the staff table, Robert asked, 'All done Mum?'

'Go gently son,' remarked Donald, feeling that he should make his presence felt.

'Can't go any other way around here,' replied the young man, placing his hands palm down in front of him, and trying to control his irritation. 'Okay, let's make a start. You'll all know how the Hydro-Electric Board's been building roads up here, and improving others, and how there's been a steady increase in the passing traffic making its way up north?'

Wondering where all this could be leading, Flora, Frazer and Yvonne glanced at each other, before nodding and making assenting noises.

'Good, good. And you must have noticed that we're getting a lot more younger people calling in now, mainly on spec, and just wanting a night's stopover?'

'Aye,' said Flora, rubbing the small of her back, 'and hard it is on the back too.'

Ignoring her, he continued. 'I've been making it my business to sound them out, and it seems that most of them would have preferred to bunk down in a Youth Hostel. But, as you know, there's nothing like that around here, at least, not yet. And that's where I think we can come in. I've just initiated discussions with the Youth Hostel Association, and there's a good chance that we might be able to build a small hostel on that spare bit of land behind the car park.'

Flora, Frazer and Yvonne turned to look at each other with obvious surprise. This was news indeed! Yvonne thought quickly, then, sounding mildly alarmed, asked, 'But … not anywhere near Rabbie's grave?'

'No, nowhere near, more over to the right,' replied Robert, having already fought that battle with his father. 'I'm thinking of a fairly simple build; just eight bunks, a bath - or shower, toilets, and a small kitchen area. I can't see us having any problems with getting it approved, so we could have it up and running by early spring. It'll run as a separate concern from the Inn, and I can't imagine that there'll be much in the way of extra work. These places are usually low maintenance. Just bit of cleaning, the usual stuff. Diversification, that's the name of the game. We'll get left behind if we refuse to move with the times. Thanks to Mum and Dad's hard work, we've already got an established business, but we'd be daft to just sit back and vegetate. As far as I'm concerned, that's not an option; we need to think ahead and be ready.' Satisfied, he paused and looked around the table. 'Remember folks, we're all in this together.'

Now Flora was quick to speak-up. 'Och, my! It all sounds very good, I'm sure. But is it wise? And what's become of all that art notion?'

He smiled at her indulgently, this was no less than he had expected from the old lady. 'I think these improvements, or, as I prefer to think of them, additional amenities, will prove *very* wise. And as far as the themed breaks go, I'll be starting up slowly - test the waters. That end single would be ideal as a darkroom, and I've got a friend whose father's a published poet and interested in doing some poetry weeks.'

Donald smiled. Now that was one improvement he was looking forward to. Georgina stifled a yawn.

'But my first priority will be in getting the hostel up and running.' Feeling that he had provided enough information for one day, he flashed the assembled group a Georgina-like smile, and concluded, 'Anyway, that's all for now. But if any of you've got any ideas, crazy or not, let's be hearing them. Let's put the Tananeach Inn firmly on the map.' He looked pointedly at Flora, then added condescendingly, 'But in a wise sort of way.'

She crossed her arms tightly across her chest and harrumphed loudly. 'Och, a'way wi' you, you cheeky young sparrow! Wise is it? We'll see, aye, right enough, that we will. And I'm not above thinking that that nasty General Wade's come back and is behind all this road building malarkey. Our Bonnie Prince must be rolling in his grave!'

*

Yvonne helped Frazer clear the table when the meeting was over. They sounded upbeat as they speculated on the changes ahead.

'Do you think we'll still have the coaches in?' she asked.

'Don't see why not,' replied Frazer. They're a big money-spinner; can't see him stopping them.'

Yvonne turned to Flora. 'What do you think Flora? You didn't sound too keen.'

'Well lassie, I'll tell you now, and I'll be telling you straight, I'm not,' she replied, looking at them both and frowning heavily, 'and that's all I'm needing to be saying just now.'

*

It came as no surprise when Flora asked to have a private word with Georgina a few days later.

Once in the office, she sighed deeply as she carefully lowered herself onto a chair. 'Aye, aye, it's time. My back and front are well past retirement, and I'm for handing in my duster. I've been having a bad time of it all summer with the lumbago and all, and I'm feart it'll lay me low for good one of

328

these days if I'm not wise. And I'm thinking it's only fair to let the youngsters have their turn.'

Georgina was prepared; she and Donald had been expecting this for some time. Still, she found herself quite moved as she agreed that Flora had indeed made a very wise decision.

*

Flora left the following Saturday after assuring them all that they would see her again at the next ceilidh. Yvonne waved and watched her pedal away, trying to decide which was the more arthritic, the rider or the machine. She turned and walked slowly back inside, already missing the old lady's calm and steady companionship. How strange it was to see someone else do the leaving; Niall had been the first, although he didn't really count - not like Rabbie, he certainly did. And now dear old Flora had gone. Who would be next? 'Please God,' she prayed earnestly, 'please, *please* don't let it be me!'

CHAPTER 38

Nature was preparing to rest, but generously gave one last show of colour before covering herself with her Autumn veil. Clusters of orange-red berries on the rowan trees shone vivid against late blue September skies, and swathes of purple, red and white heather cloaked the surrounding land.

Although things were quieter at the Inn, Yvonne wished she could rest for a while too. She had been working without a break for seven months and felt decidedly jaded, both mentally and physically. So it was with some relief that she agreed to the MacMan's suggestion that she should take the first two weeks of October off. They were planning to leave towards the end of that month themselves and wanted to tie up all the loose ends, including outstanding staff holidays.

Feeling that everything she wanted was right there, she decided to spend her break at the Inn. However, she found herself having to think again when Sandra's next letter arrived:-

King's Lynn.   *23rd September 1970*

Dear Yv,

Hello. Hope you're doing okay? This is going to be a strange letter because I'm in shock and now everything's changed and all our plans have gone for a burton! Don't ask me how, but I must have forgotten to take the pill some months back because I think I'M PREGNANT, (well, I know I am). Maybe 13 weeks gone already. You should see Tom, he's going around grinning like a big fool. It's alright for him. MEN!

We still haven't got enough put by for a deposit on one of those new houses behind the tech, and you know how I've always wanted a really lovely white wedding, but now we'll have to have one of those horrible registry office do's and I'm SO fed up. Everything's happening too fast and you know how I feel about kids. But there's NO WAY I'd try to get rid of it.

We've booked the Registry Office for the 10th of October. I think I'll be four months gone by then so I'm hoping I won't be showing much. Mum reckons she was five months gone before she started showing with me. I've got my eye on a fab A-Line coat and dress set in Baxter's window. It's in a gorgeous shade of green but a bit pricey, but Tom say's it'll come in handy for plenty of other do's later on, so I think I'll get it.

Will you come? I know it's a bit sudden, but they've had a cancellation at the Registry Office and asked if we wanted the slot. Anyway, you must be due some holiday by now? We haven't seen each other for ages. That bossy Georgina had better let you. Yv, I NEED YOU, please say yes. My cousin Penny's got a spare room in her flat now and says you can stay around hers if you like.

Tom's working on his parents to get them to give us a week in their caravan in Yarmouth for a honeymoon. (I don't think I'll be taking my bikini this time!) And we'd really like it if you'll be Godmother. Penny's going to be the other one. We can't decide on Godfathers yet, but Tom's toying with the idea of asking his boss, he's been good to him, time off and all that. Now you've <u>got</u> to come. I don't know what I'll do if you don't because you're good at stopping me from panicking and it seems like you've been gone for ages. Write back quickly and let me know.

Pots of love from Sandra and Tom.   xxx

PS.   I'll send you a proper invitation soon.
PSS. <u>You'd better come or I'll have a fit of the screaming abdabs!</u>

Of course she would go! She had enough saved up in her Post Office Savings Account to cover the fare and all necessary expenses, and, if she was careful, maybe even a new outfit. The wedding was on a Saturday, but she would have to stay until the following Monday when the trains ran properly again. The quilt was finished, and she was pleased with the result; now it would come in just right as a wedding present. The only problem was that it was as heavy as it was bulky, but at least she would only have to manage it the one way.

Then there was Alex; what should she do about him? He might think it strange that he had not been invited. She had only ever referred to him in the vaguest terms in her letters; certainly as no one special. Maybe she should write and explain that they had become closer recently, and ask if he could come too. Then again, he might not even want to go.

She decided to dash off a quick reply. It was obvious that Sandra was upset, so she tried to make the letter sound as upbeat as possible.

> ...Yes, I'd love to come, and feel greatly honoured to have been asked to be a Godmother. And it would be great if I can stay with Penny.
>
> By the way, I wonder if my friend, Alex, could come too? Naturally, he would stay in a nearby bed and breakfast or hotel, but it would be nice to have company on the long journeys there and back. I haven't mentioned anything to him yet, so it really is just an idea ...

She sealed the envelope and placed it in the post basket, where it seemed to taunt her every time she walked past. Was she presuming too much? Even if Alex did manage to get the time off, would he want to go all that way to the wedding of some complete strangers? She was tempted to remove it on more than one occasion, and it was with some trepidation that she watched the post van drive off later that day.

The Buchanan's old Humber came into view seconds later. There had been great excitement at the croft when Heather's hens had started laying, and Frazer was happy to relieve them of their surplus, an arrangement that was proving mutually beneficial. Heather was an erratic driver, and it was a miracle that the eggs did not arrive scrambled; just the one was found to be cracked on this occasion. The transaction completed, the two women set off for the croft, and soon Yvonne found herself laughing uncontrollably at Heather's colourful account of how Snowy, the goat, had devoured a pair of Lochlan's underpants the day before. The letter forgotten - for the time being.

*

Heather was in a baking mood, and the pair spent a companionable morning working in the kitchen. Both had a fine dusting of flour on their cheeks and hair by the time Alex arrived, and quickly made himself unpopular by remarking how 'quaintly ancient' they looked. Then, with perfect timing, Lochlan appeared just as the percolator started to bubble. Still on the subject of hair, the four began to discuss the scarcity of salons and barbers in the area.

'Hey, why don't you get your mate to come and open up a place around here?' Alex asked Yvonne. 'She'd have at least four customers. And I'll bet some of your female guests wouldn't mind a bit of mid-holiday pampering.'

'Good idea!' said Heather, removing the last batch of scones from the oven. 'As long as she doesn't charge Strathlochy prices. Maybe she'd take a few dozen of these in exchange for a shampoo and set? That'd be handy.'

'That's my girl!' exclaimed Lochlan, 'Bartering queen of the Highlands.'

'You can laugh Lochy, but you've got to admit we haven't done too badly out of it so far, and I'm beginning to wonder what we could swap for that mad goat of yours! How about a year's supply of underpants? Anyway,' she said, wiping her hands on her apron and looking conspiratorially at him, 'take these two into the living room and report back immediately. Remember - our little surprise?'

'To hear is to obey, O mighty one,' replied Lochlan, bowing low, before ushering Alex and Yvonne out of the kitchen.

THE HIDDEN PATH

Alex returned to the subject of hair as he attempted to get comfortable on the old horsehair settee. 'Well? You never said. Can't you imagine your mate moving up here?'

'Not really. I think she'd run a mile at the thought of it. Here, have this,' Yvonne replied, pushing a faded tapestry cushion behind him. 'She's a real towny, a real live wire, you know, always on the go - at least she was.' She hesitated, remembering Sandra's boisterous, chatty image; how different from the troubled girl speaking through the letter. 'Actually, I've just heard from her, and her...situation has changed. It seems that she's having a baby, and they're having to get married sooner than they'd planned. Poor thing, she sounds really upset.'

Comfortable at last, Alex looked concerned; he knew how fond Yvonne was of her distant friend. 'Sorry to hear that. Bit of a blow, and not the best way to start married life. But they've known each other for years, haven't they? And been engaged for some time? The fact that they chose each other before must count for something?'

'Yes. I expect she's still a bit shocked, and just needs more time to get used to the idea. She's always wanted the traditional big white wedding, although that's all gone by the board now.'

'How's her fiancé feeling about it? Tom isn't it? Did she tell you?'

'Seems he's fine. And she's really lucky there; he's such a calm, kind sort of person. I think he'll make a great dad.'

'A wedding then? And you'll be going of course? When is it?'

'Next month, and I'd like to, especially as they've asked me to be a Godmother.'

'Really? You'll be away, what ... a week?'

'About six days. Georgina's letting me start my two weeks off early so that I can travel down on the Thursday.'

He was silent for a while, then said, 'Hold on a minute, I've just had an idea. What if I come with you? I could be your escort? I don't want to push in, but it would be kind of nice. You know things can get pretty intense at the Manor, and I could do with a break. In fact, the more I think about it, the more I like the idea.'

Her heart missed a beat. 'Are you sure? But would you really want to? I mean, it's a long way to go, and it's only going to be a registry office do after all.'

'Registry office, down a mine, anywhere, as long as they love each other and mean what they say. God's not limited to churches, and marriage was His idea to begin with. So, what do you say?'

'Oh Alex, I'd love it if you could! But you'll have to let me okay it with them first.'

'Yes ma'am!'

She nestled into his arms and sighed contentedly. Family photographs were dotted around the room. She studied the nearest for several seconds, before asking, 'But wouldn't you rather go and see your family, especially if you're going all that way?'

'I'll be seeing them at Christmas, or rather, *we* will. How are you fixed? My parents want to meet the girl who's turning me into softie. Anyway, we don't need to go into all that now. I've been thinking, we'd do better to fly part of way. And don't worry about the fares; I've missed all your birthdays - so far.'

She leaned away from him. 'That's *far* too kind of you! I've got some savings, and I want to pay my own way ... or ... at least ... some of it. But what was that you just said about your parents?'

He pulled her back towards him. 'Hey! Remember our bargain? You fund occasional coffee breaks, and I take care of the rest. And naturally I want you to meet them. Don't look so horrified! They'll love you, but not as much as I do. And I know you've always gone about by yourself, sweetheart, but there's no need to, not now you've got your very own bodyguard.' Then he kissed her, thereby effectively preventing her from voicing any more objections.

Several kisses later, she asked, 'Travel agent, escort, bodyguard! My goodness, are there any other roles you want to play?'

'Oh yes! But for now, you'll just have to be satisfied with those. And I've had another idea.' He took hold of her hand. 'Now, I'm not saying this is from The Boss, but it could be. We could see this as an opportunity to deal with that other … unfinished business, and try and see your father? Remember, you were wondering how you'd feel about seeing him again? And you know I've been praying about it.'

She inhaled sharply, then, almost in a whisper, replied, 'Yes. I know.'

'And, you still think it could be … useful?'

She fixed her gaze on his hand, covering her own in her lap. So strong, so steady. 'I don't know. Maybe.'

'Well then, why don't we combine the two? The wedding, and going on a recce to see if we can track him down afterwards? You never know, he might have changed. Miracles do happen.'

She gave a small gasp. 'I doubt it! He'd probably throw a blue fit. And anyway, he could have moved half a dozen times by now. He could be anywhere. He might even be dead!'

'And if he was, would that be the end of it?' He paused and thought for a moment. 'And there are ways and means of finding out. But it's up to you; you've been hurt enough already. Too much. But the fact is, that this could well be an answer to prayer.'

As much as she knew she would be relieved to learn that her father was dead, she also knew that Alex was right - that would leave her with unfinished business. It would not be a satisfactory or decisive type of ending; after all, you couldn't do much challenging, or settling of things, over a grave! But then again, in one way, maybe it would be easier? If he was still alive, and could be traced, could she really bear to see him again, and have the courage to subject herself to more of his tirades? Or would the years have changed, even mellowed him? What if she found that she was still unable to forgive him? What would be the consequences for her and Alex then?

As though reading her thoughts, Alex went on to say, 'And if it did go badly, at least you'll always have the satisfaction of knowing that you'd have tried. That's all The Boss requires of us. We're only responsible for our own actions, not the actions and responses of others. You'd have done your part but by being willing to hear what he has to say for himself.'

There was nothing she could say; these ideas were not new to her, Charles and IIzzy had said as much. Then they had just been words, but now she was being confronted with them again, and they had come with an almost overwhelming sense of challenge, even threat. 'I suppose you're right,' she replied unenthusiastically.

'Atta girl! Maybe this is just what we've been waiting for. And remember, your father is only your human one, but The Boss - God - wants to become your *Heavenly* Father. And He'll never let you down, or hurt you; He just wants to love and care for you. You know that, don't you?'

She nodded. Yes, her head knew all this, even if her heart was not able to feel it.

'Ah, now then,' he continued, squeezing her shoulders, 'how about this for another idea? I'll try and take your second week off as well, and we escape to the islands when we get back. I think we could both benefit from having some cobwebs blown away.'

They were still holding each other minutes later when Heather called from behind the door. 'Okay you two. Let's be having you!'

They walked, hand in hand, into the kitchen. Smiles broke out at the sight of the table, laden with numerous small bowls, filled with a selection of raw fruit and vegetables; all neatly arranged around a lit fondue pot.

Yvonne did her best to join in the banter during the meal, but her mind would keep slipping back to the conversation she had just had with Alex. She was aware that she was reaching one of life's metaphorical crossroads, and would need to approach it with extreme caution. She looked over at him and smiled; he was struggling, and failing, to keep a long string of cheese from mingling with his beard. She thought again of how she had been living a sort of half-life before she had met him; it had been a stagnant, closed type of existence. But now he had brought her the kind of happiness she had only ever read or dreamt about. Along with his strong, reliable presence, had come the offer of a new life, and one lived in the openness of hope and freedom. And as for her father, he was right, she must take the chance to sort things out. She had her whole life ahead of her, and she was adamant that she did not want to waste any more of it being plagued by that awful voice and her own irrational fears.

Then, too, she needed to think about the fact that he wanted her to meet his parents - and all that that could mean.

*

Sandra's reply came five days later, enclosing the promised invitation. Much to Yvonne's relief, she sounded far more cheerful:-

> ...*Guess what? Mum's talked Dad into giving us the money they would have spent on a church wedding, now we'll have enough to put on a deposit on one of those new houses after all. Isn't that great! What a relief! And Tom's Mum's started hinting at buying us a three-piece suit and he's going to take a few hours off so that we can go to the Co-op to get some ideas. (I think we should look at the beds while we're there).*
> ...*I knew something was going on with you and that mystery man and I'm tickled pink about it and now I can't wait to meet him. I hope he's fabulously good looking, that should spice things up a bit ...*

*

With only the limited knowledge Yvonne had of her father's past, and the help of their military connections, Charles and Alex learned that former Lance Corporal Owen Williams was still alive and well - and still living in Wales.

Yvonne had quailed at hearing the news. Somehow she had coped not knowing where he was, or if he was actually still alive. He could remain a distant spectre from her past, and only his words had the power to reach and hurt her. She had no photograph of him, and his image had blurred in her memory years before. But now his physical form started to take shape in her mind, and his presence seemed to grow closer by the day. Too close.

The hateful mantra began to be particularly troublesome again, forcing her to seek Izzy's help in an effort to control the tormenting thoughts. Izzy had said it was like a battle, and that was exactly how it felt. She was so very tired of it. Why couldn't she be left alone to enjoy this new life she had somehow managed to stumble upon? Or had she stumbled upon it? What if Alex was right, and God had really been leading her along some sort of hidden path? It was a lovely idea, and she would like to believe it. In fact, part of her did. But there were times, especially after another mantra attack, when she had to force herself to reluctantly admit that she was only fooling herself, and that it was probably all just too good to be true.

CHAPTER 39

They were able to fit in one more trip to Strathlochy before they left, and, as was their custom, called in at the tartan-crazed café for morning coffee. Yvonne was in a reflective mood, and began listing all the changes that had taken place since their first visit: 'Niall's gone and left Maggie with a broken heart; Charles and Izzy have come, and the Manor's up and running; Frazer's come, and Robert's here at last; Flora's retired, and it won't be long before Georgina and Donald go as well. And I'm not forgetting Rabbie.'

'A lot of coming and goings,' Alex commented. 'But what about you?'

'Me?'

'Well, you've mentioned everyone else. What about you? How's your life changed?'

'Er, well, there's us - '

'Glad you that mentioned that!' he said, smiling.

'Then ... oh, I know, there's Heather and Lochlyn. Actually, I meant to tell you, she's invited me to go and stay with them for a few days when we get back. She's got a lot of jam making to do - '

'Ah now, that reminds me. Izzy's insisting that you come and spend some time at the Manor. She's thinking of Christmas. We'll have plenty of room; most of the guests would have left by then, and I expect my family will only take up about four.'

'She did? How kind!'

'Yeah, she's like that. She wants you to teach her how to crochet, so you'll be able to put those lovely feet of yours up.' He looked at his watch. 'That's gone fast. Right, enough of all this retrospection. Do you want the rest of that scone, or shall I help you out?'

*

The small boutique on the corner of the arcade was holding its end of season sale, and Yvonne was delighted to find a suit in a dusty shade of pink which fitted her perfectly. This, along with a pair of light cream sandals and the matching handbag she came across afterwards, also on sale, completed her outfit. Alex had already decided to wear his navy-blue suit; it was light and always travelled well. The problem about what he should buy as a wedding present was conveniently solved when he spotted a picture of a just married couple in an impressive silver-plated picture frame in the window of a photographer's shop. They emerged minutes later, having persuaded the proprietor to part with an identical frame from his own supply.

Gone was her previous reticence about disclosing her patronage of charity shops; this time she took Alex in with her. He proved to be a good customer and bought several books on basic carpentry and wood turning. When she had looked quizzically at the small pile he had collected, he explained, 'We've been thinking about turning that large outbuilding behind the kitchen into a workshop. The funds are there; it's just the time to get the project under way, and then manage it.'

Several hours later, both laden with the day's purchases, they decided to take high tea at the Strathlochy Grand Hotel, and were rewarded with the sight of a very healthy-looking Archie Loranzo. Not recognising them, he moved swiftly around the dining room, obviously none the worse for his dramatic varicose vein ordeal.

*

They were blessed with a clear sky on the morning of their departure. There was a lot of travelling ahead, and, for the first time in their relationship, they would be alone together - all day and every day.

Yvonne would have felt far more light-hearted than she actually did if it was not for the daunting prospect of the second part of the trip. Closing her suitcase, she told her herself to buck-up and concentrate on making the most of seeing Sandra and Tom again. No amount of fretting and worrying about the Welsh side of things would help, or do any good.

They drove to Glasgow, then flew to London, where they stopped overnight, before making their way by train to King's Lynn. It was just a short taxi ride to Penny's, and after making arrangements for the following morning, Alex left to book into the nearby bed and breakfast.

They met back at Penny's at half-past-ten the next morning. She drove them to the registry office, picking up her own boyfriend en route. Labels and arrows signed the way to a large, colourless room. Delayed by heavy traffic, Sandra arrived ten minutes later, looking flustered and upset. Obviously annoyed, the officiating registrar lost no time in launching into the short ceremony.

Yvonne tried hard to concentrate on the impersonal, monotonously delivered pronouncements, and decided that the only saving grace about the whole affair was that the couple really did love each other. How strange life was: Sandra had been the confident, happy-go-lucky one; things had always come easy for her, and she had been blessed with the love and support of a caring family, which, judging by her mother's continuous eye-dabbing, she still had. She had never had to chop and change jobs; hairdressing had been the only thing she had ever wanted to do, and she had done well, eventually working her way up the career ladder to become head stylist in the town's most prestigious salon. Then she had met Tom: the icing on the cake.

Alex's hand reached for hers. She looked down, and experienced an almost overwhelming feeling of gratefulness that his hands - his strong, steady hands - were now a part of her life - and a life that had changed so dramatically. Had it really been only eight short months ago that she had left for Scotland after making that foolish decision? Thank goodness that issue had been dealt with, and was now a thing of the past. Here again, her counselling sessions had proved invaluable in revealing what lay behind her reasons for making it. She had been right to believe it was a form of self-protection and preservation, although there appeared to be other, deeper, hidden, and long held motives at work - chief among them her poor relationship with her father.

The healing had started when she remembered how she had grown up promising herself that she would never allow a man to treat her the way she had witnessed her mother being treated. How strange that she had completely forgotten such a thing! This promise had lain dormant throughout her childhood, only manifesting itself when she had her first real boyfriend. As a young woman, she had been unaware of its presence and effect, only knowing that she was not able to give or receive affection from any man. Fear and flight had become her ways of coping. Charles and Izzie had gently led her along the path of revelation and understanding, until she had felt it perfectly right and natural to renounce and, therefore, negate, its hold over her during a short time of prayer. The sensations of relief and freedom she experienced immediately afterwards had been so strong that she found herself jumping up and spontaneously kissing and hugging them both. That door had been gently, but firmly, shut.

And now here she was, watching Sandra and Tom getting married, and miraculously in love herself - and even more miraculously - loved in return. And *almost* completely happy.

The couple turned to face each other to exchange rings. Yvonne noticed how pale and drawn her friend's face was, and watched as her free hand made fleeting movements over her slightly swollen abdomen. How anxious she appeared. Gone was the chatty, carefree and confident girl she had always known; instead here was a nervous and unsure young woman who was obviously preoccupied with the impending challenge of motherhood.

The allotted time over, the small party found themselves being quickly ushered out of the dismal room and along the equally dismal corridor. Photographs were taken on the office steps, after which they went to a nearby pub where a buffet had been arranged in an upstairs function room. The new bride made several efforts to appear cheerful and eat, but it was obvious that she was forcing herself to do so, and Yvonne was thankful when, at last, it was time to leave. The two friends hugged each other affectionately as they made their tearful farewells.

Alex hailed a taxi and they returned to their respective accommodation to change, meeting up again soon afterwards. They decided to go for a walk and try to find a florist; Yvonne wanted to buy some flowers for her mother's grave which they would be visiting the next day. The florist had exactly what she wanted; yellow roses, her mother's favourite. Tears came to her eyes when Alex bought another six.

They continued to walk aimlessly, until they both confessed to feeling tired and ready for something to eat. Several restaurants had just opened and the idea of a Chinese meal appealed to them. The red and gold interior of The Great Wall was cheerful and the food delicious, although they could have done without the continuous high-pitched vocals in the background. Later, he gave her a long, hard hug before wishing her a warm and tender good night.

*

They went to a Baptist church the next morning. The minister, who was 'the genuine article' according to Alex, preached on the subject of forgiveness; the timing and significance was not lost on them both. The lively service lasted nearly two hours, after which, with the praises of God's people still ringing in their ears, they enjoyed a substantial roast dinner at a nearby hotel.

Suitably nourished and rested, they walked the mile to the council graveyard. Yvonne had been nursing the roses all morning, and was relieved that they appeared to be none the worse for wear as she knelt to arrange them. The vase was only a year old, and she found herself becoming upset when she saw how cracked and stained with mildew it had already become. Even the weather seemed to be crying as the rain began to fall. She felt Alex's hand on her shoulder, and raised her own to cover his. She had always been here alone, so it was comforting to be able to share this time with such a considerate companion. If only her mother could see her now, with this fine man standing beside her. The longing almost overwhelmed her. She did her best to arrange the dripping blooms, then, standing again, was quickly enfolded in caring arms, before being slowly led away.

They walked and talked, eventually reaching the cinema, where they decided to take refuge. It was chilly, but the rain had stopped by the time they came out. When they reached the flat, Alex, who had enjoyed the closeness of the past few hours and was reluctant for it to end, said, 'Don't know about you, but I'm not ready to turn in just yet.'

She had mixed feelings. Although tired and feeling like some quiet after the day's events, she also felt the need to stay close to him, and remembering how Penny had insisted that she make herself at home, invited him in for a hot drink.

'That would be good, but won't Penny think we're taking liberties?' he replied.

'No, I'm sure she won't mind. Anyway, she told me to make myself at home.'

They found the flat empty. He settled back on the sofa, and stretched out his legs as Yvonne went off to make the drinks. The room was warm and had a friendly feel about it, and it wasn't long before he began to feel pleasantly relaxed.

She returned soon after with two mugs of Bournvita. 'Do you fancy some music?'

'Hmm, that would be nice. Something soothing.'

She went to study Penny's L.P. collection and made her choice. She carefully wiped some dust off the vinyl before placing the record on the turntable. Lowering the arm, she said, 'I can't stop thinking about Sandra. She looked so pale. I'm sure she was just putting on a brave face.' The music started, she turned the volume down, then went to sit beside him.

'I shouldn't worry, sweetheart. I've got a feeling she'll be fine. Anyway, Tom seems a decent sort, and it looks like she's got her family behind her.'

'Yes, but she wasn't her usual bubbly self, quite the opposite. If you could have seen her before, so happy-go-lucky and free as air.' She sighed, 'Now she's a married woman with a baby on the way.'

'But she's at a good age, isn't she? And they do recommend that a woman starts having the babies even earlier.'

She laughed. 'Oh heck! In that case, I'm in trouble. I'm in line for twins, *if* my time ever comes.'

'Twins! Hey, that's great! What would you like, one of each, or two of the same?'

This was a new line of talk. Although they often discussed all manner of domestic matters - usually related to the Manor - matrimonial issues, including children, were only ever mentioned in the vaguest terms.

'Er…well, if the old wives' tale is true, then I suppose one of each would be nice.'

Alex sipped his drink, trying to imagine what she would look like pregnant, and was surprised to find himself becoming aroused. Now all he wanted to do was kiss her until she begged him to stop. He put his mug down.

She could hardly believe her ears when he pulled her closer, and whispered, 'As long as they're mine.' His words knocked down all her defences. All she could think of, as he kissed her with increasing urgency, was how very, very much she wanted him too. His mouth released hers, and he began to moan her name softly as he kissed the nape of her neck. Then, pulling her blouse off her shoulder, he kissed her there too. Soon his free hand was caressing her breast. She knew she should stop him now; there was only one way this could end. But she didn't want to, she couldn't - she wouldn't! Let them face the guilt - afterwards. Surely God would understand and forgive them. They had been so good for so long. And after all, they were only human.

He raised his head and looked into her face, his own full of desire. 'I've got to tell you, oh sweetheart, I must tell you … that day … when we first met, when you walked past me - '

But she was not to learn what it was that he was trying to tell her about that day - that day when she had encountered him in the heather. Alerted by the sound of a woman's giggling and footsteps coming up the garden path, he stopped mid-sentence and pulled away. Penny had brought her boyfriend home.

CHAPTER 40

They took a taxi to the station the next morning and spent the rest of the day crossing the country. Alone in the compartment at last, Alex apologised for his behaviour of the previous night and promised that he would do everything in his power not to put her in such a compromising position again.

She stroked his face affectionately and kissed his cheek. 'Hush now! It takes two to tango. Anyway, we didn't do anything ... much, and what was it you'd started to tell me, just before Penny came back? Something about that day I passed you - '

'Ah, right,' he interrupted, giving her one of his enigmatic smiles, 'well, sweetheart, you know what I always say, that'll have to wait for another day. You'll know all about it, and soon, I hope. But not just now.' Last night had been just another of those times when his almost overpowering desire for her had been as tormenting as it had been exquisite. It seemed that another day's fasting and praying was needed, but it would have to wait until they were back in Scotland. How close he had come to revealing his secret. What a pair they were: she longing to be able to forgive her human father, and he longing to be able to reveal his Heavenly Father's will for them both. But it seemed that his timing was out; Penny's arrival at that precise moment had been no co-incidence.

To his relief, she let the matter drop, and began teasing him instead about being 'such a man of mystery'.

At last, they crossed the border into Wales, and she became quieter, only responding to his comments with nods and monosyllables. They travelled through several coal mining areas, the track running parallel with long lines of terraced houses, stepped along green, sloping hillsides. She peered out, trying to sense any affinity with the passing countryside and grey-stoned villages and towns. But although she recognised beauty, she remained detached and unmoved. How strange that

Scotland, a country with no claim on her lineage that she was aware of, had captured her mind and heart so completely that there appeared to be nothing left for this other country; this land of her parents.

*

They arrived at Nant-y-Fawr in the early evening, both in need of a hot meal and a good night's rest. Their hotel was a dreary looking, grey pebble-dashed affair, the interior of which turned out to be equally uninspiring. She unpacked, and was trying to decide where to put her case in the small room, when Alex knocked.

'It's me. How are you doing?'

'Just finished. Come on in.'

He opened the door and looked around. 'Bit of a dump isn't it?' He took two short paces to the bed, and sat down. 'I haven't got a chair either.'

'At least it's clean.'

'It'll do. Anyway, I expect we'll be out most of the time.'

She lifted her case and pushed it under the bed. He reached for her hand. 'Now look Yvonne, do you still want to go ahead with this? I don't want you to do it just to please me, and I won't think any less of you if you decide to pull out.'

She thought how kind he was; even now he was offering her an escape route. 'I'm fine, honestly. I know I've got to see him. It must be all that praying you've all been doing.'

'Atta girl! And who knows, it might just work out, but if it doesn't, then it'll be his loss. You can do triple somersaults trying to sort things out with someone, but if they won't even lean in your direction, then there's nothing more you can do. At least you'd have tried. Sometimes we just have to let things go, and leave them to The Boss. But you must have heard all this from Charles and Izzy already?'

'Yes, but now we're actually here, I think I needed to hear it again. And I'm willing to do my part anyway.'

'And The Boss will bless you for it. Whichever way it goes, you won't have lost anything you never really had.' He had a sudden image of his own father. Good old Dad: quiet, unassuming, hardworking, and steady as a rock. How blessed he had been, and still was. He pointed upwards, 'And whatever happens, He's ready whenever you are.'

She chewed her lip, yes, she knew. Over the past months her eyes had been opened to the various ways God had been revealing His love for her, and not only through Alex, Charles and Izzy, Heather and Lochlan, but also in the other Christians who met at the Manor, even in those who appeared to have no obvious faith, like Flora and Hamish, Dot and Angus, and even Donald and Georgina. Then too, she often sensed the Power and Presence of a Great and Living Force in the very land itself: from the stately dominance of the mountain ranges, to the fragile modesty of a fresh blade of grass. Now she knew who their Creator was, and she wanted that same Power and Presence to become her Living Force too.

She went to stand by the wall mirror and began to re-plait her hair, the soothing action aiding her philosophical mood, as she thought how strange it was for someone to be envious of mountains and blades of grass. She noticed Alex's reflection in the mirror; his eyes were closed as though in prayer. She felt peaceful now. At last, the awful anxiety she had felt during the past few weeks, and especially during the journey, had left her, and she was able to think clearly again. In fact, she felt so peaceful that she was very clear about her need of a Saviour, and that Saviour was the One who claimed to be *The Way, The Truth and The Life*. She had lost count of the number of times she had asked Him to forgive her for dying on the Cross in her place. She had absolutely no doubt now that there really was nothing she could do, or become, to make herself more acceptable to Him. He would accept her even with all this unresolved forgiveness business going on. He wanted her just as she was. Then what was it that was stopping her from inviting Him into her heart right now? Her head *did* understand and believe, and she could honestly say that her heart did too.

Doley ... Doley ... Doley.

No! It couldn't be. Not here, not now, now she was ready ... but Alex was speaking again.

'Tell you what, let's pray about tomorrow. We've got time, they stop serving at eight.'

'Oh Alex! I ... I ... yes, I'd like that, although ...'

'It's alright, sweetheart,' he patted the space beside him. 'Just you come and park yourself here, and let me do the praying.'

His prayer was so heartbreakingly sincere that it seemed to her that he had caught hold of Jesus's robe, and would not let go of it until He had been granted his request. She had never heard him pray like this before, in fact, she had never heard *anyone*, including Charles and Izzy, pray so earnestly. She felt herself humbled and deeply moved.

At last, the urgency left him and he spoke quietly, thanking God for the answers he believed would come. He lifted his head slowly and looked around him, as though seeing the dull brownness of the room for the first time. 'Phew!' he exclaimed, 'I needed that.'

She felt that she should say something, to thank him, and maybe tell him how she had been feeling just before the prayer, but she delayed too long, and the moment passed when he stood, and said, 'You know how praying makes me hungry. Come on, let's go and see if the food's got more going for it! But I'm warning you, I saw the menu on the way in, it's mushroom soup and some sort of stew. Looks like we're in for more of the brown stuff.'

On cue, her stomach rumbled, and she remembered that they'd had nothing substantial to eat since breakfast. Maybe it was just as well; she would probably find it easier to do what she wanted to do if she was alone anyway. Then, after they had eaten, she would suggest that they have an early night. In fact, she could hardly wait.

CHAPTER 41

Alex adjusted the seat belt of the hired car and turned to look at her. She had gone quiet again and was looking straight ahead. 'Are you ready? Shall we make a start?'

She nodded. 'I'm ready. Let's go.'

He switched on the ignition. It was ten o'clock on a Tuesday morning and their quarry would probably be at work, if so, they would return later that evening.

It took twenty minutes to reach the small village of Llanrhynfelin, during which time Alex found himself reflecting again on some advice Charles had given him just before their departure: 'Don't be surprised if Satan tries to throw a spanner or two in the works and you encounter some obstacles. Circumstances may prove more difficult than could reasonably be expected. In fact, many a time I've noticed that things seem to go very much against me when I'm set on a course of action that I believe to be right. That's why we have to be sure that it is God's leading we're following. It can be disconcerting and confusing, but hopefully you'll have the peace and assurance to guide you through, no matter how rough things could get. Anyway, you can rest assured that we'll all be praying hard for you here.'

It was good to know that people were praying; now they could go forward with confidence.

They drove slowly along Ashton Crescent, its gradual curve made up of a dozen or so detached chalet bungalows, each one in good repair and fronted by well-tended gardens, full of early autumn colour. Towards the end, they spotted a man standing beside a car. Yvonne stiffened, there was something about the shape of the head and the set of his shoulders - just something about him.

Aware of her reaction, Alex asked, 'Is that him, by that Jag?'

'Yes, I think so.'

He pulled over and parked, then put an arm around her shoulders. 'Right, let's have a quick word of prayer' She nodded. He closed his eyes and began. 'Well, Boss, here we are at last. We're asking that You guide us and help us to be sensitive to Your Spirit. Especially be with Yvonne and protect her; give her the grace and courage to do what she needs to do. If her father's going to turn awkward, then…may whatever he says … miss its mark. If he's glad to see her, then may this be the start of a genuine reconciliation; that's what we're hoping for Boss. But however it turns out, help us to behave in a way that's honouring to You. All we want is for Your will to be done. In the name of Your precious Son, Our Lord and Saviour, Jesus Christ. Amen.'

She echoed a quiet, 'Amen.'

He looked searchingly into her face. 'Ready?'

Was she? Was she ready, *really* ready to meet the man standing just yards away from her now?

Alex gave her a gentle shake. 'Yvonne?'

The time had come, the crossroads reached; there were to be no more excuses, no more delays - and no more running away. It was now or never, and anyway, she had already made her choice. Trying to sound as though she had full charge of her faculties, and despite the slight tremor in her voice, she replied, 'I'm okay. Let's go.' And with one swift movement, she opened her door and stepped out. Let him see her. She would face him, she needed to face him. And Alex was with her, by her side, holding her arm, and leading her towards the man, towards her father. But only her human one.

*

'My God! Doley! *Doley!* What the bloody hell are you doing here?' Owen Williams' tone was anything but welcoming.

Disappointed that the abuse might have already started, Alex stepped protectively out in front of her. 'Let me handle this,' he said, fixing the man in front of him with a steady look.

Owen Williams was something of a surprise. Alex had expected to find a mean, twisted looking individual, whose appearance had been affected and warped by years of spouting bitterness and causing unhappiness in others. Instead, this man looked positively glowing. Tall, well built and good-looking, with a mane of brown hair shot through with streaks of grey, he and his surroundings gave the impression that here was someone who enjoyed good health and was doing very well for himself.

'Mr Williams, I'm Alex Grant.' Any handshake could wait. 'Yvonne and I have come a long way. *Yvonne,*' he made a point of stressing her name, 'would like to have a word with you.'

Owen Williams licked his suddenly dry lips and took a step back. The last thing he felt like doing was having a word with *her*. And who the hell was this cripple she'd come with?

'A word? A word? What nonsense is this?'

'I can assure you that what she has to say is anything but nonsense.'

'Is that so? Well, I'm not in the mood for any *words*. I'm busy.'

Alex looked at the bucket of suds by the man's feet and the sponge in his hand. 'You don't look particularly busy to me. Now, if we can stop wasting time and get on with it. Maybe somewhere a bit more private?'

Owen turned his back on them and bent down to soak the sponge. 'Oh, I'll get on with it alright, and here's a couple of words for you. *Sod off!*'

Yvonne stepped forward. 'Dad, please, I only want to ask you about ... some things.'

Owen began washing the roof of the car. He glanced over his shoulder at her, and said, 'A few things to ask? Hah! That's good, that is. Shame I'm too busy.'

'But we won't keep you long. If you'd only stop and listen.'

He swung around to face her. 'That's one thing you've got right. You won't keep me long, because I've got nothing to say to you. *Nothing!* And who do you think you are anyway? *You've* got things to ask *me!* Bloody hell! Why you ... you're nothing but a ... a ...' For a moment the words of his old chant evaded him. He searched his memory, and found them lurking in a dark corner, like a venomous snake, uncoiling now, and ready to strike. 'Hah! A Doley. Remember? Let me remind you: D for Durex, O for open, L for liability - '

'Williams!' Alex interrupted the poisonous flow. 'You'll call her by her proper name! And in case you've forgotten it, it's Yvonne. That's Y.V.O.N.N.E. Now, I suggest you quieten down and have the decency to hear what she's got to say.'

Owen recognised authority when he heard it, and this b....... had more than his fair share. Whoever, and whatever he was, he was obviously used to giving orders. Nevertheless, he stood his ground as he glanced at the dripping sponge in his hand, feeling very much that he would like to hurl it in his direction. And there was no way he was going to answer any nosey parker questions, especially from the very last person he expected - or ever wanted - to see again. What could she have questions about anyway? He glared at the good-looking young woman staring back at him. Oh yes! He'd have known her a mile off, she'd always looked like her mother, but now she was like a carbon copy of the bitch.

He took a few paces back and studied the smeared paintwork on the car's boot, then decided that that took priority over the roof. The sarcasm was evident in his tone as he addressed Alex without looking at him. 'So, you can spell. Bully for you! And don't you worry about my memory, I remember her name alright.' He tossed his head in Yvonne's direction and began to apply the soap in large, circular movements, and said, 'Doley ... Hole in the Durex ... Doley! Satisfied, now are we? Does that answer your ... questions?'

Yvonne could not help herself as she let out a small but unmistakable laugh. Alex turned quickly to look at her and asked, 'Are you alright sweetheart?'

Yes, she was alright, and had been from the moment that Owen Williams had opened his mouth, for it was then that she had come to realise that his words did not hurt. In fact, they were literally bouncing off her! She had been called by that name again, and from his own mouth, he had even spelled it out, and for the first time in her life she recognised how stupid, even ridiculous, it sounded. Surely he could have thought of something more imaginative! How could she have let it influence and torment her all these years? Somehow, somewhere, and miraculously, it had lost its hold on her. She was also beginning to realise that, despite his nearness, he might as well have been on the moon for all the impact his physical presence was having upon her.

Unfortunately, her laugh seemed to rile Owen even more, and with a voice full of contempt, he went on to ask, 'What the hell are you laughing at?'

Alex was finding himself becoming more disgusted by the second at the man. It was obvious that he didn't care a damn for the daughter who he hadn't seen for over ten years.

Yvonne was quick to reply, her voice clear and steady. 'I'm laughing at that name. Don't you think it's rather stupid, even childish?'

Owen was taken aback. It appeared that the girl had grown into a right little madam. Well, he'd soon settle her hash! He looked her up and down, his face contorting into an unpleasant grimace, and sneered, 'Like you then, and it suited you. Still does.'

Alex recognised that he was in danger of slipping back into military mode and that he would have to watch himself; Williams was no raw recruit, and this was no parade ground. Nevertheless, he found himself metaphorically donning his major's cap again as he adopted an unmistakably authoritarian tone, and warned, 'Watch it, Williams! You're stepping out of line. I repeat, you'll address Yvonne by her proper name, or I'll make it my business to make sure you do.'

Owen glanced at the walking stick. 'Hah! Tough guy is it? I'm shaking in my boots. Who are you anyway? Some Johnny-come-lately? Don't tell me she's been up to her mother's tricks and pricked yours as well?'

Yvonne stared at the foul-mouthed man, and not for the first time in her life wondered how it was possible that she could have been fathered by such a coarse and vulgar individual. She could neither see, nor recognise, anything of herself in him; he was totally alien to everything she was or felt. She had been speculating at the strength of any familial feeling she might experience when they did meet, and now she had her answer - she felt none. It was as though a huge, gaping chasm had opened up between them, and he was nothing but an ineffectual and insignificant shape on the other side.

*

Come rain or shine, high days or holidays, Stella Lloyd never emerged from her bed before ten o'clock. She had heard unfamiliar voices outside, and seeing that the Teasmade was out of water, decided that she might as well get up. Pretending to tidy the curtains, she pushed the window open a few more inches and strained hard to hear what was going on down there. Owen was talking to some strangers, and it didn't sound too friendly.

'Hello!' she called. Three faces looked up at her, Owen's with a scowl, the two people with him with obvious surprise. 'Is everything alright Owen?'

'Get back in Stella! They're just … asking for directions.'

'Oh yes, and where to?'

'I told you to get back in!' He turned sharply to Yvonne, and hissed, 'Damnation! Now you've … that's it. Go on, push off! I've had enough of this bloody nonsense.'

Alex could see that things were slipping away, but he was resolute that Yvonne was not going to leave here without getting some kind of answer, some kind of satisfaction. He sent up a silent arrow prayer, asking for an extra dose of self-control, patience and wisdom, before calmly saying, 'Er, no, I don't think so. But we'll be more than happy to be on our way once we get some answers. So, what's it to be? Ten minutes of your time? Or shall we stand here arguing the toss all day?'

Stella had heard enough. Blow Owen, she wanted to know what was going on down there. Whatever it was, it didn't sound too pally; that pair might start causing a scene and she had her reputation to think about. She had worked too hard for too long to achieve some kind of respect and status in the village, and carrying's on like this outside one's property was not to be contemplated. Wrapping her dressing gown tightly around her, she hurried down the stairs and marched purposefully out. Halfway down the garden path she almost faltered at catching her first real sight of Yvonne. No, it couldn't be! She must be imagining it? Ignoring Owen's glare, she went to stand beside him, and asked, 'So, what's going on here then?'

He let out a low growl, and hurled the sponge back into the bucket with such force that a shower of suds splashed onto her fluffy pink mules. If he couldn't get rid of her now, she'd carry on and make his life a living hell for the rest of the day. And that was *not* how he wanted to spend his precious day off!

'For God's sake woman, I told you, they're just asking for directions.'

'Williams!' Alex was trying hard not to shout, even though he badly wanted to. 'Get it into your head that we're not moving until you agree to talk to us, and in a civilised manner. Now, what's it to be? Out here in the street, in public, or somewhere private? The choice is yours.'

Stella stared wide-eyed at the man. He looked as though he meant business alright. Then it dawned on her that the half past ten bus from Nant-y-Fawr would be stopping just yards away from them at any minute. Something had to be done. She put on her most appealing voice, the one that Owen usually responded to very nicely. 'Oh Owen, don't stay out here! You don't want the neighbours upset now do you? And the bus! Be reasonable now, and we'll get…whatever it is sorted out. Only I don't want any unpleasantness, you know I don't. It's not fair, think of me, I need peace. Be fair now Owen.'

However, on this occasion, Owen found her pleading tone as childish as he did aggravating, and was forced to roar, *'Stop your whining woman!* Just give it a rest!' Knowing he was beaten, he turned and headed for the gate, calling after him, 'Bloody hell! Alright, alright. Two minutes, and that's your lot.'

*

The garden was enclosed by a six-foot high fence, and was as neat as it was unimaginative. The group came to stand on the patio by some French doors, the curtains inside still closed.

Alex turned to Stella and held out his hand. 'We haven't been introduced. I'm Alexander Grant, and this is Yvonne Williams.' Her hand felt cold and lifeless in his.

Stella glared at Yvonne. So, this *was* the daughter! She had often wondered if she would show up, and now here she was. The nerve of the girl! She raised herself to her full five-foot seven-inch height, and then, almost daring Owen to contradict her, declared, 'Stella Williams, *Mrs* Stella Williams.'

Yvonne shot Owen a glance, and asked, 'So you remarried? And what about children? I hope you manage to call *them* by their proper names.'

Now this was her business, and Stella, who even these days habitually bemoaned the absence of children of their own, retorted, 'Well, what a cheek! I'm sure that's none of your business!'

'Actually,' replied Yvonne, 'I think it would be my business to know if I've got any brothers or sisters.'

Owen gave a derisive laugh as he turned to Alex. 'Hah! Listen to her! Typical. Just like her mother, always going on about bloody kids. You'd better watch yourself, or she'll reel you in - if she hasn't already.'

Obviously becoming more annoyed, Stella said sharply, 'Owen, don't talk like that! And why'd you have to go and mention *her* again? You're always going on about her. I'm fed up hearing about it.'

'Shut up Stella! I told you, this has got nothing to do with you. And look at you woman, you're half dressed, shaming yourself. Now bloody well mind your own business, and get back inside!'

The roar of a bus engine could be heard approaching, and Stella was clearly relieved when it did not stop. 'No, I won't "mind my own business". I've got a right to know what's going on.' Well she had, hadn't she? And then, as she often did, she began privately rehearsing and justifying her own situation to herself. After all, didn't she 'do' for him in every way a wife 'did' for a husband? And didn't she have every right to claim the title if she did the deed?

Owen threw his hands up in exasperation. *'Women!'* Who the bloody hell needs them? Tormenters, the whole bloody lot of them!' He glanced at Alex. 'Let me give you some good advice, Sunny Jim, and you'll thank me for it one day. Keep your flies zipped and get the hell out of it as fast as you can - or they'll give you a hell of a life.'

Stella stared accusingly at him. 'That's not fair Owen. How could you?' She jerked her head towards Yvonne, the cause of all this unpleasantness. 'And what's *she* doing here?' But before Owen could answer, she turned back to Yvonne, and said, 'Now look you, I've got a right to some peace. Why'd you come here today anyway, upsetting him? And there's nothing for you here, you've had your lot. He left you everything, didn't he? Not many men would do that, I can tell you. Left himself with nothing but the shirt on his back. And what thanks did he get? Not so much as a peep out of you all these years. And now you turn up here … out of the blue … cap in hand is it? And after me taking him in and looking after him. So don't you go making waves, or … or … I can get nasty too!'

Alex was beginning to gain a clearer picture. It appeared that, for his own reasons, Williams had been feeding this woman a pack of lies. Unless he'd had debts to pay off, he would have had all the money from the sale of the family home in King's Lynn, and would certainly not have been a pauper. He also had his doubts about the marital status of the pair; that ring finger of hers was noticeably bare. Unbeknown to him, Stella's expensive collection of engagement and wedding rings from her previous two marriages were sitting on a local jeweller's shelf awaiting enlargement. The menopause had caused her fingers to swell, at least, that was the excuse she had given the young sales assistant.

'Right, Williams. *If* she is your wife, then she needs to be put straight on a few things. First off - '

'What do you mean, "*if* she's my wife"? interrupted an increasingly agitated Owen. 'Of course she's my bloody wife!' He gestured towards Yvonne. 'I'm not like her mother; always making eyes and opening her legs to every passing pair of trousers.'

Stella whimpered. Although she made the false claim often enough, hearing him do so - and with such vehemence - was just too much for a body to bear. Ten years, *ten years* she'd been waiting for him to make an honest woman of her!

Alex gave her a cool, knowing look, before turning his attention once again to Owen. 'Looks as though that's up for debate. And if you can't control yourself and keep a civil tongue in your head, then we'll have to get a third party involved. Is that what you want?'

Stella let out a squeak and covered her mouth with one hand. Owen found himself having to think fast. What was he to do now? Somehow he had to get rid of this b...... He stood rigid, clenching and unclenching his fists into tight balls, his knuckles gleaming white.

Not particularly interested in the marital status of the pair, Yvonne took advantage of the momentary lull in hostilities, to ask, 'The only thing I want to know is why you treated me and Mum so badly? She's not here to speak for herself, but I know she would have been disgusted at the way you told me to leave the house just weeks after she died. And you didn't even have the grace to tell me to my face, just leave that note, ordering me to get out! Oh, and by the way, thank you for the money, all ten pounds of it! And I'm not after anything. I just want an explanation ... about why you treated us like that, as though you hated us. You were always so angry. Why? What had we done?'

Stella looked askance at her, then turning to Owen, asked, '*Ten pounds?* What ten pounds? What's she talking about Owen?'

Owen's face had been busily contorting into a series of unpleasant grimaces. Now the cat really was out of the bag. How the hell was he going to talk himself out of this one? Desperate to draw the conversation away from any talk of money, he flung his arm in Yvonne's direction, and exclaimed, 'Hah! It can talk. And is that what all this ... drivel ... is about?' He affected a childish voice, and mimicked, "Why did you treat mummy and me like that? Diddums!"' Then, louder and harsher, 'You're still too big for your boots, my girl. You want *me* to explain to *you!* I don't explain *anything* to *anyone*, do you hear me, *not anyone!*'

Niall's image flashed into Yvonne's mind; he had used words like these not so long ago.

Alex had been prepared to allow Yvonne free reign, but now found himself having to issue yet another warning. 'Williams! I warned you - '

However, Yvonne was on top of the situation, and interrupted, 'It's alright Alex, I've heard it all before, and I'm not surprised he can't bring himself to give me a straight answer.' She gave her father a withering look. 'He never could. He'd always start shouting and hurling insults around. Tell me, were you always like this, I mean, with Mum, before I came along? Only, I never could understand why she married you.'

Stella braced herself at the mention of *that* woman again. Despite her own distress, she was now keener than ever to discover what all this was about. It really was too bad; she didn't deserve this. But why was Owen letting the girl get away with such cheek, and lying too? Ten pounds - what was she talking about? She looked at him, his jaw was working hard, and she knew what that meant - there would be sparks flying soon. 'Owen, hush-up a bit will you! She's got her facts wrong. Tell her Owen, go on, tell her.'

Turning to Yvonne, he spoke, his voice deep and low as he fought to keep control. He'd deal with Stella later. 'Your mother, your mother. Your wonderful mother. Hah! You haven't got a clue, have you? Not a clue. And why should I tell you anything? I owe you nothing, *nothing*. I was right about you; bloody jumped-up tart! Now clear off the pair of you, I've had enough...' He turned towards the gate and threw it open, obviously intent upon leaving, even if they weren't.

Startled by the sound of the banging gate, the blackbird that could usually be found worming under the viburnum bush nearby, screeched and flew out, almost colliding with Stella. The incident unnerved her, and she found herself close to tears, as she shrilled, 'Go on Owen, tell them! Tell them about her, how she made a fool of you. You're always telling me. Tell them what she was like; how she trapped you. Go on, go on, tell them!'

Owen spun around, and gave her such a look of loathing that she took a step back. She stumbled and fell over the lawn edging, landing heavily on her backside. There was a moment of shocked silence before Alex stepped forward to offer her his hand. Mortified that it had been the stranger who had helped her, and not Owen, she accepted, bursting into tears as she did so.

Owen began shouting again, *'I told you to go back in woman. You're making a bloody fool of yourself. Go on in! This has nothing to do with you, nothing. It's nobody's business but mine. Mine!'*

But now Stella's own temper began to flare, helping her to control the sobs as she dusted herself down with quick, angry movements. She wrapped the dressing gown tightly around her, and crossing her arms indignantly across her chest, replied in such a level, controlled voice that all three found themselves giving her their full attention. 'Now, now, Owen Williams! I think this has *a lot* to do with me, *if* you'd care to remember.'

Yvonne looked with wonder at the woman; her mother would never have dared to speak to him like that. And that was not the only difference: this one looked to be in her late fifties, and much taller; her hair had clearly been bleached chemically blonde, and her face seemed to be in a state of constant surprise - probably due to her very arched, pencilled-in eyebrows. In fact, she appeared to be the opposite in every way to her quieter, downtrodden mother. If she couldn't get any satisfactory answers from her father - and it was certainly looking that way - then she might be able to get some from her. It was worth a try. 'What do you mean, "a lot" to do with you? And what was that you said about the house?'

But Owen had heard the hidden threat in Stella's voice, and had become even more agitated at the mention of money again. He had to act fast now. Before Stella could reply, he slammed his fist hard against the wooden gate, causing the two women to jump and a dog to bark in the next street. The blackbird, that had been keeping an eye on his territory from a nearby branch, decided it was time to fly away. As though trying to block out the pain of it all, Owen screwed his eyes up tightly and tried hard to keep control of himself, as he ordered, *'Shut your mouth Stella! This is over. And you two can get the hell off my property, or it's the law for you!'*

But Stella was not to be browbeaten. Buoyed-up by her indignation at hearing him call *her* house *his* property, she said calmly, 'What harm can it do to tell her what happened after all this time? She's asked, so tell her! And one more thing, Owen Williams, don't you speak to me like that, not on *my* property, you hear! I won't have it; I just won't have it.'

She paused for breath and looked at Yvonne. 'You want to know about your mother? Very well, I'll tell you, but don't you go blaming me if you don't like what you hear. She tricked him, didn't she. Going out with Evan, his big brother she was, and got herself in the family way, but he wouldn't make an honest woman of her.' Her voice began to come out in a shrill. 'Ran off didn't he, and ended up with some fancy piece from Swansea. Brought shame on the family it did, and Owen's mam and dad were devastated. Devastated they were! So, what did they do? I'll tell you what they did, they forced him ...' She gave an overdramatic flourish of her hand towards Owen. 'Just a boy, wasn't he! Forced him they did, to marry her. He was a good boy, did a kind thing, taking on Evan's leftovers, and ready to give the child his name.'

Concerned at how she would react to this unexpected revelation, Alex took a step closer to Yvonne.

Stella went on quickly. 'You should be thanking him, proud of him you should be, not coming here carrying-on like this, in public too!' She stopped for breath, feeling again the passion of all those years ago. Yes, she was mad at the man, but she just couldn't help loving him.

Knowing he was defeated, Owen had been groaning quietly and shaking his head throughout her speech. Now it would all have to come out, but he would make damn sure that they would hear *his* version of events if it was the last thing he did.

On full alert, Alex had been watching the other man's reactions closely, feeling that at last they could be getting somewhere. But he would need to be ready to intervene, Williams was a loose cannon.

Yvonne spent several moments digesting what she had just heard. Eventually, incredulous, and staring wide-eyed at Owen, she asked, 'So you mean, my mother and ... that I'm ... that my father, my *real* father ... was ... *your brother?'*

He gave a long, forced sigh, then threw his hands up once more in exasperation. The stupid little bitch had come to the wrong conclusion. He glared at Stella. It was time to play his trump card and get her away from here; she'd done more than enough damage already. 'Oh, good job! Well done! Well, why don't you blab out the rest of it? Tell it like it was? Tell her about you and me, how we'd been walking out, how you took those tablets and messed up your insides. Made yourself barren ... useless. Tell them how I've had to put up with all your whining on and on about adopting kids ... *other people's bloody kids...*driving me bloody mad all these bloody years!'

Stella had been looking at him with growing dismay, her colour draining away, her lips trembling.

'Oh, but I forgot, you're the expert, the know-it-all, aren't you?' continued Owen, well into his stride now. 'Go on then, tell them the rest. Tell them how no one forced you to swallow the damn things. Tell them all about *that!'*

'Owen, don't...you know I ... I ...' How could he mention that awful time again? Always throwing it up in her face he was. And now in front of these people too. And at last, finally overcome, she did what she had been repeatedly told to do, and trying to keep what little scrap of dignity she had left, managed to turn, without stumbling, and walk away. A minute later they heard loud, uncontrollable sobs coming from inside the house.

CHAPTER 42

Satisfied, almost gloating, Owen focused again on Yvonne. 'Now see what you've done? Stirred-up trouble. That woman …' he turned to point in the direction of the sobs, 'that woman is worth a thousand of your mother. A *thousand!*'

Yvonne calmly replied, 'I'm sure she's very worthy, but you still haven't told me if my father is your brother?'

Obviously exasperated, Owen made a great show of rolling his eyes. 'Now look, I'll tell you just once, *just once mind,* and I don't see why the hell I should do that. That woman …,' again he pointed at the house, 'that good woman thinks the world of me, and always has, but people interfered didn't they, got in the way. My brother, my *wonderful* brother, got your mother pregnant, and then bloody well went and cleared off! And I ended up having to take on his soiled goods. And by God, didn't I suffer for it!'

He paused to give a bitter, cruel laugh, remembering again how desperate his parents had been to save face in the small chapel-going village, where the birth of an illegitimate child was thought of as a shameful thing. They had owned one of the only two shops in the area, and found all the whispering and sidelong glances deeply humiliating. It came to such a pitch, that in order to salvage something of the family pride as well as the business, they came to the conclusion that the only way they could lessen the disgrace of it all was to persuade Owen to step into his older brother's shoes. It stood to reason, by marrying the girl, and taking her and her 'problem' on, they'd be doing the boy a good turn, and helping him to settle down. Everyone knew the boy would never amount to anything anyway. Still a private after four years in the Army, wasn't he? And that Stella Lloyd he always messed about with when he came home on leave was a loose piece if ever there was one. It made sense, didn't it? He'd look back and thank them for it one day.

Owen took his time thinking the matter over, and decided to take the long view in the end. He could come out of this very well if he played his cards right. His parents were in their sixties, and his father had been sickly for years. With Evan out of the picture, he would inherit the house *and* the shop, both of which could fetch a tidy sum. As for the girl, what was to stop him from dumping her a bit further down the line? All he had to do was say that she'd started messing about again, and even they wouldn't blame him for leaving her. She'd already proved that she was a tart, hadn't she?

The marriage went ahead, and the couple left for a posting to Germany a few weeks later. Business returned to normal at the shop, although it took a while for all the whispering about the shotgun wedding to die down. This one had been especially titillating, because everyone knew that the metaphoric gun had been pointing at the wrong brother.

And then, if the kid hadn't come out dead! The umbilical cord wrapped tightly around its neck. Owen wrote to tell his parents 'the sad news' and began to make his plans. He knew it wouldn't look good if he left too soon; he would wait a month or two before writing to them again and doing a hatchet job on Mary, and saying that he really couldn't live with such a woman any more. However, in the meantime, his mother's next letter arrived with some news that was to change everything. In an obviously excited frame of mind, she had written:-

...Dear Evan has come home and brought his new wife with him! The girl is called Dehlia and they're living with us for the time being but he's put his name down with the council. Her family owns a business in Swansea and he says they're not short of a bob or two. He's very sorry for upsetting us and everyone's entitled to make a mistake, aren't they? We know you'll be glad that the family is back together again. By the way, he wanted you to know that he's grateful to you and wishes you good luck, so that's nice isn't it? It's such a relief that both of you are decently

married. Now I can hold my head up again and our name is something to be proud of again in the village. We've been thinking, it's only right that he has what's rightfully his when we go. What a good job we didn't change the will after all! So, all in all, everything has turned out very nicely ...

... Ps. Don't fret too much about that baby, it's only nature's way of getting rid of something not right.

Too late Owen realised his mistake; they had gone back on their word; the Will had not been changed. At one fell swoop his promised future payout had been halved. Evan had always been the apple of his parents' eye; he should have known they'd fall over themselves to welcome the b...... back. Now he would have to stay 'decently married' if he wanted to protect his share. His mother would never forgive him if he did anything to cause her not being able to 'hold her head up again' and besmirch the precious family name! What a fool he'd been! He'd sacrificed himself in vain. It was a hard and bitter pill to swallow. Now, what else could he do - but drink his sorrows away.

Six months later, Mary announced she was pregnant again - but he knew her game alright; desperate to keep him, she'd made sure to get herself caught. Between them, his stupid mother and conniving wife had done a thorough hatchet job on him. Now he was well and truly trapped.

Yvonne was born healthy. Mary needed some kind of minor operation after giving birth, and insisted upon being sterilized at the same time. As far as he was concerned, that was the only thing she ever got right throughout the whole of their sham of a marriage. At least there'd be no more bloody kids to mess his life up!

It was several months before he could bring himself to write to his parents and inform them that they were grandparents at last. His mother's reply arrived soon after, the envelope marked in the usual way:-

STRICTLY PRIVATE

For the attention of Mr. O. A. Williams only.
... We are still reeling from the news that Dehlia has
found out that she's barren. She's got some type of
nasty infection in her private parts that's done the
damage. I keep telling Evan to go to the doctor to get
some tests done in case he catches it off her. So you
can imagine how shocked we were to hear that your
wife has had a girl. Never mind, she'll have to try
again, and let's hope she gets it right next time and
gives you a boy.

Business has picked-up nicely and your father's
looking into opening another shop. Evan says that
there's scope on the council estate and he'd like to
manage it, so that's good isn't it? I think it will help
take his mind off things ... poor boy ...

*

Three more years were to pass before Owen's demob finally
came through. However, he was restless and dissatisfied with
everything and everybody, and, as a result, moved the family
from one town and rented property to another. Always a keen
patron of the local ex-service men's club, he bumped into one
of his old Army mates one evening, who told him about a
vacancy for a job repairing television sets and radios in the
nearby town of King's Lynn. He applied and got the job, which
seemed to suit him well enough, and at last he was able to
afford a small mortgage, and the family began to settle down.

Unfortunately, his mother's occasional letters did nothing
to help bring harmony into the home, only serving instead to
continue adding fuel to his constantly burning resentment
towards Mary and the child.

His mother wrote:-

... Poor Evan's going through hell with that wife of
his...People are beginning to talk. It's nothing but
bingo, bingo, bingo and there's no meal on the table
for him ...

... She's fallen out with the neighbours so they're on the move again ...

... She's turned nasty and the poor boy's been pushed into the box room.

The looks I get! I think I will have to stop going to the Guild ...

*

Much to his frustration, it took another five years for his ailing father to pass away. His mother followed four months later, which he thought was very obliging of her. He waited impatiently for the estate to be settled, expecting his entitlement and just reward for having stayed 'decently married' all this time. He was due, by God he was! But, once again he was to be disappointed, and his fury was uncontainable when he learned that his brother had managed to come out of the whole thing smelling of roses, for not only had he been left the larger, more successful shop, but the family home as well. Instructions had been left for the smaller, original shop to be sold, and, thereafter, a sum of no more than £2,000 to be paid to Owen.

Always more comfortable with the written word than the spoken, his mother had left him one last letter:-

... After all you have never shown any interest in the family business, not like Evan, poor boy, he's still living in a council flat. He's not been as lucky as you, you've always been able to find private places to live in, and even buy your own house, and have your own offspring, he can't say that now, can he? I know you'll see the sense in what we are doing for him. It's only fair that he gets a decent roof over his head and maybe that wife of his will realise what a good provider she's married and knuckle down ...

Owen lost no time in taking legal advice, but was told that he would be wasting his time; it was up to the parties involved to reach a mutually satisfactory arrangement. The law could do nothing; the Will was binding. Sick at heart, he decided to invest the whole £2,000 with the *Sun Life Insurance Company*. That way, sooner or later, he'd have a substantial payout to call his own - and then he'd have the last laugh. Oh yes, he'd make damn sure of that, if it was the last thing he ever did!

Back in Wales, his brother sold the remaining shop, and began to enjoy his new financial status, in fact, he enjoyed it just a bit too much. Always one for the women, and now without his mother's keen and watchful eye, he could afford to splash out and *really* enjoy himself. But his carefree lifestyle was not to last long, for his wife did indeed come to realise just what 'a good provider' she had married - and now he had even provided her with undisputable grounds for divorce. As a result, the house was sold and the proceeds shared between the couple. Not overly bothered, Evan shrugged his shoulders and packed his bags - and was never seen or heard of again.

*

It was a good day when Mary had died, although it was a pity she'd taken so long about it. At last Owen was free, and now there was nothing to stop him. He'd quit the dead-end job, sell up, and move back to Wales. He'd have to rent for the time being, but he'd find a nice little property in the village when his main policy matured; something with a bit of class. He'd show them; he'd show them all! Then he'd be the one laughing all the way to the bank and holding *his* head up high - and the first place he'd be doing that would be over his parent's grave.

Things went smoothly. The house sold quickly and he turned his back on King's Lynn and his old life. He found a room to rent and took his time finding another job. Llanrhynfelin hadn't changed much over the years, and it was inevitable that he would bump into his old flame, Stella Lloyd again. She appeared to have done well for herself, having been divorced once, remarried, then conveniently widowed. Obviously thrilled to see him again, she almost fell into his arms, and it was not long before she began hinting at needing another wedding ring, and persuaded him to come and share her comfortable home - and her equally comfortable bed.

At first, he had been able to fob her off with some cock and bull story about being so heartbroken over losing Mary that the thought of tarnishing her memory by marrying again was unthinkable. However, one night he had foolishly made the mistake of revealing his *real* feelings about his dead wife when he had returned home after a particularly heavy drinking session at the club. It had taken all his powers of persuasion to get her to forgive him. He was sick and tired of her whining on about wanting to be made 'an honest woman' of again, and he had been fighting that battle for some time now, but not for much longer. His remaining policy was due to mature in just over a year's time - and *no one* was going to rob him of as much as a penny this time around. All he had to do was keep her sweet for just a little while longer - and then he would pack his bags and head for somewhere warm and dry, like Italy. And then he would never, *never* look back.

*

So what the hell was the girl doing here now? She'd already blabbed too much and upset his cosy little setup. With his head still turned towards the direction of Stella's continued loud sobbing, and attempting to inject a note of compassion into his voice, he said, 'Heartbroken she was when I was made to finish with her and…and do my duty by the family. Tried to top herself; been a wreck ever since…fragile.' And now the hard edge returned, 'And then, and get this, the biggest joke of all, the bloody kid came out dead! Hah! Born dead! What a joke!'

Yvonne was speechless, and began to struggle to make sense of what she had just heard. If she had understood him correctly, then her mother, going the way of so many young women, had fallen for a man who had deserted her in her real time of need. Her father, for now it seemed that that is what this man really was, whether she liked it or not, had somehow been persuaded to step into his brother's shoes and marry her. And then the baby had been born dead. Poor Mum, she had never mentioned another child; she must have been too ashamed, or heartbroken, to ever want to talk about it. But had the baby lived, then she would have had an older half-brother or sister. She had to know, and asked, 'Was it a boy or a girl?'

'What are you blabbing on about now?'

'The baby that died. Was it a boy or a girl?'

Owen gave her a contemptuous look. 'How the hell should I know? What's that got to do with anything? It died. Get it, it's *dead.*'

She felt a sharp pang of disappointment, and now for the first time, felt her own temper begin to rise. She was used to the fact that he hadn't cared less for her mother or herself, but now she felt distressed and appalled that she would have to add this poor dead and innocent child to the list.

'Then if you despised my mother so much, why didn't you part company then? Why did you go on to have me? There must have been something ... some feeling between you, if you stayed together?'

'Hah! Feelings is it? You want to know about feelings?'

She noticed that beads of sweat were beginning to form on his brow and upper lip, and was reminded once again of Niall.

'The only feeling I had was to get the hell out, but...'

'But?' prompted Alex, feeling sure that there was far more to his story than Williams was letting on.

Owen straightened his back and stuck his chin out, obviously preparing to make some important statement. 'I'm a man of honour. If I say I'm going to do a thing, then I do it. I took her on, and I stuck to her. And, by God, she made damned sure of that, didn't she!'

'How...what do you mean,' asked Yvonne.

'Oh, so you want to know do you? Okay, I'll tell you, shall I? I'll tell you what a nasty, conniving piece of work she was. I'll tell you how the crafty bitch made sure I'd stick around.' He gave her a withering look, and sneered, 'And I'm looking at the sickening way she did it right now.'

'What ... you mean ... by having me?'

'Hah! Not so stupid then? Played innocent, didn't she.' He paused to screw up his face and put on an affected, female voice. '"Didn't know how it happened. Must have been one of those leaky rubber Johnny's they've been sending out."' He threw his hands up in a violent gesture. 'Hah! A hole in the Durex. Stitched me up good and proper. Got it now have we? Sunk in now has it? Know what you are now, do you? Nothing but a bloody leak in the - '

'That's enough!' shouted Alex.

Stella's sobs had finally stopped, and a heavy silence followed. Yvonne studied the man in front of her, and came to understand that, in his own twisted way, Owen Williams was totally convinced that he had been the wronged party, the innocent pawn in some badly hatched family scheme. Instead of making a stand, and refusing to have anything to do with it, he had allowed himself to be drawn in and manipulated. Obviously, things had not gone the way he had hoped. But what had he hoped? Whatever had happened all those years ago was enough to cause him to spend the rest of his life plagued by disappointment and bitterness, and he had taken his frustration and unhappiness out on her mother and herself. As for that hole in the Durex claim, well, true or not, what did it matter now, after all these years? But, knowing all this, was that reason enough to hold on to her own feelings of unforgiveness? If so, wouldn't that mean that she was like him, unable to let go, and let the bitterness keep festering - like a cancer - inside her? *No*, she wouldn't let that happen. She would *not* be like him. She *would* be free. Even so, she felt that she was justified in thoroughly disliking him.

Alex was speaking, 'It takes two to tango, Williams. Yvonne's mother couldn't have had her without your...contribution. To shift the blame onto the woman, and your *wife* I might add, is downright wrong, and unworthy of any man worth his salt. You talk about being a man of honour? Well that's not what it looks like from where I'm standing. Don't you realise - and despite the way you claim it happened - that you were given a precious gift when you were given a child, and a healthy one at that?'

He turned to Yvonne and held out his hand, which she took, looking up at him and wondering what was coming next.

'She's a lovely, lovely young woman. A daughter any man would be proud of. How she grew up to be such a decent person is beyond me, especially after the years of abuse you put her and her mother through. Shame on you for rejecting her. Shame on you for throwing her away. *Shame on you!'*

Owen felt as disgusted as he looked. The fool of a man was obviously soft in the head and needed putting straight on a few things. And, by God, he was the one to do it!

"Precious gift? Precious gift?' You bloody fool! Go on then, tie yourself down, but don't say you haven't been warned. You'll soon find out she's like the rest of them. Nothing but a millstone around your neck. A sodding waste of time and space. She'll bleed you dry, suck the life out of you. They're all conniving, scheming, lying bitches. Mark my words, if you've got any sense, you'd run a mile. You'll find out soon enough how *precious* she is. She's nothing but a ... a hole - '

'Enough!' Once again Alex was forced to interrupt the malevolent flow of words that seemed to blacken the very air around them. He held Yvonne's hand tightly, wanting to get her away from the human vessel that was allowing itself to spout the poison that had its roots in pure evil itself. 'Right! You've shown yourself up for what you are, Williams. You might be Yvonne's father, but I'm telling you here and now, that unless you wake up to what a fool you've been all these years, and change your attitude, you'll keep away from her, or you'll have me ... and God Himself ... to answer to. Am I making myself clear?'

He began leading Yvonne towards the gate. 'Come on sweetheart, this is over. You've done enough somersaults.' There's nothing more to be done here.'

But Owen had not finished; he had not liked that mention of God; somehow it made him feel uneasy.

'God! God! What the bloody hell's He got to do with it? This is *my* business, *my* life. I'm the one in charge here, not any bloody God!'

Like an unexpected gift, Yvonne found that these last words gave her the inspiration, and courage, to do what she now strongly felt she had to do. She realised now that Owen Williams was a sick man; sick with a mind that had been infected and affected by the thoughtlessness and ill-judged schemes of others. He was like a man who was refusing to take his hand out of the fire, and then continually blaming and cursing everyone else for his pain. She would probably never see nor speak to him again, and unless she spoke up now, he could die without ever hearing about the One who had loved him enough to sacrifice Himself for him. And now, strange as it might seem, she was actually beginning to feel some sympathy for him. And so, yes, she knew now that she could forgive him.

She pulled back, and said in such a calm, clear voice that both men looked at her with surprise, 'Actually, God's got *everything* to do with it, and that's why we're here, because of Him.' She took a deep breath and sent up her own silent arrow prayer.

Owen visibly stiffened.

'Dad, I probably won't ever see you again. So I want you to know that I hope that you can somehow stop all this hating, that you'll be able to find some peace. I ... I ... want you to know that I forgive you ... for what you did to Mum and me.' Now her voice came out ragged and full of emotion. 'I don't understand why you let things go on for so long, but I see now that you've been ... damaged. But I want to be free to live my life now without ... I mean, I really *do* forgive you for the things you put us through ... all the things you said.'

Owen remained still. His eyes wide open with shock, and trying hard to think of something else he could insult her with.

Yvonne knew that she had meant every word. This was no act, no prearranged, carefully crafted and rehearsed speech. Her mind and her heart had felt and agreed with every word; the feelings and emotions were solid and true. She thoroughly disliked Owen Williams, and would never forget all the pain he had caused, but no longer would she allow that pain to define her. She would stop being a victim. She would take responsibility for her own life now, and she could, would, forgive him. She would let him go. In the same way that she had come to learn that there was nothing she could do, or become, to be loved and accepted by her Heavenly Father, she knew now that there was nothing she could do, or become, to be loved and accepted by her human one. The One had always loved and wanted her; the other had never allowed himself to.

Her throat began to hurt with the effort of trying to speak and not cry, and it was with some effort that she was able to continue. 'You need to let God into your life. He's the only One who can help you to let go of all that anger and bitterness. You need Him - He'll help you. Please give Him a chance. Until you do, you'll never know real peace and real happiness. But I've got to let go, let go of everything, and I do. I've got a new Father now, and One who can't hurt me - or who'll ever reject me.'

Alex gasped. Tears welled up at the back of his eyes. He made no effort to wipe them away when they surfaced and spilled over.

Unsure how to react, Owen was glad of the distraction as he glanced at him, and sneered. 'My God, I've heard it all now!'

Yvonne was really struggling, but managed to go on to empty herself of everything that she knew she had to say, and that she wanted to say. 'Please be quiet, and let me finish. He sent His own Son to die, to reach me, to help me to realise what a hash I'd made of my own life, and to forgive me. And to show me how much He loves me. I've got no right to hold on to all those bad feelings, not now I know that He took them upon Himself and suffered and … and dealt with them. He died so that I could be free of them, so I could be forgiven, and so I can forgive and know His love. And … and I shall pray that you'll meet Him, and come to know all this for yourself one day too.'

Empty at last, only to be filled again with a confidence and peace that she could hardly believe herself, she turned to Alex. And now tears came to her own eyes when she saw his. 'I'm ready now Alex, really ready.'

Alex could not speak. He had witnessed The Boss in action, and knew that he had been given the miracle he had been praying so ardently for all these months. Pulling her close to him, he put protective arms around her and kissed the top of her head. His heart was bursting with as much with love for her as with love and gratitude to The Boss who had given him this wonderful, glorious woman.

Owen was looking at them with puzzled bemusement, then, deciding that he had been silent long enough, let out a loud, jeering laugh; a sound so full of scorn and derision that he almost choked. The dog began to bark again. *'You forgive me! You forgive me!* Hah! Don't make me laugh! You've always been too soft in the head, but you've tipped over the edge now. Hah! I get it. You're one of those bloody religious fanatics. My God! Peace and love is it? Drippy, hippy flower power? Hah hah!'

He pushed past them to stand rigid and determined by the open gate, barely able to control his disgust as he pointed towards the road. 'Now get the hell out of here! Go on, get out! And don't you *ever* let me see your ugly faces here again. Bloody freaks! You forgive me? My God, that's a joke that is! Hah hah!'

They heard his laughter as they walked away. A harsh, cruel noise, full of scorn and hate. And yet there was something else in there too, something that sounded almost like panic.

Alex put an arm around her shoulders and led her away. Their steps became brisk and light, and they looked like any other couple seen out walking on a fine, clear day. Their tears already drying.

CHAPTER 43

'Are you okay sweetheart? Do you want to go back to the hotel now?' Alex's voice broke into her thoughts.

'Sorry … what?'

'Back to the hotel?'

'Oh no, not just yet, if that's okay with you. Can't we just keep going?'

'Sure thing. You just sit back and relax.'

They drove on in silence until they came across a small roadside café.

'Far enough?' he asked, 'how about a drink?'

'Good idea,' she replied, suddenly feeling very hungry.

A few minutes later, he sat back and watched her spread butter on her second Welsh cake. 'How are you doing?'

'I'm okay thanks. I think it's just starting to sink in. Actually, no, I *am* okay!'

'You had a bit of a rough time back there.'

She considered, before replying, 'Only what I expected. But it would have been nice if … well, you know.'

Alex could have said so much, especially about how disgusted he was at Owen Williams, and how disappointed and angry he had felt during the whole unpleasant episode. It was hard not to judge him; but who was he to stand in judgement over anyone? He could discern - yes - he was free to do that; and he discerned that the man had been cruelly and completely out of order.

'Well, you gave him enough chances to put things right, and I couldn't help feeling that there was a lot more to his story than he was letting on. He certainly seemed to have something to hide from that Stella. Reckon she'll be asking some questions of her own, once she gets over the upset. But as for you, it's all over now - unless The Boss has other plans. And talking of The Boss, the way you spoke about Him, would I be right in thinking that maybe something has … just begun?'

Smiling, she reached down for her handbag. 'I've got something to show you.' She handed him a small card. He recognised it immediately, it was identical to his. Printed on it were the words: *The Prayer of Christian Salvation.* His heart took a moment to catch up with his eyes when he saw that it had been signed. 'Glory to God! he exclaimed loudly.

She laughed, thankful that they were the café's only customers.

'I thought there was something going on with you last night, but I didn't dare to hope.'

'That's when I prayed it, last night in the hotel. And I didn't want to tell you…until, I mean, I just wanted to be sure that when I saw him, you know, that it was genuine, and that I wasn't just fooling myself. I remembered what you'd said about crisis faith; about how people make all sorts of promises to God when they're going through a bad time, and then forget all about Him when things are okay again. I didn't want it to be like that for me.'

'And is it?' he asked.

'No. I'm sure it's not.'

Still holding the card, he reached over with his free hand to hold hers. 'Hallelujah! I had a feeling that something had happened to you when you came into breakfast; you looked … kind of different.'

'I am feeling "kind of different."' With her other hand she took hold of the card and laid it down on the table between them. 'I know this is one decision I'll never regret. I've experienced too much of God's care already to know that it's the best thing I've ever done. I'm in it for life - and beyond.'

He thrilled at her words as he drew both her hands to his lips, and began kissing them enthusiastically.

'Hey! You'll get butter on your beard,' she warned. 'And you know, when it came to it, I found I really wanted to forgive him … and let him go. Although, it was strange, I felt that there was some kind of invisible wall around me. And somehow, and don't ask me how, I just *knew* that Jesus was actually there as well. It was amazing!'

'He was there. Like He's with us now. You'd given your life to Him. Now He's living in you through His Holy Spirit: the Spirit of Jesus. That's why you could sense His presence.' He freed one of her hands, then reached over to touch her chest lightly. 'He's right there, safe in your heart, like an invisible golden nugget.'

She beamed at him. Jesus, His Spirit, like a golden nugget, and living in her heart! She *really* liked that. And now, with Him, she felt she could take on the world! 'Oh, I *love* that!'

'And I love you,' he said. 'And you know sweetheart, you've taken my breath away.'

'Well keep breathing, you've got more driving to do yet. And if it's okay with you, I don't feel like hanging around Wales.'

'You sure? We've got a day to spare before our flight. You don't want to do some sightseeing now we're here? There's some lovely places not so far away.' Before the meeting with her father, he had thought about suggesting that they make some enquiries about her mother's side of the family, but decided now to keep that for another time.

'I'd rather not, if you don't mind. I'd really like to get back to Scotland.'

'Fair enough. Maybe we'll be able to take in a few sights when we get to London.'

*

They managed to catch the one o'clock train back to Paddington. Alex had plenty of time to think on the return journey, and came to realise that The Boss had His reasons for preventing him from revealing to her how he had always known exactly who, and what, she was to become to him. She had been through enough; now she needed time to get used to the idea of what she had really lost - and just found. He knew only too well that major life decisions were best made from a firm, steady foundation, not one that had just been rocked and undergone a radical reformation.

But how would she react when he did tell her? Would she be able to take him seriously, or laugh with incredulity? Heaven forbid that she would pad submissively behind him in dumb obedience; that was not what he wanted at all. Rather, she would hear him out and spend time talking to The Boss about it; He would know how to confirm that this was indeed His will for her. As for him, he would just have to keep on doing what he had been doing all these many months: hoping, praying, trusting - and waiting.

*

They were blessed with a peaceful night's sleep on their first night back in Scotland. Georgina's relief at Yvonne's return was explained when the latter found herself being coerced into helping at the ceilidh, despite the fact that she was still officially on holiday. This was to be the MacMan's last before they retired, and Georgina was determined to make it one of the best, and so the always popular, although exorbitantly expensive, Clansman Band had been booked. She was to be rewarded when it had the desired effect of attracting folk from many miles around.

*

Alex had debriefed Charles and Izzy about their time in Wales, and all three felt that it might be helpful for Yvonne to undergo one more counselling session.

Charles began in the usual manner, with prayer, after which they listened as Yvonne described the meeting with her father. Alex made the occasional comment, although remained silent for the most part.

When she had finished, Charles said, 'To my mind, you wouldn't have been able to point him to God unless there had been a genuine work of grace in you. By turning to Christ, and inviting Him into your heart, He was able to help you to forgive. You lay on that operating table, and trusted Him to free you from those crippling shackles of unforgiveness. You know Yvonne, you're very sensitive in the area of forgiveness, and are actually a very forgiving person. Look what happened with that chef; it sounds as though you went the extra mile with him as well.'

This was something of a revelation to Yvonne. Could it be true? It must be - why would Charles lie?

'Yes, but all the time I was there, I still couldn't forget what he'd been like. I kept remembering how he used to talk to my mother, and the way he used to treat her. But I kept reminding myself how much forgiveness I needed; and if God could forgive me, then I had no right not to forgive others, even him. And there was something you said a while back, about accepting God's love and His forgiveness, you know, about them being two sides of the same coin - and how we all need them both. That helped me to do what I knew I had to do, and, actually, what I wanted to do.'

'And the Lord will bless you for it, my dear. And don't fret about the memory side of things, it's only natural that you will remember. But you're probably aware that the sting is already fading, and it will continue to do so as time goes by. But changing the subject, what about that voice? Does it still pester you?'

'Sometimes, but I just tell it to go away. I don't believe it anymore, so it's just wasting its time. It's like I've got no room for it in my life now. It's only Jesus's voice I want to hear from now on.'

'Praise the Lord!' exclaimed Izzy.

'Amen to that!' added Charles, picking up his Bible. 'And here's something I believe He's saying to you right now:-

Trust in the LORD with all your heart
and lean not on your own understanding;
in all thy ways acknowledge him,
and he will make your paths straight.
(Proverbs 3:5,6).

She looked at him quizzically. 'He'll … make my paths straight?'

'That's right. By making Him first in your life, and by putting your trust in Him - in His wisdom, He'll be your Guide, and direct your path.'

'I think He's been doing that already, by bringing me here and letting me meet you all.'

'Yes, that's it!' agreed Izzy, enthusiastically.

'There's something I'd like to add here, about following that path,' said Alex. 'We change, get transformed - as we walk along it.'

'How … what do you mean?' asked Yvonne.

'Well, look at you! You're a great example,' he replied. 'You started reading the Bible, and then began to think seriously about what it said. I don't think I'd be wrong in saying that, from then on, you started to look at your life in a different way?'

'Ah yes, told you. Like good medicine,' remarked Izzy.

'Certainly,' agreed Charles. 'That's one way the Lord talks to us, through His written word; some would say *the* most important way.'

Izzy added, 'And talking of paths, remember that picture I had of you and the Lord in the woodland? When you couldn't bring yourself to take His hand and trust Him to lead you? That's something else you'll learn as you keep walking with Him, Yvonne: there'll be times when you'll only understand some things when you look back. Not always the case, mind you, but many times we don't see the path ahead clearly, but we know we can always trust Him. He can see the way ahead, even if we can't.'

Yvonne nodded. 'I think it was like that last week. I had a good idea about what type of reception I'd get, but after I'd asked the Lord into my heart, I felt sort of…calm, and just knew that things would get sorted out, one way or the other.'

'That was because you were already trusting The Boss to lead you, sweetheart,' Alex said.

'Yes. I can see that now. What a fool I've been, not to have made the effort to find out about Him before! When I think of all that time wandering around, just trying to find a place to settle down.'

'Well, now you're safe in Him. And I think you're discovering already that that's one place you won't want to wander away from,' said Charles. 'And you know, you learned a lot of valuable lessons on the way, and I've no doubt that the Lord will use them all one day. None of our experiences, good or bad, are wasted, if we give them all to Him.'

He leafed quickly through Bible. 'Here, I know you've read this a few times, but this seems an appropriate time to hear it again:-

What do you think? If a man owns a hundred sheep, and one of them wanders away, will he not leave the ninety-nine on the hills and go to look for the one that wandered off? And if he finds it, I tell you the truth, he is happier about that one sheep than about the ninety-nine that did not wander off. In the same way your Father in Heaven is not willing that any of these little ones should be lost.' (Matthew 18:12-14).

Yes, she had read the words many times over the past months, and as she had envied the mountains and blades of grass for the Life Force inside them, so she had envied that lost sheep.

Charles continued, 'Don't worry about the ninety-nine. They would have been left in a safe place, and probably with an under-shepherd. But for some lost sheep, it can be quite a journey. And many are like you, Yvonne, they've never heard the Gospel, and haven't a clue about how much God loves them. But for those who have heard, and then choose to disbelieve, ignore, or even rebel against Him, and still stubbornly insist on going their own way, believing that they are already fulfilled, or strong enough, to deal with life, they can end up wasting so much time. Many blame Him, or so-called fate, when they feel lost and confused on the twists and turns of their own making.'

'That sounds like my father,' she said.

'No doubt. From what you've told us, it sounds like he was brought up in a place where there was a chapel on nearly every corner. He might well have heard the Gospel, but might have felt that it had no relevance to his life, and didn't allow it to go skin-deep, never mind heart-deep. But, Praise God, you realised your need of Him - and now you're His child - and He's your Father.' He looked around him and opened his arms.

'And now you've been given a new family, and there are millions of us! Amen?'

She experienced a surge of emotion at the mention of a new family - and the fact that she was now a part of it. And it was with considerable difficulty that she managed to respond with a quiet, 'Amen.'

Charles glanced at the clock and closed his Bible. 'Well, that's it! Time's up folks. Izzy and I need to get going. But first, let's thank Him for everything. And then, Alex, maybe you'll tell Yvonne a bit more about her new family?'

'Oh yes, and not just about the brother and sisterly type of relationship either!' added Izzy, with a twinkle in her eye.

CHAPTER 44

Early the next morning, Alex and Yvonne set off for Beaulane to catch the ferry to the Isle of Brún. They joined the small queue waiting on the quayside, and watched a fisherman feeding a seal with some unwanted catch over the side of his boat. Applause broke out each time the animal leapt out of the water; the impromptu entertainment only coming to an end when the ferry could be seen approaching.

The fifty-minute crossing was smooth and uneventful, and soon they were stepping onto a landing jetty, surrounded by pristine, almost white sand. Dotted around were rocks, some as black as tar, and close by, as though on guard, stood crops of larger ones in a subtle shade of pink.

Their hotel, the aptly named Atlantic View, was just a short walk away.

Yvonne gasped with delight when she saw her room, and felt as though she had stepped straight into the pages of a fairytale. A canopy of snow-white lace fell in graceful folds from a thistle shaped crown over the bed, and pale lilac wallpaper, flecked with tiny bits of silver, set off the powder blues, subtle lilacs and deep purples of the rest of the room's fabrics. Unpacking was difficult, as time and again, she found her attention being drawn back to the sea and sky view outside her window.

She had only just managed to find a home for everything when Alex came to knock on her door, and offered to escort her to the lounge. Over coffee, they browsed through the selection of leaflets and brochures that had thoughtfully been provided by the hotel, and it soon became obvious that there would be more than enough to keep them occupied for the two full days they had on the island.

Alex was delighted, he could not have hoped for a more perfect setting for this most important of missions. This was the time he had been waiting for, and he was determined to do all he could to make it as enjoyable and memorable as possible. He watched the clouds, looking like giant balls of cotton wool, drifting silently by in the clear blue sky. Yes, there was no doubt about it now; he really had turned into an old romantic; he, who had always shunned anything to do with the matrimonial state, impatient now to secure this beautiful girl as his wife.

Dinner was a grand five course affair, and took longer than he would have liked. They chatted, occasionally falling silent to watch the setting sun cast a golden beam across the sea, now pewter grey. They joined some of the other guests for coffee in the lounge afterwards, and it was not long before he suggested that they take a stroll. Yvonne went to fetch her coat, and he took the opportunity to pray as he waited for her by the front porch.

They set off, walking hand-in-hand along the firmer sand by the shoreline; he nodding and making assenting noises to her enthusiastic chatter, the air full of the cries of gulls and the sound of the incoming tide.

He knew the time had come when she fell silent, and when he spoke, it was with a calm and steady voice. 'Yvonne, there's something I want to tell you. It's really by way of a confession, and I've been wanting to tell you for some time, but…let's just say, I've been constrained. It'll sound strange, but bear with me. I promise that every word of it is the truth.'

She looked at him, and began to feel some concern. 'Oh dear!' she exclaimed, 'that sounds serious.' She had assumed that he had wanted to finish this perfect day with an equally perfect walk.

'Serious, yes, but nothing to worry about. Come on, let's find a place to sit down. How about over there? They look smooth enough.' They walked over to some large boulders, their surfaces smoothed by the effects of a millennia of wind and water. They sat, he put an arm around her shoulders and pulled her closer. 'Cold?'

'I'm fine thanks. But before you say anything, I forgive you.'

'You forgive me?'

'Well, you said it's a sort of confession, so I forgive you!'
'You're really into this forgiving thing, aren't you?'
Smiling, she said, 'I've had plenty of practice lately.'
'Alright, so try this for size. You remember that day when we first met? When you passed me on the road near the Inn?'
'Yes ... don't tell me you're finally going to tell me what it was all about? At last!'
He smiled. 'You've waited long enough. Right, here goes. You know that I'd been praying?'
'Well, you did tell me *that* much.'
'But what I didn't tell you is that The Boss told me something about you - just after you'd walked past.'
'About me?'
'Aha.'
'But ... about *me?*'
'Affirmative.'
'What did He say?'
'Something that will radically change your life if you agree to it. But before I do tell you, I want you to know that I don't expect you to give me an answer right here and now. You'll need time to think and pray it through.' He paused to look steadily into her face, then continued, 'He said, and these were His exact words:-

"She's to be your wife, son.
I want you to marry her."

She blinked and stared at him, not sure if she had heard right. 'Pardon?'
Without hesitation, he repeated the extraordinary words:-

"'She's to be your wife, son.
I want you to marry her.'"

'Yes, I ... I thought that's what you said.'
'And that's what all the laughing was about. I was as shocked as you are now.'

She began to recall the times she had mentioned the incident to him, and how he had shrugged it off, simply saying that he had been 'enjoying an exceptionally good prayer time'. Now she knew just how exceptional! 'But ... how did He ... I mean ... did you actually *hear* His voice?'

'Not exactly. And the only way I can describe it, is that it felt as though the words had been indelibly printed across my mind. It was a kind of knowledge I was given; very clear and unmistakable.'

This was fantastic, astounding, unbelievable! But then again, was it? If the Lord was all-powerful, then why couldn't He - shouldn't He - speak to people in any way He chose? Izzy was always saying how He had told her this and that. 'And you're sure? I mean, *really* sure?' she asked.

'I'm sure.'

She looked at his steady gaze, and could detect no hint of doubt.

'But don't worry, I got it checked out. Remember when I went off to Charles and Izzy's wedding? They advised me to wait for confirmation, which I did, and plenty of it came. My daily Bible readings, and practically every sermon I heard for the next month were all about love and marriage and family life. Not to mention how my own attitude did a complete about-turn on the whole idea of matrimony. Too many so-called co-incidences, too many circumstances, all pointing in the same direction. And then there was the small matter that I found myself becoming *very* attracted to you.' He kissed her cheek, coiling the tantalising tendrils of hair by her ear around his finger. 'Guess it took The Boss Himself to get it into my thick skull that I needed a good woman to make my life complete, and that you were the one. Although, as it turned out, I didn't need much persuading.' He tilted her face towards him and kissed her gently.

She was speechless, and yet felt a sense of calm, even acceptance, at what she had just heard. She bent down to pick up a stick and began drawing a series of nondescript shapes in the sand. Somehow, she knew that this was just as it should be; that this was the logical next step. Hadn't he shown her in every way he could that he was serious about her, and that he was totally committed to her? For some time now she had been aware that everyone spoke of them as though they were a courting couple, but she had become adept at pushing the idea of marriage away - until last week - until that time in Penny's flat.

'I know it's come as a shock to you, sweetheart,' he continued, 'but it's been burning me up inside all this time, and I've been going crazy wanting to tell you. You might have taken fright and run off if I'd have spoken up sooner, especially at the beginning, after what you told me - about how you'd always wanted to escape from your other relationships. I've had to wait until things fell into place, as, I believe, they have now.'

Yes, he was right. She could see the sense in his timing. At last, she spoke. 'I *did* want to run away, in fact, I almost did.' She began to draw a large circle.

'When? Was it after that … er … discussion we had about caves?'

'Oh no! Before then. When I was having all that trouble with Niall, and I agreed to leave so that he could get Maggie in. But you were part of the reason I wanted to leave as well. Although, to be honest, and looking back now, I think the main reason.'

'Hmm, suppose it was obvious that I was more than a little interested in you, and I soon became *very* keen to get to know you more. But you didn't make it easy; you didn't exactly fall into my arms.'

She remembered how determined she had been to shake him off, and how she had failed every time - and had been secretly glad of it. 'I used to get so worked up about you. I felt that I wasn't good enough; that if I allowed you to get close to me, you'd soon find out that I wasn't worth it. I'd just be a millstone around your neck. So I decided that the kindest thing I could do for you was to leave - and let you concentrate on your work at the Manor.'

'Oh, sweetheart! I knew you were going through something, but it wasn't until you told me about that decision that I realised that we had a real problem on our hands. But I had every confidence that The Boss would sort it out. He showed me that all I had to do was to be patient, and be there for you. It's been hard, not being able to tell you, and wanting to. Anyway, I believe He was guiding you, even though you didn't know Him then. You stayed after all.'

'Yes, but only because Niall got the sack!'

'Ah yes, another *circumstance*.'

She stared hard at the circle, before dropping the stick and tucking her hands into her pockets. 'You know, I was just a week away from leaving when they sacked him.'

'Really?'

'Yes, I'd got another job to go to, in Beaulane.'

He gave a long, low whistle. 'You know I'd have come after you?'

'You wouldn't have found me. I'd already decided to ask Georgina and Donald not to let you have my forwarding address.'

'Had you indeed? Well then, guess I'd have had to have turned detective.'

She found the idea of him stalking around in a trilby and trench coat amusing, especially as he would still have his stick and limp.

He was relieved to see her smile. 'Hey, what's so funny? Stranger things have happened.'

She looked into his eyes. There was such kindness there that she had to look away, or she would do something silly, like cry. And she'd done enough of that lately!

He spoke softly. 'And so, here we are. But don't say anything just yet. There's one thing I need to hear from you. You know I love you, and you told me once that you felt the same way about me. Can you tell me again? Here, now? Somehow ... I just need to hear you say that you do.'

She picked up the stick again and drew a cross in the centre of the circle, very aware that he was waiting for her to say those words again - and how she wanted to say them. They were true, so very, very true. But what was the matter with her? Why couldn't she say them?

He gently took the stick from her, and drew a heart around the cross. 'Can't you tell me? You know I won't break yours, don't you?'

Yes, she knew, she knew she could trust him. She would say the words, on her next breath. She would definitely say them.

'After all,' he continued, 'I have it on very good authority that you aren't going to break mine.'

But now a new, disturbing question began to loom large in her mind. If she was going to spend the rest of her life with him, she had to be sure - *absolutely sure* - that he wanted her because it was what *he* wanted, and not out of obedience to something The Boss had said. She had to know that he was not simply obeying orders, even though everything in her felt that this was not the case.

'Yvonne?'

'Yes.'

'You've gone quiet on me again.'

She chewed hard on her lip, reluctant to voice the awkward question, but knowing that she had to. Falteringly, she began, 'How can I be sure that you aren't just doing...what The Boss told you to do? I mean, how do I know that you aren't ... bothered about me, just because of what He said?'

He had been prepared for this, and confessed that he had initially only looked at her because of what The Boss *had* said, and then went on to give all the reasons why he soon found himself becoming *very* bothered about her. She became embarrassed as he listed her many attributes, not recognising herself in any of them. Unable to bear it any longer, she put a finger to his lips and told him to stop. He took her hand and pressed it against his chest. 'There, can you feel that pounding? See the effect you have on me? I can't tell you how many times I've wanted to grab you and run off with you!'

She smiled and gave him a coy look. 'And what would The Boss have said about that?'

'Oh, sweetheart! You were so mixed up. He had to stop me from charging in where angels fear to tread. And a tough job of it He had, I can tell you!'

She had to think about that, remembering all the times when her own pulse had raced uncontrollably, just like it was doing now. 'Hmm, I was mixed up, wasn't I? I wonder why He didn't choose someone less...confused for you?'

'Well, I'm glad He didn't, you little minx! I was hooked right from the start. You're a maddening, fabulous mix of vulnerability and strength.' He began twirling her hair around his finger again. 'I find you ... intoxicating.'

She could have said the same about him. Over the past months she had often wondered at how she could ever have thought about walking away from him, of never allowing herself to see him again. He was perfect for her. And when he did that thing with her hair, it was all she could do not to abandon herself to him completely. The last of her defences came crumbling down, and close to tears now, she confessed, 'I *do* love you Alex. I think I always have. And I know that I always will.'

He pulled her to him and kissed her passionately. At last, he released her, and then, for a few moments, they sat silently watching the ebb and flow of the tide, the breeze blowing gently around them as her words finally came to rest in both of their hearts.

Now she had something more she wanted him to know. 'Remember when Izzy said that when we're walking with the Lord, there are times when we can only understand some things in hindsight? Well, I think it's been like that for me. I couldn't see it at the time, but now I'm sure that the Lord was trying to show me all along ...' She paused, realising that there would be no turning back once she allowed the next few words to pass her lips. Once spoken, she would have truly committed herself to this new and wonderful path. She took the step, willingly, happily and confidently. 'I don't need any more time Alex. I already know ... I mean, it goes both ways; if He chose me for you, then that means that ... that He chose you for me! That it's what He wants, and that we really are meant to be together.'

'Oh glory!' he exclaimed, then kissed her again, this time with such passion that she had difficulty trying to breathe.

At last, she asked, 'So, what are you actually saying here? Am I to take it that this is a … sort of proposal?'

A fleeting look of concern crossed his face. 'No. Not yet. There's one more thing we need to discuss.' Still keeping one arm around her, he reached for her hand with his other. She looked down at it, tanned and strong. Her breath caught in her throat as a wave of desire surged through her.

'You know that I'm not as complete in the physical way as other men,' he said. 'How did Izzy so delicately put it? That I've "been left with only half of the necessary equipment"? I want to make sure that you understand that that side of things can never change, or improve. The scars have healed, and I've had some work done on the worst of them, but they're still very obvious. I'm not what you could call a pretty sight, and that's what you'd be taking on …' he paused to stroke her face, 'that's what you'd be sleeping with, what you'd be lying next to.'

Almost overcome with relief, she exclaimed, 'Oh that!' She turned his face towards her, and then with all the love that she could feel, began to kiss his forehead, his eyes and his cheeks. 'Now look here, my *Mad, Mad Man in the Heather,* for your information, you get my heart racing too! And I can't wait to lie next to you!' Then she kissed him firmly on the mouth, thereby giving him all the reassurance he needed.

Now he knew that the wait was over; at last, the longed-for time had come. Kneeling was a painful business, and he had to balance himself against the boulder, but he was determined that this was one time his body would do exactly what *he* wanted it to do. His eyes moved over her face, taking in the lovely green eyes, huge now with expectation, the pink cheeks, and the partially open mouth that he would be kissing again soon. Then, almost comfortable, he began.

'Yvonne, my sweetheart, and the love of my life. I love you to distraction, and want … *need* … to go through life with you beside me. Will you do me the most wonderful, amazing honour of agreeing to be my wife? Will you please, *please* marry me?'

She did not keep him waiting, as she answered, firmly and calmly, 'Yes, Alex, I will marry you.' Then, looking up into the sky, she called, 'There Boss, I got the message. I said "yes". And You didn't even have to talk to me!'

He hugged her hard and laughed. 'Oh yes He did. He's been talking to you all the time!'

*

They were walking back to the hotel some time later, when he asked, 'You called Him "Boss" back there, is that how you've come to think of Him now?'

'I did, didn't I? Don't know why. It must have been a one-off.'

'Actually, you know, that's something I've been doing a lot of thinking about lately.'

'What, that you call Him "The Boss?"'

'Yes. I feel that I should start calling Him "Father" too from now on.'

'Really, after all this time?'

'Hmm. I suppose I've needed Him to be like a boss, "*The* Boss". He must have known that that was the only way I could relate to Him. But after the way He's been so good to us, watching over and guiding us, and really helping us, He's been more like a loving parent than a Commanding Officer.'

'But won't that change how you are with your own father? I mean, don't you think it could somehow affect your relationship with him?'

'With Dad? No, not at all. There was something I heard the other day that I really liked, something about our hearts. Imagine that they have small drawers, or compartments, in them; one draw for each of those we know and love. My parents would be in one, the rest of the family in another, then friends. And in the centre, Father ... my Heavenly Father. And you, sweetheart, you're right there next to Him, no escape. So you see, you're not the only one who's had a healing. I've had a kind of healing too.'

'Oh Alex, that's wonderful!' she exclaimed, feeling that Jesus was so gracious. Was there no end to His giving? How had she deserved all this?

But the giving was not over yet, as Alex went on to say, 'And you do realise, don't you, that when we're married, you'll have another father in your life?'

'*Another* father?'

'That's right. My father - a father-in-law.'

'Oh, my goodness! All these fathers! How shall I cope?'

Then, not knowing whether to laugh or cry, she did both.

CHAPTER 45

Yvonne felt that life could get no better. They had wandered into the island's craft shop the next morning with the intention of buying a few small gifts, when Alex called her over to look at a display of locally made jewellery. Her eyes were immediately drawn to a topaz, set in a white gold ring, the colour reminding her of the water near the island's shoreline: crystal clear and blue. She glanced at the others, but found her attention being drawn back each time to the same ring; there was something about the simple, honest beauty of the piece that strongly appealed to her.

Alex looked in the direction of her gaze, and commented, 'They're kind of striking.'

'Yes, and look at that blue one, it's beautiful. But what a price!'

'Oh, I don't know, not too bad. And where've I seen that colour before?'

'The sea, just a bit out from the shore.'

'That'll be it.' He moved to stand behind her, and putting his arms around her, asked softly, 'So, you really like it do you?'

'No, I *love* it!'

'Enough to wear as an engagement ring?'

She beamed at his reflection in the glass case, and hugged his arms to her. 'I … I think it would be perfect.'

He kissed the top of her head. 'Come on then, let's get you to try it on.'

It proved to be one size too small, however, the assistant assured them that a ten percent deposit would secure it, re-sized and ready for collection the next morning.

'I've been thinking,' he mused, 'that shade of gold might be hard to match later on. How about trying to find the wedding rings now we're here?'

Thus, two more rings were purchased; plain and modest bands that suited them both very well.

Afterwards, in a happy state of shock, and now with their talk full of weddings, they went for a celebratory lunch in the adjoining café.

Later, they returned to the hotel to change, before going down to the jetty to board the boat for the afternoon sea trip. This turned out to be a great success, for not only were they blessed with the sight of a minke whale, but by being escorted for some time by several dolphins that leaped and darted exuberantly alongside them, matching their mood exactly.

*

The ring fitted perfectly when they went to collect it the next morning.

'Shall we do it now?' he asked. 'Do you feel ready?'

From his eager tone and expression, she had no difficulty guessing what his wishes were, and quickly replied that she was 'well and truly ready!'

'Come on then, let's go for it,' he said.

There was nothing casual about their steps as they headed for the same smooth boulder where he had proposed to her two nights before.

Once settled, he took her hand in his, and assured her once more of his love as he placed the ring on her finger. She held it up, comparing the blue stone against the blue of the sea. Yes, she had been right, and exclaimed triumphantly, 'Look, it *is* the same! Look how they blend.'

Without missing a beat, he replied, 'Just like us then.'

Almost breathless with the wonder of it all, she continued staring at the ring, knowing that it would always remind her of this distant, magical place, this beautiful, sparkling island. She told him, and he teased her for being such an old romantic, like him.

They remained there for some time, rejoicing and celebrating their love with laughs, hugs and kisses. Then they prayed together, thanking God for each other, the rings, the island, the hotel, the whales, the dolphins, the weather, and just about everything under the sun.

*

By now, they had become friendly with some of the other guests at the hotel, and after another excellent dinner that evening, spent some time in the lounge, swapping stories about each other's travels. She felt a twinge of disappointment when no one appeared to have noticed that her ring finger now had something significant on it. However, she managed to restrain herself from revealing the fact, having agreed earlier with Alex that the first to be told the good news should be Charles and Izzy.

Amongst the group was a keen orator who took advantage of any lull in the conversation to break out with several lengthy monologues. They politely sat through his overdramatic renditions of *Henry IV: Part I; Uncle Vanya,* and even *When We Dead Awaken,* but decided to make a discreet exit a couple of lines into *The Honest Whore.*

Returning to what they now affectionately called their 'special place', they allowed the island air to bathe and soothe them, as they sat talking, planning and praying. Later, with hearts full of love for their Heavenly Father, His creation and for each other, they said a slow and tender goodnight.

*

The next morning, they hired a taxi to take them to visit a colony of grey seals on the other side of the island. The intimate scene of creamy-white, fluffy-coated pups, feeding from their docile, giving mothers, had a humbling affect upon them, and they both confessed to feeling like trespassers. Yvonne found herself quietly humming a tune that she had not sung since her school assembly days, *All Creatures That on Earth Do Dwell.* A pup looked over, and, as though appearing to be in complete agreement, began to nod its head in perfect time to the rhythm.

The taxi returned an hour later, and nature was to grant them one more blessing when the driver pointed out of the windscreen, and exclaimed, 'Look, up there!' There was no mistaking the impressive, distinctive shape of a golden eagle as it soared and glided on a current of air, high above and in front of them. They watched in awed silence, both knowing that, like the bird, their own spirits were soaring just as high and free.

*

'It's just au revoir,' he reassured her, as, later that day they stood watching the island's outline gradually disappear over the horizon. She felt the ring on her finger, tangible proof that the past few days had not just been a lovely dream, or random images caught on paper - only to be remembered for a short season, before being consigned forever to the pages of a photograph album. No, they had actually happened; they had been real. And soon she would be joined for life to this incredible, wonderful man standing beside her. She wondered how long it would be before they could return, and, if so blessed, how many little ones they would be holding when they stood here again on the ferry's deck, watching the pink stones fade into the blue distance.

CHAPTER 46

They were approaching the Inn when they met Hamish's arthritic Land Rover on the road. Alex pulled over to let it pass, but instead, it came to a noisy halt beside them. Hamish wound his window down slowly, and resigned himself to the inevitable. Flora leaned across from the passenger seat, and called out, 'And are you back just now? Was it a good time you had? And was it a tidy-like place?'

Alex turned to look at Yvonne, knowing exactly what was on her mind. 'Can't stop you, can I?' he asked.

'Sorry,' she said apologetically, 'I've just *got* to.' She held out her left hand, and began flourishing the ring. 'Oh Flora, it was *wonderful!* And look ... look ... what do you think of this? Isn't it beautiful?'

Hamish spotted the item on her ring finger, and recognising it for what it was, mumbled stoically, 'Aye, aye, and there we are.'

Flora smacked him on the elbow and reprimanded him tartly, 'Hush now, you silly old fool!' She turned to give the couple a wide smile, hoping that her new set of false teeth did not look too obvious as she peered over. It looked to be a sensible, tidy kind of ring; not a diamond to be sure, but the blue stone very attractive - and not too fancy for all that. 'Well now, isn't that just grand. Grand! Dot and I were wondering when you'd get around to it, and Mrs Mac's been looking out for it for ... och, goodness knows how long.'

Amused at Hamish's gloomy reaction, Alex said, 'Thanks, Flora. But what about you Hamish? Won't you congratulate us, and shake my hand on it?'

The older man squinted from under his cap and slowly put his arm through the window, uttering a world-weary, 'Aye, aye,' to the latest victim. 'You've done it now laddie. Mind, she's a good girl. Could ha'been worse.'

Yvonne erupted with laughter, as Flora found it necessary to give Hamish's elbow a whole series of sharp smacks. 'Och, a'way with you, you silly old divil!' Turning back to them, she asked, 'And when's the big day to be, and where? And will it be the Manor you'll be moving to?'

Recovering, Yvonne replied, 'At Christmas, and in the local chapel. We're hoping that all of Alex's family will be able to come. Some of them might have to stay at the Inn; that should please Robert.' She had been disappointed to realise that Sandra and Tom would probably not be able to attend; by then Sandra would be near her time, and it would be too much to expect her to do so much travelling. At least she had been making more positive sounds about the baby recently.

Flora frowned. 'Aye, but the lad'll be put out to lose you. He's all fixated on this rambling-bed notion.'

'Oh, I don't know Flora. He'll have enough time to get someone else in,' replied Alex. 'And I've got one or two ideas about the Manor, but it all depends on Yvonne, what she feels led to do. I wouldn't be surprised if that means taking life a bit easier, and have a breather before we ... er, start thinking about a family.'

Flora looked alarmed. She sat bolt upright, and exclaimed, 'Bairns! Och, no! But you'll be wanting to wait a wee while?'

Hamish gave another low groan, and pulled his grimy cap even lower over his face. Bairn-talk! Now there'd be no getting away.

Grinning widely, Alex replied, 'We'll see.' He turned to look into Yvonne's glowing face, 'But I don't expect we'll be waiting too long.'

Flora was now even more alarmed. 'Och, but you'll be losing them in that great barn of a place!'

'Well, actually we're hoping to have a place of our own by then,' said Alex. 'And we were hoping that you and Dot would be kind enough to help us out there, and let us know if you hear of anything going locally?'

Flora was delighted to be given such an important task, one which she would get to just as soon as could.be. 'Och, well, I think we could be doing that.' She had been hearing snippets about old Mrs MacFarlane, who had an ailing sister on Skye. Now there was a wee treasure of a house, nice and cosy it would be too, and the garden just right for a couple of bairns to run about in. Shame the old lady had a mortal fear of the telephone. Never mind, she'd pop along and see how the land lay, just as soon as could be.

Yvonne could not help herself, as, once again, she flourished her left hand in their direction. 'Anyway, Flora, what do you think? Are we being *wise?*'

Flora studied the two happy faces. She had come to know each of them well; a respectable, decent pair, and in her opinion, very deserving of each other. Dot and Angus had always held the lad in high regard, and mighty shocked they'd been when he'd been blown-up. No one thought he'd ever get over it, but he had, and a fine life he'd gone on to make for himself.

As for Yvonne; what a change in the quine! How serious and pale she looked when she had first arrived. Dear, dear, as pale as could be! But just look at her now, full of life. And glowing with a fine colour.

She nodded, slowly, sagely, and ignoring Hamish's continued rumblings that 'things were awaiting,' declared in her most solemn voice, 'Aye, aye, that you are. I'm thinking very wise. *Very* wise indeed!'

Keen to hear their news again, but with all the ins and outs of it, she went on to invite them for tea the following Sunday. And then, much to Hamish's relief, they said their farewells, and went their separate ways.

Yvonne realised that she soon she would be entering the Inn for the first time as an engaged woman, but more than that, as a *Christian* engaged woman. Undeserved and freely given, she had been offered another life. And she had said 'Yes'. She felt no fear about what might lie ahead, whether of good or bad - for this was life after all. People, places and events would come and go, but, with her Heavenly Father's help, she would adapt and survive.

She knew that she would never walk such a lonely path again, for, like a golden thread that had been woven into the very core of her being, was the absolute assurance that her Eternal Companion would never leave her.

She was settled - because He was settled in her.

> *I was lost: but Jesus found me,*
> *Found the sheep that went astray,*
> *Raised me up and gently led me*
> *Back into the narrow way.*
> *Days of darkness still may meet me,*
> *Sorrow's paths I oft may tread;*
> *But His presence still is with me,*
> *By His guiding hand I'm led.*

The End.

BY THE SAME AUTHOR

MY HIGH TOWER

Meredith did not hear the footsteps walking past her chalet. The three figures were silent, hardly daring to breath, never-mind talk; stifled shuddering was all they could manage. They felt as cold as the dawn wind blowing off the North Sea. And they were frightened. A gust caught them unawares, one of them screamed - just a small scream, but loud enough to penetrate her sleep.

Occult practices are suspected, and, for some, life on the holiday camp begins to take on darker tones. When Meredith starts to receive unwelcome advances from a female colleague, and then discovers something alarming closer to home, she turns to Kingsley, a recently arrived local Baptist minister.

Her life continues to fall apart as the frenetic routine of the camp goes on all around her. Soon, she comes to realise just how much she needs not only human, but divine intervention as well. Increasingly attracted to the charismatic Kingsley, she battles on, only able to find any real measure of peace when she can steal away - to hide in her own *High Tower.*

THE GRACEFUL SOLUTION

Two very different men come into Briony's life – both are divorced. As far as Briony's concerned, that's a 'no-go' area.

The year is 1971. Briony is still grieving when she impulsively books herself onto one of 'Halcyon's Splendid Coach Tours'.

Reuben Zimmerman, the charismatic Courier/Driver, takes a pride at being one of the company's more successful drivers. Will this be the tour that ruins his impressive record?

Briony quickly discovers that the drama is not only to be found in the surrounding landscape, but also within the confines of the coach itself.

Encountering prejudice and friendship in equal measure amongst her fellow passengers, she begins to question and challenge her own feelings and attitudes towards others.

Little does she know that the emotional, physical, and most of all, spiritual, challenges she faces on the tour, are only a type of rehearsal for what is to follow upon her return to her 'normal' life.

Printed in Great Britain
by Amazon